TOMORROW, THE WAR

TOMORROW, THE WAR

MAX WATMAN

Heresy Press books may be purchased in bulk at special discounts for sales promotion, corporate gifts, fund-raising, or educational purposes. Special editions can also be created to specifications. For details, contact the Special Sales Department, Heresy Press, 307 West 36th Street, 11th Floor, New York, NY 10018 or info@skyhorsepublishing.com.

Visit our website at skyhorsepublishing.com.

HERESY PRESS LLC
P.O. Box 425201
Cambridge, MA 02142
heresy-press.com

10 9 8 7 6 5 4 3 2 1

Library of Congress Cataloging-in-Publication Data is available on file.

Cover design by David Ter-Avanesyan

Print ISBN: 978-1-949846-76-8
Ebook ISBN: 978-1-949846-77-5

Printed in the United States of America

To West,

for whom thunder rolls

CHAPTER ONE

Down the Mountain

Summer 1846

The funeral was over. Up on Stokes Mountain, Hale Stokes and his sister-in-law Lindy had been laid to rest in the family plot. Forrest's buckboard wagon creaked as the floorboards flexed over the rutted path. Forrest clucked at the mule and held the reins with one hand, his other swatting his hat at the murmuration of gnats that swarmed and harassed him and his passengers. Enos, beside him, worked the brake against the weight of the wagon as they crept forward.

Preacher Thom, seated in the back, thought over what he had said and figured he must have done all right with it. Strictly Old Testament. He'd watched the boy, Jed, standing behind the rest of his family. Understandably dark of mien, watching his father and his aunt go into the ground. Interesting tradition they have, that they must be the ones to throw the dirt. They'd told him how to explain it—first with the shovel upside down, reluctant, but then, again, with the shovel rightways, because you can't fight against it. Jed was growing angular and tall. He's a smart kid, thought the preacher. I'll have to make a point of getting him to keep coming around. Get him down the hill, show him the newspapers, get the world into him. Can't live your whole life up there on your family's hill, three houses and a graveyard.

"You don't never get the feeling that the Stokes would want any help," said Forrest.

Jane rolled her eyes at Lena and looked up at their husbands on the seat in front. She held her hand up high, letting the gnats swarm around it.

"You don't go by feeling, Forrest," said Lena, "you just help."

"It's like when someone has a baby. You just bring them things," said Jane.

Preacher Thom sat with his back to the drivers and his elbows on his knees, smiling and rocking loosely with the wagon as it moved over the uneven road, in sharp contrast to Dr. Coyle and Mr. Tomlinson, who were straining against the incline. Mr. Tomlinson quivered and bounced with every lurch, and he held his hand against the top of his waistcoat, trying to hold himself in place and looking as if he had just belched.

"They paid me in whiskey," said Preacher Thom, patting the jug.

"Was it around here?" Enos asked Dr. Coyle. The brake bucked against his hand and the wagon pitched forward. "The accident, I mean."

"Over on the other side," said Dr. Coyle, "where that stream cuts close to the road."

"Ain't much road over there," said Forrest.

They arrived at the store before sunset and lingered in the golden light. A breeze picked up once they'd reached the flats. Forrest and Enos stood on the porch, sipping Preacher Thom's whiskey from short glasses, which Mr. Tomlinson had provided. Lena and Jane stayed in the wagon, though they rose and rested against the top rail. Preacher Thom had the whiskey resting by the heel of his boot in the rocky dirt of the road.

"C'mon, now, Preacher, give the wives a round," said Jane.

"It's a funeral," said Lena.

Preacher Thom handed his glass to Jane with an apologetic smile, topped it off, and winked at Lena. "What'll you fix for them, then?" he asked. He liked these country women, with their farm-toughened hands, sun freckled cheeks, and easy demeanors. Hard to put on airs, he thought, if you spend your time milking cows and churning butter.

Forrest, whose church clothes were just his work clothes with a dark sack jacket drawn around them, shook his head and said: "People probably would help out, but—"

"Stokes never did want any help," said Enos. Looking back to the low, lush mountain, he added that it was a sad business.

Dr. Coyle consulted his watch.

"An apple cake."

"You think so?" Forrest asked. "You think it's a sad business?"

"Sure it is."

"Can't they eat apple cake?" asked Jane.

"For the dead uns. And the children," said Enos.

"That mess of children probably don't know which one of who is—"

"Come on now," Mr. Tomlinson said. "We just put those two in the ground today. Let's not have any of that."

"Death is a sorrow only for the living," said Preacher Thom, by rote, with no more thought than he gave to the rising of his foot if he was struck on the knee. "And even in mourning, we should find solace that the departed have taken up the company of the lord."

"Stokes ain't never been of no account," said Forrest.

"Are they allowed to eat apple cake?"

"Those were kind words you said today," said Dr. Coyle.

Preacher Thom nodded his thanks and said: "You mean on account of dietary laws? I don't see why not. Does it use lard?"

Enos asked: "Do it feel different? Preaching for Jews?"

"Can I use butter?"

"As far as I know you can use butter. I'm sure they'll appreciate the gesture, more than they will quibble with the recipe," said Preacher Thom. "Same book. Same God. It's no difficulty to find a kindness for good folks taken from lives well lived."

"Known them Stokes brothers my whole life. Never thought it'd come to this." said Forrest. "C'mon, Enos, I'll run y'all by your place on the way."

Forrest had been friends with Hale Stokes, who was survived by his wife, Ethel, and his brother, Hobe.

"It was an accident," said Preacher Thom. "The wagon rolled over because the wheel broke. They'd loaded it too heavy. Which as we all know is something Hale was wont to do."

"Ain't saying it ain't in character. Just saying it sure solves things. Hale and Lindy being on that wagon what rolled, and Ethel and Hobe being up there on the mountain. Two of them get on mighty good."

Forrest and Enos nodded their farewells and took their seats on the buckboard bench in front of their wives, who each took a drink from the short glass before Jane leaned forward and handed it back to Preacher Thom. The mule, a vision of resignation, took slow steps at Forrest's first cluck, and the buckboard rattled away.

Mr. Tomlinson, now that it was just the three town folk, felt a little more at ease.

"I wonder if they'll feel the need to make it official."

"Doesn't seem particularly Stokes-like, does it?" answered the doctor.

"I think on account of all them kids they'll probably get hitched, and so the Old Man will stay out of their business."

"Seven children between them up there."

"Jed's about feral, though, ain't he?"

"I believe he is, yes."

"You think they'll be sending away for a wife for him, like they brought them sisters in for Hale and Hobe?"

Preacher Thom had come up to the porch, and he shook his head while pouring more to drink. Defender of the Virginia Jews, he thought, had a nice ring to it.

There were three houses up on Stokes Mountain. The homestead, the oldest one, had scars from Indian fights on its timber. The newest one, where Hale had lived, was now empty. One of the children would move into it when he started a family. It was hard to imagine that child being Jed, although he was the oldest.

Preacher Thom took a deck of cards out of his pocket, and the three men sat down around a little table on sun-faded ladder-back chairs that creaked in complaint.

Dr. Coyle lit a cigar and blew a contemplative stream of smoke while Preacher Thom shuffled.

"I believe," said the doctor, "that that was the first time I've seen old Horace or Charity in well over a year, maybe three."

"The old man don't come down."

"Charity Stokes looked like she had something to say."

Preacher Thom nodded along only enough to make it clear he was listening, since he'd only lived at Alcott's Brook for a decade, and knew that as far as these families were concerned he was passing through.

"I mean," said Dr. Coyle. The man paused and swore softly before folding his hand. "Does seem like the two of 'em get on pretty good."

Tomlinson had two pair and took the money from the center of the table. "The boy Jed still studies with you, ain't he, Preacher? He comes around when he wants to, I suppose. Ain't nobody get a Stokes to do anything regular."

Preacher Thom nodded. "He's a good boy. He's bright."

The men nodded, but they didn't agree.

The change in Jed Stokes was immediately apparent to Preacher Thom. The boy had lived without intent. He had done what you asked, answered you if he could, and hadn't seemed to think of the world around him as something real. He lived within patterns, Preacher Thom supposed, like a raccoon. The accident shook him. How could it not? His father dead under a pile of timber, the wheel of the wagon shattered, the mules frantically braying and screaming as they were pulled, jerked, and strangled off the road.

Well, that last part. Was the boy actually there?

You can only keep your head down, thought Thom, if everything stays the same. If there are no surprises, if nothing happens, you could live your life and never look up from your shoes, but something happens to everyone, and then the whole world snaps into focus as if you'd rubbed the morning out of your eyes.

Would it be easier to just stay asleep? To never see?

Thom struggled to keep himself out of the sorrowful ditches, and clear from weedy paths of maudlin sentiment to which he was inclined. He had hoped to find faith, but found his mood unslaked by his practice.

Poor Jed raised his head and looked around and saw his father dead and his mother standing next to his uncle. By God, thought Thom, that poor boy saw Shakespeare's Danish ghosts, the play replayed. Were things foreordained, he asked himself. What if someone like myself had been there to guide Hamlet? If only perhaps enough to keep the knives sheathed. To keep the blood off the carpet.

Thom rarely saw children as old as Jed. He wondered if Jed's continued attendance, albeit irregular, was on account of the oft-mentioned Jewish predilection for letters. His charges were usually on their farms working by the time they were in their teens. He knew them when their arms weren't strong enough to be of much use, and someone in their family decided it'd be all right if they could read a little bit. They were helpless, always, even here. They could walk to the schoolhouse—which was, truth be told, the front room of Thom's own home—and arrived more or less intact, but they seemed, as they bumped into things and dreamily drifted through the day, to be incapable. If you didn't remind them to run out to the privy, they'd pee right there and begin to cry as if something had happened to them, instead of them having done something themselves.

When they sat out on the porch and chewed through whatever they'd brought to eat, if one of them knocked over a cup of water they'd say: "The water spilled."

They couldn't imagine that their own action had caused the water to spill.

They're like savages. Superstitious savages who live in a world over which they have no agency and upon which they can have no effect, and then, one day, Jed's father dies under a pile of logs next to his sister-in-law, and Jed looks around at the world for the first time.

Imagine that. Some folks are born to understand the world is theirs for the taking, and some, having been made to understand the opposite, that they are to be taken by the world, toil for the smaller pleasures, but all are filled with ambition. What would Jed make of this?

I suppose I'll do what I can for the boy, thought Thom.

Jed started coming around on the off days when Thom wasn't teaching. Thom shared the news with him, told him about the world. Jed did seem to want to know things.

He'd sit on the porch while Thom read the paper, having taken the stairs one at a time, remembering not to skip or hop or betray anything that might reveal the child he was putting behind himself.

Thom handed him books and let him keep his copy of *The Three Musketeers*.

Thom took him down to the general store to play cards against Dr. Coyle and Mr. Tomlinson, who found it hard to maintain their smug derision while the boy raked their coins across the table and into his own pockets.

"He ain't a thing like his pa," said Dr. Coyle, watching Thom and Jed walking back up the street.

"Hale? I never lost a game of whist to Hale," said Mr. Tomlinson.

"I never knew Hale to play a game of any sort. Kept his shoulder in the yoke."

"Ain't seen him do anything but work, long as I can remember."

"Can't even recall him much liking anything, if you know what I mean, he'd come to town with a list, and he'd get those things. Most folks at that time look around the shop, they buy a candy, they buy a plug of tobacco, they lean against the counter there and turn the pages of the newspaper."

"Hale never did."

"Never even seemed to notice. Never reached out to take anything at all."

"The apple walked off away from that tree didn't it?"

"That apple tree turned to growing peaches."

They laughed together.

When Jed turned seventeen, he told his uncle-turned-stepfather and his mother that he was thinking of heading into town.

"Why you keep going down there to see the preacher? You learned enough, ain't you?" Hobe Stokes didn't trust a Christian lettered man.

Jed Stokes shrugged. He had a thin goatee that he'd fashioned as best he could in the spotted and fogged mirror after the drawings in Barrow's translation of *The Three Musketeers*. Ethel sat next to Jed at the table, their identical haint-blue eyes both bearing the same frustrating flatness. Mother and son were noncommittal, hard to read when they wanted to be.

"Y'all don't take a person seriously enough to argue with them," said Hobe. "It's right consternating."

Hobe hadn't understood, and Jed was forced to explain himself:

"I don't mean Alcott's Brook. I mean the city. I'm going down to Richmond."

"What would you want to do that for?" asked Ethel, surprised.

"What's down there?" asked Hobe, he spat into the cook fire, clumsily, and added a streak of tobacco juice to the many yellow-brown stains on his dirty gray beard. "You're looking for a woman."

"Hobe," Ethel said, "don't spit in my fire."

The man ignored her.

"There's got to be a real life down there," said Jed.

"This ain't real?" Hobe knocked on the table. "Seems real to me."

The baby, the eighth child, first progeny of Hobe and Ethel's union, was startled awake by Hobe's hand on the table, and started to cry. Ethel hurried to him, and Jed followed her with his eyes.

"There ain't room for me here."

"There's always room," said Ethel.

"Hard to argue with that, ain't it," said Hobe, quietly. "What do you aim to do?"

"I'll figure it out."

"You coming back?"

"Can't say as I know. I reckon I'll be back soon enough. Sure."

His mother was nodding over her new baby, cooing him back to sleep.

And with that, seventeen-year-old Jed Stokes walked down off the mountain on which he was born. He carried a bit of salted and smoked venison, shot and powder—he was equipped in the only way he knew, for the wild. His scattergun was looped over his back, his knife was sharp, and three good snares were coiled on the top of his possibles bag. The only difference between what he carried and what he'd taken out into the woods so often before was at the bottom of that same bag, where every bit of money he'd ever gotten ahold of was tied up in a square of leather next to his copy of *The Three Musketeers*.

With each step, the crunch of twigs under his moccasins proclaimed his freedom and his future. The world was before him. The morning was his. Everything was his. Coming out of the hills he felt wonderfully anonymous, fantastically energized.

Those hills—so steep you can't plant. So rocky you can't hardly walk. Jed had watched seed corn run down the gulley in a hard spring rain, bloated and worthless and washed away. He followed it down the hill until he found it clogged up in a swirl underneath the bared-out roots of a tall poplar. He climbed the low oak tree on the opposite side, and sat on a bough with buckshot balls loaded in his scattergun. He stayed quiet. He shot a deer there—tempted out of nervous hiding to gorge on that pocket of swollen grain. His father had praised him for bringing the animal home, but Jed figured it was easy enough to shoot a simpleminded animal. Anyway, the whole mountain was infested with hornets. A breeding ground for copperhead vipers—who would claim such a mountain?

He walked along Three Notched Road, thinking of the stories he'd heard about Jack Jouett, who had ridden his mare Sallie to warn Thomas Jefferson of the coming British and become the savior of the new nation, a hundred odd years past. Jed didn't know where Cuckoo Tavern was, exactly, but he hoped he might see it. Jouett had been sleeping on the lawn there when he heard the British cavalry. You just have to be ready, thought Jed. You have to understand what's happening, that it is happening, and that in some sense it has already happened.

This was the core belief held by Jed Stokes, that things once begun are all but finished, and that there is no sense in hesitation.

His father had waited. The thoughts Jed formed regarding his father's life repulsed him. He roared back through the years, hollering: Do something, Hale! Anything. He knew that his father had understood that his wife was in love with his brother. He knew, too, that his father, believing perhaps in the will of G-d, or in the nature of things, or simply in the absurd belief that everything tomorrow will continue to creep along as it did yesterday, did nothing. Didn't challenge the threat to his family, didn't woo his woman back to his side. He could have left Stokes Mountain. Hale Stokes could have picked up his family and left and moved somewhere.

The will of G-d. The mountain. Jed was glad to leave these behind, these gargantuan pressures, these juggernauts of insistent influence—the way it is and will be, the way it is on Stokes mountain, G-d's purpose. G-d doesn't work in mysterious ways, not for you.

Jack Jouett didn't wait. He heard the cavalry and he rode up Jefferson's mountain to warn him. He rode forty miles under a full moon and arrived at Monticello in the cold light of the predawn. Jefferson managed to evade the cavalry in the woods. He hid in a tree, some said, others that he lived in a cave. He had all his papers with him—Jed imagined him scribbling by candlelight in a shallow dirt hole, hunched under the rocks, listening for the sound of the hooves, and thinking fondly of the young man who'd saved him.

Life is just like hunting, thought Jed. How many rabbits had he shot because they stopped and looked back to check if the threat was real? And how many meals had he, himself, missed because he didn't trust his instinct and second-guessed?

In Jack Jouett, Jed Stokes saw an American equivalent of Dumas's musketeers and a model for himself. He was gallant and quick, he knew the woods, the paths. He could rise from sleep and leap to action when called upon. There was nothing left to do but find his venue out in the world, which was in front of him.

In the woods where he slept along the journey to Richmond, he awoke with a smile and greeted the chilly dew-drenched mornings with exuberance. If there was a rabbit in his snare he'd cook and eat it, and if he'd caught nothing, he'd stir cornmeal in some boiling stream water and chew a chunk of salted venison.

He came to a high place that looked down upon the James River and out onto the dusty, smoky city, roiling with activity. From the hill where he stood upon a rough outcropping of granite he could see people and commerce. There were boats in the river under sail, and smaller ones poled along the banks. There were docks and factories. Coal, cotton, and commerce filled his heart.

He found a small spring burbling out of the rocks and trickling down the steep hill to the river, and he made his camp near it.

That afternoon he shot a squirrel, and that night he slept by a crackling fire, which played dancing shadows upon the leaves. He was happy, and as the fire dimmed and the stars grew bright he barely slept, smiling out into the night sky, thinking of the city bustling below him, and how tomorrow he would walk down into it and begin his adventure.

CHAPTER TWO

The Bell Rings for Master Mr. Bodkin

Spring 1856

Raleigh stuck his hand in the flour to wiggle his fingers through the soft off-white powder, and Lo took off her cap—a man's railroad cap she'd found in the road and worn ever since—and swatted at him.

"Go be somewhere else."

The boy ran along the fence by the vegetable garden, all tall and gangly, newly light on his feet at thirteen, and drew the admiration of old man Gee, who looked up from his row of cold-weather greens and unspooled himself from his sowing. Once he had straightened up, he nodded over to the little pile of apples stacked in the grass. Raleigh brought one to Gee. Gee motioned for him to take one for himself and one for Raleigh's younger sister, Temple.

Gee hadn't said a word in years. Only Lo was old enough to remember that he had spent months with his tongue clamped in an iron branks, screwed on his head as a punishment when they were young, but even she didn't know if his silence was on account of a physical injury. Maybe he'd forgotten how to talk; maybe he gave up on it. Either way, he was the only one who could take something out of the root cellar without being scolded, which is why he had apples. Everybody else had to wait for Lo to dole out rations, and then you pretty much had to eat it in front of her. She wanted to *see* the food eaten.

"Where are you going you need to take a biscuit with you?" she'd ask. "You walk out of here with corn bread," she'd say "how do I know you're coming back? Keeping everybody alive." Smoothing the front of the dress she'd sewn together out of the better parts of three dresses. "That's what I do, and that's what I'm doing. Everything is everything."

Raleigh and Temple, thirteen and twelve, bunked together in the small, dark room next to the root cellar on litters made up of cast-off cloth and old curtains, next to crates of sweet potatoes, apples, pears, carrots, from which they pilfered nothing.

Raleigh called out a thank-you and picked up two apples. He stuck to the dirt road as he walked past the orchard and slipped behind the Old House, empty now but swept and dusted every week by Liza and Fern, who walked this same road down from the New House with their aprons pulled up to their knees so they wouldn't get dusty.

No one came to Bodkin's Hundred.

Raleigh watched them and wondered for whom it was that they kept up their show of dusting and cleaning and walking with their aprons hiked up. That'd be like Lo putting food down in the dining room for the absent family. Lo cooked for the enslaved: slices of ham, greens, and okra soup. There was no one else to eat anything, and they'd slowly grown used to eating whatever they pleased, although they were cautious not to overdo it. Peril, although at bay, was never distant.

In the afternoons, the nine enslaved left on Bodkin's Hundred packed into the little kitchen building, sat on milking stools and boxes and barrels, and said a prayer around the long table where Lo beat and cut her biscuits. Often enough, the prayer was to keep everything as it was, and to keep Master Mr. Bodkin away from the place, busy with whatever it was he was doing. (Lo also kept the gate to Bodkin's Hundred well doused in stayaway oil, a concoction of her own, with bay leaves, fennel, dill, and calendula.) They would pray "Lord, keep us together," by which they meant to ask the Lord to see that no more of them would be sold. They would remember those who had gone on. "Lord, keep Little Edward to your breast," someone would intone, remembering the young man who had decided to leave Bodkin's Hundred after Master Mr. Bodkin had been gone a year and half.

Little Edward was the impetus for the strict rationing of the stores. Lo had told Raleigh and Temple about how he had asked her for something to pack up, some salt pork and hard biscuits, before he walked off.

"You two was bitty. Temple was just crawling on the floor when Little Edward left. He was gone six nights. We thought he'd made it somewhere, too. We thought maybe he made it down to the swamp, down to where some of our people live by a big old magnolia, split in two by a lightning strike, but living still. It grows in two directions!" Lo said. She had told the story of the Dismal Swamp many times, and how Indians lived there, and white folk who had some common sense, and free blacks called maroons. "Everybody down there in the swamp knows about that tree. It keeps on living. We thought Little Edward made it. Then that man come back here, driving a team of mules."

She'd shiver.

"Three men. Said they'd met up Master Mr. Bodkin in town. They'd gotten paid, spent their slave-catching money on whiskey. This was the mule driver talking, the two other men had been walking beside him, and rolling a hogshead barrel along afore them. They rolled it right up to the House and called everybody around. There were more of us then. Them white men were grinning and spitting, dirty, smelling like whiskey. They cracked the top of that barrel off and poured Little Edward out onto the ground in a pool of blood, dead as a stone. They'd smashed all they whiskey bottles into the barrel, 'fore they shoved poor Little Edward into it. They nailed him shut in there with all that broken glass and rolled him along the road."

"Why they call him Little Edward, Lo, was he little?"

"Just so as we could tell he wasn't Big Edward," said Lo. "I'll show you where both the Edwards are buried. You can say something to them out there."

Wooden crosses tied with chair caning were arrayed like grim orchard saplings up against the trees on the western edge of the property. Lo knew the names and stories of the deceased, and had carved an hourglass into each grave marker. If the caning rotted away, Lo would retie the marker. If the marker rotted away, she'd find a ladder rung or a chairback or chop a red cedar sapling to replace the old wood. She harvested graveyard dirt for gris-gris bags there, and occasionally she would cut a chicken's throat over the grave of the woman who had taught her what she knew, and had bequeathed unto her the position she had among the enslaved of not only this plantation, but up and down the road.

"Everybody has their time," she said. "It don't stop, and you best remember that it is going to run out. Everything is everything."

Raleigh slid down where the washout around the roots of the big tulip poplar made it easy, and walked over to the bank of rocks, which were sharp on your feet, but solid enough to stand on without sinking into the mud.

Temple was skipping stones.

"Where you get apples?"

"Gee told me."

"Gee wouldn't tell you nothing," said Temple, taking hers and biting into it. She was young enough to feel the need to assert reality as she knew it, like a spell against a world, as if by stating facts as she knew them, she could keep them from changing.

Raleigh didn't bother answering.

"Did you see the carriage?" asked Temple.

Raleigh shook his head.

"Looked like a beetle, black. Two big gray horses pulling. I seen it."

Raleigh watched her, impatient for the rest.

"Did you see him?"

She nodded that she had.

Master Mr. Bodkin was, to Raleigh and Temple, like a creature from a fairy tale. Both believed in him, but neither had ever met him or even seen him in their memory.

Master Mr. Bodkin knew them, however. He'd been there at Temple's birth twelve years before, and seen her mother die on the birthing bed in the quarters by the New Barn.

Master Mr. Bodkin was the fifth Oliver Bodkin. Oliver Bodkin Jr., the first Bodkin born in the Colonies, had followed a beautiful Huguenot maiden up the James River from the original Virginia settlements, past the fall line to the abandoned Monacan village where her parents and the rest of the French refugees had settled. The lovely and gracious Martha Dupuis had 133 acres along the James, and Bodkin Jr. bought the tract next to hers in 1720 and built the Old House next to a steady running tributary full of fish that everyone called Bodkin's Creek. The clapboard-sided two-over-two hall-and-parlor building was handsome and simple, stark in its straightforward usefulness but generous enough to start a family and a farm, which they did. They planted John Rolfe's new type of tobacco, and used their influence to procure slaves from the auctions at the harbor. At its height, Bodkin's Hundred was a kingdom of its own, a city unto itself. Two hundred bound workers toiled over a thousand acres of tobacco. It had its own blacksmith shop, its own herd of sheep which gave wool to be twisted and woven into fabric from which the white Bodkin women made the clothes that they gave to the enslaved on Christmas.

Oliver Bodkin III built the New House, a structure so grand and ostentatious it seemed a direct rebuttal to the practical simplicity of the original homestead. His father was of two minds—proud of his son, his family, and money that flowed in like a river, but ashamed, in a confused way, by the pomp and display. The window frames and mantels were milled in Pennsylvania by master craftsmen who traveled to install the precious pieces themselves. The marble flooring for the foyer crept up the James on flat barges after being portaged around the rapids and the falls.

At the front and back were twin doors slathered with sunflower yellow paint shipped in from France. What Oliver Bodkin III felt most deeply, however, was that the skeleton of the great structure was his, the bricks were fired in his own kilns, made with clay dug from his own land. The big timber that framed the massive house was cut out of his woods. The wide planks of pine were from his pines. He even owned the hands that built it.

They launched the house as if it were a ship, with a grand celebration and many cases of wine. Standing in the portico, feeling expansive, looking out at the small crowd of gentry gathered around for the revelation, Oliver Bodkin III proclaimed that the land itself, nature, had built this house: it was a manifestation of Bodkin destiny.

The New House rose out of a slight swell, overlooking sweeping pastures, and was visible from both the road and the river. The drive to its three-sided, shallow steps was long and looped generously around a fountain and two old pecan trees. It quickly became the most talked-about building in the region.

When the land gave up, worn out from growing tobacco, Master Mr. Bodkin's father, Oliver Bodkin V, fenced in the tremendous fields and converted them to pasture. He built the New Barn, to the West of the New House, and began breeding horses.

Many enslaved at Bodkin's Hundred were sold at this time, as the breeding of horses and the running of fox hunts demands far less of a labor force than growing tobacco, but they were sold carefully. He looked them over in the same way he looked at his horses, with an eye to the strength of bone, endurance, and tractability. Bodkin V kept what he deemed the best, and set them to work in the orchard, the garden, or tending to sheep and cattle.

There was money in the flesh of men, as there was in horses, and the little grid of slave quarters, while not, at the time, as dedicated a breeding program as the New Barn was, turned a fair profit.

Master Mr. Bodkin, Oliver Bodkin VI, took to the back of a horse like it was where he belonged, and was riding in the first flight after the hounds while he still had his milk teeth. The one or two times a visiting rider mumbled and groused over the presence of a child at the front of the hunt, they were soon silenced by his extravagant bravery in the saddle and fluid, subtle riding. He'd burn down candles studying bloodlines in the library. All other courses of study he thought too vague. Abstractions and histories without real products were fancies, nothing but folly. He couldn't attend to anything that wasn't visceral, that didn't have breathing, tangible results. The pedigrees of the Bodkin chattel filled his mind and by the time he was fourteen he knew the bloodlines of all the Bodkin breeding stock, whether it walked on four legs or two. To Master Mr. Bodkin, all flesh became money. He broke with family tradition and did not go north, or anywhere, for his education. He took over both breeding programs well before he inherited the farm, and made rounds every day, looking in on each stallion and each mare, asking after ankles, and whether or not the horse was on his feed. Then he'd take to the grid of rutted paths among the slave cabins with the latest in a constantly rotating cast of drivers and do the same.

Driver was an impossible job to keep filled. Any driver good enough at his job to keep the peace and run things smoothly and profitably was hired away by another plantation or moved on to his own business. The other type were so vicious and drunk that they soon packed up their deep dissatisfaction with the world and took it along to their next doomed engagement. One was fired for offending Master Mr. Bodkin's younger sister, and another had been so sick with drink that he'd thrown up on Master Mr. Bodkin's mother minutes before guests arrived for a house concert. That unsavory character had found himself bumming around the streets of Richmond looking for a place to sleep, dropped off on the street by enslaved footmen who were happy to turn the tables.

Master Mr. Bodkin would look in on the pregnant, asking if they'd eaten, and commanding Lo (already the cook, and already the medicine woman's apprentice) to cook up a pot of pumpkin. He'd look in on the breeding men, kept together like soldiers in a barracks redolent with musk. He'd walk their lines and appreciate the musculature, the conformation. He'd look for eyes that shined too bright, and note which among them would sweat nervously as he passed.

His horse, Gunnery, was a regal bay with a straight line back to Bulle Rock and the Darley Arabian. He won a match race in New York and his first foal took a grand price at auction, an unheard-of $10,000, after which Master Mr. Bodkin was heard at many a party, flushed with wine, suggesting "Some sort of race for slaves! Contested over a mile! We could run fifteen-year-olds. We'd prove who has the best flesh!"

No one could tell if he was kidding. Some of his society had grown to feel that his dedication to the business of breeding the colored was ungentlemanly. They sat up a little straighter, however, when the auction announcements proclaimed that Bodkin was selling slaves or horses. Something of Bodkin's on the block was something worth looking at.

Master Mr. Bodkin married a quiet Richmond girl whose father was a lawyer and a politician.

She was a softhearted, shrinking thing, ill-suited to rural life. She didn't like the mud. She didn't like the strong, quivering flesh of horses. She didn't like to ride. In certain circles it was wondered if she'd actually ever agreed to be married. Perhaps she was simply so shy that she hadn't said no.

The feelings that Master Mr. Bodkin held for her, however, were sincere. He wanted to protect her. Missy was built of fine, thin porcelain, and he was sworn to shelter her from the crushing realities of the world. His life was messy—the breeding shed was a violent, passionate place. Missy was purity personified. He was deeply in love with her. She gave him a son, Oliver Bodkin VII.

She was too frail to nurse, but there was no shortage of breast milk at Bodkin's Hundred. Master Mr. Bodkin sat by her bedside, watching the sweat pour into the mattress. She talked through her fever dreams, her nightmares, her giddy hallucinations of a terrible world.

"Why am I in this place? Is that mud on the carpet? Have animals been in here? Where are we? Don't let animals in here."

"We're home. You're with me, at home."

"No, no. Not here."

She died when Oliver VII was two weeks old, and whatever small corners of gentleness Master Mr. Bodkin had seen in the world went with her. After her death, Master Mr. Bodkin spent his time in the barns or in the quarters, ate standing up in the mud, and rode his horses hard, kicking them over hedges and across streams. He drank. While his son toddled around the enormous New House, he preyed upon the women of the slave quarters like a raccoon in a henhouse. He was violent, insatiable. His father was dead, his sister had married and gone to Alabama, where her husband grew cotton. His wife was all that had attached him to civilization, and with her gone, he came unhinged, swept away by a river of blood and semen. He'd watch the crushing violence of the stallions mounting their mares in the breeding shed, and turn, inspired, to the quarters, where his teeth marks adorned the neck of many a black girl.

He decided he no longer trusted the slaves to breed unsupervised and designated one of the huts for breeding. He managed the copulation of the enslaved as he did the horses. Noting who among them seemed the most vigorous, and who was quick to impregnate. He'd lean against the doorframe and watch. When one slave objected to the audience, he spent the next four months with an iron branks with a two-inch bit fitted over his head and worked between his teeth to keep his tongue pressed down.

The driver in these years was a coarse and callous drunkard named Callum. One afternoon, while the two of them ripped hunks from a chicken they were turning on a spit and talked with full mouths, their lips flecked with shreds of pale meat, Master Mr. Bodkin saw a young slave brushing down a stallion.

"Is that Flora?" he said.

"Flora. She's growing up a nice one," said Callum.

Flora moved the currycomb on the animal, softly cooing.

The flush Master Mr. Bodkin felt in his chest surprised him. He had thought himself devoid of feeling, and in the brief moments he dedicated to introspective reverie, imagined himself withered, like the blackened, gnarled struck-by-lightning loblolly stump at the woods' edge past the far pasture. That he felt anything at all was a shock. That he felt it for a girl he owned was an affront.

"Whip her."

Callum raised a thick eyebrow, but he loved the whip in his hand more than anything else in life, save perhaps whiskey, and he wasted no time.

Flora shrieked when he grabbed her, but fell limp. She was stripped and her hands were tied to the high ring on the whipping post that stood in the center of the quarters: an obelisk built as a monument to oppression, a constant invocation of fear.

Master Mr. Bodkin watched as the whip cut into her. She bled. He walked off before Callum had laid his last blow, had the stallion she'd been brushing saddled, and dug his spurs into its sides.

He stormed for a week. He slammed doors and looked over figures—but the ledger book failed to hold his attention. He'd startle to find himself rocked back in a chair in the library, staring through the oil portrait of Gunnery that hung above the mantel. He could hear her gasps as if she were in the room.

Without fully recognizing what he was doing, like a man compelled to manipulate the satisfaction of an addiction he has not admitted, he sold one of the housemaids in Richmond and had Flora sent up to take her place.

The departure of the driver Callum (he'd knocked out three of a buyer's teeth at the auction in Richmond for a perceived slight) and Flora's journey up to the New House like a sacrificial lamb brought some modicum of peace to the plantation. Master Mr. Bodkin ranged no more, he had eyes only for one.

Flora's firstborn came soon, and she was pregnant again shortly thereafter.

She hemorrhaged during the delivery of her second child and died as the baby took its first breath.

Master Mr. Bodkin was beside himself, and humiliated by his emotions.

Whatever was left inside him seemed to deflate. He no longer had the stomach for business, or cruelty. The void was familiar, it had never gone, but now there was no filling it. Even greed failed to stoke him. Where once he was passionate he was now laconic. His violence turned to apathy. Anhedonia was his muse.

He sent his now ten-year-old son, Oliver VII, north to board at school and took rooms in Richmond. He hired a widow to be his cook and a young man named Harrison Hollingsworth, just graduated from the university in Charlottesville, to be his agent. Most of the horses of Bodkin's Hundred were slowly sold off, as were the enslaved. The Bodkin stock was valuable, and the whole state knew it. When Master Mr. Bodkin's stallions were walked through the ring, prices soared. The crowds around the auction block in Shockoe Bottom, down by the river where most of the slaves in Richmond were sold, were equally frenzied.

Over sheets and ledger books in his sitting room with Harrison Hollingsworth, Master Mr. Bodkin explained that he wanted to keep just enough to keep the place going.

Hollingsworth sighed. It was not the first time he'd come to this impasse with his client. Hollingsworth was a practical man, and his desire for liquidity far outpaced whatever small understanding he had, through hearsay, of the value of lineage and land. He had nothing to be nostalgic about. These were stories he had read, no realer than dragons. He thought of the investments that could be made, the capital freed, the influence bought with such a windfall.

"There is some interest, I know a man looking for a tract of land, keen to enter into conversation—"

Master Mr. Bodkin held up a hand to stop him. He would not sell Bodkin's Hundred.

He didn't have to say it, he'd said it before: "Sell the graves of my family? Sell the clay that we dug?"

Hollingsworth showed him a roster, and they discussed the value of each item on the list.

"These two are quite young, sir, but no doubt we can sell them at a good price."

Master Mr. Bodkin scanned down the list, found the names under discussion. They were Flora's children. Raleigh and Temple.

"No, not them. They'll stay. Find them a place there. The kitchen perhaps. Lo will watch after them."

"He got some sickness, I guess," said Raleigh.

"Couldn't barely walk," said Temple. "Wrapped in a blanket look like some kinda spook witch."

Master Mr. Bodkin had the flu. His doctor had thought that the clean country air, the comfort of his homeplace, might mend him. It was a last-ditch attempt. The doctor suspected that he'd sent Master Mr. Bodkin home to die, and on a settee in the library, adrift on a river of laudanum, watched over by his portrait of Gunnery, he did.

Raleigh and Temple had finished their apples, thrown the cores as far as they could across the river, and had set about an argument over fish.

"If the frogs are peeping, the fish are awake."

"It's too cold for fish," said Raleigh.

"It ain't too cold for peeper frogs. Listen at them."

The year's crop of frogs was calling out its a relentless throb.

"Frogs are so happy. They tell everybody." Raleigh said.

The children listened, and as they stood with heads cocked, the striker on the bell by the New House clanged a slow and steady knell. The somber rhythm rolled across the fields of Bodkin's Hundred with a clear meaning. Master Mr. Bodkin was dead.

Lo had put out a loaf of winter wheat bread and a tub of fresh butter. Gee held a jug of cider and poured cupfuls around.

"Fern and Liza still up the house?" Lo asked.

Gee nodded that they were.

Raleigh looked hard into the faces around the table. It wasn't sadness that he saw, but worry. Sad grown-ups would answer questions, worried ones never wanted to talk.

The bell had stopped ringing the news. The peeper frogs sang on from their puddles.

"We gonna wait and see," said Lo. "Ain't nothing we can do about it. We just have to wait and see what happens now."

CHAPTER THREE

In the City

Summer 1846

Jed Stokes did not walk into the city the next morning, as he had intended. Tasks presented themselves to him, and he soon settled into his chores.

From the snare by the big red cedar Jed pulled a strangled rabbit. His knife made quick work of the cleaning, and he threw the gut pile and the fur down the rocks toward the river, where the birds would find them. He built his fire against a nearby pine, so the needles would blur the smoke and drift it out among the trees like a wisp of heavy fog.

He spit roasted the rabbit and ate it in the crook of a massive fallen chestnut. When he finished, he reclined along the trunk of the chestnut, watched the light change against the leaves, and listened to the forest.

Under the trunk of the chestnut, Jed dug out a flat place and smoothed the dirt, where he stacked a small pallet of twigs to keep his belongings elevated. He gathered laurel and leaned it against the trunk to create a rudimentary shelter. He surveyed his work, satisfied with what he'd done. In the afternoon he walked back up the road to a grove of peach trees he'd seen and plucked a few ripe ones.

He expected to be pulled into the city like a leaf into a river hole, and although he didn't understand, or couldn't articulate, how exactly this was going to happen, if anyone had been there to ask him he'd have said that he was ready. The evidence of his activities, however, pointed out that he was perhaps less prepared than he admitted to himself. His chores, at least, he understood completely, and therefore kept at the plain and obvious tasks of survival. As he tidied his burrow, hunted and cleaned small game, built his fire, and mixed his corn mush, he told himself these were necessary. In the woods he perambulated a circle that brought him up to the gardens of some country houses, from which he snuck greens and okra to augment the peaches.

Life in the woods was easy, and it didn't occur to him to leave until his cornmeal was down to the corner of the sack, at which point he took up his coins and walked to the general store he'd seen along the road that led into town.

When the door shut behind him, he felt the stillness of the air, the dust trapped in the corners. The smoke of the lamp that had clung to the wall smelled oily and pungent. The man behind the counter looked up and greeted Jed.

"Yessir can I help?"

Jed blinked in the gray light of the store. How long had he been in the woods, he wondered? The pressure of a man's focus seemed new and strangely intense.

"Can I do you for?" The man had a mustache that looked as if it belonged to someone else, furry and fat and wriggling above his lip like it wanted to go home.

Jed knew that this was easy, and reminded himself that all he had to do was open his mouth and make the shapes of the words that corresponded with what it was that he wanted, but he couldn't make himself do it.

The glass tops of the candy jars reflected corners of light and sparkled in front of him. The coffee beans in the burlap sack that leaned against the wall behind the counter smelled of dark oil and roasted wood.

Jed looked at the barrels, and said, over the cornmeal: "Some of this."

"Yessir," said the shopkeeper, relieved that the wild-eyed man intended to purchase goods. "How about some side meat to go along with that corn? Got a good salted piece of hog in just yesterday. Nice streak of lean."

Jed nodded and dug from his purse a few coins.

The man and his mustache were jovial, and they seemed full of absurd condescension as they thanked Jed for his patronage and bowed in mock solemnity to close the deal. Jed felt a surge of anger and felt that he needed to defend himself from being mocked.

"My money's good, ain't it?"

The shopkeeper had no answer, which Jed counted as a victory. Outside, Jed saw an old flat spade leaning against the wall and he reached out smoothly and carried it off.

Back up the hill, at his Chestnut, Jed stripped the laurel stems off the roof of his hole, and while it was exposed he used the spade to dig out his floor enough so that he could sit without bending his head. The spade was old and had been left out so that the handle had dried and started to crack. Jed shook his head at this proof that the shopkeeper was a fool who didn't know the value of things or how to care for a simple tool.

He let the air move through the burrow, and then reassembled the laurel leaf cover, adding to it, and taking care that it'd keep out the weather.

Having civilized his camp in such a way made him feel better about himself.

Every day, he spent careful hours making sure his things were in place, the dirt smooth, hanging his blanket from a cord he'd fastened between two branches. He imagined, in the slanted light of the morning, that if his father were alive he'd hike himself up atop the trunk of the fat chestnut tree, sit with his leg bouncing over his knee as he was wont, and smile at the simple and clean grace that his son had made here in the woods.

After Jed learned the woods around his camp, and the few houses with gardens nearby, he gradually expanded his circles until he became familiar with the road that led to town. The houses there, small farmsteads and the homes of businesspeople, were just like those of Alcott's Brook, and he felt enough at ease. In the way that these things happen, folks started to recognize him.

Jed helped a man who was struggling to repair a fence that kept his milk cows.

"I need three hands is what I need," said the man, laughing at the futility of trying to hold the fence board by pressing his weight against it.

Jed walked over, nodding, and held the plank up steady so the man could drive the nail. They drank cool water and shook hands and Jed met the man's wife, who gave him a piece of cheese to take with him.

They asked if Jed was new around here, and he said he reckoned he was, so they figured he'd moved into a tavern up the road. Jed let them think what they wanted to think.

He felt like an explorer, mapping a steadily increasing area, although he more resembled a man wandering aimlessly through a pathless swamp. His excursions and the familiarity he bred with the folks along the road bolstered his confidence, and bit by bit, he introduced himself to the city.

In the first neighborhood he explored, the houses were like castles, with polished brass on every door, new paint, and stairs swept clean. Some of the houses had staid stone columns, or fluted wood painted white, or, and this impressed Jed most of all, iron forged to look like vines. This was a world firmly ordered, he thought, in which nature was kept at bay. The patterns—so rigid, so squared, so clearly a victory over wildness—the wrought iron imitations of leaves were like a taunt, a tease, to that which had fallen. The air was bright and breezy along the spine of the hill.

Jed stepped aside, overtly chivalric, to allow two women in hooped skirts with their corsets drawn tight to pass. They were young, their cheeks were high, their lips were red. The smell of gardenias and bergamot wafted through the air behind them. Women like flowers, stoops of polished marble, everything as fresh as snowmelt.

Deeper into town, on a street with no houses, just one business after another, the purpose of none of which were clear to Jed, there stood a black man with a cauldron of oil over a fire, frying fish. Jed bought a piece, crusted in cornmeal and dowsed in pepper vinegar. He ate standing, wiping his hands on a piece of newspaper the cook handed him.

"What fish is this?"

"Rockfish?" The black man raised his eyebrows.

Jed had never eaten fish that swam in salt water. His fish were bass, trout, bluegills, cats—muddy tasting river fish. This was firm, fat, and salty.

"It's delicious."

The cook nodded a bow, a mixture of deference and disdain.

Jed pointed to what looked like a bushel of rocks.

"What are those?"

"These here?"

Jed nodded.

"These here are oysters."

"They good?"

"You ain't had oysters?"

Jed shook his head. The man cracked six of them—unhinging the rocks and cleaving them in half, setting them atop the barrelhead next to the bottle of pepper vinegar. Jed stood, dumbfounded. The gray, tender flesh quivered against the pale white and purple lip of the inside.

"Hang on, all right, all right," the man cracked another oyster for himself, splashed some of the vinegar sauce on it, did the same on Jed's and said: "Like me."

He sucked it down. Jed followed suit.

"There you go, sir. That's it."

Jed's face was alight.

"Thank you, sir," said Jed.

The cook looked up and down the street, suspicious of this innocent white man who looked him in the eye and thanked him. Jed ate the oysters and proffered another coin but the cook refused it.

"You all right, boy. Now get on," said the cook.

Jed thanked him again and continued downhill, toward Shockoe Bottom.

Jed's life had been spent tasting almost nothing but the earth he was born on. His butter tasted like Stokes mountain grass, just as his family's pigs tasted like Stokes mountain acorns. His beans and his greens tasted the same every year, grown from their own seed, watered by Stokes mountain rain. These oysters. They were something else entirely. Jed Stokes had never seen the ocean, never watched a tide, never smelled seaweed. The oyster was a window.

Bright spots sustained Jed. He could wave to the man whose fence he'd help to fix, and eat oysters with the black cook, and feel as if he were part of something. The city itself, however, seemed to deny him, to elude him. He walked for hours each day, and came home to his burrow.

As time went on, he became more furtive. He slunk along in his explorations of the city, trying not to be noticed, adopting casual airs and slinking into shadows when he could. He saw a group of men standing in front of a barbershop, and he turned into an alley to avoid walking past them. He stuck to a pattern, a course, allowing small distractions and avoidances to distract him but never to rule him.

He cared for his burrow in the morning, when he woke, and the process became a ritual. He raked the dirt with laurel leaves, straightened the coverings, then did it again. He lit a small fire, and slurped a cornmeal porridge, or ate a pilfered apple while counting his coins. He found that when he counted them, he couldn't remember the total. He had to count them three times before he learned how much money was left in his pouch. It wasn't much.

He stole when he could. He'd loiter by the bread man's cart until his back was turned and make off with a loaf. He'd duck into the back door of a butcher shop while the butcher was chasing cats down the alley and grab a sausage.

Embarrassed to be seen by the man whose fence he'd fixed, he'd cut into the woods rather than walk in front of his house, and pause behind the underbrush to watch the man and his wife as they worked around the homestead. Their movements no longer made sense to him, but he was curious about what they did.

In early October he stopped and watched them as the sun set and after they'd gone inside he snatched a chicken from their henhouse and ran up into his woods with it. He swung it hard in a circle to break its neck while he darted through the soft fall leaves.

The first time he walked through the city at night, it was because he'd been startled awake by a crack of twigs and found himself unable to get back to sleep. Rather than cower in his burrow, he stepped out into the night. The moon shone through the yellowing leaves, and the air was crisp and clean. He stretched and walked a bit and soon found himself comfortably walking through the streets of Richmond with no concern as to whether or not he belonged there. Nothing was for sale at night, nothing was expected of him. He held the shadows around him like a cloak, and looked at whatever he wanted to look at without the prying, questioning eyes of the shopkeepers. A wandering man must explain himself during the day, but at night he was free.

Shortly thereafter he found himself resistant, and then wholly unwilling to leave his burrow under the tree during the day. He slept through the morning. Woke in the afternoon and tidied the burrow, swept the dirt, arranged the laurels, checked the snares, ate some cornmeal, and watched the sun go down. He walked next to the road, in the woods, until he reached the edge of the city, where he stopped and watched as folks returned to their houses, lit their porch lights, stoked the fires that chuffed smoke out of the chimneys and drifted across the rooftops. Once the doors were closed and the people's attention was turned inward, toward their families and their evening tasks, Jed emerged and walked through shadows. He had learned where the raucous taverns and saloons were, where the meeting halls filled with political rallies and arguments that stretched on into the night were, and he walked near them, but just out of view.

One night, on a quiet street he came across a young, well-to-do man leaned back upon a stoop, his hand dropped around a bottle of whiskey. Jed looked at the man's well-oiled beard and watched his chest move up and down under his clean, fitted gray coat. Jed carefully plucked the bottle from the man's grip, and found it to be half full. He moved on; the man stayed as he was.

The whiskey was clean and soft, like honey when he compared it to the fiery home still stuff of Alcott's Brook. He swigged, and held it by the neck as he set to walking through the lingering drifts of the scents of old clothes and burning tobacco. An argument between a man and a woman bounced between the bricks, over top of a clattering of wagon wheels farther away. He stood at the corner where the hellfire preacher hollered during the day and laughed.

He walked past low, rough buildings, and into a scraggly field to a small creek, where he knelt at the bank and parted the stiff grass. He set the bottle by his side and leaned toward the water with hands outstretched until the putrescence from the brook rose like hot air from a stove and pushed him back. In the darkness he could see lumps of filth floating in the weak stream. He picked his way along the bank which was littered with broken glass, slaked his thirst with whiskey, and walked until the creek drained into an arched culvert, where he scrambled up to the street. He had come to the docks. The air smelled of pitch.

Warehouses loomed, facing the docks, their sliding doors drawn tight and locked, the stoops that led to their offices swept clean. Hearing voices, he hugged the walls of the buildings and walked toward the noise, curious. When he came to a tall fence of pickets—the poles were thick, sharpened to points, and higher than his hand could reach if he stretched—he understood that most of the noise came from within these walls. Ghostly noises, rooted in misery, full of pain.

It didn't seem like a fort. More like a jail. He searched the wall for some point of entry, his fingers grazing the creosote-soaked timber.

There was a heavy creak, and a deep thudding bell rang out. One pull of the bell rope, the clapper struck twice, and the shuddering hung in the air. Two light chimes answered from the water.

A gate in the picket twenty paces farther on rasped open, heavy iron complaining as it slid on the inlays.

"Move 'em!" someone shouted.

Jed flattened himself against the picket wall.

"Go on, go on!"

A whip cracked.

Chains ground their links together as from the gate appeared black men, chained together at the neck and at the feet, so that they themselves made a chain. Their hands were locked to the links that connected them at the neck. They lumbered forth onto the cobblestones, trying to find a rhythm that would keep them from bouncing, pulling their collars, and choking one another. One in the middle stumbled, and a white man ran forward from behind the walls, hollered, and cracked a whip. What had been a stumble became a fall. The captive crumpled to his knees, halting the lurching progress of the terrible snake. The two men closest to the man now on the ground were on their knees. A white man rushed forth from the gate and brought the butt of his whip down hard on the fallen man's head.

"Hey, now, these is purchased and paid for goods. These boys is worth money! Get them on the boat in one piece!"

The man with the whip pulled the fallen man up, taunting him. The black men were naked. They didn't look up.

A man on a nervous filly rode out of the gate, having a hard time keeping her on task. She skittered on the cobbles, drifting and turning. She didn't like the sound of the whip or the smell of fear in the air.

A lantern appeared on the deck of a ship, and the twenty captives trudged across the road toward its inconstant light.

The horseman and his partner stayed on the shore.

The black men stopped on the gangplank, their chains thudded together like a terrifying drum.

"C'mon! This way!" called the man on the boat. "C'mon, move!"

But the black men didn't move.

"Move, damn you!" cried the man standing on the shore.

The filly skittered sideways.

One of the chained called out: "Has the bell rung?"

In unison, the reply came: "The bell done rung!"

"I said, 'has the bell rung?'" His voice was strong.

The filly was spinning around. The man standing on the shore reached for the pistol stuck in his belt.

Again, the choir: "The bell done rung."

The big voice of the leader boomed: "I stand on a sea of glass and fire!"

The black men took one step to the right, all of them. The chains clunked and the choir answered: "The bell done rung!"

Again the leader boomed: "And the lord gonna lift my soul up higher!"

"The bell done rung!"

They took a step to the left, as one. The chains were heavy and the sound they made was dull and thick. As one, the twenty plunged off the side of the gangplank and into the water. They did not shout or try to catch themselves.

They had found a moment of freedom in the space between the shore and the boat, and they had decided to stay there.

The surface erupted into sprays, and the river gave a deep, reverberating thunk. The chains pulled the men down, and foamy ripples broke against the hulls of the docked boats.

The filly broke and ran, eyes bulging, lunging while the man astride her pulled on her reins, feet thrust forward now to better leverage everything he had against the animal. He was screaming, cussing, and the filly was swinging her head back and forth, trying to shake the bit out of her mouth. With each bound forward she gained momentum, until she crashed straight into a wrought iron fence. The rider flew out of the saddle, headlong over the iron fence, and smacked against the bricks of the building behind it. He flopped to the ground, his body at unnatural angles, bleeding from his head.

There were bubbles rising in the river.

The filly backed up and shimmied herself into order; she trotted back into the gate with her head held high and her nostrils flaring.

"We have to tell somebody," said the man on the shore.

"Is he dead, too?" said the man on the gangplank.

They walked to the dismounted rider, crumpled at the foundation of the warehouse. He was lodged in the narrow space between the wrought iron and the brick, and the two men couldn't get to him. He groaned. They promised to get him help and ran off, hollering, panicked and confused.

Jed was breathing hard.

He blinked and tried to will the whole thing away. He crossed the street and stared into the slow swirl of the river, brown and thick. There were no more bubbles rising from the dead, chained together on the river's floor.

Jed turned and looked at the broken man dying against the brick wall, and saw blood in a pool under his ruined form. He looked at the lantern on the boat.

He didn't want to be here when the men came back.

He walked upstream, heading west, disgusted.

The wind picked up as he walked, and the bluster was formidable by the time Jed made it to his burrow. Looking south he saw black clouds in the dawn light. The river was roiling and frothed. The wind came in gusts on top of a persistent, relentless blow. He stood at the edge of the cliff, then squatted to lessen the blows of the buffeting wind. It wasn't raining, yet, or not raining much, more like the wind was just pushing water around in the air—he'd find his cheek was damp, but there were no raindrops. The trees behind him creaked like the old chairs on Tomlinson's porch back in Alcott's Brook. He ducked into the shelter of the chestnut and huddled against the root ball. The trunk was wide enough to cover him, and he'd swept the dirt up until it had formed rough mud walls. He watched the thin branches on either side of the tree whip in the wind. When the rain came, it hit hard. Now there was thunder, and sheets of water. Trees bent, and he heard branches snap, then boughs, then the rushing tumble of whole trunks ripped from the ground. Water seeped in, muddying his floor. He took up his things and held them in his lap, hoping that the pallet he sat upon would be tall enough to keep him from sinking into the mud.

Every time Jed felt that the storm had reached its maximum power and would soon dissipate, it grew in strength. The wind lifted trees from the mud and threw them against the forest floor. The rain came now like a wave, a waterfall. The storm raged without cessation, without respite. Jed cowered in his den, whimpering. Surely this was biblical. Surely this was the end of the world.

He had almost forgotten words, had Jed. His thoughts, so immediate for so long, had barely resembled language. They were impulsive, instinctual flashes that led to immediate action meant to preserve him and the small order which he imposed upon his world. Now, language overtook him. He was aware, for the first time in weeks, months, of how alive he was. He cried out and felt his voice tiny in the battering forces of nature.

"What is this storm, then?" he asked, "if not a reckoning? Those black men sang out their last and plunged to their death and brought forth this. Their chant called forth some judgment. They sang out, and the bell they cried for has now rung. Why have I been included in this? Am I to be washed away?"

If it was time, he thought, he wanted to be neither sheep nor goat. He felt neither was accurate. He'd had nothing with which to grant comfort, nor anything to deny anyone. Who had he turned away? No one. He'd moved from his mountain, to this hill, and he'd lived as sealed and quiet and alone as a man might live. These thoughts poured through him like prayers. He was terrified.

A tree fell across the great chestnut under which he huddled, and the tree shook but didn't move.

What do I have to do with this? It isn't my doing that cracked the sky open.

He saw, by the way the tree had fallen across the chestnut, that it had formed another layer of protection and cover. He wondered if the destructive force that whipped such fury all around had heard him and agreed. This vengeance—how could it be anything else?—was not against him.

At sunset, the clouds broke, and the storm ceased. He crawled out through the branches of the tree that had fallen across his chestnut. The sunset was glorious, streaks of color shot across the sky. He'd survived.

He gathered his things, inventoried them, and walked into Richmond.

CHAPTER FOUR

The Arrival

Spring 1856

Since Master Mr. Bodkin had died, Raleigh had taken on the nervousness displayed by the others without understanding it, the way a horse reacts to fear felt by its rider. He couldn't know what hung in the balance, but he could tell that it was big.

While they'd waited for the funeral, Master Mr. Bodkin in repose in the Big House, Gee spent more time in the kitchen with Lo than usual, sitting on the milking stool and listening to her.

"What happen then, ain't nobody know." She worked a little knife around an onion she held in her hand, dropping the cut pieces into a cauldron. When she finished she picked up a carrot. From a hook in the low rafters hung a plucked chicken, its feet tied together with a loop of twine which Lo had held when she bled out the bird over the graveyard dirt. "I guess we go down there to the swamp," she said.

Gee nodded.

"See about who is living there. Long as I have been a part of this road, I have heard about the maroons in the Dismal Swamp, and how they live free. Don't sound like no place for children," she said. Gee shook his head. "Anyway . . . they, you know?"

Gee nodded, sad-eyed but questioning. They were Bodkin children, these two, they belonged here. Not on the run in the wilds of a swamp, camped out with fugitives and Indians.

"Go draw some water, Temple," said Lo.

Temple slid off her crate and took the bucket. Whether or not Lo was overlooking them or tolerating their presence had been an issue of some debate between the siblings. Raleigh believed it was an accident. The adults were just too distracted and worried to give them chores or remember to get rid of them. Temple believed they were being allowed to stay in the kitchen and listen on purpose. Before she stepped outside she turned to Raleigh and gave him eyes that said she had told him so.

Temple was back with a sloshing bucket of water just as Lo finished the third carrot. Lo continued her one-sided conversation with Gee, and Gee nodded or shook his head in the appropriate way along with her.

"Nobody know what that boy been doin', what he learned up there in all these years. How long? Ten, twelve years? He a man now, ain't he? He left all fat-cheeked and sweet, pulling on my aprons and asking me for jam, but he's coming back a man. What's he gonna do with all this? He got a family? Ain't heard of no family, but don't see as how we would have heard about a family even if there was one. He coming down here with a child a his own? Another Oliver Bodkin pulling on my apron and asking for jam?"

She chuckled. In Raleigh's imagination all the Bodkin men, stretching back through a thousand years, had stood in this kitchen and asked Lo for jam. Hundreds and hundreds of pink-cheeked little white boys in crisp shirts, begging.

"That Master Mr. had a taste for sweets, ain't he though?"

Gee nodded, but whatever had made Lo chuckle brought a gray cloud to Gee's visage. Seeing the shift in his mood, she stopped her work and took out a tub of apple butter and spread it on slices of bread, which she passed to everyone.

Temple kicked her feet and took a big happy bite.

"Didn't always work out for everybody. I know it, old man," said Lo. "We both know it. Let it be. We got to worry about tomorrow, now. Everything is everything."

Small changes were afoot already, the first of which was the presence of Harrison Hollingsworth, who moved in while they waited for Oliver Bodkin and spent his days walking around the place, counting things, and inspecting. He carried a folded paper and looked at it now and again, and knew everyone's name. This deterred the briefly discussed possibility that now was the time to walk off of Bodkin's Hundred.

"You see? That Hollingsworth knows you. He send them men after you, you come back here dead," said Lo to the farmhands.

Fern and Liza had always kept the house as if there were people in it, or people about to be in it, but the presence of an actual guest, in the form of Hollingsworth, was novel and interesting, and it tempted Raleigh and Temple into the house, where they snuck through the familiar halls and looked for clues. They watched Fern stoke the fires in the guest room Hollingsworth had chosen, and they spied on Liza while she delivered his breakfast. Hollingsworth proved an abstracted man of simple, predictable needs, and the children followed him, as he walked the halls and corridors, listened from an adjacent room as he ate cold roast in the library. In the afternoon he walked to the cellar and found something to drink. He barely spoke a command. His pen scratched and scratched at the big carved desk in the corner of the library.

Wherever Raleigh and Temple went in the house, they took care that their routes avoided the side parlor in which lay the corpse of Master Mr. Bodkin, which Raleigh had seen out of the corner of his eye.

"Dead man in church clothes!" he said to Temple, "Up on a table made up like a bed!"

"Let's go look at it," said Temple.

Raleigh shook his head solemnly.

Raleigh had always felt that the New House had been conjured by magic—like the story Lo told about the snake rainbow named Aida-Wedo and her companion Damballah who was also a snake and a rainbow, and how they had sprung up from the earth to join together and teach us all. It made as little sense as the creation of something as grand as this house, for where could all these shimmering windows and sparkling mirrors come from if it had not risen from the ground? Now it was occupied by the dead.

"You must be Mr. Hollingsworth," said Oliver, removing a soft glove and offering his hand, over which Hollingsworth bowed slightly.

"It's hardly my place to offer, Mr. Bodkin, in your own house, but as you've just arrived can I get you anything? A glass of something? A bite to eat?"

Hollingsworth took some wood from the small stack by the fireplace and stoked the fire. They sat in leather chairs before it, each with his feet stretched out toward the glow. On the small occasional table with the alternating light and dark inlays quilted in a pattern like a star sat a bottle of sherry and two small glasses. They soon abandoned the pretense of pouring for one another and drank as friends, each according to his thirst.

"We have much to discuss," said Hollingsworth.

"But no particular reason to hurry its discussion, I hope," said Oliver. "I think we should—well, we hardly know one another. It seems to me that business is easiest among friends."

Hollingsworth couldn't help but think that this sounded like the sentiment of a man not much accustomed to business. Master Mr. Bodkin could hardly be said to have dwelt upon his son—he was rarely spoken of—but in the dozen-odd years of Hollingsworth's employ, he had been in charge of disbursals of money—at times ludicrous sums—for pianos, apartments, books, fabric. There had been special requests for payment of invoices and services regarding English wallpaper. Hollingsworth would flinch when he saw the engraved stationery of Master Tailor Solomon Stock. He was surprised to find that Oliver was a vital man, and not the wretched, corrupted wastrel that he often had imagined him to be. He had his father's eyes, and broad, flat forehead of every Bodkin. His features were darkened by the French influence on his mother's side, and this granted his intelligence an air of intensity.

"You've had a long journey," said Hollingsworth.

"The ride from Richmond was pleasant enough," said Oliver, reaching forward to loosen the top buckle on his tall boots, as if remembering from mentioning it that he was attired in breeches and boots and a sack coat of thick tweed—a costume meant for riding. "My things will follow me in the morning."

Hollingsworth nodded.

"I'm very sorry," said Hollingsworth, "about your father's death."

Oliver looked surprised, but composed himself. "Thank you," he said. After a brief pause, he continued, "And I feel that you should have my condolences, as well. My father trusted and admired you. I know that you've worked hard in his interest, and for—what has it been now? Since I went away to school, more or less? Twelve years?"

Hollingsworth nodded.

"I've been too far away I suppose, Mr. Hollingsworth. Too much time a cosmopolitan," he chuckled.

Hollingsworth was not sure what was being said, was someone being mocked? If so, who?

"Too much time gone to tolerate the savagery of this rough country." Oliver swigged and refilled his cordial glass. "It has its charms, to be sure. But what does it do to better us?"

Did he mean Bodkin's Hundred? Or did he mean to speak in more general terms? The region? Its traditions? Hollingsworth could think of numerous things bettered by each of those. His own livelihood, for one. Oliver's fortune, for another. He'd heard these lines before. The street corner preachers of Richmond, the craven, God-drunk Baptists liked to conflate, in their abolitionism, the traditions, the region, and the land into one hell-bound package. Hollingsworth kept his thoughts.

Oliver continued: "It seems to me that Jefferson's prophecy has come to pass, the South is corrupted, poisoned by its own preoccupations, corrupted by its institutions, mired in its own guilty filth."

Hollingsworth didn't attempt response, although Oliver looked at him in anticipation of one.

"We'll sort it out. I don't want it, but we'll sort it out."

Hollingsworth would be haunted and confused by those words all night, but for now he shifted the conversation to more practical, immediate concerns—yes, his old room was ready for him, yes they could arrange for breakfast to be served. Yes, they'd arranged the funeral for tomorrow. They turned to the guest list and muttered names back and forth.

The shrouded body of Master Mr. Bodkin was walked out on a board. Hollingsworth had attended to the details—the piano black coffin in the bed of the austere carriage of duller black was there, just past the eaves, and ready for him. Lo, standing off to the side, feigning servility, took note that this same ground had absorbed the blood of Little Edward, and contemplated how odd it was that the death of Master Mr. Bodkin would bring nothing but open ends.

The funeral carriage rolled to the bricked-in family plot by the Old House—a short ride—and its cargo was lowered into the hole by Gee and the three farmhands, dressed for the occasion in suits they'd keep as payment. As Gee leaned forward to pull up the lowering rope, he let drop from his palm a black feather pressed into black candle wax.

Many had come to witness Master Mr. Bodkin laid to rest, and now that he was in the ground they milled about, eating Lo's ham biscuits and drinking. A few were honestly moved, but mostly, the attendees felt that their witness of the final moments Master Mr. Bodkin spent aboveground made his death official: they were there not to grieve, but to notarize.

Raleigh and Temple were hidden in the leaves of a big magnolia, watching.

Temple recognized Oliver Bodkin from the paintings in the house—the wide-set eyes, the flat forehead—but this Oliver Bodkin wasn't stern. His dark hair was soft and long, and he had pink cheeks without whiskers. In between condolences, he looked bored.

On the cool spring morning after the funeral, when the dew was still upon the grass, Oliver Bodkin opened the wrought iron gate and stepped into the small family cemetery. The hinge had been newly greased, and the gate swung smoothly and quietly. There they were, lined up with their wives: the Oliver Bodkins. Brothers and sisters and lesser sons were interred here as well, but the Olivers had the place of distinction. They lay from left to right at his feet. A name the same as his own carved into each stone in Copperplate Gothic, slightly fresher in each iteration. No descriptions, no symbols, no credits or plaudits—just the names.

Oliver Bodkin, Oliver Bodkin, Oliver Bodkin, Oliver Bodkin, Oliver Bodkin, Oliver Bodkin.

He rolled his eyes in bored disdain, felt bad about it, and walked to the fresh earth mounded up at the new grave, next to the green grass that was his.

Oliver, being a youngish man, just twenty-five, had not lived much with the specter of his own mortality. Had not felt the cool breath of death on his neck.

There is where I will rot, he thought. *There is where my bones will turn to dust.*

Last week, the dead man had been ill, as he had been before. When he first felt the tightness in his chest, or the scratch in his throat, he must have been annoyed. A cough coming on, ameliorated with tea and whiskey. If he'd known the truth would he have dashed about? Bent himself to work? Written furious letters settling old scores, declaring hidden loves, final pleas for whatever he felt he was owed? At what point—if indeed there was a point—did he feel death calling? No longer a sickness with an end, but a sickness that would end him. The end itself.

Did he spend long with the knowledge that death was nigh, hours or days? Was he too reduced to consider it at all? Did he listen to the mumbled bedside discussions of physicians, aware of their attempts, perhaps dismissive of them, knowing the futility. Did he laugh at their hope? Or their attempts to conceal what was obvious to him? Did he know? In his youth, Oliver had seen a pig bite the hand that fed it—the pig had been right, the man who held the grain held in his other hand a long pig knife. The corn was a bribe and the pig had known: now or never. Is the doorway to death experienced in the fullness of lucidity? Or is it like a distant craving, a thirst while you're still asleep? You know it's out there, you are on intimate terms with the thirst, but you cannot turn it over in your mind and consider it. You are stuck there, as if in a spiderweb, experiencing it.

Oliver wondered if his father, upon reaching his final morning, felt a thirst. Was he urged to relieve himself? Did he itch? Or wish that the blankets covering him were tucked around him differently? It seemed likely that one dies among trivial concerns. Would he have had the strength for grander thoughts? To measure his life upon reaching its conclusion? There life was, after all, to be measured. Whatever he'd left undone, would now stay undone. Whatever he'd thought he might someday achieve, he would not.

What schemes and plans must have been dashed as the water grew shallow for all these men, here, before me. *Before me*, thought Oliver, and before me.

How many of these men had died with something left to prove? Surely even the giants among us, the kings and conquerors, must have nagging away at them some idiosyncratic collection of proofs and measures they still wished to set right. Perhaps even more so for all their accomplishments. Perhaps the man whose works were great would, by the nature of his character, die unsatisfied? Who dies knowing they've done what they meant to do? That the story of their life will be written as they would like to read it? Is it the simpler man who dies with a smile? Lays down his tools, his hammer or hoe, and rests, perhaps relieved, his accomplishments measurable, that which he has wrought being that which he intended.

These men before me, thought Oliver, each of them with their secret list, how many regrets are buried in this dirt?

CHAPTER FIVE

Virginia's Brave Sons

November 1846

"Brave sons of Virginia!"

The man stood on a box and shouted at the top of his voice, just shy of breaking into a yell, "Your time has come. It is an auspicious season. Ahead of you, heroism, adventure, and honor!" He hit that last—honor!—with a sonorous boom.

Jed nudged through the crowd, easing between the crushes of jostling men, looking for a line, a table to approach, or a door to step through.

The soapbox orator continued: "Is Virginia to be left behind in this? Is our patriotism to be called into question? Allow us, in the sight of the Maker, to express ourselves, to castigate this insolent foe. The field is ours! Reparations will be made! Insults have been hurled, injuries inflicted, and the time for chastisement is now! Brave sons of Virginia, join the fight in Mexico!

"Would you have them call us cowards? Would you have them praise Tennesseans and deprecate us? Is it not we who are called upon to deal the blow that shall fell tyranny? Sic semper tyrannis. Semper Virginia! Semper Fidelis! Step forward, step forward! We call upon you!"

Jed nudged further still. The crowd was amorphous, and while the men in it seemed ready, it wasn't at all clear where they should go.

"For honor! For justice! Be brave! We shall bring the fight to Mexico, we shall bring forth the hammer of this great state in the pursuit of the greatness of our nation. Is it not destiny? Is it not *your* destiny?"

Jed was jostled by the crowd until he came to the table and a man with greasy eyeglasses who did not look up from his papers but said: "Make your mark."

Jed's cot was in the hall in the Union Hotel, where hundreds of Virginia volunteers were encamped and waiting, crammed into rooms, and dozing on cots strung along every hallway. If the men had been quieter, it would have felt like an overflowing sanitarium, but they were rowdy, and bored, and the place stank of them, spilled liquor, and tobacco juice.

Rumors abounded, but nothing happened.

They waited for pay, for uniforms, for assignments into companies.

"You get the feeling," said the fellow casually slumped into a pillow in the cot across the hall, "that someone thinks there's a lot going on, but that not much is actually happening at all."

Jed laughed, for that was exactly the feeling he got.

The man pushed himself up off his pillow, swung his feet to the floor, and introduced himself as Percy Cooke. He was good looking and well taken care of, with a bandanna tied rakishly around his neck and no collar on his shirt. His long hair was tied behind his head. He seemed a couple of years older than Jed's seventeen, but that could have been on account of the air of confident sophistication.

"I heard that we get uniforms tomorrow," said Percy, "though I think I'll believe it when I see it."

The men had taken to wearing gray ribbons tied into their buttonholes to identify themselves as volunteers, and Jed flicked his derisively in response.

"Not much, is it. I mean, we wouldn't be a very impressive company facing down the Mexicans just all of us dressed in street clothes, with ribbons tied to our breasts. Doesn't exactly inspire fear. Have they told you what company you are to be?"

Jed shook his head.

"I don't think they've told anyone. And I don't think they know. They wanted me to move out and go down to drill at the camp at Aquina, but if I'm going to wait, I'm going to wait in Richmond, not in some crumbling fort. When we have a uniform and a boat, I'll march on to it. Let's get out of here."

It hadn't occurred to Jed to leave the hotel. He figured they'd need to ask someone.

"The trick is to walk like you know what you're doing. I could use some refreshment."

Around the corner was a saloon, and Percy bought a large jug of cider and poured out mugs for each of them, saying not to worry, he had money with him.

"Wait for uniforms, wait for assignments, wait for our pay. Somehow I don't think this was what my family had in mind when they suggested I muster into the militia. On account of some imagined history of noble service. Nonsense. I think they made it all up. Second son, however, and no place to argue. They can't send James off to war, he's far too serious."

This was more or less the truth. Percy did have a brother named James, and James was the far more serious of the two. It was also true that Percy's family was deeply self-regarding and possessed, as if it were a treasured heirloom, an inflated sense of their own history in Virginia. They hadn't sent him off to war, though, and if they had they'd have funded a company and put him in charge of it. The truth was that they'd given up on Percy years ago. Not in a dramatic way, as one would a truly wanton drunkard, but more subtly. They simply didn't expect anything of him. They hadn't exiled him from the family, but they hadn't gone out of their way for him. When he'd said he was coming into town for business—half a year ago—no one bothered to ask him what that business was. He'd been living in the Union Hotel, and when the soldiers showed up, he simply decided to become one himself. It was cheaper, anyway. In the disorganization that was the muster, it was easy enough to tie a ribbon into your shirt and move into the hall.

"I figure we're set for a hell of an adventure, though, eh?"

"You reckon?" Jed had begun to feel as if the promises made about honor and adventure were not going to be made good on. "Ain't much to be said for laying around in a stinking hotel all day and night."

"Well," said Percy, "let's improve upon that."

They were not obvious compatriots, but each suited the needs of the other. Percy needed an audience and found it fulfilling to have with him an innocent, wide-eyed country boy who nonetheless could handle his drink and knew his way around a deck of cards. Jed, for his part, was impressed. Percy was loose with his money, and Jed had never known anyone with enough to spend. Percy prioritized pleasure, which Jed hadn't understood to be an option.

Shaken by the storm and by the deaths of the shackled men in the river, terrified that the world was a dark and unpredictable place, Jed had not had his fears assuaged by the interminable waiting in the hotel. With Percy there was nothing to be afraid of. With Percy things worked out. With Percy there were card games, dinners, and bottles of wine. They walked the streets, and Jed felt himself grow taller. He lost a bit of that furtive, defensive belligerence and fell into an easy, energized camaraderie. Young men can barely exist alone. They need one another. Thusly bolstered, they lived out the waiting weeks as if on holiday, Percy's bank account never failing them.

When the company coalesced and they were moved to a fort by the river to drill, the men found themselves ill prepared. The middle of January, no more holidays, no more feasts, just the wind blowing cold off the James River where it grew wide and flat. Jed shivered in the ranks and tried to keep up with the barked commands. No one in the company understood what they were doing, and their marches and exercises only infuriated the West Point officers charged with their training.

The soldiers did their best, but their best wasn't much and the character of the group as individuals and as a fighting unit remained opaque.

A thousand men had come to this camp, including officers, but due to insufficient conditions and insufficient supplies the number was decreasing. Every other day a casket rolled toward home, or another fresh grave was dug. Some men had mumps, others had pneumonia. Coughs racked through the barracks. The post hospital was full.

Most of the officers left for Mexico first. Major Early stepped aboard the *Sophia Walker* with a few companies of men. The *Exact* sailed with another three companies. Colonel Hamtramck left by rail from Richmond, to travel overland and meet again in Port Isabel.

"Perhaps something is happening," said Percy.

"Better than waiting around," said Jed.

"Why wait around to die slowly when you can charge straight into it," said Percy. His morale, which had never amounted to much, had slipped severely.

The friends sailed on a boat called the *Summer Rose.*

"Well, if that's not just the most ironic thing," said Percy, as they made their way through the mouth of the Bay, just off Cape Henry, and the sky darkened. "Stuck on the *Summer Rose* and about to freeze to death when she's smashed to bits. How long do you think we could survive in this water?"

"Please, Percy. Stop."

Men unaccustomed to seafaring clung desperately to anything they could hold and vomited over the side of the ship as the gale churned the waves. The February wind cut through their coats like a blade, their hats were blown into the frothing brine, and most of them were weeping in the face of what they assumed was their demise. Mountains of black water tossed the *Summer Rose*, and none aboard her—not even those who knew her well—believed she could stay afloat. In the trough, there was nothing but water, all around, foaming walls of it moving with malice, a heretofore unimagined destructive force. At the crest, if one caught a glimpse of the horizon, it seemed to be untethered, slanted, completely free from the ship. Then the ship rushed down the wave, broaching, pushed sideways.

The sailors battled, blowing their high pitched whistles into the wind and screaming commands while clinging to the rigging. A mountainous wave crashed over the deck, and for a long, horrifying moment Jed couldn't see. Would he die now? He tightened his grip, and he coughed into the air when the great wave had passed. There had been a man standing next to him, but that man was gone.

The gale subsided, but the winds persisted, blowing at frightening intensity and pulling the canvas of the sails. The ship leaned hard into the rough seas. They were away from the shore. There was nothing but this ship, which seemed now woefully undersized.

Belowdecks, the bilge was already filled, and its odor thickened the humid space with putrescence. When the ship lurched, the men lurched with it, collapsing on one another and grunting stupidly while the lice scrambled to their next home.

The wind was too great for cooking fires, and the soldiers chewed salt pork cold from the stores. (Percy slipped some coins to one of the cooks and got two plates of what the officers were eating in their cabins—fat slices of roast and hunks of corn bread—which he and Jed ate quickly behind some barrels on deck.)

They buried a man at sea before they got to port, dead of an infection. In Havana they stood on the wharf, trembling and weak in the knees. One of the other boats had suffered an outbreak of smallpox, and would be quarantined at Port Isabel.

"Count our blessings, I reckon," said Jed.

"Few though they are," answered Percy.

"How do you feel about getting back on that boat?"

"Better than I feel about staying here," said Percy.

Jed nodded and spat. Percy had lost weight, and he looked mean under his salt-thickened hair.

Although the sea from Havana to Port Isabel was smooth, the men on deck were relieved when they saw a lighthouse and knew they were headed toward it. It seemed absurd to have come so close to death, to have lost men while simply getting to the war, and they crowded on the foredeck to watch the shore approach.

"Where you reckon the war is?"

"Yonder."

"Be glad to get off this boat."

They were optimistic, and the war was only something to which they looked for purpose, for honor, for a chance to prove their mettle or distinguish themselves.

Percy sighed and squinted into the horizon.

"Troubled?" said Jed.

"I can't say that I'm encouraged."

"We're here."

"Yes. I do wonder what awaits us. I'm not brimming with optimistic visions of triumph and capability."

"No."

They watched the shore rise before them, and Jed kept his thoughts to himself. He felt sure that what was to come was going to matter. They were in the army now, the United States Army, not just some volunteer regiment cooped up in a hotel in Richmond. That meant more than waiting for something to begin. This was combat, this was the theater of war.

Although it was not.

They were issued salt pork and biscuits, packs, blankets, tents. The rifles and guns were on a wagon, the cannons were unassembled, hunks of metal in wooden boxes, stacked like bolts of linen. Anyone whose uniform was incomplete could appeal to have it completed, and many who had lost their hats at sea, including Jed, asked for new ones. Jed had his knife and a few snares, his scattergun, his copy of *The Three Musketeers*, and a deck of cards.

They were not an ordered company, and the march was just a walk down a goat path strewn with rocks. They made perhaps eight miles a day—while the West Point officers pranced around on their horses, visibly frustrated, telling them that they were marching at half the speed they should be, and they'd be lucky to make Buena Vista in a week. No one knew anything about Buena Vista, so no one cared.

The ration of salt meat made for thirsty soldiers, and soon there were buckboard wagons following the ranks with groaning men who had drank from fetid standing water they'd found.

"There's sweet water at the next camp, men. We'll fill the barrels. Stay yourself until then!"

The men grumbled, ignored orders, and got sick, which made the march interminable. Men fell out. Men collapsed. The soldier who was walking next to Jed was sweating profusely, and his lips were as pale as new cloth.

"What do you make of these?" asked Jed, motioning to a squat palmetto.

The kid tried to look, tried to respond, but could only manage a wheeze.

"They ain't right, I figure," said Jed. This utterly foreign land, flat and studded with thick grasses, didn't make sense to him. Jed was a child of deciduous forests, and everything he saw seemed unnatural. "That said, you seem like you ain't doin' so good. Want I should flag one of these horsemen down? Get you some attention?"

"Ain't no occasion for that," mouthed the boy. He collapsed twenty minutes later, reeking of wet shit, eyes rolling back in his head.

"Goddamn," said Jed, sitting across a fire from Percy, having come to a small settlement—just a church and a well—where the volunteers were bivouacked for the night. "But this is rough going."

Percy had a cold look in his eye. Even in the orange glow of the scrap-wood fire he looked mean. "You want to find a pair to play whist?" asked Jed.

Percy shrugged.

More quietly, so the men around them wouldn't hear, Jed added: "We might make some money."

Percy didn't take the bait. They sat on the ground around the fire. In the near distance, over the general churn of the camp, they heard the sick men tossing and complaining in the night.

They hadn't bothered to set up their tents, and later, as Jed slept near the fire, he was awoken by what sounded like the cackling cry of a hundred madmen coming from every direction around the camp. He reached for his gun, and sat with it in the dark trying to discern where the noise was coming from and what it meant. It raised in circles, frantic and mad.

"It's Comanche," came a voice.

"It's coyote," came another.

CHAPTER SIX

The Israelites

Spring 1856

Oliver Bodkin sat not at the head of the grand table in the formal dining room, but in the center, like Christ in Leonardo's *Last Supper*, and felt it was suitable (although perhaps a little overblown), for he felt himself a savior. Hollingsworth stood at his right, frowning at the stack of papers on the table and the small purses made of thick cloth, drawn tight with a string.

The ladderback chairs had been arrayed in a semicircle, and in them sat the last nine enslaved people of Bodkin's Hundred—uncomfortable, self-conscious, and wary.

The stern portraits of previous Oliver Bodkins glowered from their gilded frames. Oliver had gathered the poor and downtrodden before him that he might deliver them, and he was filled with a jubilance he could scarcely contain. He was glad, too, for the jury of his ancestors.

It seemed to him that all he had done before this moment was meaningless folly. He had known moments of pride: he'd done well in school. He'd been richer than most of his friends, and could enjoy it due to his status as a foreigner, a southerner, which kept most from begrudging him his wealth, and him from hiding it. He had treated; he had entertained. He'd packed his salon with serious, admirable books and gathered the best minds there, arrayed them around his tea set, nestled in his purple aniline-dyed fabrics. It had felt like time well spent.

Yet he knew, here, this morning, that he was to surpass anything he had achieved. This was generous and transcendent. The task of one's being, after all, is the pursuit of perfection. A man may grow ever closer to the ideal, though he may never reach it. Life is a curve approaching the asymptote, the point of contact receding indefinitely, always out of reach.

Excelsior, Oliver, Excelsior!

Here was a chance to ride that curve, to graze the axis, and to free others from the societal corruption that shackled them—how literally did it shackle them! This was a true day.

His head felt as if it were a bowl full of champagne, and tiny effervescent bubbles cracked against his crown.

"Good morning," said Oliver. No one said a word. "Some of you, I've known my whole life," Oliver looked at Lo and Gee, who looked at the floor. "But I haven't seen you in some time, and I certainly haven't been here to express what it is that I have come to believe. I've learned a great deal. Come to believe certain things about the inalienable nature of liberty, and the rights of all to pursue it as individuals. We are, each of us, fettered. Some, more obviously than others. The shackles which bind me are mere metaphors, figments, inventions of a society. A society which harbors no good intentions for either of us. For any of us. The shackles that bind you, that have bound you, are all too literal. I have come to understand our bedrock of self-evident truths to be inclusive, to be broad in its scope . . ."

Oliver spoke on. He wasn't oblivious to the room. Even a preacher fully convinced of the power and the glory of the truth he brings can tell when his flock is drifting. It may, however, take that preacher some time to change his tack. Oliver's solution, ill conceived, was to reframe and repeat his central idea, thinking he'd break through.

There must be a way to explain this that will ring, he thought, *that will rise, that will become like music and sway them! Their very life! Their hours on this earth!*

Unable to catch their interest with his oration, he conceded and came to the conclusion. If the poetry of the moment couldn't grab them, then perhaps the final proclamation would. Perhaps it is impossible for the shackled to see the meaning of their freedom without actually having that freedom.

"My father placed a great deal of value on flesh, and loved the business of blood more than any other. I do not share these enthusiasms. I declare you, each of you, to be free."

The farmworkers looked at one another. Fern was trembling, in fear or joy he could not discern.

Oliver, looking out over the faces of the men and women who were no longer his property, was bursting with excitement, but the people before him were mute. They weren't reacting at all.

"I wish you nothing but the best. I hope your lives will be full and pleasant."

A farmhand started out of his chair and sat back down.

"Yes, yes," urged Oliver, "come forward, here you are!"

Oliver stood, found the papers that proclaimed the man free, and handed him one of the purses.

"There's $750 in there. That's enough to get a good start. This is money, for each of you. I read the ledger books, consider it . . . let us say that I've bought you for yourselves!"

He wondered if that made any sense.

Fern stuttered and spoke: "What . . . what's gonna happen to the farm? This place? Who will . . ." She stopped, and then with some confidence started again: "Master Oliver, there's things here that need to be done!" There was panic in the young woman's eyes.

"I don't know," said Oliver, fanning his hands out before him. "It won't be mine for much longer, I hope. I have no desire to run it, no desire to own it, no desire for things to continue as they have. Don't think of it again. This place doesn't own you. No one owns you. We are, today, paving the way for a different future. A civilization cannot be . . . cannot be . . . underpinned by brutality. Hollingsworth," and Oliver stood. He had lost his momentum. Why? Was it these faces? They looked so lost.

"Read them the manumission."

Hollingsworth read the paper as if he were reading a list of plague victims.

Then Hollingsworth handed out the purses and the manumission papers.

"Congratulations," said Oliver.

Still no one moved.

A spring bluster rocked the glass in the windows and whistled with a ghostly foreboding that Oliver found entirely unsuitable for the scene.

"Come on, then!" he cried. He wondered if he should have made some punch, and berated himself—how foolish, inappropriate.

The farmhands sheepishly stood. They put their hats on their heads, tipped them to the white people, and two of the three nodded and held out hands to Fern and Liza, who also stood. The little gang of five shuffled, mumbling to Lo and Gee and the children that they'd see them soon.

"Gather your things, of course!" Oliver said. "Whatever you'd like to take, I mean! Whatever is, uh, yours."

"They aren't visitors here, sir," said Hollingsworth. He had blurted it out. He had been holding his tongue for longer than he could stand.

Oliver faced him, raised his eyebrows. Hollingsworth's upper lip was aquiver, the man was furious. Was his desire to keep these people as chattel so deeply engrained? Was his sense of their natural rights so polluted? Could he not see that any man is better free? Or was it just the cost? Perhaps to Hollingsworth these men were just tools, fungible items, ambulatory sacks full of coins.

"This is their home, " said Hollingsworth. "This has been their place."

Oliver smacked the table and said: "Their place, Hollingsworth, is not for us to decide."

The farmhands and the house girls had left the room.

The two children kicked their feet. Temple had dropped her purse and paper on the floor.

"What did you expect, Mr. Bodkin? That they'd vanish? That perhaps they'd ring the farm bell and join hands?"

"They've lived their life in chains, and now they're free."

"From what?"

"Bondage!"

Should he have fed them? They could have cooked a pig.

Oliver looked at the two children teetering in their chairs.

"Why didn't you go with your parents?"

They didn't say a thing. Neither Raleigh nor Temple had spoken to a white man before.

"They're . . ." Lo said. She shook her head. She wanted to say it all, that they were Master Mr. Bodkin's children, too, but she didn't know what would happen to them, and she didn't want to hurt them, or to hurt Oliver. She knew Oliver was just trying to do his best. She chose the only path she trusted when talking with white people, which was to say as little as possible. "Their momma died."

"What about them?" Oliver nodded to the door, meaning the five who had just walked through it. "Their parents."

"That ain't their parents. Their momma died." Lo thought of Master Mr. Bodkin in the ground and added: "Both their parents died."

Oliver looked at the children. He was the only adult who failed to note that they had the same flat forehead and wide-set eyes that was displayed in the representations of his forebears memorialized in the oil paintings hung about the room.

"And you?" said Oliver.

"Me?" asked Lo.

"Yes, you."

Could he have forgotten who she was? "I been the cook here since—"

"What I mean, Lo, are they your charges, then?"

"I let them sleep in the kitchen basement, but I ain't in charge of anything, Master Oliver."

"You will take them with you, though," said Oliver.

"No, sir." She put a hand on Raleigh's shoulder, and sat on her haunches beside him. She spoke to Raleigh and Temple. "Y'all remember the story about the split magnolia in the swamp." They nodded, looking at the floor. "I can't take you down there, it ain't easy going, and we might not make it. Can't stay here, you know that. We got one year before we ain't allowed in Virginia. One year a freed black. If you need me, you come down and get me, but until then, you find a better way. Everything is everything, children. You deserve better." Now she stood. "Master Oliver, I known you your whole life. You a good man. You're going to find a way to take care of these children. You're gonna find a way to make a life for them."

Oliver turned to Hollingsworth.

"What's happening here?"

"As I told you last night" he said, "I don't know that there's anywhere exactly these . . . people can go. This place has been their whole world for many years. You can't expect them to—"

"Anyone would prefer freedom," Oliver insisted. "And I shall give these people the opportunity to achieve it. All must risk, all must experience some discomfort in their climb to liberty, is that not true? What weight has risk or discomfort on the scale when on the other side rests liberty?"

The two men were at loggerheads. Each brushed the other's ideas away as fables and foolishness. Up until this moment Oliver had considered his point won, but he saw now that Hollingsworth had merely sunk into reticence. Like a printer forced to press a book he knew wouldn't find readers, or a carpenter nailing together a structure he knew would fall, Hollingsworth had worked in quiet spite, obeying only because of Oliver's position of authority, looking forward to the moment when all was lost but the ugly joy of his vindication.

How dare he dismiss Oliver as a fool? At this moment! When there was so much to be celebrated and this . . . lawyer, this . . . lieutenant of his father's wretched auctions. Had so much time dealing with men as if they were animals truly reduced him? Or was it fear?

The coals of Hollingsworth's disagreement were fanned to a sharp glow, on the verge of bursting into flames, and just as he was set to continue, a steady scrape across the floor interrupted him.

Both white men turned back to the room. Gee was standing, slowly. He had come to a decision. He bowed to Oliver Bodkin, ignored Hollingsworth, then turned to Lo and clasped his hands over his heart. He reached down and gently took her hand in his.

Lo leaned over each child and kissed them on the head.

"Sit tight, now," she said.

Lo and Gee walked from the room.

Oliver watched them go, his mouth open as if ready to call out to them. Glancing at Hollingsworth, he saw that the worm was smiling. Not, it was easy to see, out of sympathy for the formerly enslaved, or out of any sort of rising benevolent spirit. Hollingsworth's smile was smug.

The children were now terrified. Frozen in place. There they sat. How, wondered Oliver, were they still here? How could they be sitting here? "I don't understand," he said.

Hollingsworth said nothing.

"What are we going to do?"

Hollingsworth said nothing.

That look on his face. If he were a different sort of man they'd be outside with pistols when the sun broke the horizon tomorrow. The damned clerk has a sermon rattling around in his corrupt brain. Always, a free thinking man must confront the weak of spirit, the weak of mind. Yet another walking husk, a lump of clay, a spoke on society's corrupt wheel. In the face of grand thoughts, thought Oliver, Hollingsworth could only attempt to belittle them.

Despite Oliver's fury, he held some small hope that the man had a plan of some kind. "What are we going to do?" Oliver asked again.

"I am going to return to Richmond," said Hollingsworth. "Where I will continue to search for a buyer for Bodkin's Hundred. Assuming you still want to sell it."

And with that, Hollingsworth walked out of the house.

The children were leaning on one another.

He turned from the two children and stared into the ashes in the fireplace grate.

Never would he have imagined that after he had freed the slaves, there would somehow still be slaves. He had meant to be free of it all. He wanted none of it, not the farm, the history, the horses, the dirt, the chattel.

He, Oliver Bodkin, was a new sort of Oliver Bodkin. He was not a locomotive engine, locked on the rails hurtling toward the rapacious amassing of fortune. He was a new breed, a new type of man. Something more. The next step in the evolution of his family.

He belonged in, of, and to the great cities of the world. Oliver had imagined that once he'd padded his accounts with the proceeds of the sale of the plantation he would set sail and move through cosmopolitan society unfettered. The streets where prophets and poets had tread would be his to roam. His heart cried out for ancient marble, sunsets among the cypress, opera. How many times had he imagined gazing into the depths of the Gulf of La Spezia, running his hand along the surface of those waves.

He had spent hours imagining himself in a formal garden, strolling, saying to his companion, "After I freed my father's slaves, I set out to see the world." How they would admire him.

That story began with a jubilee celebrating the Freeing of the Slaves, at which those newly freed would wail with joy and perhaps reach out to him, grasp his hands, and look into his eyes with grateful adoration.

That had not happened.

Instead, those assembled took his rejection of the institution as a rejection of themselves. I'd meant to lift them up, he thought, and I have lifted them up, they'll come to see it. They haven't tasted freedom, they haven't walked on the earth as their own masters, but they will feel it. Rejected them? I elevated them!

The children were scared, he could see that. He worked through the problem before him as if it were a philosophical proof.

Having set out to save the enslaved of Bodkin's Hundred, he felt that he must continue until they were, in fact, saved. His work was plain before him. He would propel these two children into their futures, and if he could not do it in a single day, as he had hoped, then he would persevere for however long it took. What a foolish hope, he admonished himself, to simply buy them! To purchase their next life as their lives had been purchased. If it took work, then he would work on it. It was better than all the ideas he'd ever had. He was sure of it. He turned to the children.

"You'll stay."

The boy scratched his knee.

"You'll stay with me. We'll stay together." He wasn't even sure what he meant, but it came as a relief to Temple and Raleigh, who, after all, had never considered being anywhere else.

After finding some ham to eat and sitting down with Raleigh and Temple—he'd gotten their names from them—Oliver walked around the house opening cupboards and looking in trunks until he found children's clothes. Generations of Bodkins had grown up in the big house, after all, and tucked away here and there were nightgowns, shirting, and trousers. He found a stack of dresses folded neatly in a trunk in one of the bedrooms, where the walls were a gentle mauve and two small beds were fitted with horsehair mattresses. He insisted that Raleigh and Temple sleep there. He built a fire up in the grate, and suggested that Raleigh run for some water, which was such a relief—to be assigned a task from the real world, as it had been—that Raleigh ran like a shot. He came back lugging the same beat-up bucket he'd hauled for Lo, and Oliver took it from his hands and poured it into a pitcher and a fine basin of china that sat on a lowboy. Raleigh and Temple looked at one another in terror.

This could only be the preface to their murder in some horrible fairy tale. He left them alone in the room. They sat, barely confident enough to whisper.

"What do we do?"

"I miss Lo."

Raleigh slid off the bed and fed the fire. He took up one of the shirts Oliver had left him. It was the softest cloth he had ever felt, but he didn't put it on. He just held it. They sat close to one another. When they finally slept, they did so in their clothes, atop the blankets, clinging to one another, afraid one of them would be snatched away.

Oliver divided the plantation. He would keep the orchard, the Old House, and the pastures that spread out in front of it, as well as the old barn. Everything on the other side of the orchard, where Bodkin's Hundred was new, would be sold. Hollingsworth, aghast but no longer capable of surprise, told him he was mad and that the plan was obscene, infantile, and insane, but he did as he was told.

Oliver hired a team of Italian masons from Richmond to build a brick wall to separate the New House and the Homestead, and he liked the result so much that he had them continue the wall along the road, as well, and install a gate flanked by pillars topped with globes carved from granite.

Up and down the road, in stately homes and small ones, the goings-on at Bodkin's Hundred were news. Some worried themselves with the details of how Oliver Bodkin planned to run a home without servants, others insisted that he had kept some servants. Some said, with authority, that Oliver had inherited an astronomical fortune. Others insisted that he was penniless until they saw the Italians building the wall, which seemed to shore up the former point of view. His father had turned strange, after all, running the Hundred with a skeleton crew while he stayed in town.

Why would one release one's servants, only to hire workers to build a wall? The family had lost its mooring, had descended into weird depths.

Hollingsworth asked no questions. His disgust with this arrangement, and suspicion of it, overrode his curiosity. His attention to the details of the sale was out of loyalty to his dead employer, and a sense of honorable responsibility to finish what he'd started.

When he found a buyer for the plantation, he rode out and found Oliver carrying the painting of Gunnery from the New House down the path to the Old House.

He didn't dismount.

Oliver stood, holding the painting and trying to keep the gilt frame from getting dirty.

A man named Zeb Newcombe, who had worked with Master Mr. Bodkin, had always liked the place. He'd married a wealthy woman from Richmond, Marie Collings, Hollingsworth explained. The price was acceptable. The deal was all but done.

Oliver hired the bricklayer's helpers to carry the beds and horsehair mattresses from the mauve room of the New House and put them upstairs in the Old House, and the books and the desk from the library. He took the china, the comfortable fireplace chairs, and the piano. The rest he sold with the house.

That is how Raleigh and Temple came to live at the old Bodkin place, in a room upstairs, with their eccentric half brother.

CHAPTER SEVEN

Buena Vista

Summer 1847

The camp at Buena Vista was muggy, muddy, and scarred from the battle that had been waged there. The Virginia Volunteers put up their tents in a block, next to the company from North Carolina, and were mustered to the drill field in the afternoon, where they listened to speeches. The mountain loomed above them, bare and sharp.

The battles with the Mexicans were elsewhere, but Colonel Paine drilled the troops twice a day, hoping to get them into fighting shape.

Paine lived in fear that the war would return to this place and find him unprepared. He wondered what would have happened on this ground had the troops who fought here been in such disarray. In dreams, he saw American blood flowing through the arroyos, and woke in a panic.

The volunteers were a difficult lot, however. They came and went, drifting up to Saltillo at will. Despite standing orders that the sutlers set up just on the other side of the wash give each soldier no more than two gills of whiskey a day, men were frequently drunk. Children could defeat these soldiers with toy guns. Paine worked, in a fury, attempting to improve them, but it is difficult to practice for something you've never seen and can't imagine, and the men resented the exercises.

The worse they did, the tighter Paine's attempt at discipline grew.

The summer wore on, the days grew hotter. They'd been in Buena Vista for six weeks when Paine had the horse built. It was a wooden structure, slightly taller than a real horse, with a clumsy head of planks and a ridgebeam spine that ran straight down his back.

"Not much of a likeness," said Jed.

"The man who banged that together is no artist," said Percy.

"What do you reckon it's for?"

They knew soon enough that the horse was meant as a disciplinarian tool—the punished man was to sit on the back of the horse, riding that straight, sharp ridgebeam.

"Now I like it even less."

"It's true that the artistic failings demonstrated by the horse seem now to be the least of the problems."

They were standing around a barrel by a sutler's wagon. There was a bottle on the ground, and they each held a cup.

A man from the North Carolina company approached.

"You seen that mess of a horse?"

They nodded.

The man shook his head.

"I'll be damned if I'm going to sit on a fool horse under this sun."

There were six men gathered at the barrel when they decided they ought to go and take a look at the thing. Someone had a bridle. They were all drunk. None of them could have named all of the party if asked, but they moved now as one, with intent, radiating menace. Jed was buoyed along, loving the raw feeling that something might happen, that they were dangerous. There was a wildness in knowing that they were on their way to break the law, to disobey, to do what they wanted done, and it filled Jed with excited joy. He was, in that moment, happier than he'd ever been in his life.

A saddle was produced from somewhere, and a crop, and the men took turns riding the wooden horse and whooping. Jed gave the man from

North Carolina a leg up into the saddle, and he fell over the other side of the horse and sprawled in the dirt, scrambling.

"What did you do that for?"

"He didn't do a thing," said Percy.

"Threw me over the side of that horse!"

"Not at all," said Percy, who had put himself between Jed and the North Carolinian. The man was furious, with a terrier's will to destroy, and Percy could see that it was an energy which needed an outlet.

"Look, there, that's Paine's tent, isn't it?"

Percy reached down, took up a rock, and threw it at the tent. The men laughed, and threw rocks of their own, calling out to Paine, taunting him until four riflemen came running from behind the colonel's quarters and the revelers scattered and ran away.

Guards walked the dirt between the tents that night and in the morning, many were questioned about the identities of the men who had attempted to deface the wooden horse and thrown rocks at the tent of their commanding officer. Evening found Percy and Jed at the same barrel, drinking. The North Carolinian walked up, seemingly having forgotten the tension between him and Jed.

"Now they wanna arrest us."

"No one'll tell 'em," said Jed.

"Already did," said the Tar Heel, who explained that one of their party had been revealed, and was, as of this moment, sitting on the horse itself.

Jed and Percy were stunned in disbelief. Was this painful public humiliation in store for them, as well?

Some of the other men who had been in on the frolic had appeared.

"The colonel loves hurting people, is what it is."

"He delights in these designs."

"Right devilish."

"You gotta set a man straight now and then."

They rushed to agree that some punishments might be just, which only bolstered their sense of authority.

"Set a man straight ain't a matter of humiliating."

"Ain't a matter of degrading."

"He's hurting a man."

"Hurting a man because he likes the way it feels."

Soon they were again moving toward the space where the horse was set up, near Paine's tent. Jed was again filled with a righteous and fiery excitement.

The men thought as one, and without saying anything about burning the horse, they gathered materials to do so as they moved through camp and grew in number. Fifteen men arrived in the small square. Some held firewood, and one had a bucket of pitch.

James Houser, sitting on the horse, believed at first that the men had come to kill him, and sputtered that he had preserved their anonymity, would take what was dealt to him with strength. He flinched from the flash of the knife, and found that his hands had been cut free.

"Get down from there, James."

"What's this, then?" asked James.

The mob was piling wood, pine scrub, and pitch-soaked rags under the horse.

Jed watched Percy, swept up in a mad excitement, grinning like the devil. There was lust here. Lust for death and chaos. Jed wasn't sure where it came from—it was not, when examined, a response in kind with maltreatment. It was a fire burst forth from a spark, a chaotic release, and Jed thought it the most attractive thing he'd seen.

Jed hurried to a cookfire and picked up coals with a shovel, which he hurled into the stacked pine beneath the horse. One blow, hardly more than would extinguish a candle, and the whole thing went up with whoosh. The men cheered as fire engulfed the horse.

"You! There! The lot of you!"

Paine was screaming, shirtless. In the glow of the conflagration you could see the horrible scars that decorated his misshapen body. His shoulder had been cracked when one of his own men had discharged a cannon too low and the ball shot the horse out from under him. The shoulder had not been set properly, and sloped downward. Much talk was made over the source of that injury and whether or not the soldier's aim had been accidental, what he'd intended to shoot, and what he'd truly missed. Paine had been shot through the side, as well, and scar there was a puckered pink crater. Most impressive, however, was the slash that snaked off of his cheek and roped down to his belt. How could a man survive such a cut? How, indeed, could such a thing be delivered? Paine had laid back in his saddle, riding into a stand of Apache, one of whom had sunk a spear into the dirt and leveled it at him. It scraped up toward his throat, and would have stuck into his head and impaled him but for the sweeping saber blow that Paine delivered to the warrior, which cut off his right hand. Paine took up the spear and stabbed it through the Indian to his right, before shooting a third with his pistol and fainting off the side of his horse, soaked in blood. He was left for dead. He awoke in the darkness, the battlefield quiet but for the snuffling of dogs

Now, Paine stood in front of his tent flap, looking at a mess of drunken soldiers—if they could even be called that—dancing around a fire like witches.

"I'll shoot!"

"Go on then, shoot, God damn you!"

The marauding gang ran, and Paine shot. The man from North Carolina collapsed. The bullet, slowed from its gory journey through the Tar Heel but not stopped, smacked into Percy's left hand and took off his middle finger. Percy sank to the dirt in the glow of the burning horse, clutching his bleeding hand while the Tar Heel wheezed out his last breath.

Jed paused by Percy's side.

"I'm shot," Percy said. "You should run. Go. There's no escape for me like this."

Paine was hollering for his riflemen.

"They'll hang us. Run."

So he did.

One late evening not long afterward, Jed was sitting outside his tent on a comfortable chair of carved Mexican wood slung with leather. His feet were propped up on a crate, and his head was shrouded in pipe smoke. He looked a vision of tranquility, but his mind was racing. He hadn't seen Percy since Paine had unloaded on them.

He wished he had someone to talk to. Perhaps getting his thoughts out would quit their repetitious whirling. As it stood, he couldn't stop thinking that some further mutiny was called for, or some more formal action against the colonel. Could you shoot at soldiers? Officers weren't actually allowed to shoot at soldiers, were they? Was the horse a sort of torture? Were officers allowed to torture soldiers? Could an officer devise unjust punishments without paying for it?

James Houser was in lockup, as was Percy. Jed sat and smoked and fumed angrily at the affront, the idea. He hated the army.

He heard a crunch of gravel: Percy.

"I've been discharged. Dishonorably."

"You've what?"

"I suspect they don't want to transport me, don't want to hospitalize me, and don't want to hear from me, so they've cut me adrift in the easiest way they know how. James the same. Mr. Greentop—that Tar Heel who was shot dead?—they accused him of inciting a mutiny, I suppose his sentence is time served. They don't know you were there, you don't have to worry."

"I'm coming with you."

"Desertion is a crime, Jed. Serious."

"They can't discharge you."

But it appeared they could. Percy just smiled.

"What are you going to do?"

"I'm going to make a bank draw against my accounts before the news reaches Richmond. I can probably get enough money to live nicely around here." He looked about, as if assessing the gardens of an estate he was thinking of acquiring.

Percy couldn't go home dishonored, and Jed was comforted by that idea. His friend wasn't leaving, couldn't leave. He felt his face grow hot—how selfish. How childish. He stood up, in order to feel himself more a man.

Percy reached out to shake hands, offering his left, awkwardly, which Jed accepted with his own left hand.

"How's the finger?"

"Gone."

The white dressing was wrapped around his hand and made it look like a claw.

"Never did well in penmanship."

"Send word when you settle," said Jed.

Percy nodded. Such a letter did not come, however, and Jed spent the next few months lonely and worried about his friend.

Jed's ability with a team of horses landed him a job running a wagon to and from Saltillo, to the north. The war stayed away from Buena Vista. The North Carolinians and the Virginians drilled together, but even those exercises faded as the year wore on. Jed was often excluded from them, anyway, headed to Saltillo with mailbags, or headed back to camp with sacks of onions, potatoes, fresh greens, and squash.

It was a good job, a fine responsibility, and it allowed him an amount of freedom, but it separated him from the men, and he made no new friends.

He learned, on his trips to Saltillo, of the guerrilla fighters from both sides of this war who dressed up like Indians and robbed the farmers. He heard the complaints of these farmers in the markets in Saltillo. Everyone knew they weren't Indians. Comanche wouldn't just sneak in and steal your crop and leave. They'd burn your house down, steal all the women, take your horses. The problem, as far as Jed could make out, was that if you approached any authority on the matter, local or visiting United States Army, you were told that it was Indians.

Franco, who sold onions and greens, said that it was only a matter of time until things got worse.

"If no one enforces the law, the law gets further and further away."

Jed nodded.

"If no one has a consequence, they do the next thing. The next thing is always worse. It's in the air. It's no good."

They loaded carrots and greens and onions into Jed's wagon, and Jed paid Franco, sliding an extra few coins on top. The pricing was irregular, he'd realized, and there were no invoices. He liked Franco, and he knew that Franco saved him good vegetables.

His path into the camp cut through a narrow break in the hills—the camp at Buena Vista was an enviably defensible position—and if he drove the horses up to the bank of the arroyo and onto a small flat outcropping he had found, he could watch the companies at their drills. He was not the first person who had paused in this place. There was a firepit of stacked rocks, and evidence of past meals in the gravelly sand. From here, the exercise field looked distant, but not so distant that he couldn't tell what was happening on it.

He heard whistles and commands, and he watched the patterns of the men at work learning their routes. Stop, run, overcome, move tighter, spread out in a line. While inside it, these exercises seemed designed to make you and the men around you an efficient and victorious machine. Move together, multiply your force. From a distance, it was clear that the men were simply pawns. The officer drilling them was calling orders, directions, and moving the men on the field around as if they were pieces in a game. Everyone knows—except the pieces themselves—that whatever vision of personal glory they have, they are just physical manifestations of the will of their leader.

And some of them would be sacrificed.

Jed figured it would be remarkably foolish to believe that the man leading your side of the chessboard was any smarter than the man leading the other. Looking at the men run in tighter lines, looser lines. Watching the spokes of the army pivot and position, he knew, also, that he was not watching valuable pieces. You throw away pawns to protect bishops—these men were the sacrificial pawns protecting the rooks, the bishops.

There could be no honor there.

CHAPTER EIGHT

In the Garden, Part One

Summer 1858

"I won't miss these clothes," said Rose Knaupf, in the parlor at Bonscourt, indicating her widow's weeds.

Her father smiled tightly.

"Come, now, Papa." She moved toward where he stood. He had one hand on the mantelpiece as if there were a fire in the grate, and was trying to look commanding. She undid him by leaning her head on his shoulder and evoking in him the feelings from a simpler time when she was young.

"I wish you'd reconsider, Daff," said Mr. Durand. Her childhood nickname, Daffodil, shortened to Daff, because she'd thought briefly that she was named after all the flowers, and had plucked a yellow blossom from a pasture and said it was her. She knew she'd melted his resolve.

"I was hoping my time here would end quite differently."

"You came here to make me sell Bonscourt and take me back with you to Kentucky, but I won't, Papa. I want to start the school as Jorg and I had planned. There's no reason I can't do it."

"There are many reasons you shouldn't. Did you promise him?"

"Jorg?"

"Is it some sort of deathbed oath?"

She shook her head.

"I don't understand why you'd stay. You are a young woman. You can marry again, have a family. There are many in Kentucky who would love to fold into their families that which you offer—we are Durands. You are quite a catch."

During the two years that Rose had passed in mourning, she had realized how little she wanted to be caught.

"The same money which makes me attractive to them will allow me to live here. The keeper of our house. Perhaps one of my nephews will inherit Bonscourt!"

That did please Mr. Durand. Though he still cast his response in the negative. "I do hate to return having failed."

"You haven't failed. You've been a great comfort to me. Anyway, perhaps I'll find a husband here." She wouldn't. She wouldn't even entertain the thought. She felt guilty even saying it. "When have you ever been able to convince me to do anything?"

Her father chuckled. A headstrong daughter was a curious thing. He was proud that she never budged from her beliefs, but he would have liked to have his authority respected, or to win an argument once in a while. Where did it come from, this power of will? He heard his wife answer him: *It came from you, Louis.* He moved to a chair, poured himself a thimble-sized glass of Madeira, and asked: "Well, how will you run it?"

They'd been through it all, but Rose was happy to rehash her plans.

"I think along the river here there are four or five girls. I'll advertise in Richmond for a few more. I have room to sleep at least eight girls, if anyone wants to board, and I'd still have a room for guests, or another teacher if I need it. And the attic rooms for help. I'd rather just have the girls for the day, truthfully. Who needs it? Let them arrive after breakfast. We'll have lessons in cookery, painting, French, housekeeping, literature, the kitchen garden, and music."

"And who will do that?"

"I'll do the French—"

"I mean—"

"Because of the nature of the lessons themselves the girls will tend to the house. It's important for a young lady starting out in the world not to be a stranger to the ways in which a house is maintained. You know yourself that those who do not understand that which they manage are incapable of overseeing what must be done."

"I mean the music."

"I told you! I'm going to ask Oliver Bodkin to teach piano."

"I know that people have treated you gently, left you out of the harsher elements of gossip, but surely you've heard what's said about him."

"He's always been a wonderful piano player. And I understand he kept up with it while he was in Boston."

"The way he built that wall, for instance. It's a symbol. A symbol of separation. People just don't feel that Mr. Bodkin has returned, they feel that he's somehow stayed away."

"People," said Rose, as if the idea disgusted her.

"You know he keeps those children there."

"The slave children? Where should they go? They've always lived there. I think it is an act of great compassion. I think it shows that he is a man of responsibility and character."

"He gave away a fortune, and he sold the Hundred to that Newcombe man."

"Hardly."

"Oh, I'm afraid that he absolutely sold the Hundred to that Newcombe man." Her father raised his graying eyebrows. He looked older than she remembered him, all of these two months she'd been surprised to see him in the morning, just as she'd been shocked when he arrived.

"I don't mean about Newcombe," she said. Although there could be no argument made there. Zeb Newcombe was not the sort of man who was meant to inhabit the most important house along the road. "I mean the fortune. What did he give away?"

"He set them free and gave them money! A fortune!"

"He can afford it," she said, with a dismissive wave of her hand. "Did he get a good price from Newcombe?"

"He did. Or so I hear," but her father shook his head as a man does when forced to admit a thing presupposed by something of which he disapproves. "Only because of Marie Collings. A man like Newcombe," he shook his head again in a slightly confused way. "Well, I don't think Mr. Bodkin would have sold anything to a man like that. She's a Collings, you know. The Richmond Collings. Mr. Bodkin knew what things were worth." Here, he rose to his topic, raising his eyes from the carpet where they'd been tracing the pattern. "The only reason Oliver can afford this injudiciousness is because his father knew what things were worth, and it's a shame to see something like the Hundred dismantled."

"Things," said Rose, with intent. "You mean men?"

"The whole thing, Rose. It takes a certain level of character. You can't just let anyone come up the river and buy these houses."

"You sound absolutely European, Papa. *Parlerons-nous en francais comme des aristocrates Russes?*" Laughing now, she continued: "He's a terrible man, though, isn't he? A slave catcher?"

"Perhaps the Collings woman will be a good influence."

"Bring him to heel? Does that work?"

Louis Durand shrugged, chuckled, and raised a hand, palm up. He'd avoided a fight with his daughter, and that felt good. He poured another Madeira.

"You're going to rent the fields?"

She nodded.

"Make sure they rotate the crops."

The next morning, Rose Knaupf awoke and dressed in riding clothes, which felt remarkable.

"You're going out?"

"I haven't been out on a horse in two years, Papa, I can't wait."

They said goodbye, he promised to write, and the carriage rolled off, back to Richmond. Louis Durand had been back at Bonscourt for two months, and as he rolled away Rose felt a bit at loose ends, like a hound without a scent.

She called for Frank to bring around her horse. (Frank was a lumbering Irishman at the cusp of old age whom she'd hired to keep her few pigs, the milk cow, and the horses. He lived with his wife in what had been the driver's cottage. Rose had found—as she was more than happy to explain to her father—that the work one got out of a man who was paid for it and happy to do it was worth that of four who were chained to it. Rose loved the way he talked. Loved the slightly different way in which he wore his hat.)

"Thank you, Frank," Rose said, sitting well atop the bay he'd saddled for her.

"She's a little forward, you'll remember. Likes to go. Mr. Durand got off okay?"

"He did, Frank. Thank you."

With a laugh she was gone. She was free to laugh. She'd done her duty to Jorg. She missed him, but she had found new freedom in the agency granted to widows. She had found that without a man she was free to think. Ledger books didn't trouble her—truth be told the monetary business of the plantation, which men seemed so engrossed in and presented as so horribly difficult to master, wasn't that complicated at all. It was fun, really.

She never would have called Jorg domineering—never would have said anything cross about him at all—but she did feel, in retrospect, that his presence was limiting.

Her quiet two years of mourning had been spent exchanging letters with two individuals who had influenced her a great deal. Her first pen pal was a young English painter whom she'd met when he visited the area—he'd sketched the plantations along the James and the slave auctions in Richmond and was working on a series of paintings recording the despair he had seen there. He'd sent her sketches of what he was working on, and asked her questions about detail—was this red, and here he smudged a thumbprint in the margin, an accurate representation of the bricks as seen in Richmond? She was surprised at the frisson of excitement in her chest at the sight of his thumb, and put her finger atop the print. He was her age, more or less, and handsome, and she caught herself wondering what would have happened if she'd met him before Jorg.

Her other correspondent was an excitable reformer from Ohio who had passed through the area when her husband was still alive and had been caught distributing abolitionist papers by a group who called themselves the Vigilant Society. They were boisterous, ostentatious drunks made up of the sons of plantation owners along the river, seemingly led by that Newcombe man. They had dragged Graham Gornith to the tall old oaks that grew along the road in front of Bonscourt. Gornith was slight, frightened, but stoic as the young men argued about what to do, and how many lashes he deserved. Rose stormed down the drive to the trees and interceded on his behalf.

"They'll be no murders here!" she cried. She was furious at these foolish boys. "I know you!" She tossed names at them. "Zeb Newcombe, you are not going to kill someone in front of my house!" That, she thought, was the kind of thing a place might get known for.

Graham Gornith was understandably thankful for her actions on his behalf, and took up writing to her, albeit under a nom de plume.

She rode through the new iron gates at the Bodkin place and admired the wall Oliver had built between the Old House and the New. The Old House was as charming as it had ever been, with the little slate-roofed portico and the perfect symmetry of the windows. The grounds had a weathered and settled look, the stones long sunk in and mossed over, the perennial beds long established. Her horse clopped past the orchard, abuzz with bees, the apples still small on the trees. Coming to the Old House, she tied her horse by the trough near the old barn, took the portico stairs two at a time, and knocked on the door.

"Well, I never thought I'd see a Bodkin open his own door," she said.

There stood her old friend. Dressed without pretense or affectation—fine clothes, no doubt, but no frippery about him any longer. Oliver Bodkin the man.

"So much death," Oliver said, "I'm very sorry."

She took a deliberate breath, and answered that she, too, was sorry. She'd been so cheered by the ride, and was so happy to be out, she'd not thought to greet him appropriately.

"But it is good to see you, Oliver!"

"Simpler times," said Oliver.

Oliver waved Rose to some chairs on the porch and said he had been having some tea. He got her a cup, brought the teapot out, and poured her some.

"It's good that you've returned, Oliver. I'm happy to have you back."

"Thank you, Rose. It's very good to see you. Have you children?"

She took a beat.

"No, Oliver, I do not."

"Your husband died at the same time as my father? Two years ago? I was sorry to hear it. What will you do? You are too young, too beautiful, to simply forget about life."

"Oliver, why are you treating me this way? I've just had the most splendid ride. I came to reunite with my old friend, not to suffer through politesse like some society matron."

"Sorry?"

"Are you afraid that I'm here to lure you into wooing me? Or are you afraid of what I'll think about the children?"

He gestured as if to protest, sat back in his chair, took a sip of tea, and smiled.

"I've heard two or three stories about what's happening here," she said, "but I don't believe any of them. You were always a deeply empathetic child, quick to defend the weak. I remember once you wouldn't eat the hog at our autumn party, because you said you'd known him."

"Well, I had."

"Don't think it's anything to be ashamed of, Oliver. I loved you for it. All those boys, none of them could think of a thing to do that didn't end in death. All they wanted to do. Jump a horse to chase a fox to see it die. Walk out in the woods with a gun broken over their arm to shoot whatever they find. Not Oliver, though, he's reading. Over under the tree with a book in his lap. It held a certain intrigue, I must admit."

He was embarrassed.

"But I'm not here to woo you, or tempt you. I think I can help you, Oliver, and I know you can help me. I aim to start a school, nothing much, an estate school I suppose you'd call it. I think the young ladies along this river could do with some lessons in French and music and so forth. I have in mind that I might teach them something about keeping a home, and some history." She paused and leaned forward, indicating the seriousness of what she was about to say: "It is time that we start working on the next generation, even if we must be quiet as we do so."

"That's very brave, very noble," said Oliver, still cautious.

"The two children who live here, are they your slaves?"

"No, they are not."

"I thought not. You freed them as well as the others. One of them is a young woman, I think?"

Oliver nodded.

"She'll need to know things you are not prepared to teach her."

Had Rose always had such a bright-eyed, energetic way about her? Her top lip was curved, as if she were on the brink of laughter. She sat with her riding gloves on her thigh, stared straight at him while she talked, and leaned in when she wanted to make a point.

"Can you teach piano?"

"I," Oliver faltered, "I have been teaching them both piano, and to the younger Newcombe child as well. Temple—that's her name—doesn't take to it, but Raleigh. He's a fantastic student. He should be teaching me."

"Good. You'll teach piano for me, then. Two days a week, I'd think. And Temple will come and work for me at the school. If anyone should ask we'll simply say she is your girl, and that you have hired her out. She'll do some cooking and cleaning, or rather she and I will do it together, it is valuable knowledge in itself. I'll teach her. That should help us both, Oliver. Send her to me tomorrow. I need her help preparing things. And we need to talk, she and I."

She tipped back her tea and stood. Oliver felt like butter left out in the sun.

"Wipe that look off your face, Oliver. Tomorrow, then."

Temple had grown willowy and tall, a creature made mostly of legs, with hair she cropped close to her head. Her eyes had flecks of light brown, and they floated over her high cheekbones like lanterns in a lighthouse, full of intent and direction. Nothing frightened her. She'd been raised in such bizarre circumstances of privilege—geographically limited—that she couldn't think of anything of which to be frightened. She read well, after two years of intense tutelage. She played chess well. Oliver was a good teacher, but it was clear to her that he couldn't hold the series of play in his mind, that he could never remember exactly what had come before, much less look into the future of the game and see what was coming next. He played as if the chessboard were a painting and he was trying to make sure that his palette dominated, which she supposed wasn't all that bad, compared to the rough impulsivity that ruled Raleigh's strategies. Temple understood the territoriality of the game, and could see the series of inevitable steps unfolding out into the future. Oliver said that soon there would be no sense in playing her at all.

She had wanted to wear the red gingham dress she'd made herself—a light and comfortable shift of soft fabric—but Oliver had insisted she dress as a lady would and gone into the confounded trunks from which he plucked endless crinolines and corsets. He'd found her a pale gray linen dress with rounded shoulders and a deep pointed waist. She had pantaloons with frills, and short stacked heels which sucked into the soft ground if she got too far down near the creek's edge as she walked along the bank.

It was more discreet than the road. Oliver thought it would be safer to walk along the creek and then cut along the James River through the neighbor's pastures to Bonscourt.

"You'll know it," said Oliver. "Stick by the brook, and when you get to the river take a right, walk along the bank, there'll be a field to your right, I think it's in alfalfa. You'll come to a windbreak and after that you'll see the house. There's a patio on the back that looks out over the river. I always walked that way. Hundreds of times."

Bonscourt was not as big as the New House at the Hundred, but it was an impressive place with balconies that led down to the intricate patio where she now stood, amid shrubbery gone slightly wild, by the bell, wondering what to do. Should she holler? Should she walk up to the house?

Rose came bounding out of the back door.

"I'm glad you're here. You're Temple."

Temple nodded. Rose blew across the backyard like a gentle wind and reached out her hand.

"Before we start, we should talk about pay."

"I can't . . ." Temple stuttered, "maybe you should talk to Mr. Oliver?"

"Not you paying. You being paid." Rose had an explosive laugh which showed all her teeth. "You'll need to be paid for what you do here, and we need to figure out how much."

"Oh, ma'am . . ."

"Call me Miss Rose." She looked at Temple, glancing up and down, "actually, just Rose will do nicely. Call me Rose."

Temple stood, worrying over what to do with her hands.

"Look, Temple," said Rose, "you'll be taking a rag to a floor one day, and if I haven't been paying you to do it, you'll be full of resentment. I won't have it."

"That's not true," said Temple, gaining her footing. "You'll be teaching me. It's a trade."

"Nonsense."

"I don't really need the money," said Temple.

"I think you do." She pulled on the sleeve of Temple's dress. Temple looked embarrassed. "You look lovely. But these aren't yours."

"Yes, ma'am—"

"Rose."

Temple nodded.

"No one around here will doubt for a second that Mr. Bodkin hired you out to me. In fact, they'll be comforted. So that's that. Can we begin? I've got a clutch of young ladies coming in next week, my first class, and I could use your help setting up."

They moved tables and rolled up rugs. Arranged chairs and polished the piano. They worked well together, and ate lunch in the kitchen over the chopping block—Rose sliced some chicken she'd cooked the day before, and they had cheese and apples.

"It will be good when there are children here," said Temple, "I mean, just to fill it up. It'll be nice to have the place full."

Rose nodded.

"It's not sentiment that drives me down this path, Temple. Surely there are weak-minded women—abounding—who find their value in the company of their progeny, but not me. I find peace in these echoes."

"I just meant you must be lonely sometimes."

Rose waved away the notion.

"These young ladies are going to learn and think. They are going to see that this nation is built on freedom, not aristocracy. I'm not gathering them because I need the company. This nation should continue on in the way it was begun, ever improved, ever better, with greater realizations about whose liberty and whose happiness we intend to hold sacred. To do that we must educate. Just as we must make sure that your education is complete."

Temple cut a slice of apple and topped it with cheese.

CHAPTER NINE

A New Friend

Summer 1847

Jed's hands were tied to the ring on the post by a leather strap, which cut into his wrists when he leaned out and put his weight against it. When he pulled himself up and stood tall, with the weight off his wrists, his arms got tired, so he shifted between the two positions, finding relief more briefly as time went on. The sun beat into him, and he could feel the skin on his face drying out. His lips were rough, and his eyes blinked slowly. He'd be cooked like a strip of venison soon enough, and if the wind changed and blew the smoke through the row of tents, he'd probably taste pretty good.

Goddamn that man, he thought. Damn him straight to hell. He'd bet many have called out the same. A hue and cry of complaint, a chorus of prayer against him: everybody hates Colonel Paine. Add my name, prayed Jed. Add me to list. I bet it's right long.

He was haunted by an event he'd witnessed last week, and he wondered if Paine had learned of his presence on the scene, and was protecting the officer involved by getting rid of Jed with these overblown charges. In Saltillo, at the abattoir, Jed had watched from his wagon while an officer from Arkansas listened to the complaint of a Mexican farmer, who was explaining that his sheep weren't for sale.

The officer had a dead lamb draped across his horse, and the farmer was telling the officer that the lamb hadn't been meant for market. The farmer was growing frustrated, and the Arkansan thought this was amusing. Now that the sheep was dead, said the farmer, he needed payment. He wanted to take the lamb inside and have it weighed.

"*Me pagarás lo que vale*," said the farmer. He had held his hands out in front of himself and dusted them off: they'd wash their hands of the situation.

The Arkansan shook his head and Jed had seen his boredom, viciousness, and disregard.

"*Me pagarás lo que vale*," the farmer repeated.

The officer had spurred his horse and started away and the farmer had followed, seemingly believing that this was a miscommunication which would soon be set right.

"Hold," he cried, "hold!"

The officer on horseback stopped and turned back toward the farmer, who smiled, nodding, and gestured to the abattoir, where they would weigh the lamb. The man from Arkansas, also grinning, shot the farmer dead in the street and rode off with the stolen animal.

Jed's thirst grew as he approached a second hour tied to the post in the middle of the camp in the middle of the day. He couldn't see clearly any longer, no matter how many times he tried to blink his eyes clean, and as a result he heard, rather than saw, when a stranger entered the camp. Jed concentrated on looking toward the sounds until his vision obeyed and he saw a barrel of a white man, tanned almost to the point of passing for an Indian, with a wild beard, and scrubby hair that shot out from his head in tight russet curls. He wore a leather vest over his bare chest and a Mexican hat pulled low over his eyes. He sang, and talked, and brayed like a donkey as he walked. On his vest, strapped over his heart, was a long, heavy knife with a chipped point. At his hip was a heavy Colt pistol. The song he sang (and talked and brayed) made no sense but as a sort of general lament to God, to a woman, to his brother, to the sea:

Oh, dear brother,
why have you let these waves wash me so far from home,
where the woman I love
has betrayed me.
Oh lord, my keeper,
why have you not stayed my hand,
but thrown me to my own temptations,
and let me be bashed upon these rocks.
Oh, Sally,
how I miss you,
and the tenderness with which you greeted the morning.

And then he brayed again, stopping to allow the full effect of his animal sound gather up in his lungs and pour forth. The tune was obviously improvised, as it moved without musical consideration, bouncing to and fro from snippets of folk songs and ill-tuned scales. His trousers were tucked into his tall boots, and he wore spurs that jangled like a sleigh bell with every step. As he neared, Jed could see that he was crying.

Face-to-face, he said: "I'm Crying John," and took in the scene, looking up at Jed's hands. "They've tied you to this post."

He said this as if it were news he thought Jed should hear, and Jed nodded.

"You look thirsty."

Crying John pulled the knife from the loop on his vest and moved like a swordsman. The knife was sharp and the leather which bound Jed's wrists yielded before it like tender meat. Jed's hands fell, and he stumbled. Crying John caught him.

"Let's get some water."

Jed followed Crying John to the well, and they drank from the cups that hung there until the soldiers came, six of them, and marched them both into the cell.

Crying John let out a "bah," like a sheep's, and continued to cry. After the soldiers left, Crying John asked what he had done.

"I was fixing the wagon," Jed said, "with its wheel in the ditch. Propped up that wagon with a piece of post oak, rocked it up on the wood, and held that wheel against it with the weight of my body while I tied rawhide against the axle to keep it. Wasn't going to be fixed, not by no stretch, but I figured it'd make it to the fort. Sun on my back and sweat in my eyes and no spare hands for the job. I'm leaning into it, trying not to knock it off the log. And the colonel from behind me doesn't offer to help, doesn't ask what I'm doing, just outs with how I'm no good, a waster, and threatens me with disranking."

Here Jed paused to measure the effect of his story, which seemed well received by Crying John.

"To him I say 'Those that feel it in their power to do, do exactly as they damned well please.' So he takes my guns and throws me in. Keeps me here. Ties me up before noon every day. Hangs me there for two hours."

Crying John nodded.

Colonel Paine was so disliked in the camp that when someone ended up in the jail, they were treated well. People were too afraid to directly disobey Paine, but the prisoners would be given substantial plates of the same food that everyone else ate—tonight it was a big hunk of fresh beef and some rough flat tortillas.

"I appreciate you cutting me down," said Jed, chewing a bite of his beef.

Crying John shrugged.

"I mean to say that I'm sorry that you're in here, too."

Crying John shrugged again and swatted the apology away.

"I figure I owe you," said Jed.

"They'll set me free tomorrow," said Crying John. "They can't keep me, because I'm not a soldier."

He was right. Even the colonel was so offput by this hulking bearded man with tears running down his cheeks that he couldn't find the crime he'd committed and the proper punishment. The emotional lability of Crying John negated whatever attempt at order one tried to impose, and John's answers to the simplest of questions could be confounding.

"Why did you decide to cut our prisoner down?"

"Ain't no horse fit to ride a man," answered Crying John, tearfully. "A man rides a horse. So says the Lord."

To which no one had a good answer.

Crying John was admonished and sent on his way, walking out of the camp with what he'd walked in with, as well as a tin of percussion caps for his Colt and a small sack of powder he'd managed to pocket. The soldiers watched him walk into the mountains, through the scratchy Mexican chaparral, and wondered how he'd ever survive, where he was going, and how he'd gotten there in the first place.

The next day the soldiers set out for Monterrey, and the headquarters, where Jed Stokes was to be tried for insubordination. Jed sat in the back of a buckboard on a bench. The soldiers guarding him weren't about to chain him. They didn't care to enforce these rules or bring any sort of punishment down upon one of their own. They'd lost faith in the whole system. For they were well aware that Jed Stokes was a victim of superfluity. Those in command took any excuse to get rid of a man in this army. In 1848, the soldiers at Buena Vista were unnecessary and made to feel that way.

The big mountain by Monterrey was still in the distance when Crying John showed up on low ridge astride an Indian horse. Even in silhouette there was no mistaking him, his beard and his barrel chest and the glinting reflections of the gold chain that hung from his ear. He rode along next to the troops, keeping his distance: too far to yell to, too far to shoot at.

Jed, leaning against his knees and looking out into the scrub from his plank seat, watched Crying John and his horse and wondered what was afoot.

It took two days to get to Monterrey, so they camped in the foothills where a stream rolled down out of the mountains. The horses drank, and the rifle guard soldiers—regulars, not volunteers—sat around the fire. Jed knew he should be secured in some way, but he was not. He saw, too, that there was a haversack with a bedroll on the back of the wagon.

Had they put it there for him? Where they telling him to leave? It certainly seemed that way.

He looked at one of the men by the fire, who nodded, and gestured toward the haversack without saying anything.

In the darkness of the hills above the camp Jed heard Crying John bray like a donkey. Jed stood, taking a moment to ostentatiously stretch in case he'd surmised incorrectly that he'd been invited to escape. Then he lifted the haversack on to his back, tipped his hat to the so-called guards, and walked away from the fire.

Crying John led him through the sharp creases of the foothills, the ridge canyons that rose up into the mountain. The light was fine for walking once his eyes adjusted. The moon was bright and the night was clear and warm. He followed the braying, the honking, and the duck calls up into the hills, took a right and walked along a spine of rock, which jutted out of the mountain, twisting around one of the peaks until it opened out into a flat area, maybe an acre, if Jed judged right. At the other side of the flat dirt a small campfire glowed, and Jed walked toward it, smiling. There, in the flicking firelight, sat his friend Percy. Crying John sat beside him, grinning like a boy who'd just eaten a stolen pie.

"Well, I never," Jed said.

"Sure you have, Jed, plenty of times."

Percy stood, smiled, and offered his hand, which Jed took, and then turned over to hold in his palm and examine.

"That healed up nicely."

"Didn't grow back, though."

CHAPTER TEN

In the Garden, Part Two

Autumn 1859

Oliver enjoyed thinking of himself as the headmaster of a tiny academy—The Oliver Bodkin Academy for the Advancement of the Negro. The role pleased him.

The table in the hall—once a dining room table—had become a sort of catchall for papers and books and pictures stacked around the tea tray. The Old House felt like a dormitory, or a club, where Oliver could contentedly write letters or turn the pages of the newspaper and encourage Raleigh as he worked on passages of Beethoven or Schubert.

"I think you're rushing that," Oliver said, sliding a knife under a wax seal and unfurling a wide piece of paper.

Raleigh nodded and started again.

"Very good, yes, that sounds right."

It was a letter from one of Oliver's best friends, a bookseller in Boston.

Dear Oliver,

Boston misses you a great deal. We were with Sylvie and Horatio and all those people just the other night, and I was honored and enthused to pass along the tales of your charges, whose names I'm afraid I always get wrong—Walter and Temperance? It set off quite a discussion of the natural capacity of man, both for kindness (yours), and for intellectual and spiritual growth (everyone's?). You came off as a bit of a hero, I think, by the end of the conversation. Sylvie pretends to be intent upon coming down to Virginia, but I can't see her leaving the town house—she never does anymore. She's awfully pale and nervous, which seemed charming for a bit, but I've begun to worry about her.

Here are some books. I've sent "Typee" and the new one, "Confidence Man." (Not sure how I feel about it. Seems diffuse.) Also a copy of the French magazine with Anderssen's chess game summarized.

I've also included a couple of daguerreotypes from a man I met—wonderful fellow, though intense, great beard, flowing hair, full of aesthetic ideas. He talked a lot—I mean, a lot!—about light and time. Look at the one of the Native with the rifle, he looks just like Anne when she's dressed up in chinoiserie and hoping we can have a séance—even that murderous look she gets about her forehead. Included here also some poetry for you—my gift to you!—and the music for which you asked. Enjoy, and all best, BL

He felt a pang for his old friends, whom he did miss, and wondered if Sylvie was going to be all right, and if any of them might actually come and visit. What would that be like? He thought of them here and it seemed all wrong and awkward. In placing them about the room—there, by the fireplace, Anne with her stilted diction and her powdered face—he didn't think he'd ever been happier than he was now. Temple was reading in the parlor, and Raleigh was playing piano. He had spent his life at school, after all, and this sort of studious environment felt like home to him.

Raleigh loved the photos, especially of the native with the rifle. He read adventure stories and studied maps. Oliver figured it was only natural for young men to dream of the West, of Indian chiefs, sailboats, and mining camps. There were stories of fortunes made and wilderness. It held no appeal to Oliver, but, then again, he reminded himself, fortune and freedom are already mine.

"Raleigh, I never dreamed I would have a student as talented as you are," he said. "I don't think anyone does."

The stallion named Snap came to be understood as Raleigh's horse. He was tall and lean, white with charcoal specks that grew more frequent on the bridge of his nose. He was a tractable animal with Raleigh astride him, although he drifted and pranced like a racehorse—because he was a racehorse. Under a rider who sat less well or displayed less sense, the horse grew impatient. Oliver had tried to ride him once, and Snap spun in circles until Oliver slid off the side. Snap leaned his head toward Oliver, sitting in the grass, nibbled at his lapel as if to apologize, perhaps to taunt. Snap did one tight circle around Oliver, and trotted over to Raleigh at the fence of the paddock and put his long head over Raleigh's shoulder.

What clothes they couldn't find in one of the trunks they'd brought over from the Hundred came in shop-made from Richmond, and Oliver took deliveries of bread and cheese, hams and sausages. The gardens they tended were for fun, not for sustenance. Most of the fruit in the mismanaged orchard fell to the ground the first year Oliver had the place. A nearby farmer offered to harvest it and set up a fine business making apple and pear butters and squeezing cider. By way of payment, he kept Oliver in preserves and cider. The goods added up to a fraction of the value of that which the farmer had taken, but Oliver didn't care.

Despite the fact that this relationship proved profitable, the farmer was quick to disparage Oliver, on principle. From the seat of the buckboard selling jars of Old Bodkin's Place Apple Butter he would bemoan the foolhardiness of the Bodkin scion, so degraded by the Yankees that he no longer understood how to run a farm. All along the road, which ran parallel to Bodkin's Creek, the chorus came back to him. For those families, having been reminded all of their lives that they were not as grand as the Bodkins, who had been here first, and had more, for whom the natural features around them had been named, took great pleasure in the perceived decrease and wallowed in their disapproval.

"A Bodkin!"

"Oh, his granpappy must be spinning in the grave, to see how it goes over there."

"Bodkins used to like money coming toward them. Don't seem to matter to this one which way it flows."

Across the orchard, at the Hundred, Zeb Newcombe put a foot up on the running board, spit in the dirt, and nodded along with the farmer. The cook had run a crate of apple butter into the kitchen.

"It's no way to run things," said the farmer, grinning to himself with the private acknowledgment that Zeb Newcombe didn't seem like much at the helm, either. "That," he said, "ain't no way to keep a farm."

"I never should have let him have the orchard," Zeb said, looking over to the brick wall that separated the Hundred from the orchard and the Old House.

"Was the orchard on the table?" The farmer knew well that Oliver Bodkin had begun the wall and therefore the separation of Bodkin's Hundred into two plots—"The Hundred" and "The Old Bodkin Place"—well before Zeb Newcombe had made an offer. "I'd have kept that orchard, yes sir."

Zeb nodded, as if thinking over strategies for regaining the land.

"It's not just the orchard, it's the whole place. I'd hate to try to make it through on what they grow over there. You know what it's like? It's like a city house, with a little rose garden for drinking tea in."

"Don't the servants do anything?" asked Zeb.

"Nobody doing any work," said the farmer.

"Them picaninnies?" Zeb knew them. Knew of them. He'd known Master Mr. Bodkin well enough. He'd spent enough time drinking in Richmond with his old driver, Callum—a rude and rough bastard that man was—to have heard the stories. Master Mr. Bodkin was in love with one of his Negroes, Callum had told him. He'd heard when the baby came, and he'd heard when the next one came, and he'd heard when she died and the whole empire started to slowly come apart.

It was bad for business—you needed functioning plantations if you were to catch slaves.

He wondered if they knew who their daddy was. If that foolish, pampered dandy knew himself, and if he did, had he told them?

Zeb found Oliver infuriating and mystifying. Master Mr. Bodkin had been rich, obviously, but he had worked hard for what he had, spoken directly, and treated you like a man. The disdain which Zeb Newcombe felt directed toward him from Oliver was intolerable, and if he could have located the actual insult, he'd have challenged him to a duel and shot him in the face. Newcombe's inability to locate that insult, to put his finger on it, only further incensed him.

"Never see 'em," said the farmer. "Can tell you nobody did nothing about them trees until I got in there. You should see them gardens, too. Now, for me, even if I had the money to live like that, I'd still want the land taken care of, done right. Course, I'll take all the apples he'll let me have."

Zeb nodded as if this were a noble truth, but his eyes stayed on the wall that had cut the plantation in two.

With Temple spending her time at Bonscourt, Raleigh and Oliver grew closer still. Despite the dozen years between them, they learned to act like brothers, or Oxbridge roommates. In the morning they'd ride, and when they returned they'd eat the preserves the farmer had made of their own apples on thick cuts of bread slathered with butter. They'd drink tea (shipped in from New York), surrounded by books and maps and pictures. They'd pluck up volumes and slouch into their seats. Raleigh would move to the piano and play until Oliver interrupted him.

"Listen to this: 'The mass of men serve the state thus,'" and here Oliver waved his hand to indicate that all would be clear in a moment, and that Raleigh would shortly understand that to which the "thus" referred, "'not as men, mainly, but as machines, with their bodies. They are the standing army, and the militia, sailors, constables, *posse comitas'*—that means men gathered together to enforce a law—'In most cases there is no free exercise whatever of the judgment or of the moral sense; but they put themselves on a level with wood and earth and stones.' That's good, isn't it?"

Raleigh, spun around on the bench now, with his back to the keys, nodded. "But it can't continue, can it? If the law is rotten, its continuance is impossible. Corruption poisons. It ends because it is rotten. Just as diseased plants do not grow."

"Yes." Oliver nodded, smiling. "The question, I suppose, is how long can a diseased plant be forced to survive? How long can life be sustained once it is no longer deserved?"

In the evenings, Raleigh played piano while Oliver polished the knives they'd used at supper and wrote letters.

Between the newspapers and the books sent by Oliver's friend in Boston, the two of them gathered that America was churning, and that turmoil grew inevitable. It seemed far away, but they spoke of the future often.

"There will be a need, Raleigh, for men such as yourself. Men with backbone and erudition," said Oliver. "This empire will crumble into the sand. It's the only way forward."

They'd read Helper's book *The Impending Crisis in the South*. Raleigh saw in it what he needed to.

"I do not understand the altruistic sentiment," he said, "found in so many other abolitionists."

"They don't know anyone like you, Raleigh. The oppressed are *oppressed*. You see? They don't have advantages. Education."

On the days that Oliver went to Rose's to teach piano, Raleigh would read, practice piano, or find himself feeling like a child again, down on Bodkin's Creek with a fishing rod. He loved to fry panfish in cornmeal over a campfire and sit under the poplar near the washout just as he had when he and Temple were young, before Master Mr. Bodkin had come back to the Hundred to die. The world was different then, he thought, limited. He had lived in fear and in a strange cloud of ignorance. The fish and the smell of the cornmeal toasting in the bacon fat brought back an otherworldly terror, which he attributed to his own childhood ignorance.

"That suit fits you well," said Oliver, observing Raleigh in the clothes they'd unpacked that afternoon. "I wouldn't have thought that our measurements would be so accurate. I think these sack coats are a wonderful idea, so much more flexible, so much more useful."

Raleigh had never felt anything so close, so perfectly attuned to his every movement, as the suit he had on.

"Come, Raleigh, let's ride."

Oliver grabbed two bottles of Madeira (he'd had shelves built in the low-ceilinged basement, and filled them with wines) and two bottles of claret and arranged them in his saddlebag. They cantered down the road to Bonscourt. It was Saturday, in the summer of 1859.

There were no girls at the school. The men arrived on the porch laughing loudly and opened a bottle of wine.

"Look at that suit, Raleigh!" Temple exclaimed. "You look like a gentleman!"

Raleigh bowed with ostentatious humor.

They played quoits on the lawn in the afternoon and as the golden hour faded they moved inside to a dinner of small tender hens with mashed sweet potatoes. Rose had pink shrimp in a sherried soup to start, and biscuits that Temple had made. Candles blazed at the center of the table and on the sideboard, and a fire snapped in the grate to ward off the beginnings of a chill—more for atmosphere than necessity.

Oliver, looking around at those assembled at the table, feeling the glow of the room and the happiness held within it, felt that they had built something new and joyful.

Rose gazed across her wineglass, focused on Raleigh, thinking much the same thing. "You all know the story of Pocahontas, I'm sure," she said. "The way they baptized the poor thing, then dragged her back to England to march her around in drawing rooms until she wanted to die."

The assembled nodded.

"That was for the benefit of others," Rose said. "They used her like a caged bird. Like something they'd found in a jungle, as a display of beautiful possibility. For you, Raleigh, and for Temple, the future is your own."

Oliver smiled.

"I worried," said Rose, "about what was going to happen. With you two, with everything. But when all this ends," she waved her fork around the room, "and it will end. You two will be right there."

"Raleigh and I were just talking about this," said Oliver. "It's inevitable. Either because of a war or because it is corrupt and cannot go on, rotten from the inside like a person struck through with disease. We'd said plants. Didn't we?" Raleigh nodded. "A diseased plant cannot thrive. If you have a disease, you know, one either cures it or dies."

"You, Temple, and you Raleigh," said Rose, "are part of the cure."

They were flattered.

"A toast, then," said Oliver, "to tomorrow."

CHAPTER ELEVEN

Fireworks at Saltillo

Jed, Percy, and Crying John were in Saltillo for the fireworks when the war with Mexico ended in February 1848. Whiskey flowed in the streets, and women laughed and danced with anyone who could still stand up. Bells rang for hours, and a few ambitious men rolled cannons up a hill and blasted them out into the night—one shot tore a grazing steer in half. Since there was no telling who should be held responsible, a collection was taken up and paid to the rancher, who considered the matter settled.

Jed, Percy, and Crying John were of questionable legal status, to say the least, but there was scant law in those parts, especially now that the army was gone, and they found that they could drift along the border—or where folks thought the border might be—without too much trouble.

They all agreed that they enjoyed the Mexican side better.

"Something about the color," said Crying John.

"It's a straightforward life," said Percy, "people know what things are worth, and if you want those things, you just come up with the money. These frontier people, the Texans, they believe in honor and destiny. God."

"The Mexicans believe in God," said Jed.

"But their churches," said Percy.

Crying John sang a Spanish hymn, softly.

"Their churches are different, that's true," said Jed.

"Passionate."

"A man could find amorous congress in a Mexican church."

"You can't say that about the North."

"No, you cannot."

They drifted and caroused, lived around campfires, mostly. In the spring of 1849, the mayor of a small Mexican town hired the three to track and kill a band of Apaches that had been raiding the town. The mayor outfitted them with fresh horses, fixed their saddles, gave them carbine rifles and ammunition. The price was agreed upon, and half of it was paid in advance. The men bought new hats and boots and rode out into the wild. A few nights of town food and sleeping indoors always cleared Crying John's head, and he spoke directly, looking into the fire around which they sat.

"I know the leader of that band. His name is Tsetsoyé, sometimes called Nana. He gave me this." John put his hand behind a gold chain that hung from a hole in his ear down to his jaw, it shone against his skin in the firelight.

The men waited for John to continue.

"He wears them. Watch chains in both ears. And he cut this hole in my ear and ran one of his own chains through it. He's gonna be a big chief."

"He's a friend of yours," said Jed.

Crying John nodded.

"I can't see us riding off to shoot at some friend of yours," said Percy. "We've already been paid, given horses. I'm not attached to the other half of the money."

"This is the best deal we're likely to get out of this," said Jed.

"Very little risk involved," said Percy. "I mean, in as far as if we were to say we were done with the job now."

"Tsetsoyé is a friend of mine," said John.

"I was just thinking that," said Percy. "Perhaps we should send word? Let him know that there's a price on his head?"

John came back two days later, with a fresh wound in his other ear, and a second length of golden chain dangling from it.

"Those chains look right nice," said Jed.

Crying John shot him a look.

"I don't think he's making fun of you," said Percy. "They really do. They frame your face."

"Accentuate your jawline."

"Gold looks good on you."

The men packed up the mule and rode west.

"Speaking of gold, there's more out there, I hear," said Percy.

"That's what they say."

"Let's make some of it ours."

Jed had seen the stream of settlers, the wagons struggling toward the crossing at Colorado City. The pioneers he'd met seemed frightened, skittish, but enthralled by passionate visions. They believed in impossible futures, imagined inevitable threats. They spun out tall tales of potential wealth, followed by horrible yarns of families found clustered under a broken wagon, having eaten their last horse. They told absurd, imagined stories of savage deaths at the hands of Apache and Comanche, and relished their flights of fancy in such a way as to remind Jed of the tent revivalists who would come through Alcott's Brook when he was young. The two men he'd respected—Preacher Thom and his father—had both treated the revivalists with disdain and distrust and scoffed at anyone who fell for it.

"It's like they're all caught up in some sort of revivalist tent," Jed said.

"Just townspeople chasing dreams of gold," said Percy.

There was something more to it, Jed thought.

"Gold," said Crying John. "No one argues with you. You get what you want if you have enough."

When they came to the outcropping that forced the Colorado River to run deep and created the solid ground from which the ferries out of Colorado City were launched, they stopped and set up camp. The idea was to cross the next day, after they'd eaten and rested.

They climbed to the edge of the rocks and watched the ferry launch, where a gathering of travelers was ready to board.

"Too crowded, anyway," said Percy.

There were shouts, and calls, and the settlers were getting their horses and oxen ready and standing in a short line.

"An awful lot of men working on the ferry," said Jed.

"Ticket takers, pilots, a wheelman," said John, counting them off. When he got to the two men standing by the ramp on the fore side of the ferry, and two more standing behind the ticket takers, ready to step on to the aft, he grunted a puzzled agreement.

"That big one," said Crying John, pointing out a man who moved with smooth resolve through the crowd, hulking and pale and full of menace. John shook his head as if to say that the big one looked dangerous. They all agreed.

Now only a settler and a chestnut horse were left on the bank, and the horse spooked and spun, reared up. The settler got him under control and moved on to the flat deck of the boat. The ferry lurched off the shore and started the crossing. The water was high, and from where they watched they could see the ropes bend downstream.

The ferry shuddered and stopped in the deepest part of the river.

"They aren't caught on anything in water that deep," said Percy. The first gun crack came through the air, and they all ducked, instinctually. There was a short pause, and the ferry erupted. Shots came like popcorn. The chestnut that had reared on the shore did so again, then flopped sideways into the river, dead. The people on the deck of the ferry swirled together in a mass of violence, and as quickly as it had begun, it ended. Little puffs of smoke dissipated above the current. Every traveler who had bought a ticket to cross the Colorado was dead on the deck, and the ferrymen were digging in their pockets, ripping necklaces off of the throats of the women. When they finished searching a body, they cut it open and tossed it overboard, where the corpse would spin in the current for a moment and quickly sink.

There were tears on Crying John's cheeks.

"We should go," said Jed.

They turned their backs on the West and rode up into the Santa Rita mountains.

Jed thought back to those settlers, traveling with their plans and their fears, all sunk to the bottom of the river. None of their fears had included a murderous gang of ferrymen, he was sure, and the improbability, the surprise, the possibility that death lurked anywhere, made him not want to make any plans at all.

CHAPTER TWELVE

Miss Rose's School for Girls

Early in the morning, before Temple had arrived, Rose summoned Frank, whom she had seen by the irises, tending to a shrub.

"There's an easel, Frank, I think it's gone loose."

"Let's have a look see, then, shall we miss?"

Frank had lived through times hard enough to drive him and his wife across the water from Ireland so that they might start again, and a good bit of the conversation had around that house in the privacy of their evenings revolved around how lucky they were to have landed here, with little to do other than make a life and garden and keep things tidy for Rose.

"We could do worse than living out our final days here," said Frank.

"We're not that old, Frank."

"Sure we are, darling. Anyway, just because they are the final days doesn't mean they are few." He loved that she laughed at his jokes, after forty-two years of marriage, she still found him clever. A man could do worse.

Eight easels, each with two stools (one for a palette and one for the painter) were set up in the great room, where the tall windows faced north. Rose had covered the herringbone floor with a piece of canvas.

"This one, see?" She shook the easel, which wobbled.

Frank carried a small pouch with a few tools in it, accustomed as he had become to this sort of summons. He sat on the stool next to the easel and gave it a little shake, nodding and making affirmative sounds. He looked at the feet, to see that they were still level.

"Teaching painting," he said, wistfully.

"I'm not much of a teacher, it's true, or much of a painter."

"Looks pretty enough," he said, nodding to the canvases against the wall.

Rose tilted her head and with a coquettish smirk asked what Frank was getting at. She could tell he had something in mind.

"Oh, no, no. Not at all."

"You're getting at something."

He laughed. "What if their fortunes should turn? Have they a knowledge of turnips?"

"Turnips!" She said it with a low vowel sound, turnups. "We—I teach all sorts of household skills. Kitchen skills, garden skills. These things are quite important, especially for an independent woman."

"I think this peg here, if I give it a twist and seat it a little better, she won't shake."

"Have you no faith in art, Frank? Must a thing have a menial purpose to be worthwhile?" She said it with a smile, and she was reminded of the cheerful arguments she'd recently had with her father along these lines.

"Not sure I follow you there," he said. "I suppose the girls here have little need for the ruder knowledge. Cream of the crop and all that. On to carefree lives of opulence."

"The girls derive great happiness from this, and from the elevation of their minds. The pursuit of happiness, Frank, but I wouldn't call it carefree, or necessarily opulent."

"Gentle pursuits, then," said Frank.

"And practicable contributions."

"Practicable contributions," Frank said.

"To society."

"Society."

"On the whole. Moving forward into the future."

"As one must," said Frank. "Does this seem wobbly anymore? I can't tell. Seems like it was getting better, but now it seems again as if it might fall."

Rose walked to the easel and gave it a bit too much of a shake. It didn't budge.

"Perfect, Frank. Thank you!"

Temple burst through the door from the patio into the center hall. Frank stood, smiling wryly.

"Good morning, Rose, Mr. Frank," she gave a little curtsy.

"How goes it this morning, Temple?" asked Frank.

"I've had a lovely walk by Bodkin Creek."

"Glad to hear that. I left wood by the basement door for the cookstove."

"Thank you, I've got some peaches soaking, I'll put a dish aside for you and the missus."

Frank smiled, put his hat back on his head, tipped it to the ladies, and walked back out to the shrub by the irises.

Temple started the fire with wood that Frank had left for her and set to work shaping bread and rehydrating peaches in syrup and vinegar while Rose assembled a terrine.

They'd read Antoine B. Beauvilliers's French cookbook together and found the French approach to a taxonomy of food to be both silly and irresistible.

Temple set her bread dough by the fire to rise and turned to cut a knob of butter and place it in the dish with a gold handled dome, decorated with slight pink flowers.

Every morning, while they worked, the women would assemble a breakfast to share: today, a small slice of meat sprinkled with salt and buttered griddle cakes. The clock on the mantel chimed half past eight.

The girls would start arriving at nine. Temple eyed the clock. With ten minutes to go, she took a leisurely sip of tea. It was a dare, and Rose, too, pretended not to notice the time. Three minutes clicked by like this, while the hilarity of the joke rose in them both.

"I think . . ." started Temple, feigning a dreamy face and pretending she was about to enter into a soliloquy.

"Shall we, though?"

They had six minutes.

With a peal of laughter, they rushed from the kitchen, up the stairs, and into the house, where they tore from room to room, straightening tablecloths and dusting lamps, tugging rugs and centering chairs.

Together in the center hall, Rose asked Temple how she looked, and Temple spent a deft ten seconds preening curls and wiping a clot of dust off of her shoulder.

"You look wonderful, Rose."

Temple took the duster Rose was holding, and bolted for the recesses of the house as the clip clop of the first carriage was heard on the gravel.

"Good morning, darling!" she heard Rose call to the first girl.

The first lesson that day was French, and the girls settled in with giggles and mopes, according to their personalities, continuing their rivalries or showing off their new ribbons and jewelry. Temple stood in the back, as a gesture of plausible deniability.

"Good morning everyone, Shall we begin? *Je dis*," said Rose, implying that one of the girls should continue the conjugation.

"*Je disai*," said the frail-looking girl by the window.

"Good," said Rose, "and the future? I will say? How do we say 'I will say?'"

There was silence.

"Temple, you know this."

"*Je dirai*."

The official pupils squeaked their chairs turning to look at the black girl standing in the back of the room against the doorframe. Rose nodded for her to continue.

"*Je dis, je disai, je dirai, je dit, je dis, j'avai dit.*"

"*Oui, très bien, mademoiselle.*"

Gradually the pretense of servitude dissipated, and the girls included Temple and thought of her as a friend. If Temple occasionally came up at home, the mothers of these girls would hear only a quaint continuance of the same affection that their little daughters had for their maids.

Two new girls entered the school the second autumn, and Temple instinctively retreated, but the older girls undid the ruse quickly by asking her questions and showing her their needlework. The new girls, impressionable and tempted by the mischievous nature of the transgression, adapted quickly. They'd all been raised by black servants, and the younger the girl, the more she simply assumed that Temple knew the answers to everything, since they'd been asking black servants questions their whole lives.

"Temple, why does my thread bunch along this seam?"

"Temple what does this word mean?"

"Temple, can you tie my bow?"

"Temple is not your nanny, Miss Anna."

"But she ties it better than anybody!"

Rose also taught Temple things she needed to know and which she had no way to learn without a parent or a community—pennyroyal pills, perfume, and how to soften your skin.

As she moved through the steps of a waltz on the herringbone in the great room—the half of it not given over to painting, anyway—Temple could almost believe that she was heading in the same direction as the young belles around her.

Rose grew in confidence as the time went by, and the instruction of the young ladies tilted toward the higher mind. All up and down the river, parents wondered at the things their little darlings said at the table—snippets of poetry, suggestions that there could be found a unity among all the people and things of the world, impertinent outbursts regarding the treatment of the enslaved. At first just a whisper, there was soon a general grumble of dissatisfaction with the ideas these girls were coming away with. Until one girl told her mother that she would not be attending a party in Richmond because the people at the party were "horrible shells, mere simulacra, so entrenched in their vile ways, so blind to individuality and truth that they barely even resembled humans at all!"

That was that.

The fate of Rose's school was sealed at the Hundred in the early summer, during a barn dance. The New Barn had been swept clean. The youth listened to the fiddle and tambourine music that the black folks played. The adults left the younger crowd mostly to itself (with the sharp eyes of a few especially imposing matrons to guard their activities) and gathered around the fountain on the close-cut lawn in the middle of the long sloping circle in front of the New House.

Oliver had not been invited.

Zeb Newcombe, beaming, proud, and slightly drunk, found himself involved in a conversation about Rose and Bonscourt, and while he listened to the complaints, he watched the Old House, thinking of Oliver and his Negroes.

"I've never heard such a thing as our girl said!"

"You know I did't even know what simulacra meant, I had to look it up."

"Hardly the point, dear. The point is that I feel this woman is corrupting these girls."

"It's not why we sent Maybelle there. We expected Maybelle to learn French, piano—the things she needs to know."

"That's what we expected for Alice, as well."

"Well, I certainly didn't expect my daughter to come home with a head full of Yankee claptrap. Mumbo jumbo."

"Do you know they let that colored girl sit with them at lunch?"

Zeb Newcombe turned to listen more intently. "Which colored girl is that?" he asked.

"That Bodkin girl Rose hired."

"Oliver Bodkin's girl."

"Rose hired her to do some cleaning over there at the school, housework and so on. But from what I gather she just sits right in there with the rest of them."

"She's picked up a startling amount of French, according to Alice."

"French!"

Zeb said: "You mean to tell me that the colored Bodkin girl is attending the school?"

"Well, I don't see how she could be doing that, exactly."

"At the same time, Maybelle told me just the other day that it was the colored girl who helped her read something she was having trouble with. 'I didn't know the words today,' she told me, 'but Temple helped.'" The man had made his voice squeaky and pitiable, his imitation of a girl in need of help.

It was decided that Rose was instilling in the minds of their fair daughters unwelcome ideas. By the end of the evening, every student was withdrawn.

"Where will you go?" asked Temple. She was on the verge of weeping.

"Far from here. As far as the rails can take me. To the West. To San Francisco. I'll write you when I get there."

Temple trembled, thinking of all the time they'd spent together, all the cups and saucers, all the flowers they'd cut.

"I will miss you," said Rose. "You've been a wonderful friend to have, and we will see one another again."

"Where?"

Rose smiled. Temple knew there was no answer.

"Take me with you!" said Temple. Rose took Temple's hand and looked at her tenderly, but didn't say she would.

This young girl, thought Rose, has been an important chapter in my life, but it is time to turn the page. Rose had once had a husband whom she had loved, and then, in his death, less so. She had childhood friends she no longer saw. She was looking forward to seeing her mother and her brother in Kentucky on her way west.

Rose tightened her grasp on Temple's hand. "There's nothing that needs to be said, Temple. And anyway, you've got all you need from me. You know how to wear a hat, you know what *Romeo and Juliet* is about, and I'm very proud of you."

For Temple, however, half of the limited world in which she lived had disappeared. The half that remained had become Raleigh and Oliver's—there were maps on the table all the time, and the air smelled of gun oil and leather.

Rose was her dearest friend. Her heart broke to think that Rose could bear to leave her. If the situation was reversed, she'd have stayed. Why didn't Rose stay? Or invite her along?

CHAPTER THIRTEEN

A Mining Camp

Summer 1849

After watching the massacre at the Colorado, the gang agreed they needed a solid camp and a good hunting ground. Up the mountain near a gulch that carried snowmelt, they found a broken-down run-in shed. They patched a hole in the roof and strung canvas across the front. The nights were cold, and the game was plentiful. Their moods lifted in time, and soon the three of them joked as they hunted and ranged about. A month went by before they saw evidence of any other people, when on the far side of a hill they came upon an empty mining camp.

"Ain't been empty long, though," said Jed. Pots were warm, clean, and put away—no one had left this place in a hurry, they'd simply stepped out.

"The whole of it, though?" said Percy, "women and children live here." He pointed to a quilt on which a doll reclined, tucked in. "Where are they?"

Crying John was whispering a Mexican hymn, in which he'd replaced the names of the angels called upon with the English words for various animals.

"I reckon fifteen people," said Jed.

"And not one of them home."

Crying John dismounted and walked into a small cabin.

Jed and Percy waited. Jed had his hand on his carbine—he still thought of it as the Mexican rifle. He listened to John inside the cabin.

John came out, his arms stretched wide, his face wet with tears.

"Like the sun," he sang, "it shines for you, to light the way, and bring us back, to our dear lassies and the good dogs we left behind."

He was holding a pouch of gold.

The men ransacked every tent and lean-to and cabin in the camp until they had it all. The gold was heavy in the hand.

On their horses, excited, they circled around the camp until they found the tracks that led from it. They cut across those tracks, making a serpentine pattern over them, looping out into the scrub to see if they could determine where these miners and their families had gone. They weren't Indian ponies; these horses were shod. Two hours out from the camp they heard the horses, and they ducked into cover a ways off the trail and watched as eight men, a ragged bunch of tired miners, came blasting down the trail. They wore grim, solemn looks on their faces and bounced in their saddles like they were unaccustomed to being on a horse. They had no scout, it seemed, and no rear guard, and they barely bothered to look at what was around them, bashing on to their camp.

"And where are the women?" Percy asked. "The children?"

"They'll be right angry when they get back home," said Jed.

So the three followed the tracks, the fresh ones on top of the old ones, out and away from the mining camp until they came to a small stand of trees and learned what the miners had been doing.

Four young Apache braves were hanged from the branches of the trees by their necks. A fifth—a man of some status it seemed—was tied to the trunk of a tree and had been beaten to death.

"What hell is this?" said Percy.

"Should we cut them down?" Jed wasn't sure.

Crying John rode up to the ropes and swung his sharp knife. The bodies collapsed under the tree, hands tied behind their backs. Jed hopped down and sliced their bonds. Together the men arranged the Indians around the base of the tree, and discussed what to do. Should they find the band these Indians rode for and tell them? They didn't want to be the white people who brought that news. Should they bury the dead? They weren't their dead to bury.

They rode back to their own camp and broke it down.

"We have to get out of here."

"Those miners will kill us."

"Apache will kill us if they think we hanged those Indians."

With the gold they'd taken from the mining camp, they set to wandering.

CHAPTER FOURTEEN

Brother and Sister

Spring 1860

Temple slouched around the house, pining for Rose, caught in a loop of thoughts.

Why hadn't she gone with Rose? Why hadn't Rose wanted her to come along? Why hadn't anybody said that she should, or that she could? Why hadn't anyone asked her what she wanted?

Because no one ever asked what she wanted. First Rose took her in, which, it occurred to her, nobody had asked her about, and now Rose deserted her.

Why even bother to help her, she wondered, but never bother to know her or ask her or consult her? How dare they conclude what was best for her?

Raleigh found her collapsed melodramatically on the chaise in the room they shared, staring out the window, seemingly entranced by the breeze in the willows.

"Not much to do I guess," said Raleigh, "since Miss Rose left?"

Temple didn't answer.

"I'm gonna tack up Snap, take a ride, you want to jump on Whinny and come with me?"

"I don't know."

"Go get some trousers on, Temple."

Two days ago she flared up at him and stormed out of a room when he tried to show her a drawing of a Comanche warrior—"Who cares? What is this? The frontier? Leave me alone."

But one could only stare out the window for so long.

She turned, seemed to focus her eyes like a person who has been reading and looks up to see something far away, and nodded.

"You'll come?"

The barn smelled like hay and leather and sweet feed, and Temple felt comforted by the earthy world.

"I should have gone with Rose."

He felt her words like a punch in the gut. He'd never imagined his sister diverging, never considered a world without Temple.

"Did she ask you?"

"It's funny how long it's been, how distant from our place I'd become."

"Oh, I don't—"

"It's true! I practically deserted you here."

Raleigh never would have thought so. It was the first he'd considered that they had separate lives.

"Do you wonder what's next?" said Temple.

Raleigh shook his head. In the distance, they could hear the repetitious stops and starts of the piano as Collings Newcombe, the younger of the two Newcombe boys who lived at the Hundred now, tried to figure out the chromatic descent of the chords that the left hand plays for Chopin's Prelude number 4 in E minor. After a short pause during which Oliver must have replaced Collings on the bench, the sadness of the piece filled the air. Raleigh listened to Oliver play—it was an easy piece, and Oliver could play it with feeling.

"We can't just stay here, can we?"

"Why not?" said Raleigh.

"Forever?"

Raleigh shrugged, and drew the cinch up on Snap. Temple was standing in the breezeway with Whinny on a lead.

"You never thought about it?"

"I guess not. Anyway I don't know where we could go."

"California?"

Raleigh put a saddle on Whinny.

"Or Europe."

"Europe!" Raleigh dismissed this.

Raleigh jumped Snap over a hedgerow and plunged into a trail that cut twisting through the woods. He maintained it carefully, and had placed obstacles along the course to practice jumps. He rode adroitly and with precision, posting as if he were one with the rhythm of the horse. The horse responded in kind, drifting, gliding, leaping. Watching Raleigh ride made it seem easy.

Temple had no such skill. She felt buffeted about on Whinny, her timing was bad, and she bounced awkwardly with every step. Fallen leaves and pine needles covered the path in front of her, and the loblollies and laurels blurred by her. She kept up, but she wished she could stop and watch Raleigh ride around her in a circle. He was right; Snap was gorgeous.

She whistled and Raleigh slowed Snap to a walk.

"He has grown into something marvelous."

They rode side by side, walking around the jumps, saying little, each satisfied. Raleigh at having pulled his sister from her shell, and Temple at having been pulled.

"Why does this feel like a reunion?" said Raleigh.

"I guess it rather does."

"Rather," he said, putting on airs.

"Rather, indeed."

CHAPTER FIFTEEN

Buffalo Hunters

Jed, Percy, and Crying John were flush with the money from the mining camp. They spent some time apart, thinking they might be linked to the mining camp theft and happy to have money enough to pursue their desires. They promised to meet up in a month. Each of the men had a different goal when they separated—Crying John went to see a woman he loved who ran a bar. Percy longed for urbanity. Jed looked for solitude, and camped in the back of Buffalo Lick canyon.

When they joined one another again, Percy had developed an idea.

"We should get a crew together, hunt some buffalo."

"I don't shoot things that haven't wronged me," said John.

"Then you'll run the crew," said Percy. "Drive the wagon, keep them in line."

"I wouldn't cross you, John," said Jed, and then, turning to Percy: "He'll plant you in the ground."

"He's got that air about him. He will brook no misdeed."

Jed and Percy bought four Sharps rifles and took them out onto the plains where they set up targets at 350 paces.

"Good luck, Percy," said Jed.

"I don't want you to feel bad when you lose. There's nothing to be embarrassed about."

They drank whiskey and competed for bulls-eyes. Both insisted that they had won, though the truth was that they were pretty much even.

"Maybe next time, Jed."

"You couldn't hit that at forty yards twice as big."

"Shall we try again? Loser buys dinner."

They shot until the evening made it too difficult to see.

"I guess them buffalo are safe from you," said Jed.

They hired gun boys, skinners, and teamsters. The hides were best in the winter, and in December 1856, working in the Texas panhandle, the team shot upward of 1,200 bison.

It was monotonous work, and Jed took no pride from his ability to rip through a bison's lungs at three hundred yards. He'd learned to shoot by barking squirrels. These beasts were ungainly. They stood around the first fallen cow and brayed. If you shot the lead one, they'd be so confused they'd mill around in a circle, dropping one by one. The whole thing seemed like harvesting, not hunting, but the money was good.

They fell in with a rancher named Blake "Junior" Estoppy, who let them have an outbuilding where they parked the wagons. They kept their big rifles there, too, nailed shut in a box, wrapped in oilcloth. A trunk held lead, molds for shot, and outdoor gear.

They'd take time off—Jed would spend his time in the wild, camping, riding, always returning to Buffalo Lick Canyon and the trickle of a spring where the Little Stone River came out of the ground—then return to Estoppy's Burnt Wood Ranch to rub soap and mink oil into their saddles until the leather was supple and yielding.

They ate on the porch with the farmhands and Junior and the two cattlemen, and spent their days hiring a new crew, shopping for supplies, and buying fresh horses.

Burnt Wood Ranch was as big as some counties back east: a kingdom on the Texas plains. Junior was a man with sharp edges, who blew clouds of cigar smoke through his bushy gray mustache and kept his hat on. When he was lost in thought—usually about how much he disliked anyone who had come to Texas more recently than himself, whom he referred to as "foreigners"—he tapped on the pocket of his vest, wherein he kept a French pepperbox pistol. The foreigners grazed their herds on stretches of land adjacent to his own, where once his own cattle could roam, and demanded compromises and water rights. Junior Estoppy did not enjoy compromises.

He bought every hide that the crew brought back and hired men to drive those hides north, to market with his steer. The profit was handsome, but the joy came from knowing that those bison had paid what he was owed—their deaths—for grazing on his land.

In late autumn of 1859, Percy and Jed rode a scouting mission with just their carbines and pistols and some light gear. They rode for three days without seeing anything, and stopped at dusk on the third day to camp.

"We shouldn't light a fire," said Jed.

Percy swore under his breath.

"They're right over there," said Jed.

"You don't know that."

"That's the river, down there. The herd is behind that swell, we'll see 'em in the morning. They'll be coming toward the water. We'll see them at dawn."

"The buffalo won't be bothered by a bit of woodsmoke."

"Ain't the buffalo, you know it."

He did. He knew that if they were close to the herd, and Jed always knew when they were, that they were probably close to Indians as well. To light a fire was to invite attack.

"You'll make it, Percy."

They rode down to the river and watered the horses in the light of the moon. Jed handed Percy an apple and a slice of ham.

"Junior says he shipped these apples in from New York."

Jed hoped that the expense, the luxury of a long-shipped fruit would make up for the lack of fire, for sleeping outdoors. Percy wasn't made for this.

They chewed and listened to the night.

The morning was cold, and they woke as the first gray blue light tinted the night. They were up on the horses and watching from the ridge when the pink streaks lit up the red escarpment in the distance, where the rock rose out of the scrub like the spire of a cathedral.

They sat in silence, eating another apple from the sack Jed had tied to his saddle, waiting for the buffalo while the sun cracked the sky into streaks.

"Perhaps," said Percy, "I mean, don't get me wrong I have nothing but respect for your abilities, but I wonder, looking out onto the slope on yonder side of the river, I wonder why it seems to be devoid of buffalo."

"Hang on."

"You'd think they'd be thirsty."

"Just—you know what?"

"It's no great embarrassment, Scout. Lots of us miss our mark. Don't even let it ruffle your feathers. We'll find 'em, Scout."

"Quit."

Percy laughed, and his horse stepped to the side, turning him so that his eyes drifted downstream, where he saw the clotted brown bodies of the herd coming over the rise and heading toward the river.

"Look there, Jed."

With the buffalo found, the two men turned and rode back to the ranch to gather the guns and the men and come back for the hunt.

December 1859 was the best they'd ever had. Two weeks in, Crying John had to ride hard to go find another wagon to stack with hides and another teamster to drive it.

They spent Christmas camped on the side of a hill where they built a roaring fire. Wrapped in buffalo robes, they drank their coffee spiked with whiskey. They had harvested two bison brains, which they sliced and fried in hot skillets.

"How many hides you reckon we got?"

"Each of them wagons have a thousand if there's a one."

"It's more than that," said Crying John. "Three wagons, each with twelve fifty hides, what's that?"

"Three thousand seven hundred and fifty," said Percy.

"Damn good year."

"Best I seen," said the gnarled old skinner who they'd hired. "You two is crack shots. I can't but believe how many you dropped this morning before they figured out to be scared."

Percy raised his mug in thanks.

"We going back tomorrow, John?"

"Don't sing it," said one of the teamsters.

"Hey, John, just give us the answer," said another.

But John was silent, and his attention was off beyond the firelight. Jed saw the look in his eyes and rolled sideways, over his saddle, grabbing his carbine and sliding into a ditch as the arrows came flying. When he looked up, the three teamsters were dead, stuck through like pincushions.

Crying John stood and brayed into the night like a beast, he roared and stomped. His big Colt was out, but he didn't shoot, in his other hand he held the blade with the chipped point. An Indian rode through the camp, screaming, hanging around the neck of his horse, and John turned with him, eye to eye, screaming back.

Crying John circled, breathing hard, staring into the darkness. The gun boys were hiding under one of the wagons.

"Get to cover!" Jed yelled, promising himself he'd kill as many as he could before the end.

Crying John didn't respond. His nostrils flared wide, the gold ropes that fell from his ears twinkling in the firelight.

From the darkness came a voice: "You have Nana's medicine."

"Nana is my friend, and he gave me this medicine," answered John.

"We are many, and you cannot win. We will take these wagons. But since you are Nana's friend, you will survive. Nana's medicine is strong business."

John lowered himself to the ground and sat staring into the fire while the Indians rolled the wagons away and hooked up the horses.

When the wagons exposed the gun boys, the boys ran. They died moments later, cut down amid a clattering of hooves.

The Indians took the horses, took the wagons with the Sharps and the hides. The pack mule was stubborn, and wouldn't move. The Indian laughed and put his forehead on the mule's before turning away.

The fire was roaring, and the skillets were stacked where Jed had wiped them out. There was still coffee in the pot, in front of the three dead teamsters.

"Forty-five, fifty Indians," said John.

Percy, standing up from behind his rock, was holding his arm, which was bleeding.

"John," he said.

"Percy, are you all right?" asked Jed.

"I am. Nicked me. It looks worse than it is. John? What's Nana's medicine?"

John gestured to the chains in his earlobes.

"You remember Nana," said Crying John. "That business down south. His name is Tsetsoyé—they call him Nana, now."

"You saved our lives."

John looked at the dirt, considering, then shrugged.

"Tsetsoyé is a big chief now. He wears these. Nana's medicine means I am like family to him."

The walk back to Estoppy's ranch was long. They had buffalo robes to keep them warm, but if the snow came and they weren't back they'd die. They knew it. The mule seemed to know it too. In the fading light on the first day of their walk, they spooked four deer, which bolted and ran across in front of them, seventy-five yards out. Jed had the carbine on his shoulder before he could have vocalized what was happening. The trailing deer fell with the crack of the rifle. It would have been nothing with one of the Sharps, but even Jed was surprised he made it with the little carbine.

"That was a shot," said Crying John.

"Fine," said Percy. "You win."

Crying John cleaned the deer and they walked on from the gut pile to a place where there was some sweet water that ran down off the hill. There, they took the saddles they'd stacked on the mule off the poor beast's back, unhooked the skillets they'd hung there, and splashed some corn into a feed bag for him. They roasted the venison, and hung out strips to smoke and dry for tomorrow.

"We'll be back at the ranch tomorrow," said Percy.

Jed looked at the land and nodded: "If we start early."

"I have no other plans," said Percy. "Do you?"

Crying John laughed, and sang a soft song about a river that flowed through a room in a house where a dog lived by himself waiting for his darling Rose to return from her wandering.

He stays and he watches,
he never grows old,
why would Rose leave him,
where the river does flow?

CHAPTER SIXTEEN

All Hell

March 1860

Raleigh and Temple came out of the woods next to the pasture, and Raleigh pointed Snap toward the coop he'd built and touched the heels of his boots to the horse's flanks. Snap was off, leading with his right, bounding toward the fence. Raleigh was up in the stirrups, light, and feeling the count of the paces as they approached the jump. Running smoothly, they approached, and Snap set perfectly in front of the coop, taking it perhaps a little too seriously. They were soaring, smoothly rushing through the air for a long and beautiful moment. Snap held his breath, and when the first hoof hit the ground breathed out in a rush and smoothly ran out into the field.

Raleigh heard a cry behind him and turned to see Whinny down on both front knees and Temple sprawled out in the dirt.

He leapt from Snap and a terrible fear shot through him for the instant before Temple rolled over on her back and sat up, dusting herself off and shaking her head.

"You're okay?"

She nodded.

Whinny was favoring her left hoof.

"You sure?" Raleigh steadied Temple under her arm. "You all there?"

"I'm embarrassed."

"Oh, c'mon. You know how many times I've hit this dirt?"

Temple doubted it, but she smiled and asked if Whinny was all right. "She won't step on her front left," she said. "Is it serious?"

"I don't think so. I'll wrap it, give her some liniment."

They took the saddles, hung them, and combed the horses. Raleigh rubbed salve into Whinny's ankle and wrapped it in a tight cloth.

"She's eating her grain, she should be all right. I'll be back and check on her."

At the portico of the Old House they found Oliver, sitting on the steps looking shaken.

"Are you ill?" asked Temple.

Oliver shook his head. "I had words with Zeb Newcombe. He came to gather Collings."

"Words?" asked Raleigh.

"He seems to think I'm corrupting the boy."

"With piano lessons?" Raleigh said, laughing.

Oliver didn't answer.

Neither Raleigh nor Temple knew how to go about comforting Oliver, who had never needed much from them.

"Maybe stop teaching him such sad music," said Raleigh. "That Chopin sounds like a funeral."

Oliver smiled and Raleigh gave him a hand up off the stoop.

For weeks, Temple had been a distracted, silent figure. The ride, and the fall, seemed to have shaken her out of it. It was Oliver, now, who stared off into the middle of the room and didn't seem to hear what was happening around him.

Gathered around the end of the long table in the hall, they ate a cold supper.

"Perhaps this world isn't ready for us after all," said Oliver, distractedly. With more focus: "If you'd seen that man. The look in his eyes. His eyes are like cold stones."

"I'll cheer you up. And not with Chopin."

Raleigh took a stack of Beethoven Sonatas from the shelf, and ran up the keys, loosening his fingers. Oliver moved to a more comfortable chair, and Temple stayed at the table, contentedly reading. Oliver had a glass of brandy, and if either of his charges had been watching him they'd notice that he didn't turn a page of his book.

Raleigh finished his sonata, let the last chords die, and announced that he was going to check on Whinny. "I might sleep out there, in the empty stall next to her."

"She's all right, though?"

"I think she is. I'd just feel better keeping an eye on her."

"I feel terrible," Temple exclaimed. "It's my fault."

"It was an accident, Temple. It's nothing. I like the barn."

He nodded to Oliver, grabbed a blanket, and went out. He did love the barn—the soft way the horses breathed, the smell of fresh hay. He gave Whinny half an apple and rubbed her leg, feeling for heat or swelling, and having found none he gave Snap the other half of the apple, swept the center hall, and reclined in the empty stall atop a small stack of baled hay. He turned out his lamp, and lay there listening to the mice scurry in the loft.

Raleigh felt a softly satisfying contentedness, linked, he thought, to the trials of daily life. It makes life mean something, to be upset. If Temple didn't miss Rose, she'd never understand how much Rose had meant to her. It was a fine thing to be sad about missing someone. And it was equally important to misstep over a coop and fall, otherwise, why would anyone think about how to take a jump? This was just the nature of life, Raleigh figured, and although he didn't know what was bothering Oliver, he lumped Oliver's mood in with the others. You can't live to avoid sadness, he thought, any more than you can live through a day without growing tired at the end. That's it, thought Raleigh, feeling that he'd figured something out. The tiredness one feels at the end of the day is how you know that the day gone by was worthwhile.

Raleigh had been asleep for a long time when a great commotion woke him. There was smoke in the air, but he was in darkness. He rushed to the barn door, and saw three riders circling the Old House, which was on fire. At first Raleigh thought they'd come to extinguish the fire and started forward to help, but froze when he saw that two of them had torches. He recognized the bearded farmhand from Newcombe's place and the taller, skinny one who worked with him. Newcombe had dismounted and was standing in the portico with a gun.

One of the downstairs windows shattered and flames billowed out through the broken glass and licked the sides of the house. Raleigh shirked. When he came back to the crack in the door, Newcombe was nowhere to be seen. The bearded farmhand had a horse by the reins. There was a shot from behind or inside the house. Raleigh couldn't tell. He moved back into the shadows of the center hall, shaking with fear.

From outside he heard someone yelling that they had to go, and there was a clattering of hooves. After they faded, he came again to the crack. The house was ablaze. He ran to it, but the heat pushed him back. He was crying. He tried to run into the flames again, but he couldn't make himself go forward.

He ran to the bank of the creek and toward the New House, tucking himself behind a tree. The bearded farmhand put the three horses into the stalls and came out with a whiskey bottle, which he handed to the skinny one. Lights were on in the New House. Behind him, his home was burning, and he could smell the smoke, and now he heard a bell clanging, an alarm going up. People would come, but the house was done. He couldn't fully form the thought, but he knew that Temple and Oliver were dead.

Raleigh camped for two days in a hollow on the other side of the river where he used to set beaver traps, full of despair, crying, watching, wretched with futility.

If he thought hard enough, maybe one of them would show up. Maybe Temple was hiding too. The house smoldered. People came and went, shaking their heads. On the first morning they carried a covered stretcher out of the charcoal—it must have been Oliver's body. Or Temple's. He couldn't get close enough to tell what anyone was saying. Zeb walked the property with Harrison Hollingsworth—it had been years since he'd seen him, and his blond curls had dulled, but he knew that long nose and that proud stance.

He tried to think of what to do, but felt stuck. The best plan he could come up with was to walk down the road until someone asked him what he was doing, then try to explain what had happened.

In the afternoon of the second day, Frank, the Irishman Rose had hired to take care of Bonscourt, appeared at the edge of the clearing, and put a hand out to Raleigh, gesturing him to stay calm.

"If I were you, I'd get to moving on," he said, in his lilting accent. His beard was white and bushy, and he had kindly blue eyes surrounded by sharp crow's feet like creases in paper. He squatted next to Raleigh. "They're saying you killed them both, and burnt your house down."

"I didn't."

"I can't imagine there's too many more around here but me who believe that. Or care to give it enough thought to believe it one way or t'other. No, if I was you, I'd be gone."

In the last light of the second day, Raleigh snuck through the steamy, charred wreckage of the house. There was the piano frame, blackened and bent. There was the old chaise, looking like an exploded cake. Somehow the picture of Gunnery had escaped damage. It was sooty, but it was unharmed, still in its frame on the wall above the mantel, which was now cracked and black like the skin of a horrible lizard.

Behind the picture of Gunnery was the safe where Oliver kept specie and the manumissions he'd given to Temple and Raleigh years ago.

"If something should happen," said Oliver, when he had demonstrated how to open it in what seemed like the distant past, another world, another time. Raleigh had dismissed the precaution as preposterous. Oliver had insisted he pay attention.

Raleigh touched the dial and turned it; it was gritty, and rough, but he could make it move. He went through the steps of the combination and wrenched open the door. There were their papers—freedom and money still secured in the cloth pouches on the top shelf. Raleigh took both pouches and the purse of coins.

Raleigh walked away, cautiously and mostly at night. He hadn't been more than a few miles from Bodkin's Hundred, but he knew his maps.

Sick with guilt and sorrow, unsure of himself, and unable to imagine another course, he knew he couldn't stop until he was far enough away, but not how far that was. How far did he have to go before the story of a burned-up house would be a story nobody had heard?

CHAPTER SEVENTEEN
Wanted Men

At Burnt Wood Ranch, ready to tell their story, the buffalo hunters found themselves upstaged by the presence of two coffins on a wagon.

"Yeah, they're full," said Junior Estoppy. "You're goddamn right they're full." He paced the porch, furiously smoking a cigar, looking out into the fields and cussing. "What the hell kind of season is this here, is what I want to know. Two of my hands! Shot! Getting ready for the trail."

"Shot?" asked Jed.

"By whom?" asked Percy.

"Shot by that damn Cody Farell. Owned by foreigners, he is. Or shot by his men. I wasn't there."

"The sheriff?"

"Cody Farell the sheriff," said Estoppy, angered that they didn't already know, "for now. Have to call him the sheriff." He tapped the pistol in his vest pocket. "He's a partisan murderer, far as I can tell."

Jed and Percy glanced nervously at one another. Crying John had walked away and was feeding the mule handfuls of grain, watching and listening.

Estoppy turned, taking in the yard and looking around for the wagon. "Y'all walk in here?"

"We did."

"Where's your wagons? Where's the horses?"

"Indians," said Percy.

"Indians! Why aren't you dead? If it was Indians?"

"It seems that Crying John," Percy nodded in the direction of the paddock, "has some friends among the Indians. The teamsters, the gun boys, not so lucky."

Estoppy took his cigar between his fingers and blew a slow whistle.

"Well, boys, it's a hell of a season I guess."

It was decided that Estoppy would go into town and draw some money from the bank in order to fund the comfort of the various widows and relations. When he got back they'd sit down and "figure out what to do about this situation."

He did not come back.

When the light was golden and broke across the yard in long streaks, Sheriff Cody Farell rode to the porch of the Burnt Wood Ranch and announced to Jed Stokes, who was sitting in a rocking chair, that Estoppy had pulled a gun on him and been shot down.

"We're drawing up a record of the happenings of the last couple days, starting with the attempted capture of the two rustlers." He nodded to the coffins.

"Rustlers?"

"Them two there," said Cody Farell.

"Them farmhands?"

"Them farmhands were over the hill, on Michter's Ranch, driving two hundred head of Michter-branded steer this way."

Percy, coming out from the ranch house with a tray on which he'd set three glasses and a bottle of whiskey, looked at the sheriff and then at Jed.

"The man says Junior drew down on him in town," said Jed.

Percy raised his eyebrows—what then?

"And so he shot him."

Percy set the tray on a small stool next to Jed, and as he straightened, the sheriff covered his gun, but he was unsure and moved too slow to draw it. Percy shot. Cody Farell fell backward onto the rump of his horse and slid out of the saddle. The horse bolted and dragged the sheriff's corpse for a few yards before the dead man's boot came free of the stirrup.

Crying John, leaning on the well pump and eating an apple, looked at the man in the dirt and said: "Hanging around with you is downright unsafe. Let's throw the sheriff here in Michter's well on our way out."

The men emptied Estoppy's safe before they left.

So, freed from the world, and further angered by the way it had treated them, they released themselves from whatever shreds of worldly connection they'd retained.

The next night Jed awoke before his watch and found John sitting in the light of the stars sewing gold coins, part of his share, onto the front of his vest.

"That'll be right pretty, John."

John sang a country waltz:

We should ride,
to the place,
where the sweet water runs,
cast our eyes,
on the face,
of a woman I love.

They rode to a small Texas town, where Crying John said the innkeeper was like a mother to him.

"I never looked at my mother the way John looks at Lindy," said Percy. Brazen and voluptuous, Lindy laughed hard and often. She drank coffee mixed with whiskey day and night, and ate hot Mexican peppers out of a jar on her bar. She had guffawed when John walked through the door, as if she'd been proven right, as if she'd told him so. He sat at the bar—smiling—and she walked around to face him, carrying a mug of beer. They stood in front of one another for a moment and Lindy lifted the hem of her dress from where it fell about her ankles and wetted its edge with the beer, then lifted the dress to wipe John's tear-streaked cheeks.

Jed, leaning on the bar a couple of feet away, turned his head from the sight of her nakedness. Crying John reached out and grabbed a handful of buttock.

Lindy let them have rooms upstairs, poured them cheap whiskey, and served up slabs of good meat.

"You can't stay here, though. Y'all are wanted."

"Wanted?"

"I hear tell they're putting together a string of men to come after y'all. You're wanted for the murder of Sheriff Cody Farell, and from what I hear, charges are lining up behind that. Y'all steal the gold out of a village a bit ago?" She looked at the gold coins sewn into Crying John's vest.

The gang could cut north to No Man's Land. Jed had camped at a slot canyon at the head of the Buffalo Lick river, near where Fort Little Stone protected the northern border of Texas, and had a friend there, a shepherd.

"He's a weird one. Abbott's his name. He's nice enough."

Crying John sang:

The cock in the straw,
doesn't know how it goes,
or whether he tends
or cuts down that which grows.

"He'll give us a rack," said Jed. "Ain't no law up there."

CHAPTER EIGHTEEN

The Church

"But, Mrs. Newcombe, it isn't a church. The altar, and all that was consecrated, was taken from the place. The parishioners were gathered, as is our custom. The priest, at that time, would have spoken about the good service that roof had provided for parishioners. Together, they would have remembered all the events that had taken place: marriages, baptisms, funerals. So many tears had been shed within those walls. They prayed together. It is the duty of the Episcopalian church to see to it that no soul goes untended, and that decommissioning leads not to deprivation. No one would be deprived of ministry, of sacrament, of the word. We are guided by these ceremonies, and they are not empty. Don't search for God in buildings, don't search for Him at an address, He is everywhere."

Father Rice, a well-kept man of solid middle age, only slightly worried about how proud he found himself of himself at times, sat back in his chair with the feeling he'd delivered himself rather well. He was particularly satisfied by "decommissioning leads not to deprivation," and wondered if he might find a way to include the phrase in a sermon. He reached for a pen to mark it down, and realized it would be rude.

"Oh, Father. I just love listening to you talk." Marie Newcombe felt she could hear him capitalize the pronouns. *How do they learn to do that?* she wondered.

"How long have you owned the property, Mrs. Newcombe? Remind me?"

"I bought it five years ago. We started working in earnest about a year and a half ago. Great progress has been made, and I ask nothing in return but that you might—"

"Mrs. Newcombe, I don't see—"

"But that you might, upon my completion of its restoration, bring the lovely Holy Cross Church back into—"

"It isn't the Holy Cross Church, Mrs. Newcombe, it is only a building—"

"It *is* the Holy Cross Church. A fine example of Palladian architecture, perfectly balanced, intelligently formed, and historically important."

"We have our doubts about that."

"I make no claims as to its provenance. Though we both know what I believe."

"Be that as it may, we decided," and Father Rice spread his hands out to indicate the illustrious personages he was bringing together with this opinion, "that the parishioners were better served here, at St. Lukes, and to the West, at Emmanuel. There was no need, simply no need, for a tiny old church in between those two."

Mrs. Newcombe had light brown hair, almost blonde, which she wore twisted and piled up on top of her head in a complicated mass out of which perfect ringlets fell and graced her pale, smooth, shapely shoulders. She had sharp gray eyes. The fabrics billowing about her advertised their cost, and she sparkled with jewelry.

Father Rice found her unnervingly attractive and compelling when she was in front of him, and wondered, when she wasn't, what one does with a woman who lacks humility.

Marie sighed and rearranged her shawl in such a way as to send a waft of perfume out into the air around her, so that it seemed she had exhaled rose and resinous amber. She swallowed slowly, and while looking dreamily out of the window to her left said, softly, "I suppose I could just take my carriage into town and talk to the bishop."

She was sure that Father Rice had been asked to keep her from such meetings. She might be the rocks his boat would run aground on, but the bishop was a whirlpool from which he might never return. She was an annoyance—how silly to think of oneself as an annoyance, she thought—but the bishop, that was something else entirely. If Rice couldn't keep her from pestering the bishop, what could he do? He'd choose the rocks. She feigned giving up, and made as if to rise from her chair.

"Perhaps I can come look at the progress you've made?"

"Oh, would you? That would mean so much."

Father Rice grumbled and fussed about his desk in search of his diary, no doubt to refute as many offered dates as possible.

"Today is Monday," she said. "I'll be around with a carriage on Thursday to fetch you, we'll go early, just after breakfast. We have strawberries. I'll bring you some."

"That's very kind."

She offered Father Rice a slow bow and left the room. Her servant was at her elbow the moment she crossed the threshold.

Father Rice watched her depart. He would spend the next two days attempting to come up with a reason he could not join Marie Newcombe for a tour of the grounds on Thursday morning.

"He's going to try not to come," Marie said to no one as her footman lifted her into the back of the carriage and clicked the door. "He'll have an excuse by Wednesday evening, I'm sure."

She shook her head as the carriage lurched forward.

One can't just let an institution like that crumble into dust. She settled into a well-worn reverie: They'd wanted to get rid of old Father Abby, fine, he was gone. Why consolidate parishes? There's enough to go around, and Holy Cross was more beautiful, far more beautiful, than either Emmanuel or St. Luke's. Holy Cross was a perfect expression of Jefferson's ideals—the balance! The stately rhythm. The Virginian himself would have preferred it. She knew it was his, she knew he'd designed the church himself. There was no proof. If there'd been proof we wouldn't be where we are today. They'd never leave a Jefferson church to decay. No matter. It wouldn't. She might not have proof, but once again she congratulated herself for having the vision. And the money. She loved to imagine the money. She directed it like a stream from a fountain. Or like rain falling from an angel's hand. She smiled on that which she wanted to nourish, and it grew and glowed and reached toward the sun. If something she valued wilted, she need only arc the money toward her desiccated target and it would glisten with new life.

This benevolent power made her smile. She could do anything.

"Anyway," she said aloud in the shaded carriage, unheard over the four horses trotting and the crunch of the wheels on the road: "I'd be very surprised if the Church didn't accept a gift." She knew it would work out. Holy Cross would become St Mary's Holy Cross, not that she'd claim sainthood upon herself. "Just a small tribute. A tribute."

She smelled sodden bitter ash on the air and knew she was almost home, to Bodkin's Hundred.

Temple sat in the dirt in a small shed built of stone behind what they'd always called the Little Barn. The Old Barn was over by the homestead, the New Barn was the big one with the spires for the horses by the paddocks. Little Barn was by the creek. The stone shed had been there forever, although she'd never paid it any mind. She'd never even considered what it was for or why no one seemed to store anything in it. It was the jail.

There was nothing in the room but a dented tin bowl. She had prowled the corners, scratched at the walls, pulled on the bars that crisscrossed the little window. She had kicked the door. Nothing happened. It would have been satisfying, she thought, even if someone had laughed at her, rebuffed her, made it seem as if her attempts were real.

Just after dawn—the rooster had crowed hours before, and she'd watched, recumbent, as the first gray lightened the square window—a black woman entered to deliver a cup of beans cooked with gristle and fat and a cup of water.

Temple scoffed, but she was too thirsty to resist the water.

"Ain't gonna be no more, ain't gonna be nothing else. You best take it."

Mack slapped the door with a hoe handle, and the woman flinched, put the food on the ground in front of Temple, and left the room.

After a couple of hours, Temple relented and scraped the beans into her mouth.

She guessed it was noon when she spoke through the door and asked if she could go to the privy. There was no answer. When she could no longer take it she hiked up her nightgown and squatted in the corner of the room.

The next morning the black woman who delivered her food looked at her with disgust and said "Ain't you got sense t' bury you own filth?" She set mug of beans on the ground. Temple picked up the bent bowl that was in the corner and scraped a hole in the dirt floor—the digging was difficult, due to iron bars that passed under the dirt floor. She pushed yesterday's waste into it and covered it up.

Again she waited until she was ravenous before she ate the food.

She sat against the wall all day, thinking as hard as she could. Oliver was dead, she was sure of that. Was Raleigh dead? Probably. But this. This wasn't her lot. Someone who knew her would rescue her from this. She was free. She was captive. She'd been kidnapped. Someone would care.

In the morning when the woman brought the beans, Temple leaned close and whispered: "If I give you a letter, can you see that it gets mailed?"

The woman reared back and looked at her as if she were a snake, turned, and left without answering.

In the afternoon of the third day she felt hope slip away like a boat untied from its mooring. She sat picking the clotted clay out of her toes and noticed that she no longer was sending mental signals to the world to come help her. She no longer played through the scenes in which she was rescued; the imagined door no longer burst open. She had a vague sense of surprise that it had taken such a short time for her to surrender. One more morning of beans and even the surprise was gone.

Temple sat against the wall. She rocked back and forth. Her thoughts fluttered and dropped out. Looking at the window, she'd feel as if she were about to think of something, only to have the shape of the thought dissipate like a puff of smoke blown into the air, leaving her to wonder if there had ever been a thought there.

She chewed the cuticle of her thumb until it bled. The pain was refreshing. She worried the cut in her thumb compulsively. Picking at it, making it bleed, chewing the swollen skin around it.

She ate her beans. She dug her holes in the dirt. She no longer responded when the woman came to feed her.

She'd cried the first night—how many hours ago was that? She tried to count, but couldn't focus on the counting. First she lost track of the numbers, and then she couldn't remember why she was counting.

She could hear things outside—horses, tools, people—that no longer made any sense. She couldn't see them, the barred window was too high. She was exhausted, always half asleep and confused. Almost always hungry. No one spoke to her. She hadn't made eye contact with a person in days.

CHAPTER NINETEEN

Oh, Good Shepherd

Less than an hour's ride from where the shepherd lived, Jed showed Percy and John the cave at the back of the slot canyon with the spring, and they stashed their gold there under the hieroglyphs scratched into the walls.

"Just give me a half hour head start. Ride straight toward that outcrop in the distance, and when you come to the sheep, stop and I'll come out to greet you."

"Why the pomp?"

"He's touchy."

"How do you know him?"

"I come around here, in between, I hid out in this canyon once. Stayed with him a couple times. He's a good man."

Jed rode until he saw the herd, then slowed his horse to a walk. The horse was nervous, but Jed clucked him and stroked his neck. The herd—hundreds of them—was tight against a small slope, and gathered together, the animals on the outside edge were eyeing him.

There were patterns in the herd, ripples of what seemed like intent.

The horse whinnied.

"It's all right boy, whoa."

Jed stopped the horse and looked out into the sea of white, bleating animals. He knew what was happening, and knew to wait for it to happen. A spiral began in the middle of the herd, and he saw now that two columns of sheep were turning in opposing directions, one inside the other, a wheel within a wheel. Inside the wheel was a cluster of animals, stiff legged, lurching along in the direction that the concentric circles insisted they move, like the button in the middle of a daisy, blown by the wind in the petals.

The circles were exact. A ring of sheep marching nose to tail in one direction, opposite another ring of sheep marching nose to tail in the other direction. The horse did not like the looks of this at all and Jed thought he was going to buck when the sheep rings overtook them, so he draped himself over the withers of the stallion, whispering in his ear and stroking his neck.

"Okay, big fella."

Now they were firmly ensconced in the middle of the tight central herd. They'd have to swim through sheep to leave. Jed wasn't sure how much longer he could hold the horse, and he announced it.

"This is impressive, Abbott, but I wish you'd reveal yourself."

One of the sheep started laughing and the man rose from the herd, sheepskin draped over his back. He whistled, the sheep loosened their pattern, and three dogs appeared at his feet. He gave the dogs nibbles of jerky.

"Here you go May, and Day, and Rosie, okay. That's good. It has been quite some time, Mr. Stokes."

"It's good to see you again, Abbott. Nice work."

"Modeled after the war maneuvers of the Comanche."

"They must be flattered."

"They are."

Abbott lived in a cabin, half dug in the plains, so that its walls aboveground were only half the height of a man, and one stepped down into the earth upon entering it. Two rooms, or the suggestion of two rooms, were divided by a cookstove and a shelf of dry goods. On the stove bubbled a stew of yams and onions and mutton.

Percy and Crying John had shown up on schedule, and Jed had offered Abbott some money in exchange for a few days of rest and warmth, but he wouldn't take it.

"If you change your mind," said Percy, "don't hold it in. I am obliged by your hospitality, and I would not have you breed resentment against us."

To which Abbott nodded, but said nothing.

Around the cabin was evidence of a different life—a needlepoint alphabet by the door, a small blanket, neatly folded on top of a trunk, with "Lannie" stitched along its hem. There were two children's toys on a low shelf, a rattle and a small rag-stuffed doll sewn from burlap with stitched-in dots for eyes. There was no dust or disrepair: Abbott kept his house.

Abbott would have refused the discussion, but he stayed in the cabin because if he left he knew then that they would never come back. He stayed, and he kept it in order, because by doing that he created a world in place, in which his wife and daughter might appear at any moment on the threshold and settle back into the routine that they had left when they contracted cholera from some settlers headed west who stopped and shared a meal.

They were buried on a small swell that overlooked the pond Mr. Abbott and his wife had dug to create a watering hole for the sheep, before the baby. Those had been glorious times, full of promise and possibility, and Abbott believed that his wife might like to ponder those times, if one pondered from the grave.

Abbott fully understood that he held two clearly contradictory ideas in his mind. He had buried them, he had shoveled every pound of soil that lay atop them now. He had nursed them as they died, knowing that they were dying. He had considered the placement of the graves, and indeed had begun them before their last breaths. (He did not show them or consult upon them, he thought that might be indecorous. He wanted them to die with grace and comfort.) Despite all of that, he could not shake the idea that they would return. He would catch himself—when Mrs. Abbott gets back I will ask her what she thinks I should do about the ram with the bad foot. She will know how serious it is. Or he would see a patch of prairie turnips and think to himself that he should dig them up and bring them back to Mrs. Abbott, who might enjoy them. And he would not leave the place where they had last been, because he needed—he experienced it as a need—to be sure that they would be able to find him.

While the foursome sat at Mr. Abbott's nicely burnished table—kept smooth with lanolin and smelling faintly, as did everything, like sheep—Percy asked if there was work to be done. It would be spring, soon, and perhaps in exchange for room and board they could help shear sheep, or dig the garden.

Abbott thought about it for two days, but in the end concluded that whatever trepidation he held about the disruption of his solitude (which, he allowed, was not a good motivation in itself) was not enough to justify putting these men out.

How they would fare if the Comanche came, he could not guess. He couldn't suggest that they learn the trick of becoming one of the herd, any more than he could teach them to work the dogs.

No, best to simply hope it didn't come to that.

It was the winter of 1860.

In February, Texas, just a few miles south of them, seceded from the Union.

CHAPTER TWENTY

Through the Gap

April 1860

Raleigh walked, his sadness immense—Oliver dead, Temple dead, the Old House burned to the ground. His world shattered. He found water, drank it, trudged forward staring at the ground wrapped inside an obsessive, simplistic madness. His sorrow, like the throb of a burn under a bandage, was constant.

In the foothills of the mountains he boarded a train and showed his papers.

"Where to?"

"How far does this train go?"

"Louisville."

"Louisville, then."

He paid the conductor. He took a seat on the bench in the car for black people, and slumped against the wall as the engine chugged west.

From what he had read—Voltaire, Shakespeare—he imagined that upon coming to a city, one would be attended to. Someone would greet you, perhaps imprison you, enlist you in an army, throw you in a dungeon, but to his surprise, a man garnered almost no attention in this place—he could feel his own invisibility.

In the strange streets of the bustling city on the river he was sometimes circumnavigated, an obstacle to which people would call a warning, but he was never observed. The individual trajectories of the people moving their own way toward their own goals unfolded before him like a tremendous overlay of intertwining threads. He felt safe. He wasn't alone, here, he was just by himself. No one here was thinking about a burned-down house, or a dead man named Oliver Bodkin. It was all so interesting, so beautiful, that he didn't think of himself at all.

He grew hungry and needed a place to stay but he couldn't see, in the swirl of urbanity, how to solve these issues.

The wall of storefronts before Raleigh appeared to him as a fortress of plate glass and paint, covered in indecipherable advertising. Who knew so many types of stores existed? How could so many places be dedicated to purchasing things? In the window of a barbershop, underneath a curious tin lantern in the shape of a crown painted gold and black, he saw a chalkboard sign that read "Rooms for Let / We Need a Piano Player." It shone like a guiding star.

It was the first thing he'd seen all day that made sense to him, and he grabbed it like a rope thrown to a drowning man. He needed a room, they needed a piano player, and he knew how to play piano.

He opened the door, trying to be timid, unsure of himself, and the little bell on the doorframe rang out to announce him, which startled the barber who had been dozing in the chair. The man jerked awake and looked around, spooked.

"I'm sorry," said Raleigh, "I didn't mean to."

The barber was a tall, young, black man, with carefully trimmed whiskers. He wore an apron, and under that a vest and fine looking trousers in a wide stripe.

"Oh, don't . . ." he waved it off. "You look terrible—come in here, come in." The barber said this urgently, and gestured to the chair. Raleigh sat.

"I guess you been traveling?"

He drew the curtains.

"I just came into town," said Raleigh. "I'd like to . . . do you need a piano player?"

A samovar steamed next to a wooden cabinet fronted with glass behind which rested many small vials and bowls. On a table in front of the mirror razors and scissors were carefully arrayed next to a bottle of whiskey.

The barber introduced himself. "I'm Hatforth. We'll start by cleaning you up. How long have you been running?"

"What?"

"We can't have you looking like you been sleeping in ditches. You've been sleeping in these clothes?"

He nodded and looked down, ashamed of his clothes.

"Just lay back."

Raleigh did as he was told.

"It's all right, I'll get you there."

Raleigh relaxed as Hatforth toweled him, the steam scented with bay leaves. He felt Hatforth massage his head, starting at the temples, working in circles. The straight razor slid across his cheek, snicking the stubble. Hatforth applied bracing analgesics, sharp and heady, followed by creamy unguents.

Raleigh drifted, carried away by the scents and the warmth and the physicality of the experience. Hatforth's hands were smooth and competent.

"Aright. I'll get you there. You got some clothes, then?"

"I have these clothes."

"You been sleeping in those clothes."

"Get me where?" Raleigh asked.

"Get you out."

"I don't . . . I just got here."

"What's your name?"

"Raleigh," he paused. "Bodkin."

"That name lead back to your place? Where you come from?"

"It does."

"Can't use that."

"I can't?"

"They put it out in the papers you are a runaway, and it doesn't matter how far we send you if you're going around using the name they put out in the paper. They'll catch you and send you back."

"I'm not a runaway!"

Hatforth stood in front of Raleigh, deciding whether or not to argue with him.

"What do you mean? You come in here like you been sleeping in a ditch. You look half scared out of your mind. Don't know nothing from nothing, far as I can tell. What do you mean?"

"I'll show you."

Raleigh produced his manumission from the little bag in which he'd received it, years before, flattened it out on his knee. The conductor had been the first person to whom Raleigh had shown the paper, and he had given it only the most cursory glance. Raleigh wondered if it said what it needed to say, if it were even real.

Hatforth whistled and said: "Well, damn. I guess you owe me for the shave, then."

There came a knock at the door, and Hatforth paused, then came a second knock, upon which he went to open it.

A woman entered: "I saw you lit the lantern."

"Mistake."

"Who is this, then?"

Hatforth introduced them, her name was Vivian.

"I took her for a drive in the country just last night."

"Took me for a drive," she said. There was softhearted derision in her voice.

"Did we not drive? Was it not romantic to be out beneath the stars?"

"Whose wagon was it, Al?"

"Don't ask fool questions."

"Don't give me fool answers. It was a nice ride," she said.

Hatforth started a fire and made some coffee. The three of them sat in a small room around a table in the back of the building, four tin cups on the table, three full of coffee and the fourth for portions of the clay bottle of harsh raw whiskey Hatforth set on the table between them. Raleigh coughed at his first sip, but the analgesic qualities of the drink, combined with the golden light pouring through the little window and breaking across the fabric which spilled over Vivian's knees won him.

She was beautiful. Raleigh thought of Keats—this was the sort of woman who would drive a man to write poems such as those.

Raleigh told his story.

"That's a hell of a trap," said Hatforth, Vivian nodded. They both looked thoughtful. "A helluva spot to be in. You got friends somewhere? People?"

"Gee and Lo—she was the cook, she raised me—although I don't know where they are. I do, actually. They're in the Swamp. Lo said she was going to the Swamp to stay with the maroons at the split magnolia."

"What the hell?" Hatforth said.

"And Miss Rose might be helpful—she moved to California, I think."

"Can't hardly just show up in California asking for Rose."

"No."

"You don't have a plan," said Vivian. "I mean I don't see how you *could* have a plan. Everything just crashed, everything fell apart."

"And I walked away."

"What else were you supposed to do?" Hatforth said. "They're saying you're a killer. You'd be dead if you stayed. They'd have strung you up."

Raleigh felt good to hear it said.

"At least if you actually were escaped, we'd know what to do next," said Vivian.

"Ain't got no plan for this type of thing," said Hatforth.

"I saw the sign on your window. I play piano."

"You were serious? You do?"

"Mickey be around here before too long," Vivian said. "We'll talk to him."

After a while there came a rapping on the front door, the same double knock that Vivian had used, and Hatforth went to answer it, looking at Raleigh with an automatic reflex to protect him, to hide him, to shove him in a closet or hurry him out the back door.

Moments later he ushered a young man—Raleigh thought he looked twelve—into the room. The kid was dressed in a worn three-piece suit which had been reconstructed from an adult's suit to fit him. The back of the jacket had been taken in, but the lapels had not been adjusted—they were huge. The trousers had been hemmed, but the rise had not been touched, so the crotch was comically low.

"Hello, Mickey," said Vivian.

Mickey had a plug of tobacco in his cheek. He nodded.

Hatforth and Mickey mumbled some in the front room while Vivian and Raleigh sat in the back.

"Anyway—Raleigh here plays piano," sat Hatforth, leading Mickey into the back room.

The kid shrugged.

Hatforth, behind the kid, said: "The piano player on the *Rialto* died last week. Never figured Bellows dying in his sleep—wait, we sure it was his own bed?"

The kid laughed, and said he reckoned it were.

"Don't see how we can have a show without a piano player, is what the boss says, and I reckon he's right about that."

Raleigh, looking around, said: "I'm sorry."

"What're you sorry about?" said the kid.

"I'm sorry for the death of your friend," said Raleigh.

"I ain't sorry. He was a son of a bitch and a no-good cheat," said Mickey. The kid wanted to say something else, and Vivian cut him off.

"Mickey, hush. Don't speak ill of him, now that he's gone."

Vivian looked at Mickey and Hatforth, and shook her head with a frustrated dismay, taking it upon herself to explain to Raleigh that she sang on a showboat called the *Rialto*, and that Mickey was the assistant to the manager.

This disgruntled Mickey, and he spit on the floor. Hatforth told him not to.

"You ain't got no spittoon in here."

"Don't go spitting on my floor."

"Where I'm s'posed to?"

"Walk back out to the damn shop and spit."

"Ya oughta get a spittoon in here."

"Don't spit on my floor."

Vivian sighed and turned the bright light of her attention toward Raleigh, tightening her focus to willfully exclude Mickey and Hatforth. They were nuisances, extras next to Raleigh, and his perception of this brief ownership of her full attention flooded him with sparks of joy that burst through his chest.

"I could do it."

"You play piano?"

"All my life."

"You mean you know some songs on the piano?"

"No."

"What do you mean?"

"Oliver Bodkin, my . . . the man who owned the house, taught piano, I've played piano every day. Now that I think about it, this current stretch of time is probably the longest I've gone without playing in years."

"You do surprise," said Hatforth.

Raleigh smiled at Vivian. He wanted to fix her problem. He wanted to be alone with her. He wanted to watch the light bounce off the edge of her high cheekbone forever. He wanted to supersede everyone around her.

"What you say your name was? Raleigh?" said Mickey, and then to Hatforth: "Where'd you find this boy?"

"He just walked in off the street," Hatforth chuckled.

"That right?"

The creaking barge known as the *Rialto* was painted white with red details and was pushed around on the river by a small boat with matching paint and a steam engine. The upstairs was a dormitory for the players, and the first floor was the theater. The backstage was built into the prow, and the stern was a bar and a storage room. The gallery, where the audience sat, was open on the sides. From the "abovedecks," as Mickey called the dormitory, you stepped carefully onto a spiral staircase—rust breaking through the many layers of red paint—that hung out over the side of the boat and wound your way up to Hyman's rooms, perched atop.

Vivian and Raleigh waited in the gallery while Mickey announced them. The *Rialto* tilted ever so slightly in the river, and Raleigh's feet adjusted to the subtle shifts as he riffled through the sheet music, looking over folk songs and popular songs, none of which he'd ever played. He knew he could sight-read them, but he wanted to make an impression, and they weren't the sort of thing he was accustomed to: he wanted something big. He found it.

Hyman came down from his quarters, and looked around while he stroked his belly through his vest. The chairs were stacked, the floor was swept—he was checking up on things. "Okay," he said, "so you play? They tell me."

Raleigh sat, back straight, and ran his hands across the keys of the grand piano. It was in tune, and in surprisingly good shape. The action was quick. The enclosure of the stage gave the sound some good bounce off the wall and back out into the room where Vivian and Hyman stood. Mickey was leaning over the rail, looking at the water. The first notes of Beethoven's Seventeenth Piano sonata sound just like a pianist testing out the keys of the instrument. A slightly more organized drift up a scale that resolves, but takes a breath, and fires a run like a shot out of a cannon. Then it abates, and drifts again, but then, oh, it builds, and then his right hand was fluttering like a moth over the keys, and he could feel the music. The notes on the page led him along, but he knew the piece. He'd played it every day for a year or more. His back was straight, his hands were light, when he rolled up the isolated chords before the roiling vigor that sounded like a boat tossed on the waves, he heard Mickey start to say something and stop.

The piece asked a lot, he realized, of those who had not heard it. It was always ending and starting over again. Passages of lingering single notes that sounded lost and sad were followed by purposeful, allegro arpeggios. Oliver had said that the calm parts were little bits of peace from the storm, little respites, but Raleigh had argued that they were more terrifying: "At least, when the storm is upon you, it has your full attention, when the wind dies down, and the waves subside, you have to look around and take note of all the damage." He jumped his left hand over his right in a dizzying flurry. He heard Vivian gasp. The last bit of it was his favorite, the chords galloped after one another, the motif twisted around itself, and then the beautiful one-two-three-four ring building to a rumble like thunder, and the neat little bow that tied it all together at the end. He let the last chord ring, and took a breath.

There was a moment of silence while his small audience waited to see if he was done. He stood.

"*Ir gefelt mir zaier*," said Hyman.

Mickey was shaking his head and grinning: "You say he just walked in off the street?"

Vivian was glowing. Was he imagining it? He didn't think so.

"This changes everything," said Hyman. "Everything. I have to think about this. This is something else entirely, something else entirely. Mickey go and fetch us something to eat, and something to drink. We have work, we have work." He was walking off, toward the spiral staircase. He spun on his heels. "Vivian, clean out Mr. Bellows's berth, and find what Raleigh will need."

"Mr. Bellows? Did he? Is this where?"

"Mr. Bellows did not die in here," Vivian was collecting what few things Bellows had left. The berth was barely more than a thin shelf with a blanket, a few hooks on the wall, and a small nightstand. "Mr. Bellows had a room in town."

Vivian opened the drawer to the rickety nightstand, and pulled out a couple of letters and a paper shirt collar.

"He wasn't very kind. He wasn't a good man. I knew him, though." She shrugged. "You sure can play,"

Through the portal behind her shone enough light to wrap her head in a golden glow. The sun, it seemed to Raleigh, sought her out.

Raleigh had never played for anyone other than Temple and Oliver. Oliver was proud of him, but Oliver was his teacher. He couldn't surprise him. Impress him, yes, please him, but it was a different sort of pleasure than the visceral pleasure of an audience.

"Thank you."

"You got a lot of music in you, I guess."

"I practiced. We didn't have much to do."

"Yours is a strange story," she smiled. Raleigh's heart thudded in his chest.

Mickey hollered down the stairs that Hyman wanted to see them.

The top floor of the *Rialto* comprised three rooms. Cabins—Mickey's and Hyman's—were on either side of a generous space, with luscious red carpet and an ornate round table of burnished mahogany, piled with ledger books and papers and hand bills, surrounded by chairs. Hyman stood when they came in: "This is what I think. I think we have a new concept. Big concept. Something we haven't seen before—has anyone seen it before? We haven't seen it before. Doesn't matter. It's never been on this river. This river has never seen anything like it. Never seen anything like you. We begin, as we have always begun, more or less, with some folk songs. Same old folk songs. We do a couple of the country life skits, some comedy, you know them, Vivian, the comedy. But then, a speech. I give a speech: What we have been seeing, ladies and gentleman, is a reflection of the life of the Negro as it is lived here. Left to their own devices, you see, they run amok and come to little. Entertaining, to be sure, but not much to speak of, and so on. We have here, on this very boat, a representative of another class, another world, another place! I think we have to say you are from Europe, what did you say your name was?"

"Raleigh Bodkin."

"We'll have to call you something else."

"How about Walter Raleigh Bodkin?" said Mickey.

"Walter Raleigh, I love it. But maybe not Bodkin. Too English. Too . . . colonial. Continental is what we need. If they think you got this sort of education around here, why first excuse they find and you'll be strung up from a tree. Maybe all of us. You need to be here on permission from some royal whatsit, is how I see it. Educated in Vienna, somewhere none of these people can imagine. Walter Raleigh *Babenberg*, of Bohemia. Of Bohemia! Sound good? Personal servant to an empress, perhaps? No, again, perhaps that sounds a little too much like husband? I would like to keep you alive. Protégé? Foundling, perhaps. You were found in a basket? On a doorstep you were left? Raised and educated in the courts of Europe."

"He doesn't sound European," said Vivian.

"Well, he doesn't sound *shvartser*, either. Anyway it doesn't matter. I'll be the one telling the story. What do they know from European? You might need to remember enough of it to smile, but your job is to play the piano. My job is to talk. To talk about how you prove the potential—ah, the sorely neglected potential!—of a well-managed Negro class. The potential of the colored man! Under the guidance of the finest minds of Europe, look what he can rise to. Good." Hyman swayed softly with satisfaction, before looking sharply at Raleigh: "Is that the only tune you know?"

"Not at all."

"Good, good. We start rehearsals day after tomorrow. Vivian, show our Babenburg some of the spirituals."

Walter Raleigh Babenburg of Bohemia mastered the simple songs in no time. While he practiced, he met the rest of the *Rialto.*

Tim and Tom, brothers, dark as ink and natural comedians. Tom played plump and lazy, while Tim, rail thin, played the industrious brother.

Wink, a sour Englishman with an eyepatch and craggy hands, drove the tug that pushed the barge and did carpentry work. As he moved around the barge making repairs and getting it ready, he muttered an ongoing catalogue of grievances regarding the idea of theater, Hyman, and his lot in life.

Wink doubled as the cook.

The first half of the show consisted of Tom and Tim chasing Vivian around and falling over chairs, lolling in the sun, and smoking stolen tobacco while they should be working. They had natural timing, knew just when to pause, just when to widen their eyes. Tom, the plump one, was seemingly indestructible. He could roll, fall, have things fall upon him, all without effect.

"Then!" said Hyman, "I take the stage. I will be in resplendent dress."

Wink, who was sanding a deck rail, snorted at this.

"You have to imagine the resplendence, Wink. Imagine it. Use your imagination. And I will speechify as follows:

"Ladies and Gentlemen, let me say again that I am honored to have you aboard the *Rialto* this afternoon. I hope the entertainments thus far have been to your liking. We try, indeed, we try.

"People will clap, here, and I will bow a little bow."

He demonstrated the bow.

"What you have seen tonight, in the first segment of our presentation, represents the familiar. You've heard these songs, or songs like them, all your lives. These jokes, or jokes like them, have made us all laugh. Indeed, it is but a portrait of a way of life—threatened, disparaged by some, and here exaggerated for our amusement, but not so very strange. I ask you, now, however, to open your mind to something completely alien. Something unseen upon these shores. For we have, this season, a very special guest. Raised in the palaces of the Prince of Bohemia, a Negro foundling. Tutored by the best minds of Europe. Taken in by that family as one of their own. Not knowing his name when they found him, abandoned on their doorstep, they named him after a man they admired for his intrepid exploration of parts unknown, they named him after the great Englishman, Sir Walter Raleigh. Walter Raleigh Babenberg of Bohemia is here by special arrangement, via my connections in Vienna. I waggle my eyebrows a little here? Too much? Some have said that he is proof that an educated class of Negro might rise, might learn to accomplish great things. I, myself, hesitate to go that far. For how many of us were educated in such rare air? You see? If we had among us an army of royal tutors, perhaps. No, this is far more special. This is singular. This is a precious emulsion of unmixable substances, fixed in the body of a Negro. It is, perhaps, only through ignorance of his own nature that he rose to such heights. Protected, as he was, by the palace walls. Untouched by the world. Like an apple unmet by the worm, unknown even to itself.

"And then I bow. And I do this sorta thing, indicating our Walter, and you, Walter, you have to really play to it. Should we call you Raleigh? You seem a little confused when I call you Walter. Fine. Okay, Raleigh, now, but, standing very tall, taller than that, and with pomp in your step, I want you to walk up and put your hand on the piano. And give a small bow, not like I do, but just almost a nod. Then take the bench. Take a breath. Set yourself. Then strike!"

CHAPTER TWENTY-ONE

Taken up to the House

When they came and got Temple out of the stone shed, she was broken, exhausted, and dazed. The bright light hurt and the touch of the people who had her by the arms felt foreign and strange. They were strong men, and her bare feet skimmed over the surface of the dirt path, barely touching ground. She made gestures as if she were walking, but she was not walking. They were carrying her, and her head was lolling, dizzy. Her thumb, where she had chewed on it, was infected, and the pain throbbed a steady beat, breaking her thoughts into pieces with every heartbeat.

She was dragged up the stairs to the front door, and soon stood in the center hall. The men still held her arms. They were white men. The bigger one had a beard, and they called him Mack. The skinny, meaner looking one was called Gilly, she thought. They had been talking as if she weren't there, continuing some conversation about something she couldn't understand.

Zeb Newcombe stepped out into the hall, closing the office door behind him.

She'd been in this house so many times as a child, and now it was like a dreamscape—everything was familiar, and yet entirely changed. The walls were in the same places, the tiles were the same. There was a different chair, yellow, with gold velvet stretched across the cushion. A gilt frame, ornate, with flowers and curls, wrapping a canvas that seemed to glow. In the painting, light streamed through the clouds upon a river valley. A light green sweep of meadow stretched out before what looked like a church. A few cows were standing by the river. The painting hadn't been there when she was young. There'd been a portrait of a hunting dog. It was strange to feel nostalgia for something you'd never liked.

"What do they call you?" Zeb asked.

"Temple."

"That's what I thought. I've written to Mr. Bodkin's aunt of this unfortunate, this terribly sad event. Since the death of her nephew was at the hands of your brother—the dead boy who lit the fire was your brother?"

"Raleigh?"

He hit her across the face. Quickly, with no preamble and no compunction. She gasped and wanted to cry, but stifled it. Her eyes were red.

"You best learn some manners," said Zeb. "Since the boy killed Mr. Bodkin, she wants nothing to do with you. She sold you to me."

"Sold me to you?"

Zeb slapped her again. She stared at the floor, barely holding back tears. Zeb came up so close she feel his breath when he spoke.

"You will learn not to ask me questions."

One of the men holding her chuckled.

"Take her away."

The men walked her out the door. The drive that approached the New House curved into a circle, in the center of which was a fountain and two tall pecan trees. Off the curving, well-maintained road, the farm grew more utilitarian, more regular. Gravel paths were laid out on a grid in between low brick buildings with metal roofs, impressive in their solidity. While the New House, and the grounds around it, demonstrated a certain kind of performative wealth, the side of the farm farthest from the Old House, where the New Barn towered on its stone footings, and the brick slave houses were perfectly arrayed, displayed something else. Mastery. Worth. Horses in a barn like that were worth something. The enslaved in these houses were worth too much to let freeze. All of this had been built by the Bodkins to celebrate and control what they had. It took generations of amassed wealth, and the continual creation of more wealth, to maintain a place such as the Hundred. Zeb had not been prepared, and he watched with growing fury as his accounts were depleted. The farm fell gradually into disrepair, sometimes because he hadn't noticed what needed fixing, and sometimes because he held his purse strings too tightly, allowing things to get steadily worse until they were too expensive to fix.

Temple noticed, as she shuffled between the men, that the hedges were lumpy, and the edges of the roads were weedy.

Mack and Gilly led Temple to one of the slave quarters and moved her through the door. She stepped onto a bare wooden floor, worn and dented but sanded smooth. On the back wall was a fireplace. A blanket hung on a nail in the wall.

When the men let go of her arms, she crumpled, wondering, unable to make any sense of where she was or what was happening.

She looked up at the men. The wiry one was already three steps gone, but the bearded one was looking around with a sneer.

"Wait," said Temple. The man registered surprise, and settled a smug grimace upon her. The other man stopped on the stoop. "I'm Temple Bodkin. I'm free."

In one step the man closed the distance between them and hit her with his fist on the crown of her head. She saw stars and fell sideways. She curled into herself, spitting and choking for air.

"Whoever you are, you better be outside this door and ready to work when I blow the horn tomorrow morning."

And the man left.

Temple lay on the floor, in pain. She blinked her eyes and tried to will herself to wake from the nightmare. Maybe it wasn't happening. Maybe this wasn't real. She was so depleted that she could not think but in panicked bursts of rage and frenzies of unreason.

She could smell the hog yard, behind the slave houses. On the floor, she watched a small ant walk along the groove between two planks of the floor.

She tried to push her mind through to the night of smoke and chaos.

She remembered waking up, her room filled with smoke. Stumbling down the stairs, each breath like being punched in the throat. She was falling and she couldn't see. There were flames in the hall. The parlor was full of smoke. She was crawling, trying to make it to the door. Then hands. Someone grabbed her and picked her up. When she woke up, she was in the stone shed, on the floor, still in her nightdress.

She sat up and looked herself over. She had no shoes, she had no stockings. Her nightdress was frayed, stretched, and stained. She could feel stiff mud crusted onto the back and the hem was dark.

She could walk to the river. She could walk back to the Old House. She had clothes at home. She didn't belong here, anyway.

Raleigh was dead? Oliver was dead?

Temple stood up. Raleigh couldn't be dead. Maybe he's in the Old Barn. He must be in the barn.

She stepped out of the little room and into the path. Golden sun streamed through the trees. There was a pleasant, cookfire smell in the air. Temple was wobbly, and suddenly hungry. She looked around, slowly, like a stunned bird, and walked, dazed, slow. There were people about, she saw them in the periphery of her vision. No one looked at her. Maybe she was dead. Maybe she was a ghost? She kept her eyes on the path, five feet in front of her. She saw her feet swing out in front, and she saw the pebbled ground of the walkway moving under her.

I'll just go home, she thought. I'll go back to the house. Raleigh will be there, and Oliver can explain to me what has happened. I can get some clothes, and I'll go to the river and I'll clean off in the fresh river water. I'll sit on my rock out in the stream and the water will run around me and it'll be cold and clear.

She imagined sitting all the way back in the water and letting it rush around her head and ripple at the edge of her lips. How calm and fresh it would feel.

In front of the house she thought she saw the two men who had dragged her around and put her in the room. They were up on the porch, but she was a ghost. Since she was dead, she thought, they couldn't see her. They didn't look at her. She didn't look at them. She could smell the smoke from their cigars. They were dark blurs, smudges in the shadows of the porch.

One of them called to her, but she didn't answer or acknowledge the call.

"I said where are you going?"

The smudges moved, lengthened. Temple walked. She was only going home. She lived right over there.

I live right over there, she told herself. It can't be but half a mile. Could it be more than that? Right over there, past the brick wall Oliver built. There was no gate through the brick wall. She knew that on the other side were the old garden, and the orchard, and then the Old House. She'd walk along it. She kept moving, ignoring the men who were coming down off of the porch.

"I think she's gone in the head, Mack."

"Crazy as anything, huh, Gilly? Where you think you're going?"

Temple didn't respond. She only trudged forward along the wall.

"I asked you where you were going?" They were beside her now. Walking with the casual menace of hateful men who know they cannot lose.

"I'm going home. I live over there."

"I showed you where you live."

"No, I live over there. With Oliver."

Then Temple was in the dirt, sprawled forward. They quickly grabbed her and dragged her backward, toward the slave yard to the whipping post. Zeb was on the porch now.

"She was running away."

"I wasn't running; I was walking home."

"You are home," said Zeb, "learn it."

The men put her wrists in the shackles that hung from the post and pulled the chain through the pulley on the top until she was stretched out, barely able to touch the ground. The shackles hurt her wrists, pulled on the base of her hands, and cut into her skin. They cut off her nightdress.

"Just let me go."

The whip cut across her back. The pain was immense. Like a knife slashed across her. She twisted in the shackles, but she couldn't turn or move to escape. She was sobbing. The blows came steadily, and the pain grew into a sheet of ragged fire. She couldn't see. She could hear the whoosh of the whip as it sliced through the air, and she could feel the impact of the leather. The blows were like high flames, sharper burns, pricked out peaks of an all-encompassing pain. Then they stopped. When they threw brine across her back she passed out.

Temple woke up on the floor of the brick slave house. She was on a thick blanket, covered by another one, and her head was on a pillow. Her back was throbbing. The room was lit by a candle, she watched the shadows and light play on the blank wall as she came to.

She slowly turned her head to the source of the light.

There, on a stool, sat a white woman.

She had a book in her hands, and was reading by the light of a candle at a small table, on which there were a few bowls and a crumpled rag. Her beautiful hair was piled high on her head, and fell about, caught the candlelight, and glowed like a halo.

Temple coughed and the woman looked up.

"You're awake," she said. "I brought you some blankets, and I got some poultice from old Zara. I put it on your back. I found you a dress."

"Thank you." Temple moved to get up, but couldn't.

"I'll give you some water."

She nodded.

"It's a terrible thing, what's happened."

Temple nodded.

"You never heard about anything? Any reason? Was he mad? Wild, I mean? I guess sometimes . . . your people just . . ." she sighed. "When Zeb's men saw the flames and ran over there, they heard a gunshot as they approached, and they tried to get into the house but the flames were already too high. Do you remember?"

Temple shook her head.

"You collapsed through the door, and they thought he'd shot you, too. Do you remember what they were fighting about?"

Temple drank water, but didn't say anything. The water tasted metallic, but it was cold.

"You don't know why he set the house afire? You know there was talk of a conspiracy. Some of the folks around were ready to hang you for your part in Oliver's murder."

"Hang me?"

"Oh, yes. I told Zeb to get in touch with the Bodkin woman who moved to Alabama, the aunt, the next of kin. She agreed to sell you to us, and that no charges were warranted. I never thought there should have been any. You're safe. I'll go. You should rest. They said you could have a few days to rest. I'll come look in on you tomorrow."

Marie rose, filling the room with the scent of roses.

None of what she said made any sense to Temple. It didn't seem possible. It didn't seem real. And yet, she touched the floor, and it was hard beneath her fingertips. She took the water, and sipping it felt it move through the center of her body and settle into her stomach. The water was real, she could feel it. She could feel the hunger coming from the inside of her body. She lived in an impossible world, but she didn't understand how to argue against it. There was no logic to connect every day of her life to the day she now found herself living. There was no path or sequence she could think through.

If Rose were here.

But Rose wasn't here.

If Oliver were here.

Oliver wasn't here.

If Raleigh.

Raleigh wasn't here.

It was as if everything that had happened in her life had not happened. It was as if she had woken up from a dream she had believed was reality.

CHAPTER TWENTY-TWO

Aboard the *Rialto*

April 1860

"Raleigh, you need clothes. Couple of extra collars. Some cufflinks," said Hyman. "Is Red Joe around? Have we seen Joe?"

"Have not, boss," said Mickey.

"Can we find him? Find him, tell him to take Raleigh to my cousin's shop. Put it on the bill."

"Cousin isn't going to like that, Boss."

"I don't care what he likes," he waved at the air, as if shooing a fly. "He likes, doesn't like."

"But don't come back here looking like Red Joe. A jewelry store, he looks like," said Hyman.

"Like he robbed one," said Mickey.

"Stands out."

"He's hard to miss," said Mickey.

"Subtlety is not his specialty, but subtlety? What's the point?" He shooed subtlety away with the swat of a flat hand.

"C'mon," said Mickey. Past the gangplank, he said: "Have you met Red Joe yet? He's our advance man. He works the shore, hands out bills, talks up the show. Great at it. You should hear him, telling everyone at the hardware store about how if you take a woman to the theater she'll get color in her cheeks and come home with a sparkle in her eye. He'll be in here." They had come to the door of a tavern.

Red Joe was tall and wiry; he wore kohl around his eyes. Feathers hung from his button holes, he had a necklace wrapped around his wrist, and he was bedecked in beads and odd little remnants.

"My little thug friend Mickey, how do you do."

"Can you take Raleigh here to the tailor?"

Red Joe looked Raleigh up and down, slowly, and reached out to shake his hand.

"Vivian told me about you." He mimed playing the piano on the bar. "Go along Mickey. I'll take him over. Perhaps a drink? First a drink."

Red Joe waited until the drinks arrived, tapped Raleigh's glass, and said: "I dress this way on purpose. This isn't just a collection of sentimental geegaws or things I happened to pick up. Nor is it a true reflection of my exoticism. I was raised in London. This is my costume."

"To what end?"

Raleigh looked at Red Joe's sharp features, his black eyes accentuated by the dry black kohl.

"To dazzle and wow. Do you think I could stroll into town in dusty field clothes?"

Red Joe's vest was iridescent silver and blue in a swirling floral pattern.

"Do you think they like renting rooms to red men? Confronted with so alien a persona, they sometimes forget. You think they give such a pass to my buckskin brethren? No sir. I promise you they do not. But people tend to believe what I say if I sound as if I am from London. I urge you to follow suit."

At the tailor's shop, Hyman's cousin groused about the tab, but produced a silver waistcoat in paisley, trousers striped gray and charcoal, and a charcoal coat. They bought cuffs and collars and a purple cravat. From the buttonhole of his vest, Red Joe unfastened a silver tie pin with a crested head.

"A welcoming gift," said Red Joe.

"I couldn't."

"You shall. You need something like that. Something convincingly continental," said Red Joe, with a wink.

"Now that we have some real culture," he said, nodding toward Raleigh that evening aboard the *Rialto*, "I will expand my canvassing to include the small-town sophisticates, your educators and lawyers and so on."

It was Red's idea, while they were in rehearsals, that perhaps there should be a sort of comedic relief after Raleigh's performance, to lighten the mood. Tom would chase Vivian from backstage, wagging his tongue after her like a dog, her dress in just enough disarray to spark the idea that she'd been alone when this beast made another jump for her. Raleigh would spin on the piano bench and stick out a foot, which Tom would trip over extravagantly, tumbling across the stage like a bear rolling down a slope. Vivian would make her escape.

"Then, Raleigh, you will stand, smile, and bow. The audience will laugh and it will be an explosion of relieved tension. They will hate you for your talent, you see," Red Joe explained. "It will be so strange for them—some of their children take piano lessons, am I right? Do you think any of them have heard, in the warm shelter of their drawing rooms and parlors, anything like this? Has any of their lousy little pickpocket Sunday schoolers ever even touched a fingertip to the trills, the thunder, the emotion that you have wrought here? They will be in a heightened state, overcome with emotion, admiration, loathing. So." Here Red Joe paused for effect: "You trip the fat man. Let's keep our Bohemian out of the trees, shall we?"

Wink rang the bell for dinner.

"Why can't you just tell us it's ready?" Vivian said. "You know we're only right here. We'd hear you."

Wink kept up his muttered monologue without seeming to adjust it to the fact that he'd been spoken to.

Wink was a surprisingly good man at the stove. He fished for eels to stew, bought lambs to roast, and laid in stores of potatoes and onions and apples. He had a man who made sausages, and he knew where to find good hams.

Over the big meal the team would discuss changes to the program. Tell one another what had worked, what hadn't, what was funny, what wasn't. Raleigh didn't feel qualified to add to the conversation, and no one felt capable of giving him notes on his performance, either.

After dinner, Vivian would disembark, back to Hatforth, figured Raleigh. Hyman would disappear upstairs. Mickey, Tim, and Tom would wander off into the evening, and Wink would fuss about on his little pusher boat, clanging around, tinkering, and drinking rum until he sat down with his head leaned back against the gunwale and drifted off to sleep.

The *Rialto* swayed, bumping against the pylons, and Raleigh sat alone at one of the tables in the hall with a book open before him, staring out at the light bouncing off the little crests in the river.

He wondered if he was happy. He'd certainly landed in a remarkable place. He wondered if it was okay to feel anything but guilt about his sister. Shouldn't his every breath be in mourning? How dare he watch the sunlight shatter across the river's ripples when she had suffered.

He should sit upon splinters and eat dry bread. He shouldn't be able even to hear the music he played, it was too beautiful for him. He deserved nothing. How dare he continue, while she did not? He closed his eyes and willed her death from his mind. Opened them to see Red Joe, approaching.

Red Joe nodded to a chair in asking. He sat and produced from his pocket his leather tobacco pouch. It was a two-layered affair, stitched together so as to have a sleeve on the outside in which Red Joe carefully slid whole leaves of tobacco. He rolled his own cheroots, carefully working the tobacco with a mixture of other herbs.

"Specialty of the subcontinent, 'Booz Rooz' they call it."

The rich dark tobacco soon burned a fog of smoke, tinged with strange smells of animals and flowers, skunks and cooking spices.

He puffed contentedly for a bit, still not speaking, leaning far back in his chair with his legs outstretched in front of him and jetting smoke toward the ceiling.

Red Joe sat in silence for almost half an hour, intoxicated from the drugs rolled into his cheroot, entranced by the river, the light, the rocking of the ship, fascinated by the thoughts that tumbled through his head like colorful smooth planets cruising along in their orbits, unstoppable, unbelievably heavy, pulling moons and comets to them. Pleasant when viewed from afar, if he tried to catch one, or stop it, it rolled over him like a leviathan, crushing him, obliterating him with terrible noise, tearing on away from him. He ought to have learned from his mistakes, from the panic of watching your own thought shoot out in every conceivable direction like some prismatic quicksilver vine. It was impossible to keep up, impossible to hold anything in place, impossible, even, to remember what had been interesting about this particular grain of his cerebral firmament.

He quivered, stricken, somehow joyous and ebullient and utterly terrified all at once. In the back of his mind, the tiny voice, all that remained of his sensibility, reminded him that it would all be over in a little while, you could set a watch by this, the fleeting terrible explosion of inebriation that led to a pacific ocean of joyful, easy peace. This will pass. This is not the future. This is not forever. This is just . . . this.

Streaks of calm broke through the chaos like rays through clouds. Then the clouds organized themselves. Feeling as if he had washed the grime of a two day ride from his face with a bracing basin of water, he leaned forward, blinked, and looked over at Raleigh.

"Thank you," said Red Joe.

Raleigh cocked an eyebrow.

"For letting me sit in silence. The Booz Rooz sweeps in strong, you see, and frequently renders conversation impossible. It's been half an hour,

I'd wager. Nice to have you by my side." Red Joe clapped him on the shoulder. "Would you enjoy a walk?"

"I don't know if I should."

"There's nothing to be nervous of," said Red Joe. "We can steer clear of the sorts of places where people get picked up, but either way, as I understand it, you are a card-carrying freeman. Nothing can hurt you, my good man."

His boots clacking the cobblestones in the evening light, Joe asked: "What was the name of the place you lived?"

"Bodkin's Hundred. Well, it was the homestead there, we just called it the Old House. The New House was Bodkin's Hundred."

"And you've never known another home?"

Raleigh shook his head.

"It was paradisiacal," said Joe. "Bodkin's Hundred, a garden within which you were free to roam. All of history, all of the machinations of the outside world were beyond its walls. It's a curse, of course, to know Eden. Odd, too, to be so educated, and yet so alien."

"I feel like I was educated in a doll's house."

"My welcome to you. Welcome, Walter Raleigh Babenberg, to the world outside the garden wall."

They walked and Red Joe told stories—"It was on this corner, right over there in front of the bake shop, that I first met a lady named Penelope Starr . . ."

He eventually came to his own story.

"It begins as hearsay," he said. "I was an infant when an English couple found me in the prairie grass, crying."

An English couple on a tour of the West had taken some horses and ridden out—against the advice of the hotel clerk and the man who ran the stables.

"I think they were so insistent that it would have been a relief if they'd been murdered on the open plains. Certainly I came to understand that side of them. The stableman made them put a deposit down for the horses that would more than satisfy him after the couple were killed and the horses captured by savages. They told me this part in such detail so as to remind me not only that they had rescued me from certain death, but that to accomplish that rescue they had risked their own death, albeit in a rather indulgent and pleasure-seeking sort of way, while simultaneously enforcing my own sense of my origin among the very savages that they braved to rescue me. A complicated thing to lay upon a child, I think you'll agree."

Having found him, they picked him up, wrapped him in a coat, and rode back to the hotel, where they fed him milk and warmed him by the fire.

"No one, it seemed, had any use for a foundling savage. They would tell you that they were so moved by a desire to save me, to raise me, that they couldn't think of anything but that I would stay by their side and return to England as one of their own. I think it closer to the truth to say that I returned to England as the greatest imaginable souvenir."

Red Joe insisted he was not without gratitude. They had, indeed, saved his life. They had cared for, housed, and educated him. However, they grew bored of him.

"The last two years I spent with them were chilly, and they reminded me as often as possible that I was not, ultimately, their child. Barely their responsibility at all, certainly not going to inherit anything. Before we got to the 'what shall we do about Joe' conversation, I left."

"And so the story that Hyman made up for me is your story."

"Well, certain details have been changed, no doubt," said Red Joe. "And yours has a happier ending."

The *Rialto* made its way downstream, unhurried, according to a pattern long established—back and forth across the river, stopping at Cairo last, where the green Ohio joined the muddy Mississippi. The rivers resisted one another, two wild things introduced. There, the *Rialto* would stop and take a break before starting back up the Ohio on a reverse zigzag, hitting the towns they'd missed on the way down, until they came back again to the crowded riverfront of Louisville.

Red Joe mostly stayed on the shore, arriving in the next town in advance of the boat. When the *Rialto* pulled in the day before the show, Hyman would unfurl the banner and at dusk he would light the gaslights that ringed the deck and make the place look like everything you wanted, which, Hyman had realized ages ago, wasn't all that much. What they wanted, mostly, was something to do, something to look at, something to laugh at. Lives filled with drudgery and fear, peppered with occasional flashes of passion. He had no great admiration for his audiences. They seemed stuck by their own foolishness. They stayed in their towns, rooted in these places which gave them nothing: no reward, no pleasure. The very yearning by which he profited made him disdainful. If this is what you want, he thought to himself, why should you not go and find some of it for yourself? You wait? For me? You sit and you live without music, looking up the river for my boat to come and give you some?

Leaning against the railing, smoking a cigar, with Mickey by his side, ludicrously smoking a smaller cigar—as if they had purchased cigars scaled to one another, so as not to break up the symmetry, which, for all anyone knew they had—he wiped the sweat from his broad, bald, sun-darkened brow and said: "Schmucks."

"Tell me about it, boss."

"You know what a schmuck is, Mickey?" He didn't stop for Mickey's answer, "a schmuck lacks discernment. A schmuck is starving, dying of thirst, and you give them a puddle full of water and they drink and drink."

"Beats dying," said Mickey.

"But now, here, we have something real. We have this pearl. And still, we throw it in the dirt before these schmucks."

"Tickets is tickets."

The two nodded.

On the night off, and frequently enough after the show was over, Raleigh would walk into town with Red Joe. There were barrooms in these little towns, and backroad houses full of women who danced and laughed. There were pianos to be played, and after-hours whiskey-soaked dice games on the porches of little hardware stores.

Red Joe knew the colored folks in every town. Sometimes the white folks, too.

The women took to Raleigh as if he were a kitten.

"You have a certain wide-eyed nature," explained Joe. "I think it makes people happy."

These weren't, in little towns that dotted the river, hardened and soulless habitués of the demimonde. These were, for the most part, cheerful girls with a bit of a wild streak to them and single men who didn't mind sleeping through church.

As the nights rolled on and the beer steins were drained, the dresses got looser and looser on the shoulders of the women, and the dances got reckless and close.

Margaret was the first. A young, light-skinned black girl who said that she had been owned and freed by a Mr. Turnbull, who had an office in Louisville. She ran her fingers along Raleigh's cheek.

"You about the cutest thing," she said, her dress falling open. Raleigh had played a reel—sight-read it off of some music he found in the bench in front of the stiff piano that sat in the corner. She'd danced behind him, swishing her skirts across his back and pretending she needed his shoulders to hold herself up. She smelled of sweat and perfume. Every time her dress parted, like a curtain blowing open and revealing the room you've been trying to get a look at, her soft skin would tremble and shake. Raleigh was mesmerized, and she took him back to her room as if he were a baby calf and she had a bottle of milk.

"She ain't that kind of woman, Raleigh," said Joe, two towns downriver. "She's not the sort you'd need to save yourself for and I promise you that she is not returning that impulse in the slightest. Margaret has a living to make, and only one way to make it."

"I didn't pay her."

Red Joe looked at his feet, twirling the end of one of the gold chains that linked the feathers with which he'd festooned his waistcoat.

"You did."

"Actually, Raleigh, if you must dive into the thing, she approached me. She came over to me, absolutely aglow, and suggested that I buy out some of her time so she could spend it with you. I was happy to oblige."

Raleigh thought on it a moment.

"No need to thank me, old boy," said Red Joe, with a laugh.

The showcase on the *Rialto* was a smash. Raleigh learned crawls and cakewalks in the bawdy houses and brought their sensibility back to the show that made up the first half of their performance. He'd slip in a syncopated left-hand shuffle while Vivian strutted across the stage, timed perfectly with her sway. Every eye glued to her. She'd strut right by Tim and Tom—Tim laboring, bent over pretending to be engaged in some agricultural toil, and Tom leaning on a pitchfork next to him. Tom would bug out his eyes. First he'd move only his head, following her path. Then he'd spin, pivoting on the pitchfork like a marionette. Then he'd walk along behind her, moving with her, imitating her every swish and sway while Tim played an overheated exasperation.

Vivian would stop. The music would rest. She'd turn back to Tim, Tom orbiting her, unseen, and she'd approach him, thinking he'd been scolding her. They'd pantomime reproach and apology—already dancing together before the audience realized what they were doing. They would move closer while Raleigh played a swirl of tinkling arpeggios that led up to another roiling crawl. Raleigh's left-hand rhythm, which he'd lifted straight from Schubert's "Hungarian Melody," loosened the whole dance up, and the two, Vivian and Tim, would dance while Tom orbited them, mimicking their every move at first and then losing himself in a remarkably graceful solo dance until he spun, entranced, into the area where Tim had been working, tripped, and crashed into a wheelbarrow. This would remind Tim that he should be working, and Vivian that she had been on her way somewhere. They'd dust themselves off, acting bashful, trying not to meet one another's eyes, the spell broken.

Meanwhile, Mickey would work the crowd, selling toddies.

Tom could run a fiddle and Tim would hit a tambourine and there'd be a musical interlude—a few songs that varied in their level of energy depending on how the crowd seemed to be feeling. Vivian would stand in the middle of the two with the bones. Her hands outstretched, circling, hitting triplet patterns and quick bursts of sixteenth notes across the down beats tapped on the fat, bass tambourine. The sweat on her clavicle would glisten in the candlelight, she'd throw her head back with an alluring abandon. It was hot stuff.

Then an intermission—more toddies—and Hyman would make his speech.

The trick of the show was that people ended the night feeling elevated. All the low humor, the pratfalls, and all the dancing and hot-blooded party music was a lot of fun, but somehow at the end people left feeling as if they could look their preacher in the eye.

Raleigh, however, felt no such relief.

He could barely stand to be in the room with Vivian when they weren't onstage. Her luminosity had only grown since he'd first met her, she seemed more beautiful, now. Her talent, certainly, had enhanced his feelings—she had a voice that was throaty and full of twists and turns and irony. She moved like water when she wanted to, but knew exactly how much to flick her eyebrow to make a joke. And here he was, stinking of beer and bay rum, perfume and late-night cigars.

On nights when he was unlucky enough to stay on the boat, he'd lay in his berth on the *Rialto* and wonder what it would be like to feel as if he could meet her eye. What could he do to redeem himself? Could he exorcise the filth he'd brought upon himself? Would she even notice? Did she care? Was he so far beneath her that even his debauched nature had gone without stirring in her a sense of disgust? Perhaps he didn't even exist as enough of a person to warrant judgment.

Drifting to sleep in his bunk, he played out a story in which she slipped off the deck of the *Rialto*, and on to the dock, where she was attacked by a man who wanted to drag her away. In his half dream, Raleigh overcame the villain and sent him scuttling off to hide behind the barrels like a barn cat. Vivian clung to him, sobbing, heaving.

In a little town, Raleigh won some forty dollars playing dice, and spent three of those to spend the night with a woman named Pixie, with whom he ate a breakfast of rhubarb jam on toast with real coffee before starting off for the boat.

He was in the small crossroads where the Negroes lived, and coming out of it he came to the intersection of the white world with the black—the houses stood straighter, needed less paint. The yards were distinct on the white side, one could easily tell where one person's property ended and another's began. Behind him, the shacks tumbled into one another, and the dogs seemed to mosey to and fro. You couldn't even tell which children belonged where, although he figured someone must know.

The Jew Store hovered in between these two neighborhoods, available to all. Feeling the money in his pocket, Raleigh lighted the steps up to the narrow porch, whorled by boot heels and brushed dustless that morning.

The bell rang and the proprietor turned to note his entry, returning immediately to the white woman he was talking to at the counter, without so much as acknowledging Raleigh. The woman didn't change her pace, or adjust herself to make room—physically, psychologically, morally—for Raleigh in any way. She kept on requesting bolts of fabric and returning them to the shelves. Her careful movements were focused, of singular vision. She'd run the fabric between her thumb and the meat of her pointer finger. She'd smooth it out against the bolt with the flat of her hand, purse her lips, shake her head and return it, asking to see the next one.

She bought eight yards of dark blue wool, a yard of a lighter blue in the same fabric, and a few pieces of gray calico ribbon. She paid, and walked out of the door without glancing Raleigh's way, who smiled and doffed his hat as she walked by.

"I wouldn't go around flashing my teeth at the women, if I were you, boy," said the shopkeeper.

Raleigh raised his eyebrows.

"You make a face like that at the wrong woman, you'll be lucky to be standing on your own feet after the sun sets."

"I was just—"

"You're going to explain yourself to me? I don't care what you do. I don't see you around here before, and you tip your hat to Mrs. Thompson like that, and so I tell you what I know, maybe you don't know."

Raleigh sunk into himself like a smacked child. He bought a wide-brimmed, flat hat, and a pocket watch on a chain. On the counter was a copy of *Malaeska: The Indian Wife of the White Hunter*, which Raleigh pushed across to the shopkeeper. Raleigh could tell the man thought he was faking it, trying to prove himself, trying to indicate that he was a man of letters and not some colored field hand who wanted a fancy hat. Maybe he was trying to prove something. He'd wanted a hat. Why was he buying a watch? Why was he buying a book? Was he trying to prove something? Elevate himself?

The adversaries nodded at one another, full of contempt, each glad to be free of the transaction.

Maybe I'll just give the watch to Joe, thought Raleigh, which is exactly what he did.

CHAPTER TWENTY-THREE

The *Rialto* Heads West

August 1860

Back in Louisville, after the river tour, Red Joe, Hatforth, and Raleigh ate thick slices of bread that Hatforth toasted in butter in a skillet and drizzled with molasses. They sat at the table in the little back room of the barbershop, drumming their fingers on the oilcloth, the back door slanting open into the courtyard stables. The three tin mugs were filled with coffee, paled with milk.

"I like mine sweet," said Hatforth, laughing and apologizing as he spooned in sugar. "A man should enjoy himself in the morning. I like it sweet in the morning."

Raleigh smiled. These months of simple company had changed him. These men didn't think of him as the recipient of their benevolence, wisdom, or wrath. These men simply sat beside him. The toast was golden and buttery, and when he bit it thick, damp crumbs fell onto his plate.

"It's going to be a rough time," said Red Joe, "very complicated, very involved, and I don't know how we'll make out."

"The war you mean?"

"That, too."

They laughed. After weeks of deliberation on the *Rialto*, the crew had decided to continue the tour on land, to head west, performing along the way.

There'd been a meeting.

"We don't want to be here," Hyman had said, "when the cannons start. We don't want to be here for the war. People don't know from war. Maybe it's fun, they think. They don't know. From war."

Wink was muttering about being a sailor, about dry land, talking into his beard, but clearly meant to be heard.

Tom said: "You can't navigate a showboat through a blockade, Wink!"

Mickey said: "I sure don't want no part of that. Let's see a bit of country!"

Tim said: "Kentucky says it'll stay neutral."

Hyman harrumphed.

"So as they can be in the right spot when it's over. What does it hurt?" asked Hyman. "We come back, I have the boat. We don't like it? We come back. The boat's here. What does it hurt? It's my money."

"I think it sounds . . . fun," said Vivian. "I'd love to see something other than this river."

"It's not going to leave a lot of money in the bank," Hyman mused, half to himself, it seemed, and half by way of warning. "Not a lot. Eh. What can you do? You do what you have to do. You do what you do."

"Everything is everything," said Tom.

Raleigh, who had kept to himself, was surprised to hear Lo's old saying in Tom's mouth, and nodded in agreement.

They built a plank stage with hinged poles like masts to hold the curtains. Two wagons operated as backstage, and the third, in the center, held a newly purchased upright piano. Raleigh played with his right elbow to the crowd, sitting at a slight angle so he could be seen to be smiling and they put a mirror in front of the piano, tilted in such a way as to show the people sitting behind him his visage, as well. He bought a candelabra for the top of the piano, and the light shone into the mirror and doubled.

The piano's sound was plunky, deadened. It lacked the big wooden resonance that he was used to, and had no sustain to speak of, but as he hit the keys harder, and heard the raspy vibration of the strings, he liked it. It was raw and real. What it lacked in sublimity it made up for in tautness.

"There's something about that piano that sounds like it might fall apart," he said, approvingly.

Hyman bought two horses. Raleigh would ride a bay named Chessie, and Red Joe a black gelding he called Koda, on account of it having come with the name Cocoa.

"Well, I'm not going to ride a horse named Cocoa," he said. "Too bitter, too sweet. Koda sounds close enough. He'll think it's my accent."

The rest of the crew would ride in the wagons.

Hyman had a gambler's knack for watching money leave his pocket: He loved it. Nothing made him feel more alive than being told something was going to be tremendously expensive, and then paying for it. *I'm the man who makes it happen*, he'd think to himself as he bought bolts of fabric from his cousin, mules, two barrels of whiskey, dried sausages, a barrel of sauerkraut, apples. Mickey drove the chaise around Louisville and Hyman spent money like a king.

The two of them ended up in a hotel dining room, under the chandelier, eating a table d'hôte that started with a salad of oyster crabs in mayonnaise with thin slices of celery, followed by a cream soup, followed by slices of stuffed capon. They ate slabs of beef with mushrooms and laughed over a bottle of wine. Mickey took a flower from the bouquet in the middle of the table and put it in the buttonhole in his absurd lapels, which stretched out to his shoulders.

"What I like, Mickey, here, about America, this," he waved his two pronged fork around the room and paused to take a bite of his beef.

"Yeah?"

He nodded, chewing, holding up a finger to indicate that one must have manners and patience.

"We are here. We have money. And therefore, they bring us what we want. It's all it takes, here, in America. Money. We can eat treif crabs, we can cut into this beefsteak, and dollop these sauced mushrooms atop it, and wave for more wine," he did so, "and it will happen. Perhaps they frown. Maybe. They frown. Some hard boot, some blue blood. I tell you, Mickey, this. This I tell you." He leaned in, whispered. "After this war? Even them. Maybe not tomorrow. Maybe not right away, but I tell you this, Mickey. Them? Kaput."

Having pronounced the fate of the ruling class, Hyman leaned back in his chair and ran his hands from his chest to his stomach.

Mickey forked a pile of mushrooms.

The Rialto Traveling Theatre Company left Louisville on the morning of August 15, 1860.

"Here's what we'll do," said Hyman, "we'll pull into town, naturally that will draw some attention to us, us pulling into town."

Sometimes Mickey thought that maybe Hyman was simply fascinated by the words, by the sound, by his own ability to make sounds. They'd been through this all before, but now, on the bench, as Mickey drove the mules on the second wagon (Wink piloted the first—"I'm a pilot, ain't I?"), Hyman rehashed it.

"We'll try to park somewhere conspicuous, and make a show of the stage and the curtains, which we'll leave down. We'll leave the curtains down, you see, so as to—look, there, a log in the road, watch it, son, follow Wink. Draw the curtains, you see? Perhaps the tinkling sound of rehearsal? Maybe a few runs on the keys?"

Mickey made a noncommittal noise of agreement. The chickens in the coop on top of the wagon behind theirs, the one Tim and Tom drove, were squawking. Wink had Vivian on the bench beside him, although in the afternoon, to get out of the sun, she retreated to the bed she had in half of that wagon. There were rooms in this wagon, too. In Tim and Tom's was the piano, and storage. It was like a puzzle, and it made the riverboat seem spacious. Why, wondered Mickey, would the chickens get all riled up? Were they just fighting with each other, or did they see something? Did chickens look out into the world? Did they see things?

Hyman said: "Red Joe, we send to the paper. Unless there is no paper. No paper? If there's no paper we have bills. We write in the particulars. We have the bills. You saw them. We write in the particulars. The town. The day. You think the time? We write the time?"

"Maybe we just says sundown or something?"

"Sundown."

"Dusk?"

"Half an hour before the sun sets?"

"How would anyone know when that is, boss?"

"That's true."

The Rialto Traveling Theatre Company presents
a one of a kind performance from the Olde South
See Vivian Hatforth dance The Virginia Crawl,
Laugh along with a Comedy of Plantation Life,
amuse yourself with folk songs & vignettes
and in limited engagement, from the salons of Vienna, the *Masterful*
Walter Raleigh Babenburg
playing the greatest piano works known to man.
Be amused and be amazed
by the progress of the black race
from savagery to civilization.

"I don't know how I feel, really, about that 'savagery' bit, I mean, if I'm being honest," said Red Joe.

"I don't know how I feel about any of that thing," said Tom.

"Look, yes," said Hyman. "Okay. It isn't. It doesn't—we are showmen, yes? This is a show?"

They nodded.

"And a show. If we have a show, we say, what? We say, eh. Maybe these women are like your mother? We say, come see someone reminds you of what you see at home? No. Nobody says that. Nobody says come see something like what you got at home. We say we are more. We say we have danger. Life. Shtupping. The future and the past."

"Also," said Mickey, "we printed 'em already."

The show worked. Hyman was correct in thinking that their arrival in a small town would draw attention, and since no one had anything to do and tickets were cheap, they played to large audiences.

They made adjustments. They learned, for instance, to look for natural amphitheaters, little hills they might set their stage at the bottom of so as to be more visible. They waited one day, instead of two, to perform, because by the third day, it seemed, the mystery wasn't as urgent and a fair number of folks decided they needn't know, didn't care what the Rialto Theatre Company had brought to town.

"If there's more than four streets to the town we can find a place," said Red Joe. He and Raleigh rode side by side, behind the wagons. Raleigh nodded. "In all my travels I've never been in a town with four streets or more that didn't have a place."

By the natural slope above a small schoolhouse (but far enough away so as not to infuriate the mistress by distracting her pupils) they ran the loops over the poles that held up the curtains.

"I count six streets," said Raleigh.

They looked for dance halls, taverns, and bordellos and slipped away after they helped set up the stage. They walked until they heard laughter, and cautiously approached the door. There were many places that a red man and a black man, no matter how nattily turned out they were, shouldn't enter. Many times the laughter stopped and the bottle was raised mid pour—all eyes on them until they beat it back to the Rialto wagons. Often enough, however, they were welcomed. From there it was only a matter of time until Red Joe would pitch that the evening might be made a little merrier with some music. Raleigh would run the keys once or twice. Laugh, and say it would do, then settle into a reel, just a teaser, tinkling along to get the feel of the instrument. A few drinks later, he'd be banging out rags and crawls, pounding out that syncopated left hand he'd lifted from the Schubert. The more he swung it, the better it sounded. He lagged behind the beat, and then got up on top of it. He was lulled into a trance by the interplay of the melody and the underlying rhythms. Tonight, the room was alive with laughter and shrieks, and it stank of alcohol. There were mirrors on the dance floor, and the girl you paid to dance with would twirl over one of them for an extra coin. As the night wore on, the room seemed to gather together and forget about the money, forget about everything. Things can go wrong on a floating night like that, but nobody wanted to fight, and there was enough of everything anyone wanted.

Raleigh took a break and drank a glass with a girl who called herself Poppy. She smelled like oranges and tobacco.

Red Joe was deep in conversation with a pair of bearded men, and he called Raleigh over to them.

"Raleigh, meet my friends. This is Fitz, and this is Albert. They are traveling, taking pictures, keeping notebooks. They are from San Francisco."

Raleigh nodded. Red Joe had rolled cheroots for each of the men and the thick smoke filled the air around their table. All their eyes were red. The one called Albert seemed abstracted, lost, but Fitz leaned forward, up out of his chair in a bit of a bow.

"You play very well."

"San Francisco?"

Raleigh thought of Rose. There was a strange light that shined when he thought of San Francisco, like a phosphorescent pin in his map.

"They're going to come out and photograph us," said Red Joe.

"For the *Golden Era*," said Fitz. "A San Franciscan newspaper." He laughed, and said "San Franciscan" again.

Albert leaned forward, pushing his sharp triangular beard toward the middle of the table, making his lip stiff under his push broom mustache, and trying to furrow his brow in a semblance of seriousness. He was obviously on the verge of laughter.

"Not for the era," he said "but for the *Era*."

He sat back, smacking his knee.

"Not for the era! *The Era*!"

Fitz and Albert dissolved into laughter and after they'd recovered, Fitz, gasping, said: "Albert is an artist. He photographs so that he can paint. At times, he deigns to allow me access to the likenesses, or to a sketch. I'm hoping that he'll agree."

Albert pretended, for a moment, to disapprove but then roared with fresh laughter. He took a tremendous drag of the cheroot Red Joe had rolled him, blew smoke across the top of the table, and swallowed the whiskey in his glass.

"Oh, you'll have your pictures," Albert roared, "The traveling theater troupe! It's like *Hamlet*!"

"Our mousetrap is for mice," said Raleigh. This delighted both Fitz and Albert.

"It's fantastic, really, that we might find such sophistication, and such entertainment, and such a lovely supplement," Fitz had included Raleigh, the piano, and Red Joe, each in turn. He was holding his tongue, but in his inebriation found the masquerade difficult. "I am fascinated," he said, "by the . . . the . . ." He took a moment to compose himself. "Well, by what this nation has to offer. When so often we are accursed with banalities, the very sky, the very stone, drab gray rock. And here, where nothing is expected but indigence, violence, savagery, we find mellifluity, and ecstasy enough to disenthrall us from our apathy."

Late that night, Poppy showed Raleigh the scars on her back and told him the story of how she'd run away from a plantation in Alabama via the Underground Railroad. She'd meant to go to Canada, but had somehow ended up here, on the frontier, stuck.

Red Joe and Raleigh walked back into camp in the early morning to meet Fitz and Albert, as promised.

"Hello sir," said Albert.

"So good of you to come, old boy," said Joe, stretching his Britishisms out to maximum effect in the face of the Germanic lilt with which Albert spoke. "So glad you could make it. Indeed!"

Albert set to work with the big metal box and the tripod while the cast of the Rialto got dressed in their costumes.

Tim and Tom changed from their clean, well-tailored clothes into frayed trousers with high-water cuffs, shirts made of sacking, hats they'd carefully burned holes in and crushed, and braces made from twine. Hyman wore his high-waisted white trousers and a tie too wide and colorful to be in current fashion. Raleigh changed into his formal frock coat and starched collar. Vivian was resplendent in a drop-shouldered gown of peacock green, her hair straightened, oiled, and wrapped in ribbons.

"You, too," said Fitz to Wink, and then, turning to Red Joe "and you, definitely." Red Joe was, as usual, bedecked in trinkets and chains, beads and feathers. He had rings on his fingers and silver bands woven into his hair. Fitz wanted him in the picture.

Wink grumbled but acquiesced when Vivian cooed at him.

Tim sat on an upturned box, and Tom sat on the ground next to him, rolling his eyes to the sky and splaying his feet.

Hyman said: "Raleigh, try and look serious. Look European."

Raleigh clasped his hands, one over the other, and tried as best he could.

"Now how would a person do that?" asked Tom.

"If you could act, you'd know," said Mickey.

Wink had his clay pipe clamped between his teeth. They were all arrayed around Vivian and Raleigh.

Albert smiled and ducked his head under the cloth.

"Nobody move!"

And it clicked.

"Like we have the sweethearts here before the altar, with their strange family," said Fitz.

Albert looked surprised. He hadn't thought of it.

"Ah, well. Too late. Anyway, that's what the words are for, yes?"

Fitz and Albert stuck around, and that evening they watched the Rialto's performance. The troupe played exceedingly well before an audience who, despite its small size, was wholly invested, laughing when appropriate and gasping when they should.

After the show the players and the travelers gathered around a campfire over which Wink had roasted a leg of lamb and potatoes he'd stabbed on to a saber from the Mexican war which he said he'd won in a card game.

Fitz jotted this fact down.

"The fabulous foundling," he said to Raleigh. "It's a good story."

It was the last good piece of luck the Rialto experienced. They were on unorganized plains territory now, Missouri behind them, and the first town they aimed toward was no longer there.

Hyman stood on what might have been a road in recent memory, looking at his map. He turned this way and that, as if he'd perhaps missed it.

"It says, here, you see?"

"That certainly looks like a town," said Red Joe. "Unfortunately, this does not. Did we get off track?"

Hyman shook his head, bewildered.

Mickey stood in the rutted path the wagons had followed and said: "This here is the track. Not like we missed a turn."

So they trudged forward, with the growing feeling that they were headed toward nothing.

They hadn't even seen a well in four days when they came to a small fortification with an open gate.

"There's nobody here, you can tell," said Raleigh. No sooner had he said it than he saw in the dirt in front of the open gate a skeleton, the top of its skull cut clean off.

"Not anymore, eh?" Mickey said.

They looked cautiously about. There were a few skeletons of livestock in the dirt in the paddock, rib cages bleached by the sun.

"We should take a good look at that well before we draw any water," said Joe. "I have a feeling that's where the rest of the people are." They pulled the wagon with the water barrels over to the paddock and poured water into the trough for the horses and the mules. There was not enough room inside the walls for the other two wagons, so they parked them in front of the gate, squeaked it shut, and went to look at the house, which was small and set halfway into the dirt so you had to walk down a few steps to get in. The house was a single room, with a low roof. In the corners, toward the back, there were remnants of straw litters where once a family must have slept, now occupied by field mice. The cookstove stood in the middle, and before that, a simple long table surrounded by four chairs and two stools. Everything else had been taken—whatever knives and pots had been on the shelves against the wall were gone.

"Chairs," said Raleigh, "and a table, must imply a settled domesticity that doesn't interest whoever had been here."

"We'll eat on our horses," said Red Joe, in a caricature of a Comanche accent.

They pushed open the shutters to air out the room, and Tom took up the broom in the corner.

"You best get to helping, Timothy, or I'll be sweeping your feet, and you'll never find a bride" said Tom, threatening him.

They lit a fire in the cookstove—it was getting cooler at night—and soon the room was comfortable.

Wink brought in his chest of food and a soup pot and boiled a small ham with some cabbage.

"Got to find a town soon," he said, looking into the box. "Stores be dwindling."

"There's got to be one."

"It's a different country out here," said Joe. "It doesn't conform, it doesn't provide."

"Do you think there will be a road?" asked Vivian. "South? I think we should go to New Orleans."

"There's always a passage, Viv," said Wink, "there's always a way if you stay on the right tack."

"I don't like this place."

"It's not likeable."

The cabbage was soft and pale and had soaked in the flavors of the ham, which was tender and peppery. They each had half a potato, and broth which they slurped by the spoonful.

The next morning, the two wagons they'd left outside of the gate were gone.

"The chickens!" Tom said.

Hyman looked at him as if he were crazy. Maybe he's as stupid as he plays?

"The chickens?" Hyman said, "Chickens we can get. Chickens is nothing. What about the stage? The piano?"

He spun to Mickey, remembering the box in which they kept the money: "The box."

"I have the box, boss."

Although there was nothing to say, the troupe talked all day. They looped back and repeated conversations they'd already had, they rehashed things they could have done differently.

"We're done for," said Joe.

"Who stole them?"

"We don't know."

"Will they come back?"

"Perhaps, but if they wanted to kill us, they would have, wouldn't they?"

"Maybe they'll kill us for being too stupid to leave when we had the chance."

One of them would pitch an idea, a fantastical plan for a successful future, and they'd all contribute to it until the flaw became obvious and someone else would say: "It'll never work."

"Folks, we're done," said Hyman. "I don't like it. But it's the truth. The truth is, we're done. We have the mules. We have a wagon, some water in the barrels. We have our scalps." Hyman patted himself on the head while pointing toward the door, and the brained skeleton outside, by way of illustration. "I made a wager, took a bet, and it did not pay out. I appreciate your participation in this gamble. I am sorry I did not do right by you. We have, somewhere, slipped up. Only a fool would proceed. It's time. In the morning we start south. We'll make it to New Orleans."

"We hope."

"Well, yes. I hope. From there, we head back up the river, and our barge awaits us."

After dinner, Joe and Raleigh stood in the yard, looking up into the clear night sky.

"You have to talk to her," said Red Joe.

Raleigh felt himself blush.

"She's going to stay in New Orleans. Hatforth is there. You have to try. You love her, don't you?"

Vivian was lovely in the firelight—they'd left the stove door open, for the pleasantry of it—and now that Raleigh saw her there he was so full of adrenaline that his scalp tingled.

"Why do you want to go to New Orleans, Vivian?"

She swayed a little, looking at the fire, and took a sip of rum.

"Me and Hatforth are gonna start a life there."

"We could," said Raleigh. The words were like heavy stones he had to push over a fence. "We could start a life."

"Oh."

"No listen," he said. "I . . ."

"I know you do. You have to understand though."

He shook his head.

"Raleigh," she said. She lifted her eyes from the fire and reached out for his hand. "You are a man, but you ain't my man."

With that, she stood. She took a moment to catch herself once she was standing, a little bit of rum, a little bit of the heat of the fire, a little bit of guilt about unreciprocated love. She made her way to where she'd arranged some blankets on the floor and fell quickly asleep.

Raleigh turned this way and that on his bedroll in the light of the diminishing fire. He played out the same scenarios he used to imagine while they were on the boat. He'd save her. He'd prove himself. She'd wrap her arms around him and feel his devotion. Where once these fantasies implausible but real, they now felt hollow. He was going through them by rote, like when you've memorized a poem but forgotten to pay attention to it, and you no longer hear the meanings, you just say the words.

He might have slept, he might not have. He was up before the others and standing in the cold dawn. He gave Chessie a lump of sugar. He knew he had to go. He couldn't bear it. Like young men everywhere, he was filled with shame, unable to shrug off what he imagined was a colossal humiliation. He'd rather ride to his death than face Vivian. Would rather be cut down by whomever had stolen the wagons than sit with the Rialto. He'd try for California, and figured it didn't matter if he made it.

"California," he said to the horse. "What do you think?"

Chessie put his head on Raleigh's shoulder and they stood like that, with Raleigh absentmindedly scratching the horse's far cheek and Chessie breathing deeply.

"Let's go then."

He saddled him up, filled two skins with water, and gathered a small bag of food, taking care not to take more than his share. Hyman was like a clock when it came to payouts, and Raleigh had a nice roll of money in his vest.

He was a mile away, due west, riding away from the sun, when looking behind him he saw a rider. Nervous, he stopped and turned to him. He wished he had a gun.

Lit from the back it was hard to see anything but a silhouette, and the time, as it passed, was filled with anxiety. At a hundred yards away, the rider called out to him, by name: "Ahoy!"

It was Red Joe.

"You didn't think I'd let you ride off into the unknown alone, did you? Where are we headed?"

"California?"

"Sounds grand. That's what I told them, that you had a friend in California. I think if the Rialto was in less dire circumstances, Hyman would have come out to get you back."

They shook hands.

Midmorning the following day a lump on the horizon resolved itself into a homestead and they aimed themselves toward it.

They walked next to the horses for hours, watching the house in the distance as if it might move. It was still far off when they found themselves alongside a huge herd of sheep bleating, churning, and pressing together.

Raleigh swung up on Chessie, to calm the stallion and to get a better view of the herd. Joe did the same.

He looked for the shepherd, but saw no one. The sheep were roiling and seemed, inexplicably, to be turning toward them, to be advancing in a confused zigzag. Back and forth, with their panicked eyes gleaming, and their lips trembling as they bleated their complaint. They didn't want to approach, yet they seemed compelled. And soon, Raleigh and Red Joe were in the middle of a lake of sheep. He pulled Chessie up, sat forward in the saddle, and dropped on the withers. Joe cooed at Koda that everything was fine. Koda's nostrils flared.

Raleigh heard the quick, dovelike call of a shepherd's whistle, undoubtedly human, and the sheep walked around him in a circle. Not the whole herd, he saw now, but a substantial portion. A hundred sheep broken off from the main herd and now turning about him in a vortex. They smelled of lanolin.

He couldn't help but think that if there were this many sheep here, there must be water, as well.

From the animals rose a man, bearded, wearing sheepskin—he'd been crouching, moving with them, hiding among the sheep like a fairy-tale wolf. When he raised himself up, Chessie whinnied, and Raleigh stroked his neck to calm him.

"Who are you then?" said the man in sheep's clothing.

"I'm Walter Raleigh Babenburg, sir, and I don't mean nothing by way of harm to you."

Red Joe laughed heartily.

"Well, you're all trapped in these sheep, here, on account of May and Day and Rosie," said the shepherd, who then whistled. Raleigh followed his eyes and saw a sheepdog, hugging the ground, keeping the edge of the herd tight. He was working his dogs, and they were clustering a gyre of sheep.

"And you?" said the shepherd.

"They call me Red Joe. This is impressive work, what you can do with these dogs, sir."

Raleigh took his hat in his hand and nodded.

"Where you two going?"

"California."

The man harrumphed, as if that were not a particularly bright idea.

"Come on, then," he said.

The man called himself Abbott, and was by himself in a house dug half into the ground, much like the house they'd left two days ago. He hadn't always been alone, for there were things about the cabin that spoke to a family presence, such as the neatly folded blanket with "Lannie" stitched on the hem, folded on top of a trunk. Raleigh looked at the little rag doll, thread sewn around like an asterisk to represent eyes, and wondered who had done the needlework, and who had played with it. He held his tongue. Whosoever had been here was no longer here, after all. What good are empty condolences for death or abduction? Perhaps they'd returned to the East, or continued on to the West. Didn't matter: gone is gone.

Abbott roasted a leg of lamb in the hearth.

"Course, I reckon you've no way of knowing how lucky you are by way of timing. Another month—next week—you'd have been crushed by the blue northers, driven by the freezing rain. You'd have died. You picked the finest month to travel across this land. Come any earlier you'd have found you were whipped dry by the winds, the heat. The horses would have fainted before you made it here.

"You keep right on to the west, and there's a fort, just south of Buffalo Lick canyon. You'll make it to the fort, I'd reckon. I wouldn't ride up on it in the dark. I'd wait and come up real nice, letting them see you."

Abbott rocked back, looked at Red Joe and Raleigh.

"Ah, they won't care none that you're colored, I suppose."

Red Joe offered to pay for lodging.

"What would I need with money? Ain't nothing to spend money on here! You don't talk like an Indian, huh? I don't mean no offense by that," said Abbott, hand up in a gesture of placation.

"None taken, and indeed I do not. I was found twisting in the grass by a headstrong English couple who took me home. Come to think of it, I suppose we might be more or less in the vicinity of my original discovery. I was told it was the frontier."

"Like some sorta prize!" Abbott said.

"Indeed, as if I were a souvenir."

"Hell of a souvenir. How old were you, you think?"

"We don't know. I don't. I couldn't walk, they said. Once they warmed me up and fed me they said I crawled about."

"Oh, that's about eight months, I'd say, maybe ten. Most babies left out at that age, they don't make it." He paused for a dark moment. "What happened then? They take you somewhere?" Abbott squinted when he asked a question, furrowing his brow and staring out from under his bushy, graying eyebrows.

"To London."

"London!"

"I grew up there."

"And you made your way back."

"Sorry?"

"You're back. You're from around here, you were taken from around here, and all these years later, you're back."

Misty eyed, Abbott walked to the shelf that separated one room from the other, and pulled down a clay jug of whiskey.

"Drink to that, fellows? Let's drink you a homecoming toast."

CHAPTER TWENTY-FOUR

The Fancy Girl

While Temple healed, rumors spread around the Hundred.

"She says she's free."

"What she doing here, then?"

"Says she's free don't mean she's free. She's here."

This was received with nods appreciating the sagacity.

"Her brother shot the master over there at the house that burned down. You hear that?"

"Keep away from that girl."

Temple was held in the kind of awe reserved for venomous snakes and mean dogs.

"Miss Marie tends to her every day!"

"Miss Marie bring her food!"

Marie watched Temple's hand tremble as she held the plate with a slice of ham on a biscuit.

"It's a good thing we found you and gave you a home," Marie said, as if she were talking to a kitten she'd dragged out of a culvert. "You'll feel better just as soon as you are able to be put to some use."

Temple nibbled the crumbly biscuit.

"We'll have you up at the house in no time."

The next morning, a couple of hours before dawn, Temple slipped out the door and made her way down the path. When the sun came up she was standing in the blackened ruins of the Old House, dumbstruck. Here was her world. Oliver's books, standing somehow in the bookcase, all the spines burned off. The picture of Gunnery in its charred frame, now smeared with wetted soot. The piano, with the strings all popped and the legs shattered. The roof had fallen in over the parlor side, reduced to charred timbers and sharp piles of slate.

She was on the portico steps when Zeb trotted up behind her. He didn't dismount. The horse stepped gingerly, sidestepping and huffing, hating the blackened smells and the evidence of fire. Zeb threw a lasso around Temple and tied it off on his saddle. He said nothing, clucked at the horse. Temple stumbled, caught herself, took a few steps, and fell down the stoop. Zeb nudged his horse. Temple grappled and heaved and tried to get her feet under her. Somehow, she managed to stand and run along for a bit before she fell again. Zeb dragged her a few yards and stopped. She was gasping in the dirt.

Zeb put his boot on her back and forced her into the ground.

"I could kill you right now."

"Don't."

"I could skin you alive." He pushed harder with his boot. "I could drag you behind this horse until you were a bag of broken bones and then throw you in the river to watch you drown. Is that how you want this to end?"

She shook her head.

"If you run away again, that's exactly how it will end. Now stand up."

She tried, fell. He grabbed the lasso, pulling her up. She stood. He took his rope off her and said: "I gave you a house. Walk to it."

And she did.

For the next few weeks she lived like a dog no one liked. She never saw Marie—she wondered if Marie had given up on her or become angry with her.

If she tried to include herself in meals among the enslaved, or lingered by the kitchen, she'd be shooed away.

She found scraps in the trash. Stole bits of pork when no one was looking. At night she'd walk to the garden and dig up a sweet potato that she'd roast in her room over an insufficient fire of gathered scrap wood. She'd found a spade with a broken handle in the barn and used it as a skillet.

She clung to the corners of the world, afraid and hungry, until Zeb appeared at her door one morning and said: "There's work for you up at the house. Come."

Zeb turned and walked quickly through the yard back to the house, entering through the back door. He walked up the back stairs, through the pantry, to another small room where stacks of china were arranged carefully on shelves. He showed her two white blouses, a long gray dress, stays, and a shift.

"Go out back, fill yourself a basin and get washed," said Zeb. "Get dressed and go to the pantry. You will serve at the table tonight. Tandey will tell you how. He'll show you the attic, too. Find a corner to sleep in."

Tandey was short and plump, getting on in years, and consistently troubled by the inability of the world to live up to his expectations. He'd have said that all he wanted was for things to run smoothly, but nothing short of utter stasis would satisfy him. He would like a world in which order prevailed, and in which he could quietly care for Miss Marie. The seamstresses and washing girls lived either in lofts or corners of their workplace or in the slave houses, but the maids and the liveried boys Tandey was in charge of lived up in the house. Tandey came from a line owned by Mrs. Newcombe's family for generations, and her father had given Tandey to Marie as a wedding present.

"You been inside?" Tandey had drawn himself up, although the effort brought his eyes only to the level of Temple's upper lip, and smoothed his livery, which was the same light gray fabric of which Temple's dress was made, but accented in lace, and piped around the buttonholes in light blue. The jacket was stretched to its limit. "My people been inside people for them Collings. Years and years we do that,"

"Have I . . . been inside? A room?"

"Work. Have you been inside? Or you been working in fields?"

"I'm free. I'm a free person."

Tandey shook his head. "You a slave. Just like me. If you free, why you here? You ain't been inside. Another field girl. Why can't Miss Marie get me a real girl to serve?" He looked her up and down, shaking his head.

"C'mon then," he said.

They walked into the dining room, a long room with a row of windows on either side of the table. Tandey walked to the head of the immense chestnut table, with filigree and lion's claw feet. It shone bright with polish.

"When you in here, you don't speak. You got nothing to say. They ask you something, you do it. Ain't gotta say yes. They know yes. You say "yes, ma'am," to Miss Marie, the rest of them, you just do what they say. Understand? You come to people from the left side. Like this."

He stood just behind the chair he'd pulled out, to the imaginary guest's left.

"Start with whoever to the right of Mr. Newcombe, unless it's just the family. Then you serve Miss Marie first, then Mr. Newcombe, then Johnny, then Collings. You don't never crost in front of anyone. You don't reach."

He stretched himself across the imaginary guest, glaring at Temple as if she had already committed this mistake.

"You don't reach acrost, you hear me?"

Temple nodded, Tandey sighed, frustrated. He didn't believe she understood.

"Come on, now. Let's set the table. I'll show you."

They unfolded a tablecloth and laid down silver— "I keep this silver in good polish, and I know how many things are in this box," said Tandey, staring hard at her. They put down plates for eight, as there were guests coming.

"We're serving lamb," said Tandey. "You gonna carry the tray of the cut-up lamb, and I'll put it down on the plate. You take care now you don't be slouching. You stand straight. You be quiet."

The guests arrived in the afternoon and had drinks on the porch.

Temple watched from doorframes. She didn't know the people. There were two young girls, school age, and she wondered why she hadn't met them at Rose's school—wouldn't they have attended? If such a place existed. It was all too much.

Tandey came in and barked at her to get ready, and she followed him.

The meat was aromatic, rubbed with herbs and cooked over a fire. Temple held the silver tray and tried to stand straight, but the room was spinning. Sweet onions had been roasted to a golden brown and encircled the slices of meat. The whole platter was scattered with mint. She hadn't eaten since the previous night, and then only a small potato. Her legs were shaking. She could almost hold the platter still, but she had to concentrate. The room kept skipping, as if it was going to spin around her. Her stomach was in knots and her mouth watering. She swallowed slowly, deliberately, and kept her eyes on the wall, where the intricacies of the palm fronds in the wall paper tangled and swirled. She tried not to look at the food, tried to ignore the fresh bread, golden and soft, and the knob of butter that slid sideways on top of a plate of peas.

Back in the pantry she swayed, caught herself against the edge of a table, and sank to the floor.

"What you doin?" Tandey asked.

"I'm just. I don't feel right. I haven't eaten."

Tandey gave her a glass of cool tea with sugar, and a slice of bread with butter and strawberry jam. To Temple, who had been living on scavenged scraps and stolen vegetables, the small meal had almost magical properties. She could feel, she thought, beams of light shoot through her body, out her fingertips, awakening her joints, soothing her muscles. Suddenly it seemed as if her thoughts had been like an angry swarm of bees. She focused on the beautiful sunlit tastes, sweet and sticky.

"Now take this pitcher and see if anyone needs some more tea."

She did as she was told.

She didn't go hungry anymore. After the Newcombes were done, Tandey and Temple would sit down at a small table in the pantry, with proper plates and the good silver, and they'd make themselves dinner from the leftovers, before they sent them back out to the kitchen to be eaten. They had first pick, and the food they got was as good as what the white people ate, or close to it.

Tandey filled himself a mug full of wine over the course of the dinner, pouring a little every time he walked past. As he drank his wine and they sat at their dinner, he talked about the business of keeping the plantation as if it were his own. "Was out in the smokehouse just this morning, and it looks like we have three full sides of bacon yet hanging in them rafters. We doin' okay on that, I suppose. Them hogs grow up in time, we be right on schedule. Might have to buy some in come time, but it won't be much, because they are good sides we got in there."

Temple nodded. Nothing Tandey said took up residence in her mind. She just let the man speak, and nodded when she thought he might need a nod.

"The springhouse dairy, now that's something else. I don't know what's goin' on with them cows, but somebody best be thinking on moving them to another pasture. Maybe they too old to make good milk? We running behind where I like to be. I don't like to go along with just a little bit of butter in the springhouse. I like to see we ain't gonna run into where we worried about running out. Start running out, people start worrying about where it all going. People start worrying, looking, blaming. People gonna eat your butter, just gonna happen that way, and I don't want nobody looking for who been in there eating. No, no, I like to be well ahead on things. Well ahead. Gonna have to go down and talk about them dairy cows."

Tandey would lean back in his chair, swig his last gulps of wine, and say "I'm about to get on, then." At which point he'd walk up to his room, leaving the last of the cleaning to Temple. He'd already have polished the silver, put it in the case, and returned the glasses to their slots. Temple swept, cleaned their own plates. Looked around to make sure all was in order.

Temple lived as if in a dream, unable to construct a suitable pathway of memory back to her past. The world she thought she remembered from only months ago seemed impossible. She was without a past, like a woman who had dropped from the sky. She had thought she understood herself, what she wanted, what she felt was true, and found that she wasn't anyone anymore. She mistrusted her own sight, her own thoughts. Had she seen a charred ruin? Was that ruin somewhere she'd lived? Whatever she tried to recall was like a pebble at the bottom of a creek bed, and when she reached down into the clear water she grabbed only the dirt next to the pebble.

Lacking the ability to believe in her own past made it difficult to think about the future.

She knew that she wanted to leave, but she found that she couldn't understand what her journey would consist of. Would she travel for months? For days? Would she leave and come back? She knew words that made her think she should be trying to go to California, and trying to find Rose. She was, however, no longer sure that there was a Rose, that there'd ever been a Rose. Certainly if there had been such a woman, Temple's relationship with her had been entirely imagined.

Temple thought she could picture a map, tentatively she envisioned an expanse of land, and then perhaps there some mountains, and then there was water again and that was what they called California. She'd never seen water bigger than the river, so how did she know any of this? Where had she learned it and how did she know it was real? It seemed like a long time since she'd seen a map.

She resolved to go again to the Old House. Perhaps she could find something there that would prove that she had once lived the life she thought she remembered living. That she had once been a free woman in a happy home.

On a moonless night, convinced that the whole house was asleep, she slipped shoeless down the back stairs, through the pantry and out into still dark, where she walked past the bell and toward the orchard, looking at the brick wall there, the border between the Old House and the New. She remembered watching it built, but interestingly, she remembered watching it from this side. Maybe she had always been on this side of Bodkin's Hundred.

She slipped over the brick wall, her dress flurrying out around her, and slid down to sit. Her heart was pounding, and she tried to take smooth, calm breaths while she strained her ears for sounds of horses or hounds or men.

In the starlight she saw a raccoon squeeze through the broken panel of the front door of the Old House. It must live there, she thought.

Vines grew up the side of the barn, now, and as she walked toward the house she noted that the pastures had all gone to seed.

She had a horse, hadn't she? She remembered riding.

She'd begun thinking of her memories as dreams. She corrected herself and thought that she "remembered" riding.

Her bare feet crunched the sandy gravel of the drive that led to the main road, and she "remembered" that Oliver had hired a gardener, an Irishman who lived down the road. The hedges were all lumpy. He had seemed like a nice man. Could she find him? Find his house? It would prove the existence of everything just to stand at his door and recognize his face. Which house though?

At the end of the drive, she stood and looked each way. She'd seen the gardener go home a thousand times. Which way had he turned? She couldn't remember.

Turning away from the Bodkin's land, Temple crept along the side of the road. She'd taken a path to Rose's School, hadn't she? Where did it start? Was this wisteria the one she remembered? Don't they all look the same? Failing to find the break in the woods that led to the path, she walked in the ditch.

After an hour the cry of hounds broke through the night and grew louder and more distinct until she also heard the horn and yelling.

The dogs were going to bite her, but who would the dogs be eating? Some black girl with an imagination. A girl in a dreamworld. She was mad. This was the first moment of clarity in her entire life. She had been mad. Now, she could see. Having seen, she could not bring herself to care. Let them have me, she thought.

The riders called off the hounds with a blast of the horn, and one of the men dismounted and grabbed her hands. He tied them in front of her, and picked her up (as if she was nothing, like he'd have picked up a handkerchief) and draped her across his horse. Back up in the saddle he spurred the horse, and every step pressed the breath out of Temple. She didn't cry. She didn't care. She knew the hounds had already eaten her.

At the Hundred she was stripped. She stood naked in the warm night in front of the men and looked only at the ground. She didn't try to cover herself. Someone grabbed her by the arm and dragged her to the smokehouse, where a rope was thrown over one of the rafters and pulled tight until she was dangling in the air by the wrists, her shoulders pulling out of their sockets. People were talking but she couldn't hear them. It seemed that they were asking her questions, but she couldn't understand them.

The air grew hot and smoke filled the room. She coughed, and each sharp intake of breath was ragged, and painful. She held her breath, shook her head, but then couldn't, and she'd breathe a sharp, burning acrid smoke, and cough, and then breathe more sharply. Her eyes were burning. She coughed again, and this time she couldn't stop. She coughed until she drooled, and she was sure she was coughing up blood. She passed out, and woke up choking and coughing still tied by the wrists and twisting in the rafters of the smokehouse. She couldn't see. Every ragged breath was like swallowing a cloud of biting ants. Tears were streaming out of her eyes. She coughed and drooled and heaved. She would fade from consciousness for a moment only to be awoken by her own ragged cough.

She was barely alive when they cut her down and dragged her back into the house.

Temple lay in bed in the attic for two weeks and then one day she woke, sat up in bed, and took a deep breath that did not hurt her lungs or make her cough. Tandey had helped her wash the smoke scent out of her hair.

She looked out the window at the gable end for a little while, and went back to sleep. The next time she woke up it was because Zeb Newcombe stood over her.

"Good morning, Temple."

"Sir."

"I'm glad to see that you've recovered."

"Mostly."

"I hope we can find peace here. You're very confused, aren't you?"

Temple shrank away from him.

"You're wrong about me," Zeb said. "I will not hurt you. I have never wanted to hurt you. If I wanted to bring you pain, or cause you harm, I would have stayed out of this business entirely. I didn't have to come and save you from the fire. No one commanded that I intervene on your behalf and keep your neck out of the noose—they'd have hanged you the day you arrived in Alabama, if you even made it out of Virginia."

Temple nodded, and she couldn't disagree. His words felt like an uncomfortable shoe, slightly off, but she could no longer access the capacity to argue.

"We take care of you. We'll have to make some adjustments, of course." He produced a set of leg irons with a length of chain. "You'll have to wear these. I think you get lost. I think you wander off in a daze. I want to make sure we don't need to keep looking for you. I want to protect you from yourself. It's not good to wander. You get hurt when you wander. You'll end up strung up like a hog in the smokehouse, and I might not be around to pull you out next time. That's twice, after all."

He moved the blankets covering Temple. She lay there in her shift with the strange fresh air on her bare legs watching him fasten the shackles with a gentle menace.

"I'll wear the key myself, Temple, around my neck."

She sat silent.

"You should thank me, Temple. I've gone out of my way to help you."

"Yes. Thank you, Mr. Newcombe."

Oliver had hired her out to Miss Rose, she thought, Miss Rose needed the help, and Oliver rented me to her to do the work. Hadn't she scrubbed the floors? Hadn't she been dressed in castoffs? How had she become so confused? How had she lost her sense? Maybe it was because she was so pale. She was nowhere near as dark as the house maids. Next to Tandey, she was practically white.

"Now get dressed and come serve breakfast," said Zeb. "Miss Marie is in Richmond with Collings. It's just Johnny and I."

Temple hobbled downstairs, the chain of her shackles clunking on the stairs, and set the table.

CHAPTER TWENTY-FIVE

A Welcoming, of Sorts

Colonel Tobias Hale of Tarrytown, New York, was in the front room of his house at Fort Little Stone, which was at the end of the parade grounds, flanked by barracks on either side. He'd have preferred an office that wasn't in his house, but this sufficed. His desk blocked entry into the dining room behind him, where his private life began. He was standing, prying the nails off the top of a box about the size of a dictionary. He'd arrived at the fort six months before, and found it bedraggled. The Texas Rangers had used it, but they were rough men, ill kept, with no regard for cleanliness or order. Valuable men, surely, he thought, men without whom the conquering of this land would be impossible. Still. They were slovenly. Almost willfully so.

The creation of order can only come from order, and Hale knew that as long as they fought Comanche with Rangers, no matter how deadly they proved to be, they were fighting as equals. Better to not fight than to fight a war among equals. The plains would be won by a demonstration of the superiority of God's will, the superiority of order.

He'd glazed the broken windows, painted the buildings, swept the floors. (He hadn't done any of these things. He'd issued orders to have them done, but when he listed his accomplishments, he did not differentiate.) He'd had boardwalks constructed along the front of the soldiers' quarters, and built a market pavilion with paddocks and cordons where farmers and travelers could trade. He'd created a crew of infantrymen whose job it was to clean the central street of trash and dung and to sweep the boardwalks every morning. He found a team of men who took pride in the work, who understood that it wasn't a punishment detail. He'd outfitted them with tools and given them badges. They were not a janitorial detail, he told them. They were here to control the environment, to keep the peace.

This was a chaotic, terrible place. No need to let it rule you.

In the box he was prying open was his new flag.

Before the Rangers had used the fort, it had been an army outpost, but understaffed, under gunned, and poorly run. Those soldiers had been killed, or so he'd been told, by a band of Comanche under the guidance of the Comanche chief the Rangers called Greasy Pig. As a sign of respect, they insisted, because he was hard to catch.

"Although he do smell right greasy and piglike."

Hale assumed this story was true, that Greasy Pig's band had killed the soldiers, because he'd seen Greasy Pig once, on a reconnaissance, and the Indian had been wearing the fort's flag draped over his shoulders. Hale had watched him standing by a line of women who were cutting buffalo meat and stacking it. The meat was waist high to the women, who were naked to the waist and flecked with gore, smeared with blood, glistening with fat. It was a vile scene, but alluring, in its rusticity and immediate savagery. Greasy Pig talked to the woman on the end, but she never stopped working. Greasy Pig touched her shoulder in what to Colonel Hale was a remarkably familiar gesture and walked through the swirling smoke into the heart of the camp with the flag billowing behind him like a cape.

Well, he'd thought, it had been an old flag. Although it had been deserving of a better end than it was seeing draped across that hulking savage.

Folded neatly in the box was a crisp, bright red, white, and blue flag with thirty-three stars. Hale unfolded it on his desk, but thought better of it, folded it back up to its original shape, and tucked it under his arm. He put on his hat and strode out of his office and down the planks until he reached the center of Fort Little Stone, where a flagpole (recently sanded, with a new rigging and good rope) stood.

Across the street, where the civilian half of the fort lived, the innkeeper Booth was leaning in the doorway of his hotel. There was a man, thought Hale. He kept his barroom in a fine shine, presented himself well. I'd march with that man, thought Hale, who had never marched outside of a drill. Hale nodded to him, and Booth gave him a casual wave and a smile.

Hale fastened the first corner of the flag, and then the second, and then pulled it up the tall mast proudly. He stood back to watch the wind take it. He knew that God had given him the breeze, so that the order, the law represented by these crisp colors, these sharp lines, sewn so carefully in San Antonio, could rise above the camp for the first time as it should. Hale saluted the flag without irony, turned on his heel, and marched back to his office with his shoulders straight. He was glad, but not smiling.

"Sir," came the voice of a soldier, "riders."

"Indians?"

He would never admit it, but in one brief moment Hale had believed that the simple ritual of raising the American flag might have called in the savages to surrender, to align themselves with the irresistible future. It was a foolish thought. Magical. He pushed it away.

"One of 'em a colored fella. Other'n might be Indian."

"Is that right?"

"Ride out to greet them and bring them into camp, stable the horses, and if there's no need, if nothing is emergent, bring them to me."

"What if—what was the word you said?"

"Emergent?"

"What's that?"

"An emergency. If someone is hurt, have him cared for. If he's starving have him fed."

The soldier stood still.

"This is the American army, and we are in Indian Country, and we will treat and feed any man who arrives at our fort, regardless of his color. Bring them to me, and we'll figure out who they are and what they are doing here, but until that moment treat them as you would be treated. Am I understood?"

"Yes, sir."

Colonel Hale believed that there was nothing as interesting as the Black Man. He had known a few, from a distance, at West Point. Servants of his Southern colleagues. Known was too strong a word. He'd known the names of, had nodded toward, had occasionally thanked, to the amusement of his Southern host, but what do you say when someone hands you a glass of brandy or a dish of meat? The Hales were not a wealthy family. They had hired farmhands when they could, mostly Irish, but his mother and sisters had run the house. There was no one at his elbow, slathering butter on his bread or finding the slice of roast beef cooked exactly as he liked it. The luxury wrapped around those Southerners was sinful. They were coddled. Corrupted no matter how smart, and he counted among his friends some of the smartest Southern men that walked. He wouldn't go so far as to say soft. No one would call Jackson soft—he chuckled. No, not soft. They expressed fondness for their servants, too, like that which one might hold for a hunting dog, was that it? A good horse? A being attached to you on unequal terms. Something you would protect, until protecting it was no longer a sensible course of action. Hale's mind wandered, looking for the edges on what he thought of as a subtle emotional topography. One would save a chicken, he thought to himself, from a predator, unless the sacrifice of that chicken was the last way to save oneself. When standing in front of the lion, you'd throw the chicken into its maw to make your escape. The guard dog dies first, and in that, its place is earned. That is the fulfillment of the natural way. To die first is to live in exactly the way a guard dog should live. A guard dog who does not lay himself down protecting that which he should guard is not a guard dog at all, and worthless.

Is a servant that doesn't serve, then, equally abominable?

Perhaps.

What then of the underlying assumption? If all colored were fashioned in the mold of a servant, descendants of Canaan, and they do not serve, or are set free from servitude, what then? It didn't sit well. For they are His servants, freed from Egypt, and may not be given into servitude.

There it is, he thought. It pleased him to have worked the problem through to a conclusion.

Colonel Hale was much encouraged by the experiments in Haiti and Liberia, of which he knew less than he thought. Liberia, especially, suggested that the dark race was capable of at least some form of self-governance. You wouldn't ask a legless man to walk without crutches, would you? We must offer help and support. Help and support. For a legless man will not regrow his legs. But with crutches, he will perambulate.

He heard the boots on the walkway well before the knock came upon his door, and he woke himself from his reverie and rose from his chair.

The soldier walked in and saluted clumsily—how Hale wished these men would rise to an occasion. Behind the clumsy soldier stood a black man and what appeared to be a sort of Indian. The black man held his hat in his hand and bobbed his head, meekly. Hale had seen this behavior before, among the colored servants. It was animalistic, an instinctual adoption of a supplicant pose. He wondered if they were capable of deceit.

"Welcome to Fort Little Stone, I am the commanding officer, Colonel Hale."

"Thank you, Colonel. Walter Raleigh Babenburg."

"They call me Red Joe."

The colonel didn't offer a chair. Walter Raleigh Babenburg had skin the color of a muddy river. His eyes were bright and intelligent beneath his wide, flat forehead. His features were fine, almost urbane. His suit was travel-worn and dusty but well-tailored. He spoke in clear, distinct tones. The Indian sounded British, and was dressed like something out of the *Arabian Nights.*

"Tell me, where are you from?"

The black man looked toward Colonel Hale, though perhaps not directly at him, and said: "Vienna. Please, sir, call me Raleigh."

"Vienna?" He did not sound Viennese.

"Yes, sir, I was raised in Bohemia, by the Duchess of Slezko, and lived with her in Vienna. I have been on a tour of the Americas."

"By yourself?"

"With my valet—Joe—it was arranged that I should play piano for an old friend of the Duchess, an impresario, but he fell into hard times, and I, well, I have been wandering."

"Wandering." Colonel Hale sat, stunned.

"Well, sir, I was intending to make my way to San Francisco, where I would meet the Duchess, and together we would sail back to Europe."

What an extraordinary story.

"That was a month ago, at least. She couldn't have waited for me, although I tried to get word to her. I hope that she made arrangements, if she didn't, perhaps she left instructions."

"In San Francisco?"

Could a black man with a European education navigate the doings of civilization? Or, at least, make a show of doing so? Even more interesting, would a black man making such a demonstration of his own elevation, continue that elevation when unsupervised? Or would he revert? How long until the hunting dog eats the bird? Depends upon the dog, but they all do eventually.

"It sounds preposterous. All I have thought, as I've ridden, is how preposterous it sounds; it sounds that way to me, too."

If we were thirty miles or so to the South, Colonel Hale thought to himself, I'd have to ask for proof. If we were back there among the Missourians, he'd already be in jail. Captain Hale looked at the soldier, uncharacteristically impassive and inscrutable by the door. The soldier was from New Hampshire, originally, sent out with his family among the Free Staters a few years ago. Hale turned his attention back to his guests.

"You'll never survive the trip to San Francisco."

"I'd considered that, sir."

"And yet you set forth?"

"I don't know what else to do."

"Soldier," Hale tapped his fingers on the desk, thinking. A more interesting opportunity for observation would rarely come. Why not? Better to learn a little than to send this man out onto the plains, into the storms, toward death. California!

"Could you show these men to the Inn with my recommendations? Can you pay? The army might . . ."

"This is very kind of you, but yes, sir, we can pay our way," said Red Joe.

"Well, I can't send you on to your death. Perhaps a wagon train will come along and you can join it. In the meantime, I think we should tell Mr. Booth—our innkeeper—that we have a piano player in town. Perhaps we're due for some entertainment."

CHAPTER TWENTY-SIX

The Sewing Circle

Late Autumn, 1860

Marie took Collings to Richmond to advance his gentlemanly education—dance classes, etiquette—and to introduce him around town in the series of fetes and dances meant to bring together young women and eligible bachelors. She wanted him to show up at the Christmas Eve hunt ball knowing how to hold a fork, perhaps with a friend or a girl he liked.

Collings, at sixteen, was a puzzle. Johnny, her older son, had always been a straightforward child—a miniature man crippled by honor and an abstract sense of duty. He was susceptible to manipulation from all sides. He'd fight if provoked, and he'd do anything for a woman who smiled at him. He had no profound sense of self, but he would ride a horse over a waterfall if he thought it was the right thing to do. He was no more complicated than a puppy. Collings, on the other hand, seemed impervious to influence. He watched the world as if from afar. He seemed good at certain things—books, music—but he was slow to let any skill show. Like some decadent European who would never deign to show effort.

The sitting room next to Marie's childhood bedroom was a tidy jewel box in pale colors and soft fabrics. She sat at her writing desk—she could, if she concentrated, make herself feel young sitting here—and watched the flames of her candle cast shadows where the white wainscoting met the pale lavender wallpaper. Behind her a fine fire crackled on the grate. She had bought a package of toiletries—a soap that smelled of newly mown hay and an eau de toilette of jasmine. They sat before her, the soap unwrapped, the perfume uncapped, their gorgeous, luxurious scents mixing in the air. In this comfort she let herself drift along, holding a pen she wasn't using.

Could she solve the puzzle that was Collings? He was cynical, captious. Here, in this season of dance lessons and manners, he was supposed to be smoothed, buffed out, made to understand that one must monitor one's thoughts and words. He didn't want it.

He ticked off complaints constantly. Did he do nothing but complain? About the polish on the floor, about the color of the drapery, about the way one girl danced, the crooked smile of another. He thought the man who taught etiquette was ridiculous. ("It's like he slithers, I don't like him.")

She supposed he'd make an artist. A poet?

Her parents' Franklin Street mansion had a library, and he did like that, but she suspected that he knew people would leave him be if he were in the library.

This morning she'd given him blueberry preserves for breakfast, and he'd made a face.

"What's the matter?"

He shook his head.

"What is it?"

He looked out the window as if hearing her voice made him want to die.

"Collings!"

"I just don't like blueberries."

Which was ridiculous. He did like blueberries, and she told him so.

"See, that's exactly what I mean," he said. "Never mind."

He'd need a wife. It was a good thing he was rich.

She wondered what happened to children who think too much in poor families. Perhaps it never comes up. Perhaps the common man stays nobly focused on his task—a luxury, she thought, they scarcely understand. They don't flounder about. Nor must they prove themselves. Or improve themselves. They don't even have to learn much—she thought about all the things she'd been taught, and all the things she'd tried to teach Collings, and she held it up against a list of what she imagined a poor laborer might have to learn. She had so little idea of what constituted labor, much less poverty, or how similar the shape of human life is that she struggled to put anything on the other list at all, but she faintly found "washing" and "gardening." She nodded.

She turned her thoughts to the bishop, whom she had given a dinner. They'd eaten pigeons she brought in from the Hundred, which the cook had spitted and served with cabbage cooked in parsleyed butter. They had oysters with horseradish. Slices of fried potatoes and a salad from the little greenhouse that kept the Collingses in herbs and greens until the coldest months—chervil and lettuce and cress washed clean and iced and dressed with salted egg yolks whipped into oil.

The bishop had eaten with delight, and had drunk with what bordered on rapacity.

Mr. Collings, her father, had talked of business and law. Had stroked both his gray whiskers and his round belly, and been a perfect, cheerful, hospitable patriarch. "I like a bishop," he'd said, to the bishop. "You men know the workings." He'd waved his knife in a way that would have been atrociously rude if he had not been at the head of the table in his own house. "It is you, is it not, who steward the land, keep the business going? It's the bishops, I've always said, that are responsible for the whole show."

No one had ever heard Mr. Collings say anything of the sort, but he had an easy authority, and spoke mostly in pursuit of little more than cheering people and making them feel good. Marie didn't want to mention the Church, or Father Rice, directly—she'd only wanted to make a stitch—and before the conversation came too close to her agenda she deftly steered it to some local interests, about which she thought the bishop might have an opinion. He did.

The disdain on her son's face for the mechanics of society was plain to see.

She sighed, now, in the sitting room, thinking how easy it was to have her father on her side, how useful of a man he was. Without even trying, he knows exactly what to say. She turned her attention to the paper and wrote an elegant note thanking the bishop for his company, and hoping that they'd see one another again soon.

Aside from the education of Collings, and cultivation of the bishop, her great task of autumn was the sewing of the shirts, trousers, and socks to be given out to the enslaved on Christmas. Marie, her little sister Lelia, and her mother worked together, adding all of their servants into one big list and dividing them by size—small for children, medium for women, large for men.

They sewed in the atelier, working deftly, happy to be maintaining the tradition of homespun clothes.

"I'm sure the Hundred used to supply its own fabric," said Lelia.

Marie nodded.

"Johnny is just like his father," Lelia said. "Cut from the same cloth. A war would be good for him—he's certainly suited to it, and he'll look fine with medals across his breast."

Lelia held nothing but disdain for Zeb, whom she'd described to her mother upon the engagement as: "Common. A slave catcher without education, interests, or respect for human life." Her mother had told her she was being hysterical.

"Collings, though," said Mother.

Marie laughed. "Not him."

"No," said Mother. "The sword is not for him."

Marie's mother had found, in what she referred to as her antiquity, the most comfortable iteration of herself she'd ever known. She enjoyed being imperious, and had no qualms about displaying her wealth or her wisdom. At Marie's age, she'd had still clung to the last threads of girlish shyness and harbored some thoughts she kept to herself. Now, she fancied herself a monarch. She'd have had a fanfare announce her if she could have figured out how to do it. She tied her hair up in the same complicated bun that Marie did, but she no longer let the ringlets and curls fall about her face.

"He will focus on his studies and steer clear of the clubs. Let the warriors have their glory. You keep his nose in the books."

"The new country will need men of intelligence," Lelia said.

Lelia spoke with confidence. She'd studied at the Augusta Female Seminary in Staunton. Although she'd fallen in love with her husband—a physician—and married him at a young age, they had delayed the birth of their son William until she was thirty. At her home they spoke of a practical and scientific future, and she had nothing but disdain for the aristocratic ways that her mother and older sister adhered to, which she felt to be the wilted leavings of European nobility. "It's like we're French, or something, it disgusts me. Didn't we fight a revolution?" She'd been given three servants upon her marriage, whom she'd freed at once, and then hired back to do the housework, cook, and watch young William as ostensibly free women. They lived in her house and she paid them. They knew that she no longer had the right to sell them, because she'd told them that, but they weren't sure if they were free.

"Collings wouldn't last four minutes at war," said Mother. "I may have many misconceptions regarding the talent of my own grandchildren, as one should, but I shall not insist that they are suited to that which they are not. You'd have an easier time getting Johnny into the priesthood than Collings into the army."

"He's off to Hampden-Sydney, come the new year."

"Good," said Lelia.

"I've dropped a stitch," said Marie.

Her mother set down her sewing and came to her side.

"There, see?"

"You'll have to ladder back."

She was already undoing the yarn.

"It's not too far," said Mother.

"Will Johnny join the cavalry?" asked Lelia.

"If there's a cavalry," said Mother.

"I've been asking," said Marie.

Lelia turned to the bolts of fabric, and with her back to the other women and a trace of a smile asked if Zeb knew anyone.

"I've been asking," Marie said again.

CHAPTER TWENTY-SEVEN

The Paris of the West

February 1861

Rose arrived in San Francisco, took a suite at the brand-new Asiatic Hotel, and liked it so much that it never occurred to her to leave. The flowers there were frequently replaced, and the briskly efficient attendants dropped off generous bowls of fruit without being asked. She loved the drawing rooms with pianos and thick carpets in which she could settle down with a sherry; she adored the open and airy dining room, with its rows of columns. A castle built on commerce, she told herself. It seemed the most American thing of all, and she loved it. It was exactly what she had wanted.

In the little cafés attached the bar, actresses lingered and flirted and when Rose returned from the opera, she often found the singers themselves installed around a table, eating a late snack or drinking champagne. Making friends was easy: she was good looking but not so young as to be threatening, she was smart but liked to listen, and money flew from her fingertips.

For someone accustomed to running a plantation house, the price of champagne was laughable.

She did not look back. The great loves and strategies of her past became as artifacts in a museum, fossils, insects in amber, interesting, but no longer relevant. She moved forward, her life started exactly where her feet were planted, and went on from that point. She missed Jorg as one misses the characters of a book. Once upon a time she had been engaged with the fortunes of a man named Jorg Knaupf, just as once she had clutched the kerchief that hung down from the collar of her blouse while she read *The House of the Seven Gables*, and just as once she had tutored a young woman named Temple. Now, she was at the Asiatic.

She liked the concierge who worked in the mornings named Mr. Peabody. He smelled nice, had a mustache which hung over his lip as if a dust broom had been pasted there, and was in possession of many props and accoutrements with which he fiddled and fussed while speaking. He had a watch and pince-nez and the silver chain upon which they hung. He had a pen and a small sharp knife for cutting cigars with which he would tap his table, a polished podium by the marble columns which flanked one of the stairways. When asked a question to which the answer was not immediately apparent he would look off at one of the potted plants around the cavernous lobby and blink regularly, slightly faster than the beat of a human heart, as if willing himself to speed up. He punctuated his sentences with little taps of the folded knife on his desk.

Rose found the entire production ludicrous and charming.

"Mr. Peabody," she asked, "have you about the premises a heavy walking stick that I might borrow or purchase?"

"A walking stick, Madame?"

"There's a lot of dogs out there," said Rose, "on the street, I mean. I'd like to walk, and I want something sturdy in hand, something to shoo them away with if it comes to it."

"Oh!" said Mr. Peabody, "I hope it won't come to that." He locked his eyes on his favorite ficus and blinked.

"That would be better for everyone involved," said Rose. "But if it were to come to that, I'd like to have a stick."

"There's much of this city that might not suit you, Madame."

"All the more reason for the stick, Mr. Peabody."

Mr. Peabody's various affectations would have been far less entertaining had he not also been tremendously effective. He had a working knowledge of the wine cellar, a cache of tickets to sold-out entertainments in his vest, and a preternatural ability to locate solutions. He did not begrudge his clientele their wants. Rather, he found joy and solace in the idea that there were in the rooms of his hotel hundreds of people with desires they'd perhaps never understood but which he could slake.

"Ma'am, if you might excuse me, I believe I have something that would suit you."

He came back in four minutes with a mahogany flagpole. The top had a heavy golden ball as a finial, and the bottom was capped with a brass cup. He bowed as he held it out to Rose.

"Left here after a political rally and forgotten. Quite solid, but not so heavy that it will grow tiresome. That brass ball, I'd think, would discourage a dog, or anyone else."

She thumped it on the carpet, held it at her side as if she were Joan of Arc calling the troops into battle, and cast a beaming smile at Mr. Peabody before walking out into San Francisco to contribute her little bit to the joyful theater of the street.

She made circles around the hotel, careful to note the direction home, and moving outward only as her confidence in her environment grew. She found equal pleasure in solitary moments of quietude and hurried city business. She nodded to the private constables hired to protect the families in wealthier neighborhoods, and she laughed with the untended children for whom she bought apples or pears.

The world, as represented in San Francisco, was a wonderful place.

What foolishness had she been raised to believe? Who would hold the agricultural ideal as the pinnacle when clearly, culture was bursting, exploding, and lively here, where it was all set to play out in its fantastic collisions and wild diversity? As she walked along the edge of the neighborhood where the Chinese lived, she was electrified by how they moved and spoke. The Chileans, the Italians, here was rice from Peru, textiles from China. She leapt at any opportunity, clattered her staff on cobblestones and tapped it on curbs. She felt good.

Did she look odd, striding through neighborhoods with a flagpole? Well? Perhaps. It gave her joy to think that she was now a part of this fabric. That someone might be newer to town than she and think of her as the Woman with the Flagpole.

Men such as her father were able to continue their lives, live out their ideas, because they were never confronted with a contradiction. Along the James River, all the families lived the same lives. That is why they took to her ideas so badly, and why they hated Oliver. They had never been forced into confluence. If you'd only ever talked to people who agree with you, how could you absorb anything new? That is what is so wonderful about a place like this, she thought. Lives all around you with different goals, different ideals.

She shuddered to think of the provincialism, the staid manners, the earnest rectitude into which she'd been raised. She wanted nothing to do with it. She had moved for good, and for the best, she told herself. She'd liquidated everything—in addition to Bonscourt itself, she'd sold the books, the silver, the carpets. She'd hardly needed the money—there was the Durand trust set up to protect her livelihood against untoward events, the dowry she'd contributed to her matrimony, and the fortune Jorg Knaupf had brought with him, which was substantial. She'd consolidated it all, put it on an overland express to the Wells Fargo and Company Bank, and told the receptive bank officer—Mr. Neale—to look out for interesting investments. "Productions, publications, entertainments, that sort of thing. Nothing too big."

Mr. Neale sent word of an opera in need of a backer. She invested and earned out within two weeks.

A newspaper called *The Golden Era* hired a new editor and briefly ran out of money; there was Rose Knaupf to step into the breach, soon after which she found herself invited to salons and gatherings among the growing literary scene. She felt that they were on the cusp of something exciting.

She would pick up a copy of the *Era* on her walk, and bring it back to the hotel to read after lunch. She loved Edward Jump's cartoons, and the tipsy, eccentric, and jovial San Francisco that was its favorite version of itself. She found in the humor, the excitement, the wry tone of the newspapers proof that these San Franciscans were flexible people, with quick, complicated minds. She had a leather-topped table by the window in the sitting room of her suite and a comfortable chair in front of it where she would spend the afternoon with a couple of newspapers spread out flat, a book, and her correspondence. A bottle of wine or a pot of tea was never more than a bell ring away. From the street below she could hear the wonderful hum of the city—coachmen calling out warnings, men selling vegetables, arguments, and barking dogs. Half of her attention was usually given over to a happy contemplation of the city, her situation, and her life, while she turned the pages of the broadsheets, focusing on items here and there, pausing to take in a bit of news more carefully, then breezing on.

One afternoon she turned to the inside pages of the *Golden Era* and found herself so startled she stood right up.

She quickly sat back down and turned the page backward, seeing if she could undo what she'd seen. Coming to the page again, she saw the same picture. There, in the middle of the page, was a report from Fitz Ludlow regarding a traveling theater group called the Rialto, and there, in the middle of the page, was a drawing by Albert Bierstadt of the same. The caption said he'd taken a photograph of the troupe, and listed the names. The thin, aristocratic-looking man in evening dress standing as if about to be wed next to the singer was identified as Walter Raleigh Babenberg, of Vienna. It was clear to Rose that he was Raleigh Bodkin, though it didn't make any sense at all that he would be.

She rang a bell, and while the porter came to see what she wanted she wrote on a calling card that she very much needed to speak with Fitz Ludlow and Albert Bierstadt and would appreciate it if they could come to her at the Asiatic this evening for tea, and perhaps bring a copy of the photograph of the Rialto players, which Bierstadt had taken, and which she would like to buy.

She ordered claret and Madeira, nuts, rolls, and an assortment of cold meats with caper sauce, pepper jelly, and mustards.

CHAPTER TWENTY-EIGHT

The Piano Player at the Fort Little Stone Hotel

November and December 1860

Dressed in his suit, Raleigh waited at the back door of the inn for the innkeeper, Booth, who soon stepped out on to the porch, looked around with the authority of a man who owns what he's looking at, lit a cigar, and nodded. Booth was a formidable man: tall and bald, with broad shoulders and arms that looked as if he spent his time swinging an ax rather than pouring beer. He had a bar towel over his shoulder, and a mustache waxed into points. His nose had been broken more than once. "You play piano?" Booth asked.

Raleigh nodded.

"What's your name?"

"Raleigh, sir."

"This isn't some forsaken plantation, Raleigh, you can answer me when I ask you something. You're a man." He absentmindedly kicked a pebble at one of the cats lurking in the shadow, apparently intending to compare the actions of a man to that of a cat. "Cats are fine. There's a lot of 'em, though. Better than rats. Up to a point, because then you don't have rats but you got cats. What then? Dogs? You play piano?"

"I do. I worked on the *Rialto*, a riverboat. And we had a wagon theater troupe for a while, but it broke up."

"What the hell are you doing here?"

"Headed to California."

"It's November, you'll be dead in a week. You aren't going to California."

"That's just what Mr. Hale said."

"And the colonel gave you a place to stay?"

"No," said Raleigh.

"There's a few rooms up there we keep for colored folks. You can play for one. I'll feed you, keep you in beer—mind you we'll see about that, I ain't having you drink me out everyday. We'll see how it works out."

Raleigh nodded. "Thank you."

Booth held the door and walked Raleigh into the barroom. "Lala and Tula, the cooks." He indicated two women in messily laced bodices and layered skirts too big for kitchen work, who leaned against the bar and scowled slightly. "They'll cheer up, just as soon as I open the spigot."

"And this is Millie. She helps behind the bar."

Millie, a Creole girl with long braids, laughed and said hi.

Lala spit tobacco juice into a spittoon.

"Get on, then," said Booth. The two girls gathered their skirts and tromped into the kitchen, where to Raleigh's surprise the sound of cooking did commence. He'd figured them for fast girls.

The room was open and bright, dominated by a long, shining, wooden bar. Strong chairs were arrayed around square tables of the same wood as the bar, and just as clean. The kerosene lamps were polished, and in the middle sat a squat woodstove with a pile of wood squared around it like a fence to keep people from burning themselves. In a side room, a massive stone hearth held a generous fire, in front of which a table as long as the bar stretched. The piano was an ornate square grand, on a riser next to the bar. The outside had been cleaned and polished, but there was dust on the keys when Raleigh opened the top.

Booth handed him the towel from his shoulder.

"We do all right. We're a way station for the stagecoach, and we've got the mail behind the bar. Sometimes your better wagon train folks need a break, and they'll stop in for a bit. The soldiers come in, they all get a night off, we try to arrange it with Hale to keep the ones what don't like one another on a different schedule for nights off, so as to keep the fights to a minimum."

Raleigh explored the keys. The piano was a little stiff. The notes decayed quickly, but it had a woody tone, wasn't as banjo-like as the one he'd had on the wagon, and built up a ghostlike resonance in the room which he liked. Raleigh made a left hand striding figure and played a B chord over it, then pulled his ring finger down a semitone to D to shift to the haunting B minor. After a quick rest he thunked the first three chords of Schubert's "Hungarian Melody." Another brief pause, during which he counted himself off, and he repeated the opening chords but this time kept going, spooling out the filigrees as if pulling yarn from a skein, building the song over itself, pushing the pattern a little higher each time. First they climb a hill, he thought, as he lost himself in the music, and could feel in it the sway of the folk dancers. He could see them dancing around a fire, drinking apple brandy. The little touch of cheer was the brandy, he thought, that flashed through but couldn't replace the mournful underpinnings. They were besieged and melancholic, but he always thought of the peasants together. It wasn't a lonely piece, they were pushing back against the current. Stopping, turning. Sometimes he felt each return was a new character, a new face in the firelight telling their story to the others. He fought the urge to speed up, instead played harder, reined it in like a horse who wanted his head, and let the tension build as the song cascaded out in ever-growing complexity before softening for its denouement.

He took up his fingers from the keys.

Lala and Tula had come back into the dining room, and Lala whistled low.

Millie was beaming at him from behind the bar.

He smiled at her, and with his eyes still on her hit the bigger strides of the Virginia reel. He let it slacken and sway, he let the resolving run gush like a waterfall. Lala and Tula were swinging arm in arm, and he stepped it up, got in front of the beats to propel it a little. Wrapped it up in a half-tempo flourish with semitone frills thrown all over the edges, and laughed as he pounded the final chord.

Booth patted him on the back and stuck a dollar in the pocket of his jacket.

"Have you eaten, Raleigh?"

"I have not."

"Take a seat at the bar, and let's get the man some hash."

Red Joe appeared at the door and strode confidently to Raleigh.

"Booth, this is Red Joe. He was on the *Rialto* with me."

"My pleasure," Red Joe bowed, "I went to buy tobacco."

Raleigh tried to hide his tension—Red Joe, in regalia, was a sight.

Booth, however, laughed.

"You play piano, too?" Millie asked.

"Alas, I do not. I was more of an advance man."

"Guess you'll have to pay for your room, then," said Booth.

That night the room seemed to light up. There had been nothing to do, no reason to be there except to quickly drink and then to pay one of the women or decide not to. Now, men lingered. They nodded their heads to Raleigh's music—he kept it upbeat, but threw something intense in whenever he felt sure the drinkers would barely notice. People bought drinks for one another, they stayed and drank and tipped the women just for talking. The room was full, now, and the patrons didn't just sit and stare at one another and feel the loneliness of the place or the loneliness of their lives.

A couple of days later Abbott came in with a skinned lamb over his shoulder.

"Don't walk that through my barroom," cried Booth, laughing.

"What?" Abbott spun, feigning ignorance of the lamb he was wearing like a stole. "Walk what?"

After he gave the lamb to Tula in the kitchen, Abbott sat by the fire in the dining room with Joe and Raleigh. Joe bought Abbott a bottle of whiskey.

"Take it home," said Joe. "It's the least we can do."

Abbott shrugged, poured them glassfuls, and said it was the least he could do.

Raleigh played and Abbott laughed and clumsily danced with Tula while Joe leaned on the bar.

"Y'all friends with Abbott?" Millie asked.

"We are."

"Good."

Lala brought out a tray of charred rib chops, which Booth said were too good for the customers, and the seven of them—Lala, Tula, Millie, Booth, Red Joe, Abbott, and Raleigh—sat at the long table together and ate. They pushed the last two chops around the table, each unwilling to take one, until Abbott laughed, took a chop in each hand, and fed them to the cooks.

Word got out among the townsfolk that there was something interesting to see at the inn, and another crowd started showing up, as well, from the civilian side of town. The banker and the trader who funded expeditions for furs and explorations for metals came in together, sat for dinner, and listened to Raleigh play. They came back in a couple of days, with their wives. The sutler closed up his supply shop early and brought his wife in with her friend the schoolmistress before the soldiers got there. He tipped Raleigh a dollar, and Raleigh played Beethoven for them while they ate.

"It's brought a new sophistication to our small town, Mr. Booth, and I appreciate it," said the schoolmistress. She was young, tight-lipped, and tried not to look at Millie or Raleigh the whole time she was there.

Judge Philpot came in every Thursday, now, to sit at the bar, next to the piano, and eat dinner with which he drank two beers and a glass of brandy afterward. He'd leave when the infantry men showed up.

"Can't abide young men who drank too fast," he said to Raleigh. "Though I don't begrudge them their youth or their impatience. Guess if I was headed toward a war, I might be impatient, as well. Happy to know that we're on the right side of the line, here," the judge said, "not like them Dark Lantern folks. We're Free State here in Fort Little Stone. Ain't we Booth?"

"That we are."

Lieutenant Pip Crawford stood at the judge's elbow.

"You can't leave the coloreds in the devil's hands," said Crawford. "The dark race is the devil's pawn. They need guidance. They are slated to their lot."

"Slated?"

"You're an educated man, Judge, and you know as well as I that the descendants of Canaan are put upon this earth to serve. Tell me what a servant without a master is worth?"

The judge shook his head: "There be no justice in searching for a man's worth that way, Lieutenant."

The judge tipped Millie and Raleigh, nodding to each of them, and said good night to Booth. He ignored Crawford.

Crawford drifted over to the gambling table and made jokes at the expense of a soldier who was losing to Red Joe.

"It's not right to rib a man who takes a risk when you take no risk yourself, Lieutenant Crawford," said Red Joe. "You're welcome to join at any time."

Crawford snorted. He was no gambler. The games he played were rigged.

Millie had pale green eyes, a tambourine, and a great sense of tension and timing. Late, when things were smoky and wild, she'd stand next to Raleigh, striking the tambourine and laughing with her head thrown back. Raleigh liked Millie, liked her tambourine and her laugh and the way she'd lean against the piano when he played Beethoven, as if it was all too much and she was just too overwhelmed to go on. When they played reels and crawls he'd invent little trills, extra filigree, and send them to her.

"You best quit that," said Lala.

Raleigh feigned ignorance.

"She's Booth's wife, you know. Yeah, you can pick your jaw up off the floor there, piano boy."

CHAPTER TWENTY-NINE

A Christmas Party

December 1860

"Well, it seems as you've had a time," said Marie, sitting imperiously at the foot of the table, across from her husband, who was shaky, damp, and obviously hungover. Her boys Johnny and Collings were already out with the kennel master, looking for good runs and fixing the coops on the fences. They'd straightened up before Marie's return, but she'd noticed the notches on the newel-post and the general smell of tobacco and whiskey that wafted from the rugs and couches in every room.

Temple placed a tray of bacon on the table, eyes down.

"Why is she in braces?"

"She runs," Zeb waved it off. "I had one of the servants wrap the chain in velvet—it drove you crazy, listening to her drag that around." He spread some butter. "Anyway, I thought I should protect the floor. Scratched it up."

One of the tiles in the foyer was cracked and there were the prints of horseshoes on the stairs. This is what happened among men left to themselves. She supposed she was lucky he hadn't lost the house in a card game.

"We're hosting this weekend," she reminded him.

He nodded and said: "The boys are out looking over the coops now."

"Yes, but also the ball."

"Of course."

"I sent Tandey with the wagon."

He nodded again, and stretched his legs out to the side of the table. He drank black coffee from her Limoges, into which he'd splashed brandy from a pocket flask. He'd attempted to do this surreptitiously, at the sideboard, but he was incapable of subtlety.

It's impossible to make him care, she thought. Impossible to make him understand. She remembered what she had found attractive about him—his wildness, the smell of the horse on his clothes, his reckless violence which she, in her naïveté, mistook for courage. It had all been so refreshing. So unlike the world-weary, sophisticated, well-heeled suitors she'd otherwise received. Her father entertained a vision of Zeb as what he called "an honest man," some sort of vigorous representation of an agricultural ideal. There had been Newcombes in Virginia for long enough for them to show up here and there in the histories, and Mr. Collings had come to believe that a Newcombe rode with Patrick Henry in the gunpowder incident, which Zeb never denied. Her mother never liked him—"He's not quite one of us, though, is he?" Her sister hated him. Even better.

Over the intervening years, Marie had come to agree more with her mother and sister.

She needed a man who rose in reputation, who became a leader, who broadcast an air of command, and she found that he was not here. The appeal of a lusty swashbuckler fades. She'd thought she could refine him. She'd thought that by now he'd understand how important the coming parties were, or, at least, that he'd understand how to use his silver. She was powerless to change him, because he had no idea that he was failing. He was so utterly devoid of manners—she watched him now as he pronged jam with a fork—that he had no idea he lacked them. He wasn't even embarrassed. Those without manners hold us in their sway, she thought.

"It's Collings's last Christmas," Marie said. "We should do something for him."

"His last? It's not his last."

"It's not the same."

"He'll be back."

"Once he's at Hampden-Sydney it won't be the same."

Zeb recoiled for a second, sunk into thought or frustration.

"What?"

"Well, something."

Zeb made a gesture indicating he'd conceded the point.

"I was at the bank," said Marie. "This morning."

Zeb tried to look nonchalant, but she swore she saw whatever last color there was in his sallow cheeks fade. So he knows.

"I was told, I'm sure it's nothing, but I was told that my account was overdrawn."

"Overdrawn?"

She picked up a small piece of toast and took a bite.

"There must be some mistake. I'm headed in for some business, anyway, I'll clear it up."

He did know. He had invoked a line of credit, and that credit had run out. What Marie thought she was spending she was borrowing, and yet she kept up the work on this church. She kept pouring money into things. When he'd been alone, free to travel and work, he'd made money. He thought of the bounties. He thought of the rewards. He thought of the simple times he'd spent running down escaped Negroes and bringing them to justice. Old Mr. Bodkin had paid him handsomely, the Master Mr. Bodkin, those were good times they'd had. God the looks on those faces when he'd poured that boy out in the driveway—he'd loved the house then, it was true. The house was his idea, but she was the one who had trapped him here. And she never spent a moment considering depriving herself of a single desire. To see something was to have it!

It was irresponsible, he told himself.

That afternoon in Richmond, Zeb visited Mr. Collings in his study at the Franklin Street mansion. He had a whole story worked out about how the bank must have made some error, and now he needed a cosignatory to extend a line of credit, but Mr. Collings started in before he could make the pitch.

"I'm so happy to see you, Zeb," Mr. Collings rarely looked excited, but he certainly seemed so. "We have, here, sit down sit down, we have a big opportunity ahead of us. Perhaps the biggest."

He went on to explain that he understood, from sources in Washington, that the South was soon to be blockaded.

"Nothing in, nothing out," he said. "However! I have arranged a warehouse, on the coast, in England, and I'm going to fill it with cotton. I've arranged purchase of two million pounds, and I've arranged the ships to sail it over. I've signed a contract for ten cents a pound, and if I'm not mistaken, we'll see a handsome return on that if we hold it. We'll have to be patient, of course, but I foresee a tenfold return. Imagine being the last seller of American cotton in England, Mr. Newcombe. It's exciting. I wanted to be sure to include you. There's a lot of money to be made."

"Of course, Mr. Collings," said Zeb. "That's very generous of you."

"We'll draw a little off that line first thing," said Mr. Collings, with a wink. "Helps one with the patience."

They shook hands, and Zeb left, dizzied by his luck, with the promise that $5,000 would be deposited in his account before Christmas.

Tandey was arranging candles, hundreds of them, in the banquet room, where a buffet was being readied. The hunt would be back by one o'clock, and they'd have a punch in the dining room, where he'd set out a platter of smoked tongue, chicken salad, and a ham. The guests—those who had not ridden today—would arrive by three. There were long tables against each wall, soon to be laden with oyster stew, lobster salad, venison roasts, and two turkeys. There were confections of spun sugar and nougat and orange styled into pyramids, and a molded calf's-foot jelly in swirls of bright colors. There were small fancy cakes and burnt almond ice cream in a wooden box lined with salt and ice packed in hay. Around the room there were jeroboams of wine. Each would have an attendant, in livery, ready to pour the wine into one of the hundreds of crystal glasses that were lined up, glistening on the tablecloth.

Out in the yard, the enslaved had gathered for a party, as well. They'd been allowed to kill and cook a pig, and the fires had been well tended since last night. The pig was washed in vinegar, and there was a pot of okra soup bubbling over the fire. They'd cleaned out the center hall of the barn, and they sat on boxes and danced and listened to the fiddle and tambourine music. There was a barrel of whiskey, and everyone was drinking—men and women pulling off a ladle that was dipped into the cask. Some precocious children seemed wobbly, as well.

Temple had asked Tandey if he wanted to go.

"No ma'am."

"But it's a party."

"So is this here. This is our party."

Temple understood that Tandey thought the party in the barn was beneath him.

It was Christmas Eve, and the Bodkin's Hundred Hunt Ball was the social event of the season. Christmas gifts were given to inside servants: a coin for each of them and new clothes. New boots, as well, in high polish, for the four liveried boys and for Tandey. Tandey's jacket had been made a size bigger, and his brass buttons no longer strained. Miss Marie—or someone—had added to the filigree of Tandey's uniform. He had epaulets, now, and stitching around his cuffs. They'd also given him a new tie. They did not give Temple shoes or money, but they did give her a new dress.

"You do look wonderful, Tandey," Temple said.

He bowed and thanked her.

"Your job is to be helpful," said Tandey. "I'll be out by the door." This would allow him to receive Christmas gifts from most of the visitors, all of whom knew Tandey, and he smiled at the prospect of the many coins he was about to pocket. "You move about the room, and you see a glass someone put down you take it up. You see a platter looks like it gonna fall off the table, you slide it back. Make sure the food don't look like it's disappearing. Make sure the platters stay full. You stay out the way. Don't bother nobody."

The room grew loud, stuffy, and thick. There was a constant din of laughter, of people in vacuous holiday talk. As Temple moved through the hall, head down, shuffling, she heard snippets of more serious conversations. She heard the name "Abraham Lincoln"—she'd read the debates in the newspaper two years ago. She remembered. Mr. Lincoln had said that self-evident truth, that all men having been created equal: "That is the electric cord in that Declaration that links the hearts of patriotic and liberty-loving men together, that will link those patriotic hearts as long as the love of freedom exists in the minds of men throughout the world." She'd been taken with the phrase, and she and Oliver had discussed the idea of an "electric cord" linking things together.

These memories came at her so hard she was momentarily dizzy, and she scolded herself for drifting back into her invented past. Disappointed with herself, she gathered a platter of sliced meat, which she took to the kitchen to refresh.

An audience had gathered around Marie, who stood next to an urn filled with twigs of holly. Her eyes twinkled in the candlelight.

"My people have been here for a long time, as I think you know," she said, "a Collings was with Spotswood in 1716, a member of the expedition, a Knight of the Golden Horseshoe. We *are* the Old Dominion. We built it. We built it with honor and benevolence and while I find it unfortunate that it appears we will have to defend it, we will. Because a Virginian stands against barbarism."

"It's our way of life," said one of her audience.

"It's more than that," said another. "It's the path to the future."

"We need to sever ourselves from these gray northerners."

"Open up our ports!"

"New Orleans, Galveston, Tampa, the sun shines on this nation, we will build a new Mediterranean!"

With the platter newly filled, Temple walked the perimeter of the room, a quick-moving figure against the bright yellow paint, taking her short steps, dragging the chain that fell between her ankles.

Zeb and Mr. Collings had slipped into the library and stood by the fireplace with small glasses of brandy.

"I hate to talk business, Zeb, at a party," said Mr. Collings, "but I wanted to let you know."

Zeb knocked back his brandy, poured himself another, and lit a cigar.

"We're ready. I've spoken to my friend at the Mercantile, and they've extended a three hundred thousand dollar line to us. It's a big play, but they have every faith that we shall succeed. I have the papers."

He tapped his pockets. Zeb moved to the desk and made a show of reading the contracts, which he did not fully understand. He saw the number, terrifying and exhilarating, and scratched his name across the bottom.

A group of women were talking, and Temple could see that their faces were animated by a cheerful cruelty.

"Well, at least she's gone."

"That woman."

"I'm so glad to have you instead of Rose Knaupf. I'm just so glad you bought Bonscourt."

Temple slowed down, just behind the women.

"Did you hear that she lives in a hotel?"

"In San Francisco?"

"It's just been built. It's called the Asiatic."

"She lives there?"

"Like some sort of . . . I don't even know."

"Like an opera singer!"

The women were overjoyed with this stab, and they threw their heads back in raucous laughter.

Temple felt the stuffy, thick air of the hall choking her. She set the platter down, slipped out of the main room to get a breath, and found herself in the library. She could smell lingering cigar smoke. Someone had been here recently but she was alone.

She opened the small window and let the cool air rush to her face. The party sounds were distant, and the dusk was purple on the other side of the narrow casement.

I'm trapped in a castle, thought Temple. I'm trapped in a castle like a fairy tale. I'm the princess, held by the dragon, waiting for St. George. There's been a spell put upon me, a spell that makes me unsure of whether or not I belong, whether or not I am, truly, the princess.

She knew. She heard them talking about Abraham Lincoln—he'd been elected president—and she knew she'd sat at a table and read his words, and talked with Oliver about what those words had meant. And Rose, too. They'd all sat there and discussed the speeches, the poetry of them, the flair for the theatrical. They had talked as free people. Not, perhaps, as equals, but as student and teacher. She could, for the first time since she'd been locked in the shed, put in her mind precisely who she had been, and how it had felt to be that person.

Temple looked around the library. There were ledgers and books—encyclopedia, collections of military history, Walter Scott. Next to it, a shelf of poems—these must be Collings's. The gentle boy who used to come play piano. She'd seen him, earlier, looking morose and disdainful. Edmund Spenser's *Faerie Queen*—she touched the spine, she thought of Una, and how the wizard had tricked the Redcrosse Knight into believing she wasn't true to him. Una had overcome. Una had gone forward.

I am trapped, but I will move forward.

Moving quickly, she went to the library desk, where there was a pen and paper. She dipped the pen, nervously looking behind her to the door of the library. She'd soon be missed, but there were a couple of glasses on the end table by the fire, she'd pick them up. What should she say? She decided to write in French, that much less likely to be discovered, that much less likely to be believed as coming from her. Rose would believe it, though. Rose would know.

"Ma cherie, ils disent que je suis mort, pourtant je vis. Captive! J'avais asservi!"

She folded the paper and dripped candle wax on the edge to seal it. She wrote "Rose Knaupf, The Asiatic Hotel, San Francisco, California" on the outside, and secreted the letter away inside her dress.

Turning from the desk, she grabbed the two glasses from the end table, swept some cigar ash into them, and walked out into the party. She was different, already. She'd been scuttling along, staying on the edges, but now her eyes were up. She'd go forward. She'd overcome.

The guests were tittering, drunk, their faces flushed, their eyes loose in their heads. From the pantry came a commotion. Someone was bellowing. It was Johnny, surrounded by his cavalry hopefuls, banging pots and tapping their glasses with spoons. One of the glasses broke, and the young man just dropped the stem on the floor and kept on walking.

Johnny was carrying a tray on which there was a great ring of plum pudding. The center of the pudding was a lake of brandy, which Johnny had lit on fire. They were singing, commanding attention:

> Then I wish I was in Dixie, hooray! hooray!
> In Dixie Land I'll take my stand to live and die in Dixie,
> Away, away, away down South in Dixie,
> Away, away, away down South in Dixie.

Johnny found himself in the middle of the room, with a burning platter of plum pudding in his hands, and nowhere to set it. He looked about as they ended their song, wondering where to go, smiled when he noticed a gaggle of young belles, standing by one of the buffet tables with their eyes on him, and reeled in their direction, but as he did so his feet tangled in one another, and he toppled forward. The tray fell before him, and the brandy, invigorated by the rush of air, burst into more violent flames, shooting out across the floor like a sheet of fire. The pudding, upended from the tray, landed with a wet flop at the feet of one of the maidens, who screamed as it splashed upon to her.

Temple watched this all as if it were trapped in molasses, as if each moment of the happening took half an hour. She gasped as Johnny turned to the maidens, and caught her breath when she saw the young woman who was spattered with plum pudding. She knew her—the girl had been at Rose's school.

Temple moved forward, elegantly, efficiently, and coming up to the young woman, said: "I'm very sorry ma'am, please come and I'll help you get cleaned up."

Temple had her in the pantry, alone, in seconds. The girl looked confused—she saw in Temple someone she ought to recognize, but couldn't place. Temple took the letter from the folds of fabric, pressed it into her hands.

"Mail this."

The girl nodded, wide-eyed, and Temple turned to get a cloth to wipe the pudding from her dress.

A call went out that it was time for the cakewalk, and the party rushed forth to the circle in front of the house to watch the enslaved perform their imitations of the promenade for the thirty minutes a year during which they were encouraged to feel superior.

CHAPTER THIRTY

Winter in No Man's Land

Winter settled around Fort Little Stone, and Raleigh bought a buffalo hide from the sutler and thick wool socks. The days were slow, and the girls at the inn would bring out a rich stew at midday and put it on the long table for everyone. They included Red Joe and Raleigh in these meals, which were convivial and joyous, with a big fire in the grate and an open bottle on the table.

To everyone's surprise, Red Joe had befriended the schoolmistress, as well as the doctor, the judge, and a man named Ernie Crab who had drifted into Texas from New Orleans thinking that he might start a newspaper, but found that there wasn't much to report, or many people to report it to, and took a job with the army running the telegraph. Each of them had a few books, and Joe organized a system by which those books could circulate. He'd gone to the sutler shop and bought some fine paper, and in his exquisite, English-school penmanship written little book plates for each of them: Ex Libris Judge Philpott, and so forth. They were charmed. It gave everyone something to talk about and new things to read.

Colonel Hale sent a note to Joe asking to be included. "It has come to my attention that a certain organization has been made here in Fort Little Stone, by which bound volumes might be shared amongst those of us so inclined. I have a few books of interest, and I would be happy to have some more to read."

"Further proof," Hale had said to his wife, "that the prejudices underpinning this nation are misguided. Put a savage through school in England, you get a gentleman."

It was a happy time, for the most part. At night, when Raleigh lay in his small room on the rope bed, under his buffalo hide, he'd hear the horses in the paddock behind the Inn, and he'd think of the Old House and of Snap. He missed Oliver and Temple, and although he knew there was no sense in it he would wish, sometimes fervently, that they weren't dead. Alone, with the winter air stinging his cheeks, he would allow his boyish feelings and let flow his more childish thoughts: perhaps the world was magical, perhaps things could be changed if you thought hard enough on them. He would send those spells back across the map, eastward, hoping to reverse time and revive his sister and Oliver, to make the world as it was a misunderstanding. In sleep he dreamt of them, and of riding those lush fields, and of golden Virginia light caught in the wings of mayflies on the edge of a hayfield.

Folks grew weary of the cold, and although they were not, in any real sense, any more constricted than they had once been, the soldiers chafed. They'd get drunker, and fight more, so Booth kept his shillelagh leaning on the back bar, the top thick as a man's arm, and weighted, it was said, with a pour of lead. The myths about Booth were grand and terrifying, and the soldiers believed them all. Booth had spread them himself so as to be able to more easily keep the peace. He'd told stories about swimming to shore from a sinking whaling vessel, and how he'd killed three men in a bar in New York with a glass and a spoon.

The men to whom he referred had died, but it had been in a fight among themselves. He'd had some excellent rum, and some good sugar, and they'd all three of them arrived in the morning together and sat there wheedling one another until evening. Eventually, they ran outside, knives drawn. Booth appreciated that they'd had the generosity of spirit to vacate his bar before the murdering began, and that they'd made it equitable and managed to all die.

Red Joe was gambling in the side room with the soldiers at the long table, while Raleigh took a break and leaned against the bar to drink a beer and talk to Millie.

Pip Crawford was at his usual spot, on the corner. "Since when you let Indians in here?" Crawford said, loud enough for Joe to hear.

"I run a bar in the middle of No Man's Land, Pip, everyone with money is welcome," said Booth. "You're just sore your men are losing."

"I've no idea if they're losing."

"Anyway, he's English."

Pip Crawford harrumphed.

Joe called out, his voice clear and royal: "It was Indians, you know, who left me on the plains to die. It was savages what attempted to end my young life. I'm not too fond of them myself, Mr. Crawford."

The men around him laughed. He lost a couple of hands on purpose.

On New Year's Eve, Colonel Hale threw a party in the mess hall and invited the civilians. All day the smoky char of a whole steer roasting on a spit wafted through the fort, making everyone cheerfully hungry. When they rang the bell, townsfolk, children, and soldiers poured into the hall, where the cooks passed out slices of charred beef drizzled with chili sauce, wrapped in tortillas and halves of fire-roasted sweet potatoes, drizzled with molasses. The quartermaster poured cups of pale whiskey.

The officers and the enlisted men mingled, and no one talked about the cold or what looked more and more like a war back East. Folks were still laughing when Red Joe and Raleigh walked back to the Inn in a light snow, passing a flask.

"That Pip Crawford is a dangerous man," said Red.

"I don't know," Raleigh said.

"You've led a life insulated from harm, my friend, and you don't know a snake when he rattles."

Raleigh shrugged.

"I believe he's a truly dangerous man," said Red Joe.

"To us?"

Red Joe didn't answer, just blew a cloud of smoke around his head and passed the flask back to Raleigh.

CHAPTER THIRTY-ONE

Rose and Fitz Have Tea

Fitz had waited in the lobby of the Asiatic hotel for only a few minutes, but those minutes had been full, and his thoughts had ranged widely. He was slightly, only slightly, under the influence of morphine, and the world seemed to turn and ripple at the edges, as if it were printed on a scrim and floating in front of him. He saw himself in this lobby as if from afar. Was it, in theme, Abyssinian? Oriental? Theatrical? He watched the ficus leaves ripple and chuckled at a group of happily smug visitors while he sank into cushions that felt so soft he wondered how they were made or what of. They must be horsehair, and with that, he dreamt of the horse and its tail, thudding across a green pasture in the evening. What must the wind feel like to a horse, he wondered, freedom? Escape? Pure pleasure?

A uniformed youth leaned in, indicating that Mrs. Knaupf would receive him. Fitz rose and followed. He needed to get back to New York, to his bride Rosalie. Bierstadt would be there soon, and the mere thought of the two of them unchaperoned was enervating. He trusted Bierstadt, sort of, but he knew Rosalie. And yet here he was, on a ridiculous errand, following the bobbing head of the hotel servant while his young bride entangled all of New York in her long curls. It's not as if he were going to leave tonight, he reminded himself. This wasn't a delay, it only felt like one. The young servant of the hotel had a golden braid, which wrapped around the top of his red hat. A flat circle, under which the boy stands ready. Under which he leads forth. All day, he stands under the red disc, ringed in gold like a halo.

The servant knocked on a door, bowed, and vanished.

Rose Knaupf opened the door with a smile and looked over his shoulder.

Fitz bowed slightly, and said, "I regret, Mrs. Knaupf, that Mr. Bierstadt is already on his way back East, and couldn't join us."

The young man was slim and his eyes were pale. His beard grew out from his chin with a divot in the middle, as if it were parted in two, and Rose wondered if something had happened to him to cause this bifurcation or if he twisted it while he sat. (The latter.)

She brought him into the sitting room, offered him wine, and made him a plate of meat. She forked the slices herself, and asked him which sauce he would like.

"Mustard," he said, "unless you have a favorite. Whichever one you like."

They sat in wing chairs next to one another by a low table upon which they rested their delicate plates. The wines were there, in front of them. Rose poured and ate a nut.

"Mr. Hart speaks highly of you, Mrs. Knaupf."

She nodded. She felt, momentarily, a flushed awkwardness she had not felt in years. Not only did Mr. Ludlow not know why he was here or what she wanted, he didn't know what to do or say. She smiled at him and felt stir inside her the young woman who once smiled at the country boys. She had felt, then, the power to bewitch. She had learned, since, that half of that power might be hers, but the driving force behind it was the unrelenting desire felt by the young men. Mr. Ludlow smiled back and took a sip of wine, praising it with a small nod. Rose did not seem to have sparked anything within him, and she wondered if he were entirely etiolated, or if she had grown old and invisible.

"I saw a piece of yours, Mr. Ludlow, and I think it may be of great importance to me."

Fitz settled in, happy and receptive. Nothing was so pleasant as praise, to be read and appreciated was all he wanted. As she unwound the tale of Temple and Raleigh, her tragic neighbor Oliver Bodkin, he was at first surprised, then momentarily lost, and finally embarrassed. Never for a moment had it crossed his mind that the Creole piano player would be anyone other than who he said he was. Fitz grew angry with Red Joe and Raleigh, then annoyed with himself. By the time Rose had unwound the story of the brother and sister raised by the scion of one of Virginia's foremost families and thought to have died in a fire after she'd left, he was truly angry.

"And then here he is, brought back to life in your story in the pages of the *Golden Era*."

"The man I met said he came from Vienna," said Fitz.

"And did that seem likely, Mr. Ludlow? That he was a baby found among the rushes? Raised by a queen? Wandering in the desert?"

"It wasn't really the desert, Mrs. Knaupf, just, really, right by—" Fitz couldn't remember the name of the place.

"Metaphorically, then."

He shrugged and took a sip of wine.

"Rather a tall tale, isn't it?" Rose asked. She let it sink in.

Fitz lashed out.

"You cared about these people? Temple and Raleigh?"

Rose had just eaten a piece of toast on which she had carefully arrayed a smear of butter, a slice of pickle, and a sliver of ham. She nodded and chewed.

"But you left them? There? In a slave state?"

Rose, still chewing, nodded again.

"My father was a ticket agent on the Underground Railroad in New York, he helped those who escaped find their way to the stations, to the railroad. He was dedicated to freedom, to abolition. We are about to launch this nation into war—I don't doubt it for a second, Mrs. Knaupf, it is the sacrifice of wealth, and your Southerners will not sacrifice it easily.

They don't feel they owe the black man Freedom. I went to school with them, I preached to them as an apostle would. They will defend themselves, their traditions, their corrupt and vile way of life."

Fitz settled himself against the arm of his chair, set his glass down, and rose unhurriedly back up until he sat straight. He spoke slowly: "Why, then, if they were important people to you, if you knew them and loved them as you say you did, did you not arrange for their passage to safety and liberation?"

"Well, that's no simple thing."

"The simplicity of such a task is beside the point. It is no small task to rescue a child from a well, and yet one would not be discouraged in the pursuit of a rescue."

Now they sat in awkward silence. For Rose had never imagined that Fitz Ludlow would grow angry.

"You're making me feel terrible," Rose said, with the understanding that making her feel terrible was a truly offensive act. Something that simply wasn't done.

"No," said Fitz.

Rose was aghast.

"No," he said, "you have made yourself feel terrible. I am simply pointing it out."

Rose struggled and fell back on the manners instilled in her. She poured more wine and offered Fitz some sugared almonds. It was almost impossible to be in a room alone with such a man, she thought. At least, if this had been a party, she could have engaged the attentions of someone else, or come up with a reason to drift away. They spent an awkward ten minutes or so, before Fitz suggested that he had taken too much of her afternoon, and began motions toward leaving.

At the door he stopped, hand resting on the brass knob, and turned back to Rose. He dropped the photograph Bierstadt had taken on the small table by the door. "You know," he said, "it's not too late to set it right. Find this young man."

A few days later Rose received the letter Temple had pushed upon her old schoolmate at the Christmas party.

Rose sat at her leather-topped table at the window, listening to the barking dogs while ice melted around a small, elegant decanter of Martinez cocktails. The drinks had brought a flush to her neck and made her feel rather more expansive and jovial than was proper for the task at hand. She tapped the end of the pen against her eyetooth distractedly.

"Well," she said aloud, "it is good news."

Dear Raleigh,

I'm sure this time has been difficult for you, and above all I hope this finds you well. I wish I could somehow say everything at once, for there is much to say, and I'm anxious to give you the information I have.

Of course I heard news of Oliver Bodkin's death, and I was told that you and Temple had died in the fire, as well. I was also told that the fire was started by you. I've never been able to bring myself to believe that, although without any evidence to the contrary, I put it down to as something confounding. Life is, after all, full of confounding events.

That all changed when I saw a picture in the Golden Era*—if the Pinkerton has done his job you'll have that newspaper as well as this letter. There was no doubt in my mind, not even for an instant, that the performer standing in the middle of the picture, looking proudly at the camera as if it were his wedding day, was you, Raleigh Bodkin. I summoned the writer and pressed him for details. Odd man. Rather distracted. Perhaps abstracted is the better word. You met him, Fitz. He praised you highly, exclaimed you were a first-rate piano player (which we knew) and that he'd had a wonderful time with you.*

So you were very much on my mind when I received a letter, written in tremulous hand, "Ma cherie," it read "ils disent que je suis mort, pourtant je vis. Captive! J'avais asservi!"

It was badly addressed, just the city, the name of the hotel, and my name—if it weren't for the fame of the hotel, I'd never have received it.

It's from Temple. A second note came a few days later from one of the girls at the school, saying she'd put it in the mail to me because a house girl at the Hundred gave it to her. She thought about it for days, she said, feeling as if she'd seen a ghost of someone she used to know. Of course it was Temple, I can tell.

She's alive.

It says she's captive. "I have been enslaved!" (How good is your French, Raleigh? I can't remember.) But more importantly, that she's alive.

There's a war coming, Raleigh. We should get her away from there, away from Virginia. Go to her. Bring her to me in California. I'll pay to get you both here. Send me word via the detective. Good luck!

She sat with another cocktail for twenty minutes wondering what the proper salutation would be, settled on "Godspeed," and rocked back in her chair with a dramatic flourish, wondering if she should go to dinner or ring to have something brought to her room. She was satisfied. This was as good as solved. She'd set it in motion. She rang the bell to summon a servant, and walked to her dressing mirror to powder her nose in anticipation of his arrival.

CHAPTER THIRTY-TWO

Crawford's Time

March 1861

Lieutenant Pip Crawford hated Texas. He hated the windswept plains, the canyons, the steers, the dust, the Mexicans, the beans, tortillas, Fort Little Stone, the pale shallows of Little Stone River, the scrub brush, the sage, the occasional tumbleweed, the pioneers who tottered along in their wrecked wagons blindly stumbling toward whatever weak betterment their feeble imaginations evoked, the dusty rocks and thirsty cattle, the Spanish churches, the post oaks, the canyons, the false heroism embedded in the mythos of self-reliance, the lie of exceptionalism, the horse culture, the heat, the pines, Catholicism, the Jews of Galveston, and the Comanche.

He had found some value in black folk. As he had drifted west, turned out from one town after another—here a small fraud, there an upset mother—he had drifted away from respectable employ and toward the more direct methods of personal enrichment. He rustled cattle first, but became frustrated with the scale of the operation and turned to luring the enslaved into traps, promising freedom with the help of a free black that he'd hire, then returning the slave and collecting the reward.

The looks on their faces! Oh, that moment of delicious revelation when it occurs to them that they are being taken back the way they came, that they are captured, that their escape had failed. Foiled by the man who emboldened it. Pip loved to ask them questions about their masters, whether they were kind masters, what the master might have in store for an escaped slave.

The free blacks he used as bait, those who weren't the worst kind, resisted the deal as soon as they came to fully understand that the freedom they'd been told to offer was never going to arrive. Pip sold the freemen on the spot at a discounted rate, saying he didn't know who they were, where they belonged, but the master was welcome to them. Those he did not sell he'd left gutted and sunk to the bottom of a river after they'd asked for their pay.

The devil has sway over this place, he thought.

The devil makes folks believe they are owed that which they are not owed. Makes these freemen forget their place. Grows a will to thievery in the breast of the lower races, thievery and resentment, against which Pip felt he must defend himself. For if he let it flourish, if the corrupt impulses were unchecked, would not they turn on him?

Pip thought of himself as the rod which spared would ruin the child, and applied himself to the thrashing with a sadist's zeal.

The farther west he traveled, the more he believed that the country was in need of a higher class of men and women. In many a barroom he'd have been heard to say that all the pestilence, the problems, the death that was hiding in every shadow was on account of the savages and the Negroes which held this place in their clutches, with the devil behind them, calling the shots.

His own project was bathed in the light of purity and justice and honor. His role, as he saw it, was not that of thief. He was, rather, a messenger. The slaveholders needed to understand how fragile was their hold over the devilish charges they thought they owned in pacific mutual beneficence. The arrogance of white men astounded him. These comfortable men, raised in the captivity of luxury, a prison of comfort, insulated from repercussions and reality, with no real sense of the chaos that began at their hedgerow, just beyond the gate, where the savages competed for basic resources. These fools—the colonel, for instance, Colonel Hale, with his absurd ideas of order and propriety. One cannot bring order to hell.

Colonel Hale was so easily fooled that he was taken in by Comanche who knew how to dress for dinner, as Crawford had seen. He'd seen the Indians ride in off the plains, four, five, twelve at a time, and show up with hats on, a cravat wrapped around their throat, a throat the thirst of which was slaked with what? Blood? And Hale bowing to them, sniveling at them, opening the storeroom and feeding them on jams and cake. Here, have of my wine. Here, have of my stores. No sense of the contagion, the common rot of their various ingrained misdeeds.

You lie with dogs, Colonel, hence your fleas.

Here was the colonel before him now.

Crawford called upon the carpet, to stand before the desk. Crawford was sure the colonel thought himself better than anyone at the Fort. The colonel, snuggled with his woman in a nice big house with a big desk thrown down to block our passage to the softer, domestic corners. Crawford was accustomed to being dressed down, discovered, asked to move on. There were men who called him out. He had heard fools so bent in their misunderstanding of this world that they had called him corrupt. He did not let such insults linger, for he was quick with his fists. He wondered which of the sniveling who had felt his fury had crawled to his betters to complain. He would revisit his anger upon them, once their identity was revealed. He looked forward to it.

When Colonel Hale spoke, however, what he spoke of was not a reprimand. Far from it. The fort was being closed. They had to leave someone in charge, and that someone was Pip Crawford.

"I'm honored, sir," said Crawford.

The colonel's desk was a riot of papers. Behind the desk, Hale, seated, and behind Hale, a tall safe. Past that, a chest, open, papers and records neatly stacked inside.

"I suspect," said Colonel Hale, "that leaving you in charge of this fort will not end well. I do not, for a second, want you to misunderstand my relinquishing of command as an act of faith.

"I am following orders. Officers are needed, and we are to leave only one here, the lowest-ranking officer present, to assume command. That's you. I don't think there is any matter at hand that will cause you to rise to an occasion of any sort. Please do not attempt to leverage this into more than it is, or to find in this an opportunity for heroism."

Pip Crawford stood straight, looked at the wall, and nodded. He wished he hadn't.

"I will leave to you these keys," Hale gestured at a ring on the desk, "and I shall leave you this map of the immediate surroundings, and this inventory ledger. Please continue to monitor the stores. Arrangements will be made to transport the cannon and so forth, once we figure out where they are needed. I am also making arrangements for some of my personal items—this desk, for instance—to be shipped back to New York. There are a few plates and so forth, there, on the pantry shelves. Eat what you like, too. I will be sending for my wine and so forth, in the cellar. Leave it alone. You'll have a dozen men—including the cook and quartermaster."

"Yes, sir," said Crawford.

"Hold fast, as they say on the ships. The best strategy here for you is to have none."

Crawford knew that these West Pointers held the cadets of Virginia in disdain.

Pip Crawford wasn't a cadet, and hadn't gone to the Military Academy in Lexington, but he had lied and said that he had so as to join the army as an officer. He was frightened by this lie, told impetuously first to an officer in a barroom, and then again at an ad hoc enlistment office, standing next to the officer, but he soon realized that what few graduates of that institution were in Texas were far too decorous to challenge him, even if they suspected him. To tell a Southerner he's lying is to stand before him with pistols in short order. Or perhaps they were too genteel to contradict him. He wondered if they talked among themselves. They must. Over the course of his service, he'd so internalized the lie that he now took offense at slights he imagined were aimed at his pedigree.

"I suppose it will be convenient for you to be here," said Hale.

"Why's that, sir?"

"I'd think all the Virginia men would drift back to Mr. Jackson, won't they? Won't you? It's the honorable thing," said Hale.

Is he baiting me?

"Whole thing will be over soon enough. I can't imagine we've got a war ahead of us."

CHAPTER THIRTY-THREE

A Letter

March 1861

The telegram from the office of the Pinkerton Agency in San Francisco explained that the client, Rose Knaupf, wanted to find a black man thought to be in the territories, that they'd narrowed it down, and that Liston "Lee" Bostick was the Pinkerton agent closest to where they thought the man might be, so Bostick saddled up. He loved lonely rides across the big country, with a gun on his hip and hardly any accountability, and he enjoyed the search, which progressed well with what information they'd given him. He was hot on the fellow's trail—a swath of dancehall girls and librarians who remembered either a rollicking, sweaty young man who stayed up all night or some sort of European colored Paganini of the piano. Bostick had not immediately realized that this was one and the same man, until he heard the story enough times—the wagon, the stage, the piano, the "Red Englishman" who came to town, and the colored woman who sang like an angel. He had them, he was in their wake, and then . . . poof. The traveling Gypsy stage run by a fat little Jew had kept going on past where the road ended, ridden off into the scrub, and somehow dissolved. He'd found word of some of them headed south, but not the Indian, and not the piano player, so he worked his way along a curve headed northward, looking for the trail to light up again, but suspecting it wouldn't. Bostick did not look forward to reporting back what he increasingly felt must be the reality of the situation, which was that someone who was desired here among the living was no more. He liked a chase, he liked a point to it, he liked knowing progress was being made. It's one thing to be on a hot trail, but another to ride along in this forsaken bleakness with the increasing suspicion that Mrs. Knaupf was hurling good money after bad. It offended his natural economy. ("My natural economy" was one of his favorite phrases.) They were gone, probably dead, but he had been encouraged by the agency to continue until he ran the Negro to ground, and he was a Pinkerton, after all. He'd see it through.

He came to Fort Little Stone deflated, found it much engaged in leaving, and made his way to introduce himself to the commanding officer, as per his orders and despite the fact that this was far from the most effective way to infiltrate a given situation. What could you do?

Military men respond to the concept of organization, thought Bostick, which is why it is important to show them your badge. It reassures them. As soon as he had his hands out of his gloves he pulled the Pinkerton insignia from his watch pocket, made a slight nod, and introduced himself to Colonel Hale.

"Thank you for seeing me, Colonel, I'm sorry if I've interrupted."

"You must be tired," said Hale. "It's a hard road this time of year."

Bostick nodded.

"We're moving back, we're packing up." Hale motioned around the room. "It is a time of great upheaval, as I'm sure you know. I'm sure I don't have to tell you."

"Well, then."

There was a pause, as Hale struggled to hurry the conversation along. What did Bostick want? Hale distrusted the idea of private law enforcement, if it was the law Pinkertons enforced. Like a mercenary army, a police force for hire, he suspected that what they enforced were whims, the whims of whomever paid them. If they took an oath at all, he was sure it was not to a higher duty, or to support the public peace. Did they swear themselves to themselves? Like Catholics, he thought, their fealty lay elsewhere.

The disarray around the room—the boxes stacked with papers and ledger sheets, the books down from the shelves, was not ideal. He liked a good, straightened room. He needed order in the world that reflected the order in his mind, and he needed that order—of mind and world both—impressed upon those who would entreat. He'd dragged his six-foot, claw-footed, leather-topped mahogany desk out to this . . . wasteland . . . for that very reason. So that those who might approach him would have to sit across it. And here it was, covered in papers, stacked with books.

The dining room, he thought, was still in order, and there was a fire. It was farther into the house than he typically brought his business—the desk was a barrier, too, between the domestic and the military—but the table there could stand in. A naive Mexican design with no subtlety or elegance to it at all, but it was a polished expanse of wood.

"There's a nice fire in the dining room, Mr. Bostick, come, I'll pour you a drink and warm you up. Let me hang your coat. Something of interest, here," said Hale, as they entered the dining room. "You see these rocks? They built these fireplaces from rocks quarried nearby. I was fascinated to note the petroglyphs, see them here?"

He pointed to a scratched in picture of a dozen longhorn sheep standing bunched together around a man.

"What a celebration it must have been to domesticate animals! Incredible to think about, that these men lived here, and hunted and gathered, and then they figured out how to steward. They brought the animals to them, cared for them, managed them. We have no proof, of course, but this, it only makes sense that this is an announcement of that accomplishment. Can you imagine? Knowing that for the first time in history the survival of your clan would not be dependent upon luck?"

In the fireplace, a few logs of post oak were ablaze. We're not rationing anything anymore, he'd told his wife, no need. Might as well use it all up, and he felt the same about the cellar.

"A glass of whiskey, Mr. Bostick? Wine? Better to empty it here than to have it break on the way back to New York."

"Whiskey, then. New York?"

"Tarrytown. You know it?"

"I've a brother in Yonkers."

"Not far at all."

Bostick had never visited his brother.

"It's all luck, though, innit?" Bostick asked.

"There is that."

The two men settled into Windsor chairs on either side of the table, Hale with his back to the fire, which was hot enough to make him shift to the side. He poured out whiskeys. The Pinkerton was a broad, thick-handed man. He looked like a brawler. Hale wouldn't want him in the infantry, but he'd be a fantastic addition to a guard squad, or a quartermaster. Anywhere physical authority was needed. Hale was momentarily distracted thinking about how little he liked the flimsy—that's how he thought of him, flimsy—man that was the quartermaster at Fort Little Stone. Jimmy Thorne—weak-minded, blubbery, drunk. We should do better than that. Would he be able to close out the stores? Would he be able to manage the disbursal? Resist the occupation, if it came to that? How long until the United States property could safely be moved? How long until we get wagons down here with men?

"I'm looking for a man," said Bostick.

"I'm glad to help." He wasn't. He didn't like intrusions, he didn't like his men having to answer to outside authority.

"I've had word from our office in San Francisco. There's a client there who would like to find a Negro."

Hale made a sour face.

"Not like that, Colonel. I'm a Pinkerton, not a slave catcher. He's a freeman. Goes by the name of Raleigh."

"And what's this fellow done wrong?" Hale would not budge. Don't come blasting into my camp, he thought, with your meaningless badge and your beaverskin hat and start asking me about the people who live here. My people. No, we circle our wagons.

Bostick laughed.

"Wrong? He ain't done wrong. You mind?" He gestured to the bottle. So coddled, these officers. Ain't Tarrytown near West Point, wondered Bostick. "You go to the academy up there? West Point?"

"I did."

"Well, then."

"What's this man done?"

"Oh, that. He ain't done nothing. He's got a sister, and he thinks that sister is dead, but as far as I can tell the story goes that she ain't and for some reason my client, our client, in San Francisco is keen that he receives this information. I've got a letter with me," he patted his pocket "what tells the story, but I don't read letters that ain't addressed to me, and now you know what I know. Came in a telegraph from San Francisco." He reached into his vest and pulled out a telegram, flicked it but didn't read from it, just held it, as evidence.

"Client requests the location of a free Negro by name of Raleigh, a piano player in a traveling show, gave the last known location. Mail train—why they didn't just send a letter I don't know, send a telegram to tell me to wait for a letter—came with an article from the *Golden Era*—that's a newspaper in San Francisco—and a photograph. And a letter from the client to this Raleigh. You want to see the newspaper? That I will show you. There's only what? Two hundred people in these parts? Is one of 'em a colored what plays piano or no?" Bostick leaned his elbows hard on the table and raised his eyebrows, with all the airs of a man giving you your last chance to comply. He had a feeling the trail had just gotten hot again.

Hale did not like this broad-shouldered thug at all.

"Were you in the military, Mr. Bostick?"

"No, sir."

"In the military, there are certain unshirkable duties, requirements that cannot be avoided, responsibilities."

Bostick stared at the man, counting along with the words without meaning as if they were music, one two three, two two three—he'd sung in the church choir, as a boy, and it soothed him to think of music, calmed him down. He was going to punch the colonel if this went on for much longer, and he thought to himself it would be a simpler world if that could be avoided or if he could somehow talk himself into just, perhaps, slapping the top of this ridiculous stretch of table at which they sat while the colonel continued to speak. He was saying:

"And my responsibilities include the governing of this town. As the commanding officer of the fort, I am the de facto mayor. The judge has some—"

Bostick rapped the tabletop, just lightly. "The judge wouldn't by any chance be a colored fellow who plays the piano?"

"The judge has influence and we operate in congress together to steer the various civic decisions. Just last year—perhaps it was two years ago, no, it was just last year—we had to decide whether or not a road should be constructed between the blacksmith shop and the carpenter's. The blacksmith is army, you see, and the carpenter shop is not. But the traffic between the two had caused a rut, and we weren't sure who should be responsible for the grading, the hauling. Should we sink planks in? We have a good quarry," he gestured to the fireplace, "lots of rock around these parts."

"Colonel."

"These citizens are my responsibility."

"Colonel, please."

"And I'll need a file with your name, your badge number, the office of your superior."

"You're kidding me."

"Just, if you could write those there, perhaps. We don't have a form for visiting law enforcement, but if you could just, you know, scribble the pertinent information there."

"Scribble?"

"Just as long as it's legible."

Bostick envisioned, momentarily, the geyser of blood that would erupt from the colonel's neck if he were to simply rip his head off of his shoulders. The thought of it made him chuckle, and the chuckle combined with the imagined murder calmed him down. He gathered up the pen and the piece of paper.

"Very well," said Hale. "I believe the man you're looking for is here."

"I was thinking that might be the case."

"He plays piano at the inn, and he lives there."

After the Pinkerton left, Colonel Hale addressed the paper. It read: "My name doesn't matter, I am a member of the Pinkertons. We never sleep. Mr. Lincoln owes his life to the actions of my leader. Watch yourself."

The Pinkerton walked through the parade grounds with his big coat pulled around him and his boots stomping in the icy snow. Through the windows he saw soldiers and heard them moving, packing, and yelling out to one another. By the smells from the kitchens he judged it must be getting on to supper. The whiskey felt good in his belly, but he was angry, and he needed to shake that off before he got to the inn. He stopped, pulled a thin cigar from a pouch in his coat, and having lit it, stood, puffing and concentrating on the satisfaction of the smoke while he looked around the barren ice field that was the center of the fort. God these miserable foolish cunts, he thought. I found him, though, and that is what we came for, innit? Gotcha. He filled himself with smoke, blew it into a cloud, imagined himself warmed by that cloud, and walked on.

With the cigar between his teeth, he entered the inn and rubbed his hands together while he surveyed the polished wood, the warm stove in the barroom, the blazing hearth in the side dining room, the clean sturdy tables. Surprisingly nice place, he thought. People had held high hopes for what was going to happen in Fort Little Stone. Too bad for them. As he moved toward the long bar, he could smell gravy, garlic. Mushrooms. Someone must've dried mushrooms? Birds roasting?

He saw his man—he suspected it was he—leaning against the end of the bar and making eyes at the Creole woman who was smiling back, but clearly not reciprocating fully. The balance of love there tilted toward the fellow, as it often does, and as has led to many a sad song. Somehow he'd expected a more substantial person. Raleigh was frail. I've been darker than that boy after a week on the trail. That little chin looks like it'd break into bits once struck. He laughed. Figured he might as well get some food. He removed his hat, put it upside down on a stool next to the one he intended to occupy, then slowly removed his gloves and dropped them into the hat. He turned, smiled to the Creole and asked: "Is that birds I smell cooking, Miss?"

"Just out riding the plains?" she said.

"It's cold, truly. And I'm hungry."

"It is birds. We have gravy, and potatoes. Not much by way of menu, pickings are slim this time of year. I'm sorry."

"No apologies," said Bostick, he put a hand up, he wouldn't hear of it, wouldn't dream of having her apologize. "I'll take some beer—there's beer?"

"We've beer from the Germans, down in Texas."

"I'll take some beer. Maybe a pour of whiskey. And a half a bird, with your gravy and potatoes. That'd do nicely."

Millie nodded.

"And I'll take a word with Raleigh there."

She froze. So did Raleigh. Well, then, that was that. He was right. She didn't correct him. "Nothing to it," he said. "No bad news here. I'm about to make your day."

Raleigh was standing straight as an arrow, terrified. They'd come for him. Someone had claimed that he'd killed Oliver, and here they were. Raleigh looked to Booth, who was already hustling down with his shillelagh. Raleigh's eyes were wide. Booth was focused.

"I believe I heard Millie ask you a question," said Booth.

"Whether I was riding the plains?"

"I'd like an answer," said Booth.

Bostick drew from his cigar, assessed.

Booth spoke slowly: "Who are you?"

Bostick turned to Raleigh.

"Well, then. You've got a lot of people intent on protecting you from good news around here, which makes me wonder what sort of bad news you deserve to get. I wonder, sure, but it's no business of mine. I'm Liston Bostick, go by Lee," he held out a hand to shake, "and I'm a Pinkerton. I've a message for you from Rose Knaupf. Sit a spell," he tapped the stool next to his "they're bringing me some food. Can I get you anything? My expenses are covered."

Booth poured Raleigh a whiskey. "On the house, Raleigh, you know that. This goes wrong, I'm right here."

Bostick drank his whiskey and settled himself, brushing some imaginary dust from the arms of his jacket. He blew a cloud of smoke, giving Raleigh time to absorb the first bit of information.

Raleigh left his drink untouched.

"From Rose? How would she? You have come from Rose?"

"She hired us, knowing we are nationwide. She had narrowed it down, a bit, but she needed some coverage. She saw you in the newspaper—did you know you were in the newspaper? I have it for you here." He tapped his jacket pocket. "She saw your picture, and she had me track you down to tell you that your sister is alive."

"No. She died. It was a fire."

"The message I was given stated that Mrs. Knaupf understood you to think that your sister had died, but recent information has come to light that she did not. I have a letter here for you from Mrs. Knaupf, as well as the newspaper. I'm to bring back word from you as to what you intend to do."

He slid the newspaper and a letter toward Raleigh, and took a sip of beer. This Raleigh character was young. You could see it in his cheeks, his hands. A man gets battered about, as the time goes, especially a black man, and this man ain't been battered much.

The chicken arrived, and Bostick nodded to Millie, who gave him a knife and a fork and a square linen cloth. She motioned to his glasses and he nodded to both of them while drifting the napkin to his lap like a leaf falling from a tree. He loved the unspoken communication between a patron and a tavern keeper, the smoothness with which one's will could be made felt, and the competence with which it was fulfilled. He knifed a piece of the roasted bird onto his fork and fell into a pleasant contemplation of barkeeps past in an effort to discern which sex was more suited to the job.

Raleigh's hand shook as he took up the newspaper and saw the photograph that Bierstadt had taken. He turned to the letter, and slid his thumb under the wax which sealed it. Unfolding it, he felt the world around him disappear.

That all changed when I saw a picture in the Golden Era*—if the Pinkerton has done his job you'll have that newspaper as well as this letter.*

He looked at the man at the bar, who was pulling a lump of mashed potatoes through a pool of gravy. Bostick looked up from his food, still chewing, and smiled at Raleigh.

He swallowed and said: "Well, then."

This isn't true, Raleigh thought. It isn't possible. Perhaps it isn't even happening.

Raleigh read on through the strange words, so difficult to digest that he read some of them three, four, five times or more. Enslaved! Was Rose saying that the house girl at the Hundred *was* Temple? Even the consideration of these names was dizzying. Everything he had left behind, come back at once. Everything he understood, dismissed. Half of that which he had grieved, restored.

"Why would Rose write this to me?" Raleigh asked.

"I think she'd like you to know. She makes it clear, innit? Clear there, innit?"

"Why would you make these claims?"

"Me?"

"What is . . ." Raleigh faltered. He was furious.

"Shaken up, that's understandable," said Bostick.

Raleigh took a breath and said: "How do we know?"

Bostick looked up from his meal, eyebrows raised. "How do we know that she's found your sister?"

Raleigh nodded.

"Well, then," and he set aside his fork, wiped the gravy from his whiskers and took a sip of whiskey. "We interviewed Mrs. Knaupf, to find out what she suspected she knew. She believes that the woman who wrote the letter is your sister. We had an opportunity to send a man around—not to the place itself, mind you, it seems clear that such an action would put a great many people at risk—but we arranged for the girl who sent the second letter to Rose to have an interview with a Pinkerton in Richmond, and it seems that she knew Temple—that's your sister, Temple?—knew her when they were in school. She is sure that the house girl at the place called the Hundred was one and the same."

In the mirror behind the bar Raleigh could see the fire burning in the second room, past the long empty table. He watched the flames flicker and cast firelight, watched the dance between the fire in the hearth and the flames on the candles in front of it. They moved together, and he thought of the air and the wind, the draft in the room, the way the candles ducked to the side if the wind blew hard against the front of the building and the way the fire seemed to pulse and shift and pull at the candles. Bostick had neatly sliced off the leg of the chicken at the joint and was chewing through the meat with evident satisfaction. The world seemed impossible. How could Bostick still chew?

"She's sure of it?"

Bostick assured him she was.

Raleigh felt everything inside him clunk and rattle and then start again. Like a locomotive pulling from a station, his mind began to rebuild itself, almost from nothing, for every principle upon which he'd operated was obliterated and replaced. Was Oliver alive then, too? No. None of this could have happened if Oliver were alive. But his sister was. He looked at his hands on the bar, considered the knuckle of his pointer finger, each puckered ridge where the skin bunched over the joint held flat against the wood, two parenthetical ridges around the whole, and then two main creases over the knuckle, one behind the joint, and one right on top. The creases echoed down his finger like ripples in water. He wondered if he should drink some of the whiskey in front of him, thought perhaps he should, but couldn't make his hand move to pick it up and bring it to his lips. Even the thought of it exhausted him. The air was like thick mud. His blood was in his feet. He felt every slow breath he took, and thought that if he focused on it he could see the place where his mind was telling his lungs to take in air. He could stop it, he thought. He could cut that connection. He tried for a moment to see if he could stop himself from breathing. He couldn't, he could only stand and look.

"It takes a second," said Bostick. He could see in the young man that he was shocked, almost broken. "News like this isn't easy, it takes digesting. You should sleep on it. Think about it. You'll be happy, promise. And we can talk in the morning. You can tell me what you want to say to Rose. This is good, it's good."

CHAPTER THIRTY-FOUR

A New Plan

March 1861

Abbott, overwhelmed by the work of running a herd of sheep, had neglected necessary repairs for months. Jed fell naturally back into the rhythm of tending to a farm. He repaired a hole in the chicken coop, fixed the fence boards in the paddock, and rebuilt the slats in the picket fence around the garden.

Percy took down the front door, planed it, repainted it, and rehung it so it would swing freely and close cleanly. He found a three-legged stool that had snapped and was leaning against the wall of the run-in shed, dismantled it, and sanded each surface. He found an old ax handle and cut a replacement for the broken leg, whittled the tenon down to fit the mortise, and tapped a wedge in to hold it.

"I don't think that's level," said Jed, observing the angle of the seat.

"It's strong." Percy gave the stool a shake to demonstrate. "It'll pitch you forward a little and keep you attentive."

Percy painted the stool barn red and took to sitting on it while they ate. One afternoon, after their midday meal but before they broke off into whatever needed to be done before evening, Abbott said that he'd go in to the fort, to the general store, and pick up some supplies.

"I need to talk to Thorne—the quartermaster there—and see if they're buying any mutton. Usually good for a few. I'll send a letter to my wool man."

Crying John wanted to go along, but the shepherd dissuaded him.

"There aren't strangers about in these parts. New soldiers, sure, but people are either passing through in a wagon, headed West, or they live here. I don't see as how you all would be served by advertising your presence." He looked around the table, his eyes resting on both men, grinning. "Don't worry about me," he said. "Jed and I have known one another for a spell, and I ain't told nobody about him being out here yet, have I?"

"Course not," said Jed.

"We should give you some money for the supplies," said Percy.

Abbott nodded.

The shepherd took some money from John, got on the mule, and rode into Fort Little Stone, where he bought flour, sugar, tins of peaches, jugs of cider, bottles of whiskey, and a box of candles. He bought matches, lead, and powder. The storekeeper gave him a remnant of tough cloth for patching trousers, and then teased about the condition of his hat.

"It is a sorry thing. In bad shape," Abbott said, pulling it off his head and considering it. "But she is mine, and I love her as if I made her."

"I think the credit for the construction of that hat in its present state is all yours, Abbott, dubious as it is."

Abbott took a little bow.

At the end of the row of barracks, on the porch of the colonel's house, Abbott saw the quartermaster, Thorne, sitting on a crate and spitting tobacco juice into the dirt. How Thorne had ever managed to convince anyone he should be put in charge of managing the supplies, Abbott couldn't imagine, but then again, these wide open spaces work on a man. Maybe he'd been different when he got here, though it was hard to imagine Thorne as anything but the bleary, disheveled troll perched atop a crate.

"Hardly workin'," said Abbott, upon approaching, "and no better acquainted with the barber."

"Ain't you one to talk."

"Might have some big ewes gone too long in the tooth here before too long, happy to bring them in for you."

Thorne shook his head. "Ain't nobody here."

"I took notice there ain't many soldiers—they on a maneuver? Running a drill up in the mountains?"

He and the quartermaster liked, generally speaking, to poke fun at the training and drilling that the soldiers engaged in, as if the Indians they were here to defend against were British soldiers.

"They ain't out, Abbott, they gone. They taking 'em back east, to the war."

"All of them?"

"Just 'bout."

The crate was a munition box, Abbott noted, locked and new, and there were another four stacked against the wall of the house behind Thorne.

Abbott wanted to continue, wanted to ask who would be here to keep the Comanche at bay, who would buy the mutton, and who would secure the trading post so he could sell his wool, but he knew that Thorne was not the man to ask.

"I'll ask the colonel for a moment of his time, I think," said Abbott.

"Hale is gone with 'em. Crawford is running the place."

"Crawford?"

Thorne nodded and spat.

"He inside?" Abbott asked, nodding to the house and stepping toward the door. He peered in through the sidelight. In the front room, which had functioned as Hale's office, he saw Hale's desk in a state of disarray—empty glasses, tipped bottles, cigars stubbed into the wood, and the safe behind it open.

"Well," said Abbott, tipping his dusty hat, "you let me know if you need anything."

At the inn, Abbott sat at the bar and drank a beer.

Booth, who had put up his broom when Abbott arrived, leaned on an elbow, poured out two whiskeys, and raised his glass. "Good luck," he said.

"Much obliged."

"Business isn't much, but I'll buy a lamb if you've got one."

"Should have," said Abbott. "I'll bring one to you next couple of days. You can just put it against my tab."

"Might not be the best of bets," said Booth, "I don't know how much longer we'll make it with the soldiers gone."

"We'll make it right in the end, I ain't worried about you, Booth."

Raleigh called a greeting from the top of the stairs and came to sit with Abbott at the bar, accepting a whiskey from Booth. He looked good, thought Abbott, healthy. There was a glow about him that Abbott hadn't seen before—more tooth in his grin, more light in his eyes.

"Strangest thing," said Abbott. "Y'all remember that kid I told you about, the one who was hiding out in the canyon?"

They nodded, it had been an interesting story.

"He's back, and he's got friends with him, two of them. I used to think the kid wasn't as hard as the life he had fallen into, but I ain't sure anymore."

Booth looked worried.

"Oh, no," said Abbott, "it's good having them around. I like the company, and they been doing some work around the place. I ain't worried about nothing. I wonder, though, what they done to get there. Some outlawing, for real. You see any marshals? Rangers? Anybody looking for anyone?"

"Pinkerton came to town," said Booth, "from the agency."

"Looking for someone?"

"No," said Raleigh, "or, I mean, yes. He was looking for me. He gave me a letter. Someone I had lost touch with, someone I thought was gone."

"Good news?"

Raleigh nodded and the three men clinked glasses. Abbott nodded to them and put his rough hands on the bar, suggesting that he had one more thing to say before he hoisted himself from the stool.

"If you see that Crawford around, well, hell, I don't know."

"He ain't worth a damn, Abbott."

"Like to sell him some mutton, I guess."

"I'll ask him for you."

Abbott nodded, and went out to load his purchases on to mule.

The sun was just sinking when Abbott got back from the fort, and he made a cobbler. They all laughed at the beauty and the sweetness while tapers burned in the sockets of Abbott's tarnished candelabra for the first time in years.

"Strange things afoot at the fort," said Abbott. "Nobody there."

"Nobody there?"

"Colonel Hale—he's a fine man, I've sold a lot of meat to the colonel—has gone on back East, they said, left the fort in the hands of his lieutenant Pip Crawford. Ain't but a handful of men there. A few civilians. Right interesting they are, too. Colored fella who plays piana and his friend the English Indian. Of course they're fixing to leave, too."

The following day, Abbott saw two soldiers on a buckboard wagon and followed them by having the dogs move the sheep along. He knew by the way he moved and the wild wisps of his hair that the one driving was Thorne. The other one looked enough like Crawford for him to lay money on the line. Hidden in the sheep, he got close enough to watch them where they stopped at the top of the hill. Two riders, also soldiers, but from the newly formed Confederate Army, approached them. The two on the buckboard dismounted, handed over a canvas bank sack, and took the horses the others were riding. The men in gray got up on to the wagon and drove it back the way they'd come. There, in the bed, were the crates of munitions that Abbott had seen on the porch of the colonel's house.

He related his story to the men back at the cabin. "It's a wonder what them boys are up to."

"Did you see anything else?" Percy asked.

"Nah," said Abbott, "although I did take a gander into the house, looking for Crawford, and I saw Hale's desk, all wrecked, and the safe behind it, just flapping open."

Percy raised his eyebrows and looked at Crying John.

"Crawford is selling guns to the Confederacy," said Percy. "Man could make quite a fortune selling off one army's guns to the other army. We ought to go in there."

"And what?" Jed asked.

"He's still got soldiers!" said Crying John, who had understood Percy's intention from the start. "We're wanted men. Robbing a fort ain't laying low."

"It's true we're wanted men," said Percy.

"I ain't intended to build on that," said Jed.

"Can't undo it, though," said Percy, "unless, we go and intervene on behalf of the army, and stop this rampant criminality in its tracks."

"You are full of shit," said Jed.

Percy laughed. "It might work on a judge."

Crying John had rocked back in his chair and was looking at Percy with gratified respect. "We going in there and just, what? Ask him to empty the safe?"

Percy nodded. "I suppose I'll put a gun in his ear before I ask him."

"I have relationships," said Abbott. "I can't be party to this."

"That's understood," said Percy, "That's fine. You must grasp, though, that there is no fort any longer. They're all going to leave. You won't sell any meat to them until the war is over, if then. There won't be a trade done on these plains without an army to secure it. Your wool business will drift away on the winds of war. Anyway: after we take the money they've made, we'll ride off into mystery and be gone. We won't pull you in with us." Percy held up his hand, missing its finger: "No man with stripes on his shoulder has done me any favors. They owe me something. They threw me out of the army for shooting me. I can't go home. We'll take the money, and we'll ride down south to Mexico. We'll buy a ranch, run it together. Call it Tres Pistolas."

"All for one and one for all," said Jed.

Percy nodded, then turned to Abbott and said: "I don't mean you wouldn't be welcome, if you'd like to come on I'm sure I speak for all when I say you're welcome."

Abbott shook his head.

"There were actually four musketeers, you know," said Jed.

"I've listened to you talk about the Three Musketeers," said Crying John, "never understood how there were four of them." In the excitement, Crying John neither cried nor sang.

"We'll give you a share," said Jed to Abbott.

"Think of it as rent," said Percy.

CHAPTER THIRTY-FIVE

Big Changes

March 1861

The news that his sister was alive unleashed in Raleigh a riot of analysis and anxiety. He was overjoyed to learn that she was breathing still, but mortified to think that he had left her there. He'd spent a year knowing that she was dead. His grief had been his cornerstone. It hadn't mattered what his name was, what he did, where he went.

His relief upon releasing the guilt he carried with him that he had not been the one to die was replaced by the feeling he had failed her. His contrasting emotions were like an apple tree neglected for decades, the boughs and branches crossed and tangled. To trim one was to reveal another. It seemed impossible to gain any real knowledge.

She was chained while he wandered the country playing piano, enjoying himself. He should have been hurling himself against the walls. He should have rescued her. How unworthy of a man is it possible to be?

The soldiers had left, and as the early spring grasses grew in the mud the town sunk into an ugly, abandoned disarray, like a room from which all of the furniture had been taken.

Crawford had never demonstrated any talent in leadership, or any proclivity to command at all. The only reason his artillery unit hadn't disintegrated was because the men under him knew the guns and the drills. Aware that they were sailors without a captain, they had placated Crawford's ego and operated independently.

Every morning the corporal, Paul Lewiston, mustered the ten privates left at the fort.

"Good morning, soldiers!"

"Hey there, Paulie."

"Seen Crawford?"

"Or Thorne?"

General laughter. The quartermaster and Crawford were often together, but neither seemed interested in managing the stores. The soldiers had fallen into drinking in the barracks and bringing choice foodstuffs to the cook throughout the day.

"Are we fighting Indians today, Corporal? Or taking on the Confederates?"

More laughter.

"Moving forward," said Corporal Paul Lewiston, "on the list, here, I see we need to sort and pack the tack."

"Breakfast, Paulie."

"You were there with us. You know we're not fit to start work. Let's go see what the cook's got."

"What does the cook have?" Paulie asked.

"Well, I know he's got some peaches."

"And a brick of Mexican sugar."

The corporal asked what he'd said he was going to do with those things.

"Cobbler, I think he said."

"Cobbler."

"That's what he said."

"And there's cream."

"All right then," said the corporal.

Opinions among the men left at the fort were split. Half of them felt that they'd been left out in the middle of nowhere and deprived of a sense of purpose, while the other half felt that there was no need to hurry toward a war. (There was no agreement over whether or not there would be a war or how long and serious that war might be.)

Only the corporal felt that he had any duty to continue the work they'd been assigned, and much of that sense of duty stemmed from the fact that it was his job to sell off the cavalry horses, in which he found a lucrative business.

Crawford moved into the colonel's house, began drinking his way through the wine cellar, and paid no attention to the soldiers at all.

Tula and Lala had left with the soldiers, and Booth was planning on shutting the place down. He'd bought some of the cavalry horses from Corporal Paulie, a mule team, some tack, and a wagon.

"Can't stay here," he said, one afternoon to Raleigh and Joe. "Comanche are going to blow in as soon as they realize there's no more army. Or Confederates. Either way, I don't like it. What about you two?"

"Our friend Raleigh is in what I can only call a delirium of indecision," said Joe.

"You're welcome to join. We're California bound. Must be a good place to sell beer. Play piano."

Raleigh looked at Millie.

"Sounds grand, don't it?" Millie said.

He stared into the wood of the bar. He'd told Rose, via the Pinkerton, that he would go and get Temple and wire her from Louisville once they got there. He had no idea how to do any of that.

"Doesn't it sound grand?" Millie said again.

"I have to tell you the truth," Raleigh said.

Booth grimaced, and Red Joe put a hand on Raleigh's forearm. Millie stood akimbo. He unwound the whole story to Booth and Millie.

"Jesus's shit, Raleigh," said Booth.

"What's that mean?" asked Millie.

"Means it's a lot of story."

"What are you going to do? You have to go rescue her. You thought she was dead." Millie said.

"I don't know how to," Raleigh said. "I want to, but I can't figure it out. I can't travel into Virginia as a free black with old manumission papers, no proof of address, no job. They'll hang me."

"Wait—who taught you to play piano?" asked Booth, who was still piecing the story together, smoothing out the wrinkles.

"Oliver."

"Your—what do you call him? Your keeper?"

"No," said Millie. "Not keeper."

"I've never known what to call him," said Raleigh.

"What if you weren't free," said Joe. "What if you were a slave?"

No one understood.

"What if we played that you were a slave? Free blacks can't move about, but an enslaved black, with his master? He could. It's just in the telling, isn't it? We're theater people, aren't we? We're players."

"Whose slave?"

"Mine."

And so Red Joe unspooled a plot that had been rolling around inside his mind since Raleigh's frustrations had first manifested themselves. He would masquerade as a South American planter—"José Rubio, from Brazil, on a mission to buy slaves for my plantation."

"The most obvious problem, here," said Booth, "is that you don't look like a South American plantation owner."

"It's a costume, Booth. It's nothing."

"We could help," said Millie. "I can cut hair."

They had Joe in a chair over a drop cloth in the middle of the room in no time, with Millie at his shoulder. Raleigh and Booth took up chairs and gave advice, which was unnecessary and largely unheeded.

First, gently, she rubbed the makeup from his eyes with cooking fat.

"It's been years," said Red Joe. "I've put more on, but I don't know that I've ever taken any off."

"Don't open your eyes."

"I don't intend to."

"We'll get you seasoned up and roasted here shortly."

She worked again over the eyes with water.

With two sharp chops of the scissors she lopped off both braids, leaving the sparkling threads he'd twisted through them, tying them with a ribbon and wrapping them in a newspaper.

She ran to Booth's room and brought back a new white shirt, hair oil, combs, witch hazel, a cravat.

"I can't take Booth's things."

"You can," said Booth.

She set to work with the scissors.

"You're going to be very handsome."

"Wasn't I already?"

"Even more so," she said.

She dusted him off with a towel, slapped his cheeks softly with witch hazel, put droplets of oil on his scalp, and ran her comb through his hair until it shone and lay flat.

"From mystic to planter in one hour," said Booth.

"I can't believe it's you," said Raleigh.

"It isn't. It's José."

The front door slapped open, and Crawford moved unsteadily across the threshold, followed by Thorne, who was flushed and wet-lipped.

"Ahhh, Millie, you lovely thing," said Pip, "bring us some roast, eh?"

"Ain't you got a mess over there?" Millie said.

"I prefer the mess here," he looked Millie up and down, slowly. "You need to relax," he said. "I could help."

"You're writing checks you can't cash."

Millie had long put up with the lechery of soldiers. This was nothing new and nothing surprising.

"Millie, some drinks," said Crawford.

"You know, Pip, I think we're closed today," said Booth.

"Y'ain't."

Pip noticed that everyone was out in the middle of the dining room, gathered around Red Joe, who was sitting shirtless in a chair, polished up and gleaming. "What the hell devilry is this?"

"You should go," said Booth.

"I'll take a beer, a whiskey."

"I think you've had a skinful."

"Beer and a whiskey. Same for my friend here. Unless this is just a place for savages to shave now."

Pip took a barstool on the corner of the bar and made a show of ignoring the friends gathered in the middle of the room. Thorne slid stupidly onto the next stool, grinning.

Booth objected, and Millie touched his arm and said it was fine. She'd get them some beer.

"All right, Pip, here you go," she said. "Two whiskeys, two beers."

"How much for a shave, Millie?"

She shook her head.

"You only shave Indians?"

Thorne chuckled again, Pip drank his whiskey in one gulp.

"Seems to me that I'd pay a good price to take my shirt off and be ministered to here. A dollar. How about it? Two dollars. That's high money, Millie. Maybe you throw in a little washing?"

Booth came up out of his chair, raging. He leapt forward, and Pip, with a liquidity to his movement which belied his inebriation and suggested a lifetime of evasive maneuvers, stepped to the side and gave Booth a push, which sent him straight into Thorne. The two men toppled to the ground. Thorne had a knife out, but Booth had a strong hold on his arm. Pip pulled a pepperbox pistol from his vest, and took aim at the two men rolling on the floor. The idea that he might be about to put a ball into Thorne gave him pause enough for Red Joe to leap from the chair and grab at him, but he wasn't fast enough. Pip spun, and shot, and the ball caught Joe in the neck. Millie screamed, and Raleigh leapt forward. Pip fired his other ball and the shot went wild, shattering a window behind him.

Pip turned to see Thorne sink his blade into Booth's shoulder and push the bartender off of him. Thorne and Pip ran out the door, and Raleigh and Millie were left with the bloody men.

Booth hauled himself up and held his shoulder, which was damp with blood. "I'm fine," he said.

Raleigh looked at Joe stretched out on the floor with his eyes on the ceiling, pale and confused, then dropped to his knees in the growing lake of blood and took the shot man up in his arms. Joe took shallow breaths, and every moment was like a thud. Joe seemed to want to say something, but his throat was mostly gone, and no sound came. Raleigh squeezed his hand and watched his friend die.

Raleigh was sure that Booth was talking to him, but he couldn't make any sense of it.

"We'll get authorities," Booth said.

"What authorities?" Millie said, holding a rag to Booth's wound and crying.

If the words meant anything to Raleigh at all, he ignored them. He stood—covered in blood. He tried to will the events to happen again and change the course. He tried to reach out his hand and pull Joe back into the chair. He tried to throw a lantern at Pip, or break a glass into the fireplace.

Full of anger and despair, wanting revenge, he turned from the body, walked to the door and across the camp, past the locked-up storefronts and the mostly dark barracks.

Thorne, out of breath, sat wheezing on the other side of the big desk, which Pip had methodically ruined, staining the surface with coffee circles, spots of grease, and dollops of mustard. Cigar ash coated the surface, overflowing from a soup plate that Mr. Hale had left behind.

"It's about time someone shut that Indian up," said Pip.

Thorne's eyes were drifting in horizontal nystagmus, his drunken muscles unable to hold them straight. On the desk was a fat bottle of brandy they'd been drinking earlier in the evening, and he gripped it and swigged from it twice.

Had Crawford shot Booth? Thorne wasn't sure. Killing an Indian might go unnoticed, but you can't go around killing white men. People get strung up for that.

Both men were considering the death of the other and how it might help them. Crawford was slightly ahead of Thorne, having embarked on a baroque mental preamble to the act.

Thorne had no direct plan, but when he blinked hard and made the figure of Pip before him stop drifting to the left he remembered the knife on his belt, and he thought about how much money Crawford had made off of these deals and how much of it ought to be his own. He thought about what it would mean to have the whole share. He might tell his superiors that Crawford, after shooting up the saloon, came after him. Better yet, he could say that after he confronted Crawford for selling out the stores, Crawford had attacked him. It was self defense.

Thorne laughed, thinking that a dead man can shoulder all the blame and can't argue back.

"Hey," said Thorne, "maybe we should be cuttin' that straight? We split down the middle, huh?"

Pip affected shock. Thorne wasn't sure why he'd said it. He was going to stab the man in a second. Why bother?

Pip laughed.

"Oh, my friend. Who understands better than I do the lessening of what one is due?" Pip pulled a long swig from the bottle of brandy and said: "Hale thought he was sticking it to me. Getting the better of me. Many have thought this. I ever tell you about that bastard cheat in Charleston?"

Thorne nodded; Pip had.

"That man accused me of stealing. Cost me my job."

"You were, though. You were stealing."

"Was I?"

"You told me you were."

His knife should be buried in Pip Crawford. Why were they still talking?

"I have not treated you fairly, I think," said Pip.

He turned to the safe and fiddled with the door until it swung open—he never locked it, didn't know the combination, just made it appear to be locked. A man like Thorne would simply assume it was and wouldn't try.

A safe without a pistol in it is like a trap without bait, thought Pip, picking up the gun. It'd be self-defense. The man was drunk, angry, and had jumped at him with his knife.

Raleigh left Booth's barroom as the sun set and walked the edge of the street, keeping close to the buildings, which cast long, jagged shadows across the dirt. His perceptions were heightened to a strange and surreal degree. He was dedicated to the idea of killing Pip Crawford, but swimming in strangeness. His knees and his hands were wet with blood. It felt warm for the first time of the year. He and Joe might have left tomorrow. The first few precocious cicadas had crawled up out of the earth and were singing. Pip Crawford was about to die.

A scurrying in the shadows across the road startled him and he ducked under an eave. He saw three strangers, and knew instinctively that these were the outlaws Abbott had told him about. They, too were headed for the front door of the colonel's house, and they had guns.

Jed stood in the shadows in between two buildings across from the colonel's house, leaning on the wall next to Percy. Crying John had crept forward to the door and looked in. Returning to them, he told them what he'd seen. His cheeks were wet, but he spoke clearly, without singing.

"They're about drunk as hell," he said.

They laughed.

"Easy money, then," said Percy, as he pushed himself off the wall. "Let's go." He led the way.

Pip Crawford stood up from the safe, and slowly turned toward Thorne, who also stood.

"You're a bastard, Pip."

"Well, perhaps."

Pip shot and missed. The bullet shattered the doorframe behind Thorne. Thorne pulled the bowie knife from his belt and lunged.

The bullet meant for Thorne crashed into the doorframe just by Percy's hand as he reached for the knob, and Percy—without stopping to ask how he'd been seen through a solid door—assumed it was meant for him. "I'm not going to lose another finger to these rotten shiteaters!" He lifted his boot and kicked. The weakened door fell open, inward. Percy had his pistol in hand.

Two shots were fired so quickly that they sounded almost as if they were one.

Raleigh had watched the three men come to the door and had heard the shot, and watched them kick it down, then heard more shots and the cries. Now, overwhelmed with confusion and curiosity he snuck forward, came to the doorway and saw that Pip was shot, Thorne was dead, and the room was full of smoke. The three men were crouched by the safe, emptying it.

Pip looked up at him, clearly dying, and tried to reach out.

Raleigh ran to saddle Chessie and swung up on the stallion's back.

They'd killed Pip Crawford, and Raleigh's first thought was that the blame would quickly be shifted to him. Booth and Millie wouldn't reveal him, but he had followed Pip out of the barroom, and Pip was now dead. He would follow the outlaws to Abbott's. And what then?

He didn't know.

The alarm bell clanged as he rode out of town in the last light. Outside the fort, he picked up the three men easily enough. He could hear them, jubilant, and see their silhouettes against the flat plain.

He rode at a canter to match their pace, so as not to gain on them, and as he rode he was crushed by sadness over the death of Red Joe and bewildered with frustration regarding what he could do next. He needed to get to Virginia. He did not believe he would fare well in a military trial on the death of Pip Crawford, if he attempted to pin the crimes on outlaws no one had seen. No, he needed to keep them within reach. He needed to know where they were. If he could point to them, he wouldn't have to defend himself, and if he didn't have to defend himself, he could continue in his plan to rescue Temple.

Here, his thoughts foundered. How could he rescue Temple? He'd needed Red Joe. Without Red Joe he was stuck.

Ahead, Raleigh saw the rider with the slouch hat cut off to the left toward the slot canyon. Raleigh pulled up, worried for a moment that he'd been discovered. He heard coyotes in the distance, off to the south. They'd surrounded something and were confusing it, bouncing the echoes of their barks until it seemed that there were a hundred coyotes.

What if the outlaws could help him? Abbott had said they were on the run, had spent years evading lawmen. But what leverage did he have against them? He couldn't just ask for their sympathy. He needed the upper hand. Could he threaten them? Turn them in if they didn't help him? Wouldn't they shoot him?

He followed the single rider, considering the future as they cantered toward the slot canyon where the river began.

Pip Crawford stayed alive long enough to tell Corporal Paul Lewiston that the company safe had been robbed by three men who'd ridden out of the camp on horseback.

CHAPTER THIRTY-SIX

A Meeting in the Canyon

At the slot canyon, Jed drank from the pool in the rock by the mouth of the cave and tied his horse to the hitch there so the animal could drink as well. He scrambled into the darkness, and without a lantern found himself listing the things that might hide in a cave. Snakes. Mountain lions. Coyote. Wolf. Wild pig—that'd be a mean beast to meet in a cave. He kept his hand against the wall to guide him, half expecting to feel fangs sink into his wrist.

"A'right, snakes. Git. Go on. Git outta here now. I'm just walking past, not gonna mess with you. Ain't good to eat. I don't think. Git. Go on. Outta here."

When he thought he'd come to the right spot, he lit a match and touched it to the wick on the stump of candle from his pocket. He lifted the light to the wall to look for the pictograph of a bison under which they had hidden the sack, and saw it, scratched into the rock. The fat hump, the rear legs just a touch too long, the animal leaping, but already wounded, the arrow buried in its heart.

He mounted the candle on a rock, affixed with a drop of wax, and looked down into the crack under the pictograph.

"Okay, snaky. Okay. Gonna just."

He picked up a pebble and clattered into the hole. He'd wait a moment.

"Okay. Warning shot. Just run along."

He plunged his hand into the blackness until he felt burlap against his fingers and pulled the heavy sack out into the open.

All their money, the gold, the notes, most of what they'd earned as buffalo hunters and as rustlers was in the sack. He didn't know how much they'd hauled out of Crawford's safe, but he figured together this was enough to buy a spread in Mexico, if the three of them went in on it.

He dumped what they'd hauled from the safe out onto the ground, divided it into four piles, held out Abbott's share, and combined the rest, which he dropped back into the hiding place.

Three Guns Ranch, thought Jed. All for one. He liked it. Tres Pistolas.

He tied Abbott's money sack closed and hung it from his saddle horn. As he rode up and out of the slot canyon, through the narrows, where he could reach out and touch the canyon walls, he dreamt of a ranch house with a porch overlooking a paddock, just like Estoppy had. Good head of cattle on the range outstretched before him. They could hire a Mexican girl to cook for them, and they could watch the sun sink into the desert every night. John could go back and get Lindy, invite her down if he wanted. Jed didn't see any reason why she wouldn't want to come. They'd live so calm, so peaceable. They could find land near Saltillo; they knew people there. They had friends. With the right amount of money their lives could be different. With a big ranch they'd be real members of the community. Relied upon. Looked up to. Percy could get involved with the government. Jed would look after the cattle. It'd be an idyll.

He rode carefully, quickly but not hurriedly, relishing every coin he spent in his imaginary Mexican future. He saw himself at the tailor's shop, getting a nice vest. He saw himself sliding money across the polished wood of the old Saloon in Saltillo to Martina, the barmaid there. She'd be happy to see him, he thought, happy to see that he'd grown so successful.

He reached the lip of the massive bowl that constituted Abbott's ranging plains, and looked out across the expanse. He saw the herd, over on the far slope, a mile away. The sheep looked like a field of flowering shrubs in bloom.

Abbott's squat hut sat in the center of the bowl. Soldiers surrounded it.

Looking again across the expanse to the herd, he tried to see if Abbott was with his sheep. There was a tighter cluster near the center of the herd, which made Jed think that Abbott was hiding there, protected by Rosie, May, and Day herding the sheep around the shepherd in sheep's clothing.

He thought about his Sharps. He was too far to shoot the soldiers, and it looked like there were eight or ten of them. He backed the horse up, and slipped out of the saddle, staying low, worried and watching.

He could hear yelling, but he couldn't make it out.

Puffs of smoke came from the windows at the front, and two soldiers fell. A volley of shots answered. More shots from the cabin, and two more soldiers fell. For a moment, Jed wondered if Percy and John might hold the soldiers off, but then another volley of shots came, and soldiers rode to the back of the hut and lit the roof on fire. He watched for a moment more, and said as close of a thing to a prayer as he'd ever offered up.

He rode fast through the chaparral back to the slot canyon, where he tied the horse so it could drink, and scrambled, quickly this time, without room for fear of snakes, without caution, scattering pebbles as he went, obscuring footprints in the cave's floor, until he reached the stone. He lit a match to check on the pictograph, and saw the familiar red shape against the tan wall. He plunged his hand into the shadows, and found nothing.

He pressed his face against the wall. Where was it? He lit another match. Had he moved it? Had he put the sacks somewhere else by mistake? He lit his candle and spun around. Then ran to the front of the cave, to double-check, was he in the right place? He'd just left here. Moments ago.

By the spring at the mouth of the cave there stood a light-skinned black man with his hat to his chest like a preacher.

"Hello," he said, "Raleigh Bodkin."

Jed went for his pistol.

"That cave is a mile and a half deep, you know," said Raleigh. "I wouldn't think you'd be able to find something in there, if you didn't know where it was. I know where it was—there under that leaping bison, slid behind the rock—and I know where it is now."

Jed stepped forward. The black man wasn't wearing a gun.

"You will never find your gold with me dead."

"What gold?"

Raleigh laughed.

"I was there. I saw you smash into Crawford's place." Raleigh held up a placating palm. "You did me a favor there. He shot my best friend."

"You stole from me?"

"Can what's been stolen be counted as stolen? I'm not sure. I haven't taken it, though, I've only found a new hiding place."

Jed figured he should just shoot this man, get it over with.

"I need your help."

"You ain't off to a good start on getting somebody's help."

"When we're done, I'll give you the gold."

"There's more gold out there in the world. I don't care. That gold wasn't hardly mostly mine, anyway." *Although it is now*, he thought.

"Fair enough. Allow me a moment, before it comes to that, to tell you a story?"

And so for the second time that day, Raleigh Bodkin told the story of his life and how his best friend had been murdered in a meaningless bar fight, and how he'd followed them out there, because he recognized they were headed toward Abbott's place, which meant they were the men that Abbott had been talking about. He'd almost given up hope on being able to rescue his sister, but then he'd realized that the men best suited for the mission were the men at Abbott's.

"You're a friend of Abbott's?" Jed asked.

Raleigh nodded.

Jed was leaning against the canyon wall.

"I hope he's all right."

"What do you mean?"

"Soldiers got there before I did. Percy and Crying John, they're dead for sure. I think Abbott was up in his sheep."

CHAPTER THIRTY-SEVEN

A Narrow Escape

It was as clear a matrix as had ever presented itself to Jed—he could either shoot Raleigh or help him. It felt, surprisingly, better to think that he might help him.

If he'd been inclined to think it through, he might have come upon the insight that helping Raleigh to deal with the repercussions of the death of Red Joe was easier than mourning the death of his own friends. Easier, too, to have a task. Having something to do was easier than riding off alone and reminisce. He was a wanted man, again. He didn't have a crew. Without Percy, he felt adrift. He had nothing to look forward to, and he needed to move on.

"I reckon you've got me up against it, ain't you?" Jed said.

They rode back to the fort, slowly, roundabout, to avoid the soldiers.

"We'll have to hurry, " said Jed.

"You're wanted."

"I am."

They needed supplies. They needed a wagon.

In the storehouse they found sacks of feed, a sack of cornmeal, two sides of salt bacon, some beans, a crate with a kitchen kit—a couple of pots and pans, plates, cups, salt, coffee. They took powder, shot, rope, and sugar. Raleigh held up a small box that said "Pellier's Gardens, California."

Neither Jed nor Raleigh had ever seen a prune, but they smelled good, and Raleigh took a bite and thought it delicious.

All of this they stacked in an unmarked covered wagon that was out by the stables. Raleigh pulled two mules from the pen and yoked them. Even the stable was empty.

"Where do you think everyone is?"

Jed shrugged and said: "Looking for me?"

From the barn they took some leather and a few combs and picks. They snuck up the back steps of the inn and took Raleigh's few possessions—the little pouches which held the manumission papers, the money, the letter from Rose, and some blankets. Raleigh paused to look around.

It had been a happy time.

"Don't," said Jed.

They climbed into the schooner, knickered at the mules, and lurched to a start.

At the edge of town the last of the soldiers stood watch with torches.

"You better get in the back," said Raleigh.

Jed slid into a space between boxes and covered himself with a blanket. Raleigh whistled a little tune, overacting. The wagon stopped.

"Evening," said Raleigh.

"Ain't that the wagon from over there by the storehouse?"

"It is. I'm borrowing it to run an errand for Booth."

The guard had recognized Raleigh.

"For Booth?"

"The innkeeper?" Raleigh asked.

"I know who Booth is."

"Well, I'm helping him out."

"Ain't he laid up?"

"That's why he needs the help."

"Who told you you could take it?"

"The wagon? I'm not taking it."

"Who did you talk to?"

"I paid Thorne last week."

"Paid him?" The guard laughed and the other two men on the side of the road laughed with him. "Paid Thorne? He put that in his pocket, I bet you."

"I speak no ill of the dead," said Raleigh.

Someone coughed, and one of the soldiers said: "That's true, Ronny. Thorne met his end. Don't muddy him."

"I ain't muddying him, and I ain't changing the truth of him, neither, Paulie. Thorne was a thief and a bastard."

"Some friend you are."

"I have not breathed one moment on this earth as that man's friend."

"He's done, Ronny, he met his end."

"I heard you the first time, Corporal."

"Y'all have yourself a fine evening," said Raleigh.

"Go on, then."

When they were a few hundred yards down the road, Jed climbed out and took his seat on the bench.

CHAPTER THIRTY-EIGHT

Catastrophe

"We came as soon as we heard," said Marie Newcombe, rushing into her father's study, where he was propped up on a settee, pressed into pillows, looking pale. He'd been before a judge and collapsed, grasping at his chest.

Zeb held back, nearer to the threshold.

"And I'm glad you did," said Mr. Collings.

She smoothed his hair and knelt by his side.

"They told me you fainted," she said.

"Oh, I don't know about that."

"But they said that you had trouble breathing, and you said something that didn't make any sense, and then you collapsed."

"I said something? Ah well, much of what I say doesn't make sense. A bit of dyspepsia, I think, darling, nothing to be worried about. Just found that I suddenly had to sit down. I'm not a young man, and I'm afraid the passion of the argument must have gotten the best of me."

She lay her soft hand on his forearm, and looked at him with concern.

"If it's all right, my dear, I'd like a word with your Zeb. Just a moment. We have some business."

She pouted, but acquiesced and went off to find her mother and discuss dyspepsia.

Mr. Collings motioned to a chair.

"I'm sorry to be receiving you in this state," he said, gesturing at himself. With his mussed hair, in shirtsleeves, he looked ten years older, utterly devoid of authority. It made Zeb uncomfortable.

A more refined man than Zeb would have attempted to comfort Mr. Collings, but Zeb held only disgust for the pale, frail, wire-haired old man before him. In his mind, a display of weakness was only something to be exploited. He flopped gracelessly into the chair by the old man's feet and raised his eyebrows.

"I've gotten word," said Mr. Collings, "that our ships did not make it through the blockade."

The color washed out of Zeb's face. Mr. Collings continued.

"One was sunk, the other two were captured, taken to Haiti, I believe."

Panic gripped Zeb. He was tangled in a vine, and he couldn't get free of it. Sunk. He was on that note for half—$150,000. He was already in debt. This was ruin. His first thought was that it wasn't true.

"Is there proof? How do we know this is what happened?"

Mr. Collings was surprised: "The captain and crews disembarked, mostly unharmed. I believe they managed to rescue most of the crew of the sunken ship, as well. Not too many casualties. The captain sent word. Said once the first ship went down, there wasn't much to be done. They were outgunned, outmanned, out shipped. It was a gamble. We lost. Oh, well."

The old man chuckled merrily, and reached for a small bottle on the table by the settee.

"You fool," said Zeb.

Mr. Collings took up his medicine and shook a bit of powder into a glass, swirled it with whiskey, and drank it.

"Ah, well, it was a gamble," Mr. Collings grinned and patted his belly where it rose from under his rib cage, and took a wheezing breath, followed by the rest of the drugged whiskey.

"You foolish old man. How could you do this? How could you be so stupid?"

Zeb was standing.

"Watch yourself, boy," said Mr. Collings. "You are stepping out of bounds."

"You call me a boy? You played a game and you've ruined us."

"I'd hardly call it ruin. It's unfortunate, but so it goes."

"You fool."

Zeb was furious, red faced. He had lifted his hand at the man on the couch, about to strike him, when Marie reentered the room.

"What are you doing?"

"This fool has ruined us."

"Stand down, boy," said Mr. Collings.

Marie was horrified.

"Ruined us?"

"We invested," said Mr. Collings, merrily, the powder in the whiskey floating him along, "in some cotton. I'm going to try again, of course, not ruin, just a setback. A setback."

"I can't try again! That was it! That was everything—more than I had! I needed that. Come Marie, we're going."

"I'm not going anywhere," said Marie, "I'm going to tend to my father."

Zeb stormed out the door.

CHAPTER THIRTY-NINE

Homeward

The wagon they'd taken from Fort Little Stone rattled across the high plains of No Man's Land, heading east through the scrub and the grass. The first task was to get Jed out of the region in which he was a wanted man. Raleigh had already helped him begin his disguise—he'd given him some of the less extravagant of Joe's clothes and told him to shave, given him a comb and told him to brush his hair in the river. Jed didn't look gentlemanly, but he had taken a big step, more dashing than dangerous.

That night they made a fire, ate a little, and rolled out blankets.

Jed lay on his bedroll and listened. He could hear Raleigh, sleeping, and beyond him the snoring redundancy of the little spadefoot frogs hiding in the grass. He liked Raleigh, although he wasn't sure what that meant. Despite the fact that he was, in some strange way, a hostage, or here under duress, he found the kid comforting. He could always shoot him. The thought relaxed him. He wasn't exactly coerced, he told himself, because he didn't give a shit. Let the kid keep his sense of advantage, though. Let Raleigh believe that he was pressuring him. Don't tell him the lever ain't lifting anything.

He let sadness wash over him, remembered the flames on the roof of Abbott's hut. Percy and Crying John had died. Maybe that's another reason for not shooting the kid. Maybe there's been enough death, or maybe he just didn't want to be alone.

And if it got to be too much, he would just leave. He didn't have to shoot him. He didn't have to discuss it. He could stand up and leave right now. He wasn't bonded here.

But he felt for him, really, and that was a fresh experience. The kid was stuck, and he had also lost his friend. It didn't make them the same. It did make Jed feel something, though. Something other than loss and grief.

To the stars up in the humid sky he gestured, and almost said aloud: "Ain't that right?"

Anyway, he never was good at figuring out what to do. Preacher Thom used to tell him to be his own man. It'll be good to see Virginia, too, been a long time. He drifted off thinking about the forest, the oak leaves, the smell of the Virginia dirt.

Just before dawn, a crack jolted Jed awake, and he sat up, hand on his gun.

The night had turned. The wind was whipping. Lightning flashed, and he saw low thick clouds in the east, which showed the first blush of dawn like the pink edge of a terrific bruise.

"Shit."

Raleigh was already up and trying to calm the mules.

Jed tossed his things into the wagon and took the lead of one of the mules. The animal pulled back, whale-eyed, wanting to stomp him. He tried to calm the animal, but the mule flashed his teeth and bucked. Jed settled in, boots apart in the dirt, center low, with the lead tight in his hands. The mule danced lightly sideways, and brought his front feet up again as another crack of lightning shot through the sky.

The clouds moved fast, and on the horizon clumps of heavy darkness like pillars seemed to hold up the cloud cover. The sun shone through in spots, and cast just enough light to bark off of pale rocks and set everything in surreal contrast. A tall bur oak whipped in the wind, snapping back and forth, pale gray and ghostly in the weird light. It was blown first in one direction and then in the other, which Jed took as a bad sign.

The mule reared again, and Jed sunk his boot heels in, trying to hold him.

With a leap that was like water Raleigh gained the mule's back. The mule spun hard to the right, and Raleigh called for Jed to let go.

Raleigh rolled perfectly with two bucks, and then the mule stood, dazed, trotted three yards and took a few steps to the right before standing still and waiting for a command. Raleigh patted him and walked him over to his friend, and they sniffed at one another while he completed hooking them up. They were comforted by the familiarity, and assured by the clear fact that there was, now, a task.

"We've got to find somewhere to go," said Jed.

It sounded ridiculous, out on this flat expanse. There was nowhere, nothing.

Jed looked at the clouds. He could see, a few miles away, the bank moving to the left while the closer one was moving to the right.

"It's going to be a twister. Come on, then."

Under clouds with all the intricacies of a black eye fading and falling across a man's face, Raleigh trotted the mules, banging the wagon back to the rocky trail and turning to the east. No Man's Land stretched ahead of them for miles. Both men knew there were no towns here. The unclaimed land between Kansas and Texas was empty, unmeasured, home to nomadic tribes, prairie dogs, and grouse.

The lightning came in regular, jagged dashes, like swords thrust through the air, thick and fiery, full of menace. You could see, thought Raleigh, how the ancient world developed animism, how the Greeks would think that lightning came from the hand of a god, and how the same myths would be reflected in the primitive people of these lands. Look at the manifestation of physical power. How could you not attribute it to something more than yourself, and then call that thing a god?

"There," said Jed, "what's that?"

In the distance they saw what looked like the light of a fire reflected. They could just make out a small seam in the earth, like a cut on the top of bread, no more than a change in color, but full of promise.

"Is that a bluff?" Raleigh asked, "Some rocks?"

The sun shone like a pale skull behind the colossus of cloudscape. The clouds moved faster now, behind and afore, thick and black and low to the ground.

It's not will, Raleigh thought, comforting himself. These clouds hold no intention. They are meteorological, not metaphysical. Looking at them, however, did nothing to assuage his fears. These clouds, and the bursts of hail and sideways sprays of rain that fell from them, radiated menace.

"If that there is a rock bluff, and we can tuck into it before this figures itself out, we might be all right," said Jed.

Raleigh held the reins, and the mules pressed forward.

In the distance the columns of baleful clouds had come together and formed a tremendous thorn. The wind came in sputtering bursts and then blew harder, and then harder still. Behind the thorn of cloud, its narrow point dragging across the plains, the sun shone for a moment and then the black ceiling covered it up and plunged the scene into a hellish purple darkness.

In the flatness it was impossible to tell how big the twister was, or how far away.

On the wind they heard a voice, and squinting into the spray of rain they saw a man, an Indian with a soft round face, waving to them. They were at the rocks, a bluff on the other side of a small river. The man was waving them to the ford, twenty yards upstream. The mules balked, but Raleigh got them in and once they felt the solid ground under their feet they pulled the wagon across. The man waved them, come on, come on. He showed them a spot to tuck the wagon in against the bluff. Motioned with his hand that they should follow, and they ran toward a campfire in the mouth of small cave. Two dozen people huddled under the shelf—men, women and children. The man patted their shoulders and shook their hands. He was smiling.

"We saw you coming. We worried you wouldn't make it," he said. "I'm Albert."

"Jed," said Jed. "This here is Raleigh."

Raleigh bowed a greeting and wished that they had invented names.

"Thank you," said Raleigh.

Albert said something to one of the women, who produced two shirts of white cotton, sewed in the loose Mexican style, embroidered with flowers and open at the neck. The woman's hair was wet.

"You are wet. Take these. I sent her for them when it looked as if you might make it to the river."

"We don't have anything to trade."

"A gift," said Albert. "You can help me. After the storm."

They turned to look outside. It was disconcerting not to be able to see the twister anymore, to know that it was over their shoulders. The shirts were crisp and very clean.

"Sit," said Albert. "We will have time."

With his back to the wall, the storm raging, Raleigh tried surreptitiously to see who these Indians were. The adults were tattooed with lines and triangles on their faces and across their chests. Albert, underneath a pale leather vest stitched with ornamental shells from somewhere far away, wore a white shirt like the ones he'd given them. A woman who sat close to him and watched him speak in the way that wives do wore a silk scarf of pale lilac tied across her chest clasped with a large cameo set in gold. Many of the men and women had complicated jewelry—white women's necklaces and rings, earrings and bracelets.

From the fire one of the younger men took a stewpot. He set himself to work with a pile of hand-sized loaves and hunks of meat from the stew, slipping a piece of meat into each loaf after he'd split it open. He dropped pieces of hot pepper and herbs on top and handed them out, two at a time. First to Albert and the woman, then to Raleigh and Jed. Raleigh bowed again, and smiled. The food smelled delicious. Noting that Albert had not started eating, Raleigh put his hand on Jed's arm.

"Wait," he said.

When everyone had been served, Albert raised his food and smiled. He said one word in a language Raleigh didn't recognize, and all fell to their meal.

As they ate their last bites, the sun broke through the thick clouds and hit the steaming prairie floor. The thick air seemed to hold the light, and the land was quiet, but for the rushing water of the little river. The grasses had been battered and muddied by the storm, so strong that it trampled the earth instead of cleansed it.

The mules stomped but looked no worse off. Raleigh fed them each half an apple from the wagon.

Albert was the chief of a band of Taovaya who had not agreed to leave and enter the Wichita nation. They were a small enough group to go unnoticed, mostly—although to hear Albert tell it they had not always been so—and they had augmented their population with a few white people who had fallen away from the wagon trains to the West and with a couple from another of the Wichita tribes. The tribe from which the couple came had dwindled, and they felt they were the last of their kind. They were proud of this, and Albert said that they kept themselves slightly apart. Albert himself claimed some Spanish heritage—he was the latest in a long line of Alberts, he said—"Not an Indian name, after all"— descended from a conquistador who had fallen in love with one of his ancestors and abandoned his European ways to live with the Taovaya.

"He became a great chief," Albert said, "and made many profitable trades. His knowledge of strategy and the weapons he brought with him allowed us to defeat a neighboring tribe who had beleaguered us for many generations."

Albert showed them a rusty old flintlock and said it was the conquistador's gun.

"We don't roam like we used to, there's no reason to. We trade with the Comanche, we trade with the wagon people. We have Kansas," he gestured to the north, "and Texas."

He took them on a tour of the village atop the bluff, where the tribe lived in eight beehive-shaped houses. The white people had been adopted into families and lived in the houses with married couples to be taught how to survive. Albert explained that they didn't have a vote, yet. They were as children. If they became married, and had children themselves, Albert would have a house built for them.

The twister had missed the village, and the repairs were minor, but Jed and Raleigh gladly helped patch the grass walls. They leaned on the posts that held up the houses and made sure they were stable. They walked the perimeters and looked for cut furrows that would allow varmints in.

Albert led them to a structure which he said they kept ready for visitors. "You are no inconvenience. You have helped us with our tasks today, you've earned our hospitality. Tomorrow, I would like it if you would accompany me into the field, so we might find where the twister did its work, and see if it's turned up anything of interest. You'll come with me and we'll hunt!"

He didn't wait for agreement. He smiled and clapped his hands. The gesture made Raleigh think of some plump and mischievous king. Albert turned with a flourish and walked from the building.

The next day they went out with Albert and his dogs. A quarter mile from the camp the tornado had shorn and split what few trees there had been, cleaving whole halves of trunks, pushing the grass flat into the dirt or tearing it out in clumps. The wind had brought manmade things from far away, barn doors and fence posts. They slowly walked the torn land, taking game as the dogs flushed it—Raleigh bagged two grouse, Jed got another, and Albert shot a hare.

Raleigh liked this horse, a calm and understanding animal. He barely held the reins at all, and he felt the horse shifting to keep him in the saddle.

Albert thought they should see if there were deer hiding in a small patch of shaded hollow. Jed nodded and drew his Sharps rifle. He put it on his shoulder to feel its weight and readjust, then relaxed and nodded at Albert.

At the chief's whistle the dogs crept forward, and then stopped. The one on the right had his hackles up. Albert whistled the dogs forward but they wouldn't move. Albert clucked to his horse and was halfway to the dogs when the red wolf broke from the shadow of the pit and ran for the closer of the two dogs. The wolf was fast, and the dog leapt forward. They were three feet apart when Jed's rifle banged, and the wolf dropped stone dead. He reloaded quickly, turning to the shadow, to see if there was another wolf coming, but none came.

Albert had been right, there had been a mule deer in the shadow, but the wolf had found it first.

Back at the village, Albert demanded a feast be cooked in celebration of the thwarting of the wolf. "My dog!" he scratched the dog behind the ears, "lives because of your fast gun."

"These Indians have strange ways," said Jed, while they were alone in their bungalow waiting for the feast to begin. Raleigh asked what he meant.

"They don't act right, somehow, I don't know. The bread, I guess. The way they are organized, the things they have."

"They have taken things on, you mean."

"I guess that's it," said Jed.

"They're all by themselves, opportunists."

"You're trusting."

"I like them. I've never felt so welcome."

The feast only increased Raleigh's sense of well-being. There was dancing. Albert produced a barrel of wine—Jed raised his eyebrows as he took a mugful, as if to say "See? Where did this come from?"

"They're traders. They trade for these things," said Raleigh.

"Or thieves," answered Jed.

"Well, what's the difference? You've been both, I believe."

Jed laughed.

The party lasted late into the night, and the Indians sang. Albert named Jed "Friend of Dogs," and gave a toast in his honor.

In the morning, Jed sensed a presence in the room before he was awake and reached for the rifle, always by his side, to find it wasn't there. Arrayed around the edge of the room, eight Indians he had not seen before.

Raleigh choked on a snore and sat up to survey the room with wide, frightened eyes.

These Indians were rough, and they smelled ripe. Their faces were blackened with grease and soot, they scratched and slapped at their skin, picking vermin off and flicking them in the dirt, they squatted, cold-eyed, armed with arrows and knives. Their hair was parted in the middle and twisted into long braids. One of them had ermine tails tied into his braids. It was he who spoke first.

"You are lazy," he said, "and you sleep too deeply."

"Good morning," said Jed.

"Maybe," said the Indian. "You are Jed Stokes, a wanted man. Who is this?"

"Doesn't matter, nobody."

"Should I kill him here or take him with us?"

"We aren't going with you."

"Albert sold you to me," said the Indian. "I don't think he understands how much the reward is."

"The reward?"

"You are a wanted man. Dead or alive. Maybe easier dead? Little more money alive."

"How much did you pay for us?" Jed asked.

"Slaves don't poke the business of their masters."

"Slaves?"

"Albert sold you to me."

"How much is the reward?" asked Raleigh.

The Indian looked at Raleigh, slightly amused and wholly disgusted.

"There is no reward for you."

"For him, how much is the reward for him."

"One thousand dollars."

"That's pretty good," said Jed. "They want to hang me, I guess."

"They will get their wish."

"I have it," said Raleigh.

"Everything you have is mine, I bought you. You have money, give it to me."

"That ain't going to work," said Jed.

The Indian looked at one of his compatriots and laughed. They talked briefly, chuckling. Neither Jed nor Raleigh understood a word of what was said, but it was clear that the two Comanche had come to agree upon something.

"Let me see your money."

"Don't, Raleigh."

"I take your wagon, I take your food. You pay me $1,000. I leave you your guns, and you walk."

"We'll need horses," said Jed.

"It's none of my business if you steal horses from Albert. I'll kill you if you lay a hand on mine. Let him kill you for stealing his."

"Let me go to the wagon, and get a canteen and my pistols," said Jed.

"And our saddles," said Raleigh.

The Indian laughed.

"I wonder how long it will take Albert to find you and trap you again? I'll come back in two days and buy you again."

Raleigh took the money out of his pouch, and counted a thousand dollars to the Indian, who slid the guns across the floor to them and grinned with a crazed malice.

On the walk to the wagon, Jed said: "We need to stampede all the horses. The Comanche horses and Albert's horses. They let us go for sport. They're going to hunt us."

At the wagon they grabbed canteens, a small bag of apples, and a hunk of ham. There were villagers milling about. What did they know? What did they think was happening? It was early in the morning.

"Why do you have a thousand dollars?"

"I saved up."

Raleigh had used the money that Oliver had given him when he was a child. He figured it was money for freedom, so it was put to good use.

"I owe you," said Jed.

"You don't."

They took their saddles and walked as casually as they could into the paddock where they found the horses they'd ridden in the hunt yesterday. They fed the horses each an apple and said hello, slipped the saddles over them, and tightened the cinches.

"Ride in the herd as long as we can before we cut east," said Jed.

"Are we going to make it?"

"Keep your head down and hold on."

Raleigh had the shotgun that Albert had loaned him yesterday, and Jed told him to load it.

Jed checked his pistols.

"Guns don't scare these animals," Jed said.

"Open the gates," said Raleigh, "then go in that paddock where the Comanche horses are. We're each going to have to hurt one of them. Just poke him in the hindquarter, use a knife, not too hard but enough to draw blood, he'll kick the horse behind him, and they should all run after that. Do it again if you have to. They'll kill us for this."

"They'll kill us anyway," said Jed.

Jed slipped out, opened both gates, and rode into the herd of Comanche horses. The men made eye contact, and Raleigh brought out his knife and jabbed the haunch of the nearest horse.

The instincts of horses did not disappoint, and chaos soon arrived. Once both herds of horses felt that something was wrong and started to run, they joined together in one surging mass, biting each other and competing for the front. Jed and Raleigh rode leaning forward across the withers, their legs pressed in between horseflesh as the steeds reclaimed their wildness and ran with wide-eyed fear.

There was no directing them, they would go where they wanted, and they ran north, away from the bluff and the river.

Raleigh heard shouts, and he thought he saw an arrow—a worthless expression of frustration—sink between running horses. He dropped his head and looked back under his arm like a jockey. There were men at the end of the village, shaking their fists.

Raleigh stroked the neck of his horse and settled in. The herd wasn't panicked any longer, they were just running. Pressed together, running for themselves, now, sweating and frothing. After half an hour he felt them start to tire. He sat up. There was Jed, only a couple of horses away, riding well.

They made eye contact and nodded, and pulled their mounts to the right, as if choreographed. They took to the grass, smiling wide. Raleigh had never felt so free.

CHAPTER FORTY

The Freshman

Marie resigned herself to returning to the Hundred, for she had promised Collings that she'd take him to school to get settled, and no one else was capable of the task. She wanted to show the boy that all was well and let him set forth into his education unperturbed.

Her father had passed her a check in excess of the tuition that Collings required for school. She knew that Mr. Collings would have no member of his family appear to be anything other than flush. Mr. Collings told her the boy would need books and ready cash for laundresses and nights out.

"When I was there," Mr. Collings had said, "I made my most profound friendships and connections over a cup of ale. Implore him to be not tremulous."

Odd, she thought, how a man can be so clear, and solve so many problems, without seeming to admit that those problems exist. Was it to their credit as a sex? The coach cruised smoothly down the road, buoyed along by the elliptical springs of which her father was so proud.

His pride was her comfort, she thought.

She thought of her older son, Johnny, and his rough gallantry. Perhaps some of that had come from her, too, and the prideful nature of the Collings family. She was accustomed to crediting every aspect of his personality to Zeb, so clearly was he the inheritor of his father's ways.

She'd worked so hard. Children pull at you. First they weigh you down—she put her hand on her belly, and thought about the weight there, and how it had shifted her walk and made her put her feet out in front of her like a duck. She'd hated it. She hated everything it was—raw and painful and physical. One should be demure, postured, and self-sufficient. One should not be a burden. The burdens, needy and dependent, stuck to her, depriving her of sleep, of time. The luxury of time, unnoticed until it was too late. Pain, too, she thought, but that was ours to bear, although she was unconvinced that she deserved any punishment for sins committed by the ancestor of her sex.

I am in a black mood, she thought. She watched the trees and when they broke into farmland she tried to remember whose acreage it was.

She had worked to better the children. She plied them with bribes and attention to keep them at their studies, hoping that a little learning would temper Johnny's proclivities to physical exertion and bloodshed. She'd even entertained, briefly, that he might rise to become the model cavalier—the finest expression of their class. Bookish Collings lacked the physicality, but bookish had a role, as well. He would be able to move this new nation forward. We'd need a crop of parliamentarians soon enough. College would keep him out of the war, and when it was over, a couple of years of law. Perhaps a voyage. He'd take his place. The new South would need worldly, sophisticated leaders, intelligent men who could carry forward the traditions begun by those who founded this nation here, in Virginia. It's who he is.

When she thought about the future she felt her son deserved, she thought of it in reverse, as what the state deserved. If one had told Marie Collings Newcombe that she was thinking of what was best for her son, she might have smiled, but she would have answered that she was thinking of what was best for their way of life. The two thoughts were inseparable. What was good for her son was good for the new nation, and the good of the new nation depended upon her son.

This reverie moved her from her dark place, but only briefly. She thought of the tangle and the mess that Zeb had made. His stupidity, his arrogance. Collings couldn't embark upon the life that she envisioned for him, and which the nation required of him, if Zeb sullied his name.

She had a wealthy woman's understanding of money, which is to say, no understanding of it. Money would be sorted out.

A reputation, however, was fragile. She'd seen the worst! Rose Durand married that Knaupf man, and he filled her head with ideas before dropping dead. Oliver Bodkin! Look how they talk about that family now. It didn't take long at all. One generation lost its grip on the next, and that generation hurled the family into ill repute. She had to make sure that the pressure of history was felt.

Zeb was an animal, driven by impulse, by fury, by lust. He didn't feel any obligation to anything.

The thought that all which she had found attractive—the brutishness, the rough hew of his character—was what now repulsed her was a thought she'd visited so often that she had smoothed it the way the mirror on her armoire had the print of her thumb worn into the silver where she reached out to tilt it.

She needed to exert her influence. Collings should never forget who he is, where he comes from, and how he fits into the world.

The world, thought Marie, is an orderly place if properly tended. From the window of the coach she saw a field of winter barley, planted as a cover crop and being cut by a phalanx of fieldworkers. From a distance it looked idyllic.

She could not, from the window of her coach, see any discomfort or note the inadequacy of their shoes, their scarred backs or blistered hands. From her vantage point they weren't undernourished in body and mind. If she'd been shown these things, she would have insisted that the condition of the individual was an individual matter, and that a whip was not proof of the cruelty of the master, but rather proof of the corrupt nature of the beaten.

To her, the enslaved were part of a pleasant, well-managed land. The colored people would not, on their own, plant a winter crop and cut it into the soil in preparation for the spring planting. They needed guidance to accomplish this, and through that guidance they were kept busy and found their worth in that work. The spring crops would grow well. Everything in its place.

So it was that when the coach turned into the drive at the Hundred she was aggravated to see untrimmed hedges along the drive and the bowl of the fountain green and in need of scrubbing. The two boys in livery who were supposed to greet people were nowhere to be seen. The front doors needed cleaning, the stairs needed sweeping, the gravel needed to be raked.

After instructing the coachmen to water the horses, brush them down, and turn them out, she strode into the house full of imperious fury.

Temple was in the hall, pretending to dust a vase.

"Why would you drag that greasy rag across my vase?"

Temple turned to Marie and curtsied, smiling and mumbling something in welcome.

"Don't mumble. Why are the stairs unswept? Where are the boys? And where is Master Newcombe?" Turning her voice up to cast it into the house, Marie called out for her sons.

"I don't know ma'am," said Temple.

"You don't know what?"

"I don't know."

Marie stepped to Temple, smacked her sharply across the cheek, and said: "Then find someone who does."

Temple's cheek stung as she turned and walked back to the tangle of small rooms—the pantry, the china closet, the inside kitchen—where she would find Tandey. She wanted to cry, but she took a deep breath to steady herself.

She'd felt the absence of Mrs. Newcombe, and hadn't liked the roaming, threatening wildness of the men here by themselves. It felt volatile, dangerous.

In the weeks since she'd sent the letter to Rose, her enthusiasm had slowly weakened. She didn't know how long it took to get a letter to California, or if the letter would be mailed. What would happen next, even in the best of circumstances, was vague. If she thought to herself that she'd be rescued, she couldn't put together who would do that rescuing or how they would do it, what it would look like when it arrived, or how it would play out. Her helplessness was compounded, she felt, by the chaos into which the house had been thrown. Tandey told her that no one knew what to do anymore. That no one was receiving any instruction at all regarding the farming or the crops.

"Them rough boys, Mr. Mack and Mr. Gilly, they supposed to be minding," Tandey said, "but they just sitting around getting drunk."

When Temple had learned that Miss Marie was coming back, even if just to take Collings to school, she had been delighted. The mistress of the house had comforted Temple, and as the rush of confidence that came from the revelations at Christmas faded she came to desire the kinder, careful hand offered by Marie. She had begun to think, yet again, that she might be the victim of her own mind. Perhaps her memories were fantastical. It was a miserable plague, she felt, to be burdened with this madness, caught up in your own lies about yourself. Temple had been scolding herself, telling herself that the imagined world of California and some dream of a past no one had ever heard of did her no good at all. There was no leaving this place, there was nowhere to go. She had to make her life better out of the things she had, like Tandey. He derived pleasure where he could. He lived in harmony.

Temple had hoped that she might somehow exploit Marie's kindness, find a way to build the relationship with her that Tandey had. For Tandey had nothing but good things to say about Miss Marie. They'd been together since Marie was born.

Temple's face was stung, and she thought of the viciousness in Marie's eyes. There was no home for her there. She'd have to find another way.

CHAPTER FORTY-ONE

Across the River

Jed and Raleigh rode evasively for two days. They backtracked and took high positions where they could to see if they were followed. It made for slow progress.

"It ain't easy to outrun Comanche, kid, but I think we did."

Raleigh's life had become something he'd read about with Oliver, an adventure story, and he found it thrilling. He was growing out his beard.

"I think if they haven't shown up by now, they haven't figured out which way we went," said Jed.

"If we didn't tell them we were headed East, they wouldn't think we would be, right?"

"A black man and an outlaw, headed toward civilization? If I were Albert, or that stinking Comanche with the rodent tails tied up in his hair, I'd be looking for us on the trail to Mexico."

The next morning, Raleigh shot a prairie chicken.

"I guess we'll see if anyone is following us now," said Raleigh.

"We gotta eat sometime. And if they're still on us, we might as well shoot a couple Indians."

They stopped and let the horses graze while they made a fire and ate the bird.

"Don't matter how many times I've seen it, I can't believe it," said Jed, in the saddle, looking out over the half-mile crossing of the Mississippi River, Memphis on the other side. "Once we get over there, I guess we're back."

"Still got a way to go, but I know what you mean."

They were headed southward, down to the where the river narrowed a bit, hoping to find a private ferry or a fisherman with a boat.

"We get a train," said Jed. "We sell these horses."

"Should we sell them or find a stable? We might want them on the way back. I like mine quite a bit." Raleigh patted the horse on the shoulder. "He's a good ride."

"There's a war."

"It's a chance, for sure."

"The way back?"

Raleigh looked down, suddenly embarrassed. He hadn't thought about it.

Jed laughed hard once. "We ain't maintaining proper hostage-and-captor relations."

Raleigh shrank from him, sputtered something that didn't go anywhere.

"You saved my life once," said Jed, "and bought my life another time."

Raleigh tried to speak again, but he couldn't get around the words.

"You're going to have to lighten up," said Jed. "Let's find a stable."

At Wyanoke, on the Arkansas side of the river, Jed arranged for the horses to be stabled, fed, and exercised for two months, paid in advance. He didn't trust the arrangement, particularly, but he saw no option.

They found a black man with a rickety little boat just bigger than a canoe who agreed to take them across the half mile of brown, menacing water.

"What would you call this boat?" asked Jed, grinning.

"A skiff, maybe?" Raleigh said.

"The death of us?"

"You can swim?"

"I've jumped in a creek."

"Well, hold on to the boat if we flip."

"We ain't gonna flip," said the fisherman.

"No offense," said Jed.

"Y'all get settled up there," said the fisherman, grinning as he snapped the sail taut and the boat was pulled into the wind. It leaned hard, and the water was just at the gunwale. He laughed, and pulled on his sheet, making it tight. "We going, now."

Steamboats chugged on the river, throwing black smoke. Their man was cutting straight across. The wakes of the steamboats frothed and churned and came at them head-on. The little boat stank of fish guts, and there were dried bones and scales cast all about the floor.

"Why ain't y'all just get a ride on the steam ferry? Cost about what you gave me."

"We thought this would be fun," said Jed, "We like to arrive in style."

"You got business in Memphis?"

"Farther on," said Jed.

"Back East," said Raleigh.

"You heading the wrong way," said the fisherman. "Right thing to do, stay on the West side of this river, get out of here. Head North. Ain't no good business happening back East. Not these days."

"Didn't say it was good business," said Jed.

Memphis felt like trade and commerce, as if it vibrated with schemes and deals.

"Been a long time since I seen anything like this," said Jed.

"You've been a long time on the plains?"

"And Mexico. I was in the war. Well, sort of. I make it sound like something. I was in Mexico, and for some of that time I was in the army. I did miss trees."

Raleigh agreed. "Proud-pied April, dressed all in his trim."

"Ain't it May?" Jed asked.

"Fair enough."

"Let's find something to eat. And some drinks."

They walked Memphis, which was tighter, smaller, and more segregated than the cities Raleigh had been in. He stuck out, or rather, the two of them together did. They saw nowhere to buy food until they found themselves in the ward populated by only the poorest of whites, where the black folk clustered as well.

All through the town, as they walked, the reality of an approaching war was apparent to them.

"You take note," said Jed, "of how everybody is talking about the war, but they're all talking about how it isn't going to happen?"

"But it's all they're thinking about. They can't deny, but they don't want to believe."

"If it ain't happening, you'd think they'd talk about something else."

"How are we going to get there?" asked Raleigh. "These people are keyed up. We can't go places together."

"We'll begin the charade. I'll buy a suit tomorrow."

"I'll buy the suit," said Raleigh. "We'll begin there. I'm your valet, after all." He bowed at the waist.

On the commercial street where they stood, laundry had been strung between the buildings from the windows of the shopkeeper's apartments above. A white man had parked his vegetable cart near the corner, and his draft horses stood, blinkered and still, licking the bottom of their empty feed bags.

"Look, there," said Raleigh. He'd recognized the lantern burning in front of a barbershop. It was the same one that Hatforth lit in front of his shop. Black and gold tin, shaped like a crown. "I know that sign."

He walked quickly, and Jed followed.

"I don't think I should follow you," said Jed.

Raleigh slowed a step, allowed Jed to get in front, and they walked through the entrance to the barbershop, where a little bell announced their arrival.

There came a flurry of movement, and before they could act or speak Jed was in a barber chair with a straight razor at his throat and Raleigh had his palms out, facing a man with a gun. Both barbers were black, in crisp white shirts.

"Hold up," said Raleigh. "Slow down."

"Slow down," said Jed.

"Nobody is talking to you," said one of the barbers.

"What in hell is going on here?" said the other.

"Nothing," said Raleigh, "and let's keep it that way."

Jed made as if to speak, and the man with a razor to his throat pressed the blade against his neck and said: "I'll let you know when I want to hear what the white man has to say—which will be never."

"Why'd you bring this man here?" the other barber asked Raleigh. "He keeping you?"

"He's my friend. He's helping me."

"Don't come in here with that. Walk in here sounding like one of them that feels saved by their Master. He ain't taking care of you, he owns you."

"You misunderstand. I've hired him."

The barbers looked at one another, unsure of what that could mean.

"He's a wanted man," said Raleigh. Jed's eyes flashed at him. "He's wanted by the Confederacy. He stole from the Confederate Army, and after that I hired him to help me free my sister. I saw the lantern. My friend in Louisville has the same one. Hatforth."

"Don't say names."

"Sorry," said Raleigh. "I'm sorry. I just thought I recognized it, and I know it means you can help. I need help."

They relaxed. The razor was put away, but Jed was told to stay where he was, in the chair, and to not speak.

"We aren't interested in what you have to say."

Raleigh explained the mission, what they were doing, and when he was done one of the barbers let out a low whistle, and the other said: "I don't like one bit of this."

"For one thing, railroad don't run that way. For another, it don't run for freemen."

"I'm trying to free her," said Raleigh, "she's been made a slave."

"That's the part I feel."

"And you say the man what has her is a slave catcher?"

Raleigh nodded.

"Certainly does motivate," said the razor-wielding barber. He turned then to Jed, and said: "White man. Why are you helping?"

"Raleigh is my friend. He's saved my life twice, at least. Three times, if we count that razor in your pocket."

The barbers considered whether or not the series of abolitionists, freemen, and coconspirators that constituted the Underground Railroad should put themselves at risk for a white man and a freed black who wanted to ride the secret paths back. Back! The wrong way. It was like getting to the pearly gates and telling St. Peter you wanted another shot at it. Why would anyone go back?

However, it must be said that the leaders of the cause snuck into slave states to wrest the bonded from their shackles.

But this is a personal mission. Brave, perhaps, but of questionable motivation.

Was the desire to rescue a sister somehow less important than the desire to rescue a stranger?

Could the train even run backward? Is there a difference between sneaking in and being smuggled in?

The barbers asked around and found a sympathetic brakeman on a cotton train bound for Petersburg, Virginia, out of Grand Junction, Tennessee, who agreed to take Raleigh and Jed, and they rode to Grand Junction under a false floor in the back of a wagon, an uncomfortable journey of two days.

Every time the wagon lurched to a halt, they froze, terrified, their hands near their guns. There was a simple three-knock code meaning all was good—ta ta TA—for which they waited earnestly.

"I feel like a chicken waiting to be let out of the coop in the morning," said Jed.

"It can't come fast enough," agreed Raleigh.

"Waiting for good news or bad, just bring the news."

The air holes behind their heads, covered with a thin cloth, let a faint light fall upon their strange bed.

"It's like practice for a coffin," said Jed.

They squirmed to find comfortable angles. They couldn't sit up, but they could lay on their sides, and they found themselves face-to-face, like lovers, heads resting on their hands, supported by cricked elbows, close enough to feel the warmth of the other man. They spoke in the language of confessionals and midnight divulgences. Both men had had few opportunities for connection, and those they had been closest to were dead.

Jed told Raleigh about the death of his father. He told the story in full, including details that he wasn't sure he'd ever confronted himself. He turned onto his back, stared into the wood grains.

"I heard, lots of times, not fights. But Ethel comparing Hale to Hobe. Hale was my pa, Hobe my uncle. She thought my uncle was smarter, stronger. I think it might have been between them, the sisters."

"Your mother and your aunt were sisters?" Raleigh was still up on his elbow, carefully watching Jed speak, attending to his story.

"They were. I reckon I've heard tell plenty of brothers or sisters who were at each other like two roosters when they were young, but sorted it later. Never grew out of it. Them two, my lord. Mountain wasn't big enough for the both of them."

"How'd they manage to meet and marry like that?"

"Country ways for Jewish folk. Rest of 'em have barn dances and so forth. Easier to marry off two sisters into one family than to go off looking for another. Marriages are arranged. And even the most hating of sisters will bind themselves together for a cause. I reckon brothers would, too."

"Did they, your father and his brother?"

"Conspire, you mean? Nah. The women liked 'em, or pretended to, and that was enough."

"But it wasn't enough. In the end."

"Far cry from the end. Wadn't enough for Edith. She commenced to comparison. Badgering. 'Why don't you do you like Hobe do?' I guess early on, there'd been a couple of years when Hobe did do better than Hale did. I was too young to understand it, but I guess they didn't split up everything even. Grandpa would cut slices out on merit, I guess."

"And Hobe's family got the bigger slice?"

"Nobody told me as much, but I think they might been set up a little better."

"So you think they did it. I mean, on purpose?"

"Might've."

"You don't look Jewish."

"What's that mean?"

Raleigh considered it, and said he didn't know.

"That's a lot, to kill a brother," said Raleigh.

"Easier to imagine killing a wife?"

"I can't imagine either."

They both lay on their backs, now, Raleigh drawing figures along the wood with no real intent.

Raleigh told Jed about Red Joe.

"It was more than just his facility with the world," said Raleigh. "I don't think I'd ever had anyone treat me as an equal."

"Your sister."

"That's true, but it's different isn't it? We're in it together, thrown into it together. Born on a strange island. I'd been holding hands, navigating with her, since before she could speak. Since before either of us remember."

"It's a different thing, it's true."

"I never thanked you," said Raleigh.

"Thanked me?"

"For killing the man who killed Joe."

"Not sure I'm ready to take credit for that shot. Anyway, I think you did thank me. Back there at the cave."

"Thank you."

"Sure, then. You're welcome."

"I loved him like a brother," said Raleigh. "He taught me so much. Savoir faire."

"What's that?"

"Knowing how things get done. Knowing how to navigate the world."

"I know what you mean, there. The man they shot at Abbott's? We joined the army together, years ago. His name was Percy. Met him in Richmond, in the Union Hotel. You know that place?"

"I don't."

Jed looked over, startled. "No, I guess you wouldn't."

Raleigh laughed and said he guessed they might have let him cook or play piano.

"Dances and all that," said Jed.

"I think so."

"I ain't spent much time amongst those folks, you know, but I think I remember that lots of them have a soft spot for being entertained by Negroes."

"They seem to."

"I guess you been using that to your advantage."

"I don't know that I'd call it an advantage."

"No, I reckon not." Here Jed paused, and even in the humid darkness Raleigh could tell he was thinking. They were so close that it would have been more comfortable if Raleigh had hugged Jed, if they'd drawn into one another like mother and child.

"There's a little bench, there, on the bales, you can sit. We stop fifteen times for water, count them. Keep track, that's how you know where you are. It'll take about twenty hours to get to Petersburg. Keep your wits about. When we do stop, climb up to the top of that bale there and tuck in behind. Someone might close this door, but the latch is busted, it won't stay closed, just be quiet and let them. Couple of the crew don't know you're on. Count the stops then start looking, there's a point outside of Petersburg where the train slows way down, and there's going to be a red quilt tied into a tree there, it'll look like a camp, there'll be a fire. You need to get off the train there, and someone will meet you. When the train first slows you'll see two silos right next to the tracks, one them is painted with a black heart, the other painted with a black diamond—we'll be going real slow—and then about a quarter mile you'll see the quilt and the fire. You won't see me again."

"Thank you."

"You didn't see me this time, either, come to think of it. You got water?"

They held up canteens.

"Here's a twist of chewing tobacco. Don't smoke in the cotton."

Half an hour later the train lurched, chugged, and started rolling on the tracks.

The door to the freight car was open, and they had a ledge on the bale, as the brakeman had said they would, and a view out the door. They left just after dawn.

Raleigh watched a flock of small birds landing in a hayfield. Hundreds of them, in groups of a couple dozen, each group going a little farther into the field, like waves. The hay was pale green and calf high, and the light caught in the wings of the birds and glowed bright gold.

Jed was cutting a plug of tobacco. They had corn bread and salt meat for later, and the canteens were full. Jed had a new suit, rolled up in paper in a flour sack they'd tucked into the bales with their bags and the long guns. Jed kept his pistol on his hip.

The train rocked along, and both were mesmerized by the speed at which they traveled. Through the open door, framed by the worn wood of the freight car, they saw fields of corn, cotton, tobacco, drying sheds, horse barns, and potato fields. They rose up into the mountains, and the forest closed in around them. Through a break in the trees they saw a crossroads, a general store with three men leaning on the porch out front. They watched a man in overalls with a long switch, herding a small group of skinny dairy cows toward the milking barn. He looked heartbroken, downtrodden, but you could tell, even in the brief moment that they had him in the frame of their view, that he loved those cows, and that he didn't blame them. He looked as if he were asking them for help, as if he were trying to explain that they would have more food to eat, and better food to eat, if they made more and better milk.

They saw young animals in pens—piglets and lambs and steers. They saw leafy greens in neat rows. The train shot across a bridge, and up the creek from where they crossed they could see a race and cluster of buildings—a lumber mill with the wheels turning. The light faded in the leaves.

Each time the train stopped Jed took his hunting knife from his belt and carved a small notch on the doorframe, and as it grew dark he notched the eighth.

"We'll need to sleep. We'll take shifts. You go first, and I'll wake you up when we stop again," said Jed.

In the early morning, they stood at the door of the freight car holding everything they'd brought. The train had made its last stop for water, and they were looking for the silos. The train was moving slow.

"Still, sort something to jump off of it," said Jed.

Raleigh nodded and said: "Don't get run over. Jump outward—look, there's the fire."

"Who's first?" asked Jed, but Raleigh was already moving through the air. Jed held his breath and jumped as far away from the train as he could. His left foot went sideways on a rock, pain shot up his leg, and he rolled across the gravel into the grass, where he lay still, gasping.

CHAPTER FORTY-TWO

Seduction

Collings left for college—a firm handshake, hand on the shoulder from his father, an imitation of the same from his older brother, followed by some chiding and a playful, pretend sock on the jaw—with his books, his trunk of clothes, the money his grandfather had given him, and his mother.

Marie looked at the back of her son's head—he kept his face to the glass as the wheels rolled—his lovely hair brushed smooth and resting just at the top of his collar, childlike. Was this his last moment of childish wonder? She supposed that wasn't how it worked, exactly. The wonder was extracted from you bit by bit. She wondered what Collings saw. He hadn't missed the town house when they'd moved here, even at that young age he'd been focused on the next thing, devoid of the neophobia so commonly found in the young. Johnny was a provincial child, she thought. It was he who wept for his old room, the old staircase, the old courtyard. Zeb had dedicated himself to showing Johnny around, to entertaining him and making him brave. He'd done this casually, with impressive competence.

If there had been a high point in her marriage, that must have been it. The feeling she'd had then was more than just optimism, more than satisfaction. She'd opened her eyes each morning with anticipation and confidence.

She'd felt that everything had worked out, that life was proceeding along its course. She couldn't find the spot at which this had changed.

When Marie departed, Temple embarked upon a new strategy. She'd thought it through, in the dark hours before she slept, while the twittering and gossiping of the other house girls kept her awake. They ignored her, even ostracized her, and only allowed her a spot in the attic because Tandey reproached them and furrowed his impressive white eyebrows and told them to hush. They resented that Tandey would protect her, would care for her at all, but that just meant they left her alone. She stacked a few boxes to cordon off her corner, and when she put her head down it was almost as if she had her own room. She had gathered a tangle of cast-off rags, linens, and old clothes and made a litter, just as she'd slept on in her childhood in the kitchen basement.

See, she thought, you have always been here. You slept on a pile of rags below the kitchen. What led you to believe that you were anything other than a slave girl? Of course the other girls kept away from her—she was a madwoman in their midst.

Temple listened to their gossip, their empty-headed strategies. They looked no further than the next day, the next moment. The girls perceived no future, no alternative—all they desired was a shred of comfort, and what they truly wanted was to know that they were slightly more comfortable than their peers. They had grown up together and treated one another like sisters in that they took their closeness for granted and competed for what limited, simple resources existed.

The currency in which they traded was sex, and what they wanted was to stay in the house and work indoors, as opposed to living in the quarters and working in the fields. Working in the house meant food, warmth, and uniforms. Working in the house meant status. Although as Temple listened to them she wasn't sure.

Temple, having grown up on a farm, knew a little about the physical act of sex, for even Oliver's remaking of the Hundred couldn't erase sex and death. What she knew of human sexuality, unfortunately for her, had come from Rose, and had mostly to do with the seduction of a husband among the upper classes. (Certainly there'd been practical matters—Temple knew how to brew pennyroyal tea to induce menstruation.) The lessons, delivered as if they were pilfered lumps of sugar candy, were teatime fare, a smiling conspiracy between her and Rose to set Temple upon a path that never existed. Rose told her that "Men like to know that you will care for them. That you'll be there to make things better. They think their lives quite difficult, you know, they believe they suffer. They believe in nothing so much as their own misery, and what they want in a woman is someone who is going to alleviate it." She told her that men didn't know the things they were truly attracted to. "If you ask them, they'll say they love your eyes. And everyone knows how they feel about breasts and legs and so on, but everyone's got those, and the man who is attracted to you will love yours. What they don't know is that they're attracted to the way you smell. They're attracted to the softness of your skin. They're attracted to the way that your being is in contrast with theirs. Think about how he amuses himself, what he likes in the world. A bookish man, one who dithers and enjoys flowers, needs a woman with a strong head to coach him, to guide him, to lead him." She'd said, more than once, that men didn't know themselves. That if you were to ask they'd insist that they want a woman who shares their interests, but they don't. They want a woman who appreciates what they are interested in, but not one who is also interested in that. "Sure," Rose had said, "Percy Shelley wanted a wife who was interested in literature—his."

Perhaps, Temple thought, it was Rose who was mad and had pulled her into the delusions from which she now suffered. Could one catch madness? Share a misapprehension? Perhaps Rose, a widow, childless, had lost her grip on the way of the world and brought her into a fantasy. The white women didn't seem to think too highly of Rose.

Whatever it was that the girls on the other side of the attic were talking about, it bore no relation to anything Rose had discussed, and sometimes Temple could barely unpack the meanings of their nightly gossip. Things were left unsaid, spoken of elliptically, or with words Temple had never heard. She knew, however, that the girls engaged in—actively pursued—sexual activity with the men of the house.

If Temple had spent a few seasons in the attic of the Hundred, she would have learned that the girls were cast aside quickly. Any infraction, invented or otherwise, was enough to have a girl returned to the fields or worse, sold southward. New, younger girls would replace the ones who had just left. Somehow, the new girls believed that their weak hand held a winning combination to the game that was played on the Hundred. This was never proved correct, but it wouldn't have mattered, because their consent in this trafficking was illusory. Out in the field, where the dismissed toiled, most knew that whatever consent they thought they'd contributed was a fabrication. It was a long and complicated rape, the discarded women came to understand. There was no comfort in this understanding.

Temple had no such knowledge, and slowly unfurled a plan of her own. She figured that in Rose's equation Zeb was a hard man, a physical man, and that what he'd desire would be a soft, yielding woman. She pocketed herbs to put in her cleaning water, and made her body smell good. She softened her skin with kitchen oils. She kept her eyes wide and smiled readily. If Zeb said anything intended to be funny, she made sure to be seen stifling a laugh, or to chuckle softly just within his hearing. Whenever she could put a soft hand on his, to steady a coffee cup or take away something, she did so, making sure that her touch was softer than warm butter.

She dare not engage in this incitement when Marie was in the house—she heard among her attic mates disappointment when the lady of the house was present.

"Did you get Master Collings settled?" Temple had asked.

Marie looked up, surprised, as if she'd been asked by one of the laying hens.

Temple didn't wait for an answer: "Big portion of a young man's life, I'd imagine, leaving home. I'm sure he'll do fine, ma'am."

Marie didn't answer.

"You've got a lot to be proud of there," said Temple, leaving the room to continue with her tasks.

Marie went back to Richmond and to her father's side shortly after she'd returned. Temple carefully constructed her new character and put herself on display.

It'd been just over a week when she walked into the pantry after setting up the dining room for the evening meal and was ambushed by Mack. He'd been leaning behind the door, waited until it shut, and then grabbed her by the back of the neck and propelled her forward into the smaller china closet, where he spun her to face him and pushed her up against the wall across from the shelves with the plates. He was a big man, and he pressed his belly against her to keep her where she was. The stink of tobacco juice and whiskey rolled off his beard like fog rising from a river.

"You prance around, you'll get what you asking for, slut."

Temple whimpered. Mack shoved a knee between her legs.

"I see you. I know what you're doing."

She shook her head in response.

"Thing is, boss don't like it if they like it. Whores like it, and he don't go in for that. Too good of a man." He laughed a rough, short laugh, put his hand on her, first at her waist, then up to her armpit, then down her front until he held her between her legs. He pushed her hard against the wall.

"It's the church what taught him that," said Mack. "Taught him that if a woman wants it, she ain't worth giving it to."

With one hand still between her legs, pushing her back into the wall, he put his other forearm across her neck, pinning her head back.

"You want it? Lift them skirts for me then."

She whimpered.

"Too late to be scared, girl."

Keeping her head pinned back, he gathered up her skirt, a handful at a time. He was drunk, and clumsy, and as he struggled to reveal what he wanted, Temple gasped and squirmed to make it more difficult.

The back door slammed open and Gilly called out to Mack, who in his fumbling frustration with her clothes had lost his motivation. He pushed her aside, gave her a disgusted sneer, and walked back to see his friend.

CHAPTER FORTY-THREE

To the Swamp

Jed was still on the ground when two men came out of the tree line, both dressed in rags, like drifters, but with an intensity of purpose that betrayed they were not. They were thin, and they wore slouch hats, and one had a long scruffy beard. The other, the younger of the two, had a pink gash that ran along his cheek, a knife cut, straight and clean. From battle, thought Jed, not farming.

The older one spoke: "You're hurt."

Jed shook his head.

"Hell you ain't," said the younger. "You're hurt. What'd you do?"

"Stepped on a rock," said Jed.

"That's hell luck."

"I wish you'd stop invoking the devil," said the man with the beard.

"I ain't invoking." The young man said "invoking" petulantly.

"Hell this, hell that. Got enough on this earth to compare things to without reaching out into the realm of the devil, which anyway you don't know what it's like. Don't help nothing, saying something is just like the devil."

"Fine, Pa, I'll keep them God damned hells to myself."

Jed accepted a hand from the young man and heaved himself up off the grass, wincing, and tenderly testing to see if the ankle would bear weight. It would not.

"It's sprained," said Jed.

"Maybe broke."

"Ain't broke," said Jed, grimacing.

"There's a safe doc in Richmond," said the older man.

"Safe for runaways," said Jed. "That don't apply."

"Ain't nothing to be done with them," said the father to the son. "They can't go on."

"Put them up somewhere" said the son.

"For how long?"

"We don't know," answered the son, "because we don't know if his foot is broke."

"It ain't," said Jed.

"We don't know," said the father, "and we don't know how long it'll take to mend."

"Can't stick him somewhere safe without knowing for how long. Nowhere wants him for more than they have to have him."

"Can we get to the swamp from here?" Raleigh asked. "The Dismal Swamp?"

"He can't walk with a broken foot."

"Is there a horse we could buy?"

"We might find a donkey."

"That will take a saddle?"

The father and son took them to a safe house, where they hid in the hayloft. Jed wrapped his ankle tightly in some cloth the farmwife gave to him, and slept with it propped up on a bale of hay.

In the morning, a donkey with a tattered saddle on his back was tied to the hitching post. They walked until they came to the edge of a dark, damp forest, and scanned the tree line until they saw a notch cut into a cypress.

The father had said that they should follow the notches into the swamp. "That's solid ground, and it'll lead you right to a settlement of maroons. If your woman is there, they'll know her. Someone'll probably come along and ask you what you're doing there before you find the settlement. Tell them you heard the bells ringing for little Ida's funeral, and you come to pay your respects."

"That's the password," said the son. "You say the wrong thing you'll end up sunk in that swamp."

"We heard the bells ringing for little Ida's funeral, and we have come to pay our respects," said Raleigh.

The swamp was thick, rough going, and they moved slowly through the underbrush, looking for the notches carved into the bark of the black gum trees and tupelos. The air carried the rich reek of rotten matter, humus and mushrooms, moss and vine sap. But for the narrow strip they walked, the land was soaked, and the forest that spread out from either side of them opened up in places where the gum trees gathered around small ponds from which fat cypress grew, their airy hips like hands reaching down into the water. All around came creaking and humming, the leaves teeming with insects, the canopy alive with birds. Underneath the hooves of the donkey the black earth was rich and fecund.

They walked for some time without speaking and then Jed asked if Raleigh had given the donkey a name.

"What makes you ask that?"

"You just seem like the sort of man that might have. Given him a name, I mean." Jed paused briefly and when Raleigh didn't answer, he said: "I ain't saying anything against you. I'd just like to be referring to this animal proper."

"I have been calling him Hob," said Raleigh.

"A'ght, Hob." Jed reached forward and patted the donkey, the old dry saddle creaked. His boots were no more than a few fingers from the trail, which was almost invisible any more than ten feet ahead of them. They looked for the notches. When the marsh came up close to the trail and they walked along next to the loose black mud, the smells grew more intense, a rotted miasma caught between noxious and satisfying.

Jed said: "You know how from a ways away a dead thing smells kind of sweet, but when you get up on it, it'll make you retch? Whole place smells like that."

They drifted along, caught up in the search for the trail markers and happy in their sparse conversation. They'd almost forgotten their mission when a voice came out of the shadows and asked them where they were going.

Raleigh looked into the shadows and saw no one, so he said into the air that he'd heard the bells and had come for little Ida's funeral, at which point three black men with guns stepped out on to the path.

"And this here?" They gestured at Jed.

"He's my friend. We're together. Also, he's hurt, and we need help. We've come to see the medicine woman Lo—she used to go by Lo—she told me she lived by the great split magnolia."

Two of the men stayed in the wood and the third led Jed and Raleigh to a clearing, encircled by small shacks, made carefully but without plans and from what was at hand. The shacks encircled a tall magnolia tree split in two by lightning or wind, and caught, as each half fell, by the low branches that each held a half of the old trunk in place. Over time, the branches had rooted into the ground, and the tree had become an interconnected grove of trees centered around the bifurcated trunk. The leaves were thick and the overall effect was of two magnolia trees growing close together. If one stepped inside the shelter of the canopy, the cleaving was made clear, and many a secret conspiracy among the children of the settlement had been hatched in the notch of the tree, where the wood had weathered. The shack to their right seemed hung on a stone chimney which, itself, looked as if it were about to fall in and pull the siding down in a heap behind the small porch—from the shadows behind that porch came a shriek.

"Raleigh! Raleigh Bodkin, my Lord, that is you. You can grow a beard, little boy, but you can't hide yourself behind it! Not from me."

Wobbling out of one of the doors came Lo, older, her gray hair twisted in long strands and gathered together behind her head. She wore a flowing kaftan died in crimson, yellow, and purple, and leaned on a staff of twisted cypress. She had chicken feet and stones stitched into a complicated necklace, and from within her billowing sleeves one could hear the rattling and clinking of baubles and charms. While she walked with purpose, there was a labor in each step she took. She let her walking stick fall by her side and they embraced, and she kissed him, and held him again, and then backed him up in her arms to look at him, and then hugged him again.

"Raleigh Bodkin," she said, amazed, appreciative.

Raleigh looked at the shack behind her, and saw Gee, smiling wide, his gray beard gone white. Raleigh picked up Lo's stick for her, and walked to Gee, who slapped him on the back as they embraced.

Lo made a compress of comfrey and garlic for Jed's ankle, and wrapped clean cotton cloth around it, tightly enough to hold it still and press against the swelling.

Jed exclaimed that he smelled like a sausage.

"You blown up like one, too. You stay off this. Stay right there."

She had him laid up on a cot on the front porch with rag-stuffed pillows elevating his ankle and propping up his head.

"I'm'a give you something to help you rest, now, too."

She handed him a draught of tea she made from the poppies she grew, and he drifted calmly on a painless sea of golden stupefaction.

"Raleigh! You are a man now, for sure, ain't he, Gee? But can't fool me none. I see that red colored forehead."

Gee raised his eyebrows at Lo, and she settled herself. He felt sure she was about to mention the boy's father, and how were they to know if the boy had been told? Who knew what he knew?

The reunited sat in ladder-back chairs around a small square table in front of the little house.

"First," said Lo, "terrible thing that happen to Master Oliver, wasn't it? You stop that, Gee. I can't help but think of Master Oliver as Master Oliver, means young one I guess somehow too, anyway, that little boy grown up just to die like that. I heard about it. Course we heard about it. They said you all three died in that fire. I never believed it."

Gee shrugged, indicating that perhaps she believed it some.

"I thought Temple had, as well," said Raleigh. "Then I got word Zeb Newcombe took her. Enslaved her."

"You got word?"

"From Miss Rose."

"Rose Knaupf?"

Raleigh nodded.

"I heard she got run off, out West."

"She wrote me a letter."

"That right?"

"I'm going there. We are. To get her."

"From Bodkin's Hundred?"

Raleigh nodded.

"With that man?"

Raleigh nodded.

"How do you know him? He's a friend of yours?"

Raleigh couldn't have evaded Lo's questions if he'd tried.

"He is my friend. I mean, he is now. We've become friends. I . . . He's a wanted man. He has a treasure, out there in the desert in No Man's Land, where we came from, and I hid it and captured him so he would help me. Because my friend Red Joe—an Indian, an Englishman, an Indian who was raised in England—is dead, he was shot in a saloon. I needed someone."

Lo stared at Raleigh. As she had told him, she could see the boy under the beard, under the age so recently acquired. The story sounded fantastical, and she'd heard that Raleigh had been raised up on white-man stories after she'd left. The James River served as a conduit for goods but also for gossip and information. As a healer and a woman who knew herbs and could help people, a good number of people had wanted to curry Lo's favor, to develop a bond with her, and one of the prices she had made known was information about the Bodkin plantation, about Raleigh and Temple. She'd been starved for news since the fire—word did not get off the Newcombe place. Her emotions, now, were conflicted. She was overwhelmed with motherly love to see Raleigh, and deeply suspicious of what he was saying.

"How did this all come to be?"

"I guess it's a long story."

She nodded back at Jed, and said he wasn't going anywhere too soon.

Raleigh and Jed stayed in the swamp for a week.

Raleigh told Lo stories about his adventure—about Red Joe, Vivian, and the *Rialto*, about life out West. She listened with the heartfelt, bewildered attention that a grandmother gives to a grandchild explaining a life lived far away, holding hard to the details she recognized, and letting the mystery of that which she didn't understand impress her.

Eating Lo's cooking was, for Raleigh, a remembrance, an invocation. He said as much: "I've missed these biscuits, Lo."

It made her feel good to know that she hadn't been supplanted by all this worldly experience.

Raleigh helped out and met the community. They lived free, far from the white man's world. They did not worry much about the war to come, but they were curious about what would happen and who would do what. They were separate, and the world outside of the swamp was interesting in the way that news from across the sea is interesting. The Russian Tsar had recently emancipated the serfs, and if someone had brought this news to the swamp it would have been discussed with the same intensity.

Although there was some talk among the younger men of joining the first Union army that got close.

"The war will be over by the time a Union army gets close," said Lo.

After a couple of days, Lo allowed that Jed might rise from his stupor on the litter she had set up on the porch and walk to the table. He was all grateful expressions and gallows humor, kept in the best of all frames of mind by the poppy tea. She took to him.

His limp was terrible, however, and he grabbed a stick from the underbrush to help himself along.

Gee held up a hand indicating that Jed should wait. Jed obliged, and Gee appeared with an intricately carved, well-oiled length of bald cedar, topped with a ball carved of darker wood, and wrapped in wires of silver that had been melted into the seams. Mysterious symbols wound up and down the shaft, as well as vines and flowers. Jed did not recognize the hoodoos on the stick, but he felt them.

"He makes those. They are powerful, and it's an honor to be given one," said Lo. Gee smiled and nodded. "I believe he thinks it will help you on your quest."

Jed gave a little bow, and thanked them both.

"It's beautiful," he said. "People don't," he started and then paused, clearly moved. "People don't give me much."

Gee nodded as if he knew that were true and patted Jed on the shoulder.

Jed had his foot up on a stool and was dressed in his new suit. His cheeks were shaved clean, and Lo had evened out his tuft of whiskers. He'd oiled his hair back and polished his nails.

"We do need to get you some boots, though," said Lo. She sent the word out, and the next day a pair of fine stovepipe boots in soft, fawn-colored leather arrived.

"You're a rich man," said Lo.

"No, ma'am" he said, embarrassed, "not me."

"Lose that quick. Humility fine and good, but the man you are walking as now don't have none. So get used to it. Rich man act like he deserves. Rich man act like what he sees is already his. Rich man believes he rich because God loves him and because he's right about things. You are the master. You see? The master. A rich man traveling light. You need to make excuses for that. You're sorry you don't have the proper clothes for dinner, and all that. What you gonna do for money?"

"I have some," said Raleigh.

"Stop by this address." She took a scrap of paper from the folds of her kaftan. "Ask for a man named Haso. He'll sell you a stack of checks from the Cape Fear Bank in Wilmington, North Carolina."

Raleigh wasn't surprised by Lo's competence—she was, in his eyes, the definition of competence—but he was surprised by her worldliness. Over the week while they'd worked on their parts—teaching Raleigh what it meant to be a slave, and Jed what it meant to be a master, as well as finding details for their costumes—a hand-me-down shirt for Raleigh, a watch chain for Jed—they'd also discussed the swamp and the railroad that led to it. The swamp was a terminal, a free place. Runaways landed here, as well as free people like herself and Gee who wanted to live away from the compromises that the white world insisted upon. Nobody owned property here, in the swamp, she explained.

"You want to build a house? You ask the people nearby if this is a good place. If it ain't a good place, they show you one."

Now that the blockade was up, the runners and smugglers needed somewhere unconnected to any nation or state.

"The Swamp is separate. Lots of people need a place like that," she said.

They planned their route one midafternoon while the swamp was alive with insect and bird calls, over tea that an English blockade runner had traded Lo in exchange for hiding his boat in a creek for a week. Jed noted the implication—it was Lo who got tea. Raleigh took this for granted.

"Grey's Tea, he called it," said Lo, "Said he got it from a place called Jackson's in London. Piccadilly Street." She said the syllables distinctly, having made an effort to remember the name. "Delicious, isn't it? It's good we're talking about Captain Stephens, because he's going to run you up the river."

She leaned forward, pulled a whittled and polished stick from the tangle of her hair, and placed the sharpened point on Mayo's Island, in the middle of the James, where the rapids begin.

"Stephens can't take you past this. But he's docking here, and he will drop you at the docks."

Jed looked at where she was pointing and remembered the men he'd seen on those docks.

"I stand on a sea of glass and fire," he said.

Lo looked at him, startled to hear a black spiritual in a white man's mouth.

"I saw something there. A long time ago. Slaves on a gangway. I haven't thought about it for a long time. They sang a song back and forth."

"The bell done rung," said Lo.

"That's it," said Jed. "They sang out that the bell done rung. They sang about a sea of glass."

His voice came slow. He'd been drinking poppy tea for six days, and the world had a magical warmth and an extra glow.

"What happened then?"

"They all jumped. They were chained together on the gangway, chained by their necks, by their feet, and they preached and sang. Then they jumped." He shook his head, lost in the remembrance of the moment.

"Better to be free. Least the last choice was their own," said Lo. "Captain Stephen will drop you at the docks, and you'll go see Haso. He'll sell you horses, too. You got money for horses?"

Raleigh nodded.

Everyone seemed satisfied. Gee went off to fish, and Lo walked over to a man who was waiting for her attention in the shade of the big magnolia.

CHAPTER FORTY-FOUR

Marie's Truth

Marie looked about the room assigned to Collings—one of six in the attic of an oddly shaped building called the Alamo—and helped him unpack some books. She smoothed his shirts and hung them, introduced herself to the porter (and slipped a coin into his hand), hesitated, groused about nothing at all, tucked a stray curl of her boy's hair behind his ear (chiding herself as she did it for babying him), and departed.

He was caught between youth and manhood, just as the college looked caught between seriousness and pretense. College didn't seem like much to her: buildings, lawns, young men lost in thought or walking with their friends and speaking too fast, playing at being serious, playing at lawyering or science or whatever it was that held them. It didn't seem much different than Johnny and Collings playing at war (Johnny leading the charge) or setting up a theater in the great room for one of Collings's meandering productions. It was hard to imagine that her own father's most fond moments passed among these buildings, but it was less difficult to imagine Collings settling in. Collings wanted to stretch out, and needed a couple of years of pretending, developing his own tastes, and arguing with peers.

First he'd have to get through what would no doubt be an overbearing visit from his grandfather at the end of the week.

Take your grandson to lunch, she'd said, and see if anyone you know is still there. She doubted it, but to suggest this would be to remind Mr. Collings of how many years had gone by, and the man, especially in his current fragility, would come to that on his own. He'd spent too much time on the settee in the library with his powder and his whiskey at hand. A ride out to Hampden-Sydney would do him good.

She'd warned Collings to take it easy, not to lead him around too much. Don't make him climb stairs if it can be avoided. Make sure there's somewhere to sit, make sure they eat at a reasonable time.

Collings had nodded, bored.

"He'll expect you turned out well. Make sure your shirts are pressed," she'd said, while Collings stared out the window, a portrait of ennui, bored almost to the point of perishing by the unfathomable stupidity of the world sliding by, but finding even in that a respite from the relentless prattling of his mother.

He'd turned to her with a malicious glint, she could see him deciding which horrible thing to say. Collings had said: "I'm perfectly happy to entertain him, but I think Mr. Bodkin was right when he said that my future was my own."

"Mr. Bodkin?"

He nodded, "Yes, Oliver Bodkin. He told me not to worry about legacy, about tradition, but to understand that the only person living my life was me."

"Oliver Bodkin said that?"

She'd made the boy impatient, and he glared at her and said: "Yes. I just told you. Oliver Bodkin."

"What an absurd thing to say. And from a Bodkin." She could not help but hold that family in the highest regard, despite the strange and ignoble end of its reign among the founding families of Virginia. This, in part, was why she did not like to speak of the dead man. "When did this happen?"

"The last time I saw him. The day he and Father fought."

"Oliver Bodkin? And your father?" Now even she thought she sounded like an idiot—she must stop asking, must stop saying the man's name as if it were a question. "I didn't know they'd fought, this must have been some time ago."

"Oh, no. Not at all. I was there playing piano with Mr. Bodkin, Chopin I think, and Father came to get me and they had words."

"Words?" She caught herself asking questions again. She couldn't help it. The idea of the two men speaking, much less arguing, was preposterous. What could they say to one another? Her husband and her neighbor didn't speak the same language, or they did in only the most superficial sense. In years past she might have relished the idea of her brute of a man, standing on the carpet in a Bodkin's house, horrifying, scorching Oliver Bodkin like a beam of strong sunlight on a violet. This no longer amused her.

"Oliver told him, told Father, that he ought to investigate some Northern colleges for me, that I was bright, and musical, and that I should be allowed to live as I choose and do as I please."

"I'm sure he said no such thing." Was there anything as vicious as a young man?

"He did. He said that to Father, and more. He said I'd like Boston and New York. Father got cross and yelled and acted like a brute. Mr. Bodkin didn't seem upset by it, which just made Father even angrier."

"Well, this must have been a long time ago. I never heard anything about it. Was that all that was said?"

"It wasn't. I said it wasn't. And I told you it was the day the Old House burned down. It was the last time I saw Mr. Bodkin."

He went back to staring out the window of the coach and broadcasting his general dissatisfaction with the world.

"Your grandfather will be here on Friday."

Collings nodded.

Marie had worried the shirts, unpacked the books, tipped the porter, tucked the stray hair, stepped back up into the coach and departed. Good place to be if there's a war, she thought. He'll be safe. She recalled the gleam in Johnny's eye when he spoke of the cavalry—clearly if it were up to the young men of the South there would be a war. There would be a war because to not have a war would be a disappointment, or worse, it would besmirch them, call them out as cowards. Boys like Johnny would rather die, would march toward death, would invite it, before being called a coward. What creatures they were, these hot young men. Why can't they just be clever? She didn't know that she'd ever met a boy who wasn't either mired in his own malaise or as hot as a stallion.

She contemplated what Collings had said as if it were a rough stone in her gloved hand, turning it, feeling every snag and hook, and that which she had steadfastly avoided thinking about for the better part of a year came to her. Now it was she who watched the countryside go by, wrapped up in her own dissatisfactions, caught up in her own troubled thoughts.

The men had fought. She still couldn't bring that into focus—how would each comport himself? Zeb's physicality, his grit, the cigar stains on his fingers and the way he stood square at everyone. Oliver, so casual and assured, so superior, casting words about that Marie was sure would have no meaning to Zeb, and laughing as he did so, which Zeb would think was laughter directed at him, which to some degree it would have been. Zeb must have arrived furious and grown only more so. She knew that Zeb was suspicious of Oliver, of his influence on Collings and of his intentions with the colored children.

More like pets than servants, they'd agreed. What a terrible and corrupt notion, she thought.

Zeb had gone riding that night, out with the night patrols—a stupid waste of time, but men will ride and drink with other men and if it makes them feel that they are protecting us, then so be it. He'd gone out, and said he'd be home late. Mack and Gilly had gone with him. She'd been roused from sleep by the clanging of the bell and the bucket brigade being organized to draw from the well and throw useless puddles at the conflagration. Steam hissing and men hollering and Oliver nowhere to be seen.

Something about the way Zeb had told the story to her—first he'd found the girl running away, then when he told her again he'd rescued her from the fire—cast the whole affair into confusion. But it was a confusing night. And so many had worked so hard to curb the flames. They were sooty, and sweaty, and muscle sore. She'd had a keg of beer brought up, and even allowed a few of the servants a cup.

I knew, she thought. I knew then and I know now. Still, she danced around what she knew, and wished she could avoid confronting the thought.

But she could not.

There, in the carriage, with her youngest behind her, she could not go on evading or distracting. She was stuck, looking out the window and thinking about that which she did not wish to consider.

He is a violent man, and I've always known that.

She'd called it something else. Strength.

She considered the months she'd spent avoiding him, the excuses. The blessed excuse—she caught herself, sent a little prayer asking for forgiveness for thinking that her father's ill-health had provided her a convenience. She stayed in Richmond whenever she could, distanced herself with work on the church, or with her father, scribbled letters to men who didn't care to hear from her, didn't care about what she had to say, and why? Just to avoid the possibility that she might have to talk to Zeb. She'd have to, now, she decided. If only to make sure that the rest of her life was not a sham. She'd confront him.

What was it that bothered her so? *I have been trying to preserve a way of life*, she thought. Trying to preserve traditions, and gentility, and the benevolent hand that ruled over the sweet sunny South, and he was dismantling it. Through example, through action, through good works, she had tried, as she saw it, to keep order and justice and prosperity.

What, she wondered, would be loosed upon these lands? What would happen to these fields? These houses? These people? Even the blacks. What would happen to them?

Why must everyone resist? Why, when she says that she wants to renovate the decrepit chapel, repair it, bring it back to the vision Mr. Jefferson had of it when he drew the plans—she knew, with passionate intensity, that it was Mr. Jefferson who had designed the church, and that the incompetence of the priests was why that was no longer common knowledge. They didn't know! They shrugged as if it didn't matter. There she was with money and her intentions clear, and they resisted.

She felt herself fold in on herself when she thought of money. Had Zeb ruined that? She pushed the thought from her mind.

Eighteen years she's spent! She chided herself, remembering the time before Johnny, and the time in between, so not all of these eighteen years.

She had been a girl, and then, what? Lustful girl woman, animalistic, a succubus. She knew, and was ashamed, that her fervency had started well before the marriage blessing. She'd held on—a credit to her ancestors, superior people, who even in the throes of this madness could resist, could hold on to purity because they understood, and therefore she understood, what was important. She'd dreamt, perhaps too much, but she'd saved herself for the marriage bed. It's the action that matters, she assured herself, then as now, not the imagining. Who among us escapes temptation? No one. Some might linger upon it a little less, but what happens in the cradle of one's own private heart happens only there.

Then children and the house in town and then out to the Hundred without so much as a pause. The whole of her life rushing forward. And if one stopped and thought, in some rare private moment, some holy crumb of time during which nothing was needed of her and she had the wherewithal to think about things, what did she see? She saw her life ill spent on the sudden flush she'd felt as a girl. A girl asked to make decisions she should not make, the repercussions of which were unimaginable. What does "the rest of your life" mean to a girl of sixteen? How dare anyone ask a girl to play at these stakes?

She'd dreamt of Zeb, even before she had met him, when he was but a figure in the doorframe, standing on the porch, announcing that he was here to see Mr. Collings. She'd spy glimpses of him, seated before her father's desk, slouched, all confidence. She'd bring in a pot of coffee and hold his eyes as long as she could stand. Back in the kitchen her mother would be counting the spoons—perhaps she should have given that more thought. Although there could be no doubt as to the victor in a contest between his dark, wild eyes and her mother's suspicions that he was made of inferior stuff and wanted to use her, even a spoon at a time, to gain a foothold on the next rung of the ladder. His gloves on his knee, the way he rippled with strength and danger. He set her aflame. She'd run upstairs to her frills and her lace, soft fabric everywhere, drapery and finery and featherbeds, throw herself upon the bed in a fit of melodrama and dream of him kidnapping her.

She wanted him to ruin her.

Her friends and her mother thought she was in love. Her sister understood she wasn't. If they'd known how visceral her desire was, if they'd known what it was she saw when she thought of him. But there was no language available to a girl of sixteen. So she, too, called it love.

Maybe this is the foundation of all marriages, she thought, as difficult as that is to imagine. Or, perhaps—and she and her sister had come to agree upon this—it would do just fine as a foundation for this one.

They'd been wrong. She'd survived on lust for months, and then been lost in a haze of pregnancy—a wretched, spellbinding business—and then in her maniacally heightened state after Johnny had been born she returned again to lust, and then Collings, and more of the absurd weight—not her figure, she'd never minded her figure, she'd been proud of her babies inside her, the physical pull, the heaviness, the swelling, the constant reminder of her physical form.

Then she shed girlhood like a skin she'd outgrown, shook her new self into being, and found that she was someone else entirely, with nothing left in her marriage that interested her. Nothing about Zeb amounted to the sort of man she wanted to be married to. She wished he had kidnapped her. How simple, how romantic. She'd rather have suffered the consequences of such an impurity than this slow debilitation. She'd have been rescued, forgiven, or if not forgiven at least settled.

And now the boys would be gone, but he would not.

And this. (Still she couldn't speak it.)

She'd suspected all year long that Zeb knew not where the line was, that he was not, at his core, civilized. He couldn't tell the difference between us and them, between white and black. He was common. He had no quality. To improve, an individual must have, hidden within them, something superior. There was no prince hidden within Zeb. There was no changing him.

She found Zeb in his office.

"You don't look happy to be here," he said, wryly, still thinking he could make a joke, unaware of how deeply she had turned and the fury she was barely containing.

"Collings told me you fought with Oliver Bodkin."

He didn't answer, just looked surprised.

"Did you?" Marie asked.

"I didn't like Oliver Bodkin. I don't know that it ever . . . we never came to blows." He laughed. She could see how unfair such a contest would be.

"I have put it away, deep inside myself," her lip was quivering, "and ignored the nagging truth. I can't ignore it anymore."

"Relax, my darling. Can I get you something? You've had a long day, and you are upset—of course you are. You've dropped your baby off at school. Your child is grown. It must be hard for a woman—"

"Stop. It isn't that, and no," she refused the small, elegant glass he held out to her, so he drank it and set it back on the small round table next to the decanter of brandy.

"Get some rest, Marie, we'll talk when you feel better."

Something opened up inside her and she blurted out: "Did you kill him?" before she could cork it.

"I understand. It's hard to watch them grow. Go off on their own." He went back to the brandy, poured another, drank it. "The slave boy killed Oliver Bodkin, then lit the house on fire. Everybody knows that."

She heard it, and she wanted badly to believe it, as everyone did, because it was so much easier to simply lay the blame on the degeneracy of the darker race. She saw the rope of thought, like a lifeline in turbulent waters, and she wanted to grab it, would love to grab it, hold it and close her eyes and float in peaceful delusions. This, she thought to herself, scolding, is exactly why you should never have brought it up. If it had gone unsaid, it simply wouldn't be at all, but now it was out. It was real. She'd said the words. She knew he'd killed Oliver Bodkin.

"He was a *Bodkin*," she said. "You are a violent man."

He shook his head.

She went on: "Of course you are. You were the most feared tracker and slave catcher in Virginia. I have no illusions about what that entails. Never have. Though I believed you understood that there are lines one should never cross."

"Get some rest. You're upset. That boy Bodkin kept went crazy. That's what happens. What do you expect?"

"I need to return my father's horses," said Marie.

CHAPTER FORTY-FIVE

The Charade

Captain Stephens mastered the SS *Dafoe*, a four-hundred-ton side-wheel steamer built in Scotland.

"She ain't the best looking, but she hauls good, and turns quick, and she'll make Nassau full of cotton as soon I get her turned about and out of this river." Captain Stephens was a tall, dark-eyed man, deeply tan. "She'll make twelve knots under full steam," he said.

Raleigh and Jed stood at the aft gunwale with the captain, who kept his eyes moving, scanning the water.

He looked through his telescope at a still-distant gray mass. The water was wide. They hadn't made it into the river itself yet.

"Without guns, we trust ourselves to be faster than the gunships. Once we're in the river, there won't be anywhere to run. Doesn't matter how fast you are if there's nowhere to go."

The captain looked up and down the shore.

"Usually the *Virginia* is about, that's our side, but I don't see her. Be nice if she were."

Raleigh asked, haltingly, if they were under chase.

"Of course we are, lad. Look here."

Captain Stephens handed Raleigh the telescope, and pointed.

"Are they going to catch up to us?"

"The real question is whether or not they've got compatriots. Smaller boats, hiding here and there, ready to dart out and take us. The race is on. They won't come within range of the guns at Rockett's. Once we hit that river, we're going full steam."

He put his telescope to his eye again and said: "Ah, yes. Duck."

There was a whistling scream as a shell from a ten-pound Parrott gun flew into the water off the starboard side.

"Not a bad shot for a first try."

"They're shooting at us?"

"It would seem so."

"Is that against the law?"

"A fine question I hope to never have the opportunity to ask. They aren't Navy boats, if that's what you're asking. They're privateers. Pirates. Hired—with a wink—by the Navy. They catch us, they keep the prize." He paused. "We're no better, I suppose. Anyway, the good news is they don't care about the crew, so if we survive, we'll walk away. If we can walk. Test of your mettle, if you see what I mean. Where's the line? When do you throw in the cards?"

A shell exploded in the water, closer than the last shot.

"I wonder how many guns she's got."

A barrage of scatter shot balls, each the size of a thumbnail, slammed into the deck from the port side.

"Ah. There's her partner in arms. Stay low, lads."

The captain crawled forward on his belly and hollered down into the engine room. A shudder moved through the boat, and they lurched to a greater speed.

"Always like to make them think they know what they are dealing with," said Captain Stephens, crawling back toward Jed and Raleigh, who cowered against the metal gunwale. "Save a little. I said we didn't have guns. That's not entirely true. There's a punt gun in that dingy there, eight foot long. Who wants to slip it into the oarlock and give that bastard off the port side a reason to back off?"

The gun was a battered, brutal machine, layered with thick fat to keep the salt water from pitting it.

The captain slid into the dinghy and opened a case of shot that was on the floor. Raleigh and Jed crawled in behind him.

"I was looking forward to shooting some ducks. Hopefully we'll have some shot left."

He slid the massive gun into the oarlock clasp and rearranged a couple of sandbags to hold down the stock.

"She kicks like a damn mule, now, watch yourself."

He pulled a shell from the box; it was brass based and had a paper tube that was a foot long.

"We'll wait until they shoot again, and then we'll poke our heads up and get a bearing."

Within twenty seconds lead balls bounced again across the deck of the SS *Dafoe*. They lifted their heads from the dinghy and saw the small gunship, a steam-powered skiff, coming right at them, no more than two hundred yards away. There were men on the deck, manning the gun on the prow, and scrambling about.

"I don't look forward to killing, but I'll not have people firing on the *Dafoe*. Good luck!" The captain slapped the trigger on the punt gun. The blast was enormous. The men shook their heads, their ears ringing.

"Let's see how that felt," said the Captain, his voice muffled and distant in their newly assaulted ears, but his face agleam with pride and humor. He liked a battle.

They looked again at the little skiff, and saw that the men were now laying on the deck and the skiff had turned.

"See! There we go. I'm going to call down to the engine room. Count to ten, then send another blast over, would you?"

Raleigh picked up a lead ball from the floor of the dinghy and slipped it in his pocket.

"Well," he said to Jed. "It is exciting."

The ship behind them landed another shell in the water, closer.

"I think they're missing on purpose," said Raleigh.

"Why?"

"What sort of prize is a sunken ship?"

"You think they're just trying to get us to surrender?"

"I do, but I don't think the captain is the surrendering type."

They laughed.

They loaded another shot, got their bearing, and blasted it toward the gunship.

When the captain came back he was grinning from ear to ear.

"I'll take you both on, if you like. You want to run blockades? There's money to be made here! We've only got another couple of hundred yards, then we're in the river and close enough to Rockett's Landing that they'll stop shooting at us. One more volley from that punt and the little one won't want to follow, anyway."

The smoke from the engines filled the sky above them, and the steam was hot and stank of boiler metal.

The smaller gunboat was aside them, 150 yards off, running parallel, but falling behind. The *Dafoe* was the faster ship, running without cargo.

The captain watched the man at the gun on the prow ready it, and just as he was about to turn it toward the *Dafoe*, he shot the punt again. The man fell backward.

"Looks like he might have fallen in," said the captain, "what a pity."

The gunboat was slowing down, giving up.

"Tangled with the wrong Englishman."

The meeting with Haso was smooth and uneventful, though it felt peculiar to Jed to be back in Richmond, which had changed enough and grown enough to be both familiar and strange at once, like a dream of a place that resonates with, but doesn't resemble, the place you know it to be.

With new horses, tack, a stack of blank checks, additions to their wardrobes, and some gear and provisions, they started out of town on the old Indian road, which led out to the Huguenot settlement and to Bodkin's Hundred. They stopped at plantations along the way, were asked to lunch, were asked to stay the night, and Jed tried on bits of his character. Fumbling a little at first, he settled into it. He remembered what Lo had said, to simply believe that he owned what he looked at, that he was the master of what he saw, and all else would fall into place. The cane was an excellent prop—it leant him an exoticism.

He owned a sugar plantation in Brazil, he explained, and while he was sure that this foolish war would soon be over, he had experienced the blockade himself, and felt that he needed to increase his stock. He was on a mission, therefore, to buy slaves.

Families pressed for money and fearful of the future were quick to oblige the inquiry, and Jed found himself inspecting lines of people, and listening to their owners list their faults and qualities.

He was disgusted.

He refined his pitch as they went. He figured out that the plantation owners along this river didn't want to think of what was coming as a war. "These acts of aggression," they would say, and Jed adopted these phrases as well. He saw they held pride in their new nationhood, and wanted recognition.

"What do they say of our plight in Brazil?"

"When one nation is bent on the destruction of wealth, and another provides the finest cotton and tobacco to the entire world, what would they say? They say it is a shame."

Although gentlemanliness did not come naturally to Jed, he found that if he kept Percy in mind, if he spoke as Percy would have spoken, and moved as Percy would have moved, he was allowed in this genteel world. He cast himself as a bit of an eccentric—again the cane helped—and combined that eccentricity with his residence in Brazil to mask any errors of manner.

He also made sure that he was waited on by Raleigh, who helped him through.

"On account of my injury," he gestured toward his leg, "I have become quite reliant—rather too reliant I fear—on my boy. I need him with me."

Raleigh would help him up from chairs, and hover near, and would manage to slip in and touch the fork he should be using for the fish course.

"I'll need a cot for my boy. I find that the leg troubles me in the night, and I need him by my side, for I cannot rise without him."

They had private moments, therefore, and were able to keep Raleigh out of the slave quarters or the barn. They debriefed along the way, in whispered guest room conversations.

"Selling me a man," said Jed. "Talking about that man right there before him as if he can't hear? As if he can't understand the words?"

"Remember not to treat these people as your betters," said Raleigh. "Treat them as if you belong. Maybe think of them as if they owed you money."

"I worry someone is going to recognize you," said Jed.

"I am a stranger here, because we never left home. Perhaps among the slaves, but they haven't seen me since Lo was the medicine woman, since I was ten, twelve years old. Anyway, we learned, in the Rialto, that whoever you say you are is who you are."

"And the beard," said Jed. "Which becomes you. You look smarter."

"I noticed," said one gray-haired patriarch with some condescension, "that you wear a pistol. Is it customary for a gentleman to proceed as such? I mean, in Brazil. Like a bandit?"

"The roads of Brazil are rife with criminals," said Jed, with a slight nod. "I have been pleasantly surprised to find no need of self-defense in your fair environs."

They rode in the morning, covering the couple of miles between the big farms in an hour or two, and then stopping at the next plantation in time to be invited for lunch. They stayed in character as best they could along the way, but they couldn't help but talk about the business at hand.

"This is terrible, worse than the army," said Jed. "To walk down a row of men and listen to someone describe them like they were selling you a horse."

Raleigh nodded.

"This one has bad teeth, but he's strong. This one here needs a strong hand, or he'll laze about. It's worse than selling you a horse. I think if they were selling a horse they'd just praise the horse. They'd lie and inflate his value. They can't but help to run these people down. Something worth so much you think they'd at least try and talk it up. You'd think, seeing how important these colored people are, important enough to fight a war over, that they'd be held in some regard."

The road down which the horses walked was like a tunnel of green, and for a few hundred yards a mockingbird flew from tree to tree, singing at them. He cycled through six songs, one of which sounded like the squeak of a wagon wheel in need of grease.

"Mockingbirds are fascinating," said Raleigh.

"They sure like to give you a hard time."

Raleigh laughed. "I read in a book by Charles Darwin—he sailed around the world, visiting islands and taking note of what he saw there—that the birds of different islands were different, despite being the same. They were the same sort of bird, but they were different depending on where they were."

"Well, yeah. You take note of the idea that out there in the territory, people don't sound like they're from here."

Raleigh nodded. It was more than that in the Darwin, but then again, maybe it wasn't. Maybe it was that simple.

"People become what they have to become," said Jed. "Think about Abbott."

"What had he become?"

"Well, now that's a right good question. Sometimes I think that he figured he was part of them sheep he kept."

"Some sort of spell."

"Some Comanche medicine."

"You ever ask him what happened?"

"His family? Cholera. Caught from some pioneers they took in."

Raleigh envied Jed the sharp cuts he could make, the bare common sense with which he operated. Raleigh would think on details and motivations, underlying currents. He analyzed things, turned them over and worked on them. Not so Jed, it seemed. He wondered if it were learned wisdom, or if he'd been born that way, which reminded him of the various types of mockingbirds and the mutability of being. No one is born any way, he thought. Folks become what they are.

At a bend in the James River, secluded in a wood between two farms, Jed and Raleigh made camp, lit a fire, and sprawled on blankets while the hobbled horses grazed.

"It worked like a charm."

"You bought the slaves?"

"I arranged for the purchase of four slaves. I paid for them. Well, we signed a contract. I wrote a check for deposit, and told them my driver would be passing through in two weeks to collect them and pay the remainder. That gives us a deadline. Once people start cashing checks that don't pay and no one is showing up to collect the slaves, we need to be gone."

Raleigh nodded.

"That was a good idea, that your driver would be coming back through."

Jed was thinking about a man who he'd met in Texas, who told a story about traveling down the coast on a small sailing boat in Florida, selling the same two black men in each town. He'd sold them over and over, and they'd escaped each time and met him and done it again. He was going to give them a share and drop them off with the Seminole. They got caught just north of St. Augustine, and while he had managed to squirrel his way out of the jam, he figured his compatriots were hanged. He took a boat to

Havana and spent a year drinking and swatting mosquitoes on the money he'd made.

"I do wish we were buying them and freeing them," said Raleigh.

"They're going to be relieved, if they're told, that they aren't going to a sugar plantation. And anyway we ain't got the money for it. Everything we do brings us closer to getting run out, hanged, or shot. I don't reckon either of us are welcome, if they know who we are or maybe even if they don't really. I don't hand the man the rope. We'll do what we came to do, and we'll move on." Jed thought for a moment, eyes to the evening sky, and then said: "They'll all be free, soon. The war is coming. It won't last long. There's too much honor around here and not enough iron."

Raleigh considered it. What happens after that? He'd been free most of his life—and yet free from what? He'd been in hiding, first on the grounds, like a walled garden, a hidden fortress. Then he'd played a part on the stage. He'd felt the pressure to leave, to move on, to stay on the edge of the town. Free, but only in the sense that he wasn't owned. Now, ironically, in his costume slave garb, masquerading as chattel, he found his greatest sense of freedom. No one looked at him now. He was free because he didn't seem to be free.

Like a dog, thought Raleigh. If a dog is walking with someone, you are comforted, you know the dog is accounted for. If a dog shows up alone, you are nervous. That's a wild dog. Wild dogs are dangerous. A safe dog is a dog that gets fed, and gets disciplined and rewarded. That's how you know the dog will behave. Wild dogs get shot.

But, Raleigh thought: *I'm only pretending.*

He wondered if that was what was required. The appearance of servility draped over an underlying freedom. For a man who knows that his life is his own to pass unhindered through the world must he simultaneously appear as its servant? Was this true of Jed, as well? Less obviously, but still true?

"Tomorrow's the day," said Jed. "It's right down the road isn't it? They told me it was an hour ride or so. We'll get to Bodkin's Hundred in the morning."

Raleigh nodded, and realized that Jed probably couldn't see him in the fading light so he made an affirmative noise. He was frightened of the future, but excited for it.

CHAPTER FORTY-SIX

Homecoming

Jed let out a low whistle at the top of the drive, raised his eyebrows, and twirled the ends of his mustache, which he'd twisted to rakish points—this is the place?

Having been so long away allowed Raleigh a fresh vision of the grandness of the Hundred—the massive brick house rose out of the small swell of a hill, fronted by a portico with a half circle window and four looming two-story Doric columns, the windows arrayed in perfect symmetry. The shallow stairs from the sandy gravel expanded out, squared off—Raleigh remembered walking the ninety-degree edge of the marble, stepping only on the crack so as to cast whatever child's spell he'd been thinking on. The drive made a sweeping oval around the low grass, the fountain, the two pecans, and caused you to approach the house from the side and take note of the H-shaped doubling of the grand building, the four gable-end chimneys, oversize windows sparkling along the center breezeway behind which the approaching guest might spy a line of statues and potted trees. Raleigh'd spent his time pissing against the poplar on the bank of Bodkin's Creek out back, blind to the grandiosity.

The horses walked slowly on the curve that led to the front doors, and Raleigh looked to his right, trying to see over Oliver's brick wall and through the orchard, straining for a glimpse of the ruins of the Old House.

When Raleigh and Jed reached the apex of the oval, two black boys in livery trotted out and took ahold of the horses. Jed dusted himself off.

"Go get the master, boy. My man can take these."

Jed slid off his horse and Raleigh handed him the cane that Gee had made.

"Look after their feet." Turning back to the young boy in livery holding both the horses, he asked: "Is there a smithy? Good. Show my man where he is. Show him the stable." He flipped a coin to the boy, "Give us some grain. Water them. If they need shoeing, go ahead with it." Jed turned on his heel. Raleigh had been dismissed.

It had been years since Raleigh had spent time on the Newcombe's plantation—once Oliver had built the brick wall they didn't cross it. The old road that had connected the houses, where he'd watched Fern and Liza walk from the New House to the Old, was still there, but it was weedy and stopped abruptly at the wall. Things had changed enough that he didn't have to feign awkwardness. The familiar details just pricked out the overwhelming strangeness of the place.

The boy in livery led him to the barns, pointed to the water.

"That smoke is the smithy. This here is empty stalls."

Raleigh nodded thanks. Hiding inside his beard, and keeping his hat low on his brow. He watered and brushed the horses, leaned against their sides and asked them for their feet, dragging his hoof-pick around the edge of the frog to carefully pluck out little stones and packed-in dirt.

The whole time he was looking and listening, as awake to everything around him as if he'd been hunting. Every dapple of light, every skittering bug—Temple was here, somewhere. A woman walked across the barnyard, and when he saw her his heart leapt. It wasn't Temple, but his hands shook at the sight of the stranger, and he dropped the hoof-pick. He stood and leaned against the horse kindly. The horse was shifting, putting his weight on his back legs, whale eyeing him, picking up on how excited and nervous he was.

"We'll calm each other down. We'll calm each other down. We're doing fine."

The horse snorted and swiveled his ears to Raleigh, and Raleigh ran his hand along his back and stroked his flank before leading him to the stall.

With the horses in their stalls, and their noses buried in feed, Raleigh walked around to the paddock side of the barn to check that the stall doors, which led to the paddocks and pastures, were latched closed. The horses needed rest, and he wanted to separate them from the horses here. As he touched the latch on the second door, clicking the metal back and forth to make sure, a horse nickered behind him. It was Snap. He'd grown out, he looked more formidable, more solid. The stallion took a step toward Raleigh and nickered again. Raleigh stepped forward, into the grass, hand out, and the horse nuzzled and smelled, then stepped forward and dropped his heavy head over Raleigh's shoulder. Raleigh pressed against the horse's cheek, whispering soft affections.

"You best watch it," came a young voice. One of the young footmen. "He mean."

"Doesn't seem mean," said Raleigh.

"Well, he is."

"I have a way with horses," said Raleigh. "I suppose."

Snap picked up his head, stepped back, and snorted at the kid, then turned back to Raleigh and nickered at him again.

Raleigh reached in his pocket and found a sugar cube, which he gave to Snap.

"Seems like he likes you. He dropped Master Johnny right in the dirt."

Raleigh smiled. Of course he did.

Jed was shown into a drawing room near the front door by a plump but rickety old black man in a wildly detailed livery—more or less the same uniform that the two young footmen had worn, but stitched with gold threads and sewn with extra buttons. A higher rank, thought Jed. The black man seemed a little dreamy, almost distant, and just so slightly flustered, as if the things which should have been familiar to him were not. As if the rote motions of welcoming a guest the Hundred were not rote. Was Jed unwelcome? He looked himself up and down. He thought he had it right. He felt that he looked the part. Travel weary, perhaps, dusty from the road, but rich. He straightened his collar.

From the hall came in a tall man with a little dart of a mustache and sharp, mean eyes. The man was down to his shirting and his breeches, and held a handkerchief to his lip. With a start Jed noted the blood blossoming on the white fabric. Oh the shoulder of his shirt, at the seam, was a wet bloodstain the size of a zinnia.

"You're hurt."

"It's nothing," said Zeb. "A little swordplay."

Jed bowed slightly and said: "Jedediah Sullivan, sir, of Villa Amador."

The men shook hands, and Zeb introduced himself.

"You have a beautiful home, Mr. Newcombe."

"I got your note. Mr. Sullivan." Zeb dabbed at his lip, offered a chair. The blood seemed to be slowing. "You're welcome to rest here. Pour you something to drink?" He did so. "I'm happy to have you. There's nothing I can do for you though."

"Nothing?"

"I ain't the sort to run, Mr. Sullivan, I don't operate from the back foot. I'm not selling."

Jed rubbed his hands together thoughtfully, accepting and lighting a slim cigar.

"That is too bad," said Jed. "I've heard good things. I welcome your hospitality—road weary. Perhaps I can convince you."

Zeb laughed. The cut on his lip had stopped bleeding.

"Are you sure that you are all right?" Jed asked.

"We were fencing. He caught me in passing. Do you fence?"

Jed shook his head.

Zeb shrugged.

"My boy enjoys it. Thinks it gets him ready. Villa Amador? You don't sound Brazilian."

Jed smiled as if praising Zeb for this observation. "I'm a Virginia boy, but I married into sugar. Ready for what?"

"For the war. He'll do all right."

He'd seen these men in the army, young men of the cavalry who came with their own scarves, their own hats, always so eager to ride, never afraid of death. Percy had said that they believed their privilege excused them from risk, it never entered their minds that they might be the one to die, or if they did imagine it they thought about it as a glorious moment, their end heroic, and the clouds parting to reveal the hand of god reaching down to pluck them up into heaven. They never saw themselves trapped under what was left of a horse, bones shattered, wheezing their dying breath while some battlefield urchin held them still enough to pick their pockets. Jed wondered now, as he had then, if the dying had time to reflect. If, in those dirty moments, they noted how wrong they were. Did they admit defeat when the cannonball knocked the horse from under them, or at least wonder why they'd thought to practice fencing?

Jed sent word that they'd be staying, which Raleigh took as a good sign. Raleigh made a space for himself in the hayloft above the stalls. He swept it and arranged a pallet, brought up the bedrolls. No one except the young servant in livery noticed him, and he tried to keep himself out of the way.

In a lonely stretch of weedy grass behind the barn, far enough from the path to be anonymous, he circled some rocks to make a ring for a fire and tipped a crate over to sit on. There, he made himself lunch with the provisions they'd brought—a slice of ham and a toasted hoecake. He made coffee, and drank it slowly while he looked around the grounds. His position gave him a good view of the quarters, the washerwomen, the path to the gardens and the kitchen.

The fences needed paint. The barns were mildewed on the shady side. The weeds grew tall in the culverts.

He scanned the faces for Temple.

They'd come here on evidence, but things change, and it was possible that she'd escaped or been sold. If that were the case, then he'd pick up the trail. He'd find her. If she had escaped, she'd be looking for him. If she'd been sold, there'd be a record of it. *Not available to me*, he thought, *but to someone*. To Jed. Would Jed continue? Eventually the outlaw would grow tired. Raleigh guessed that an outlaw's life was a constant reckoning of risk and reward. At some point the scales would tip.

Raleigh idled on his crate, watching carefully as the servants of the plantation went about the business of the Hundred, until he had finished his coffee. He brought the crate from his fireside to the breezeway of the barn and sat in front of his horses with the tack and a tin of mink oil—just a man with a job.

In the afternoon, he saw a black man walk over to the dovecote with a box coop and come out with two dozen pigeons, warbling and cooing. He walked over, stood in the light at the open door of the barn, and called to Raleigh: "You Mr. Sullivan's man?"

The birds in the box at his side were gray brown and they thrust their necks through the slats and looked around with their frightened yellow eyes.

Raleigh nodded.

"He says to come on up to the shoot, he needs you to load his guns."

Raleigh nodded and followed the man with the box of pigeons. Jed had felt sure that none of these white people would recognize him, but Raleigh found he had no confidence in his beard, and only a little in the general blindness with which white men looked at blacks.

Behind the house, Jed, Zeb, and Zeb's son Johnny stood on the patio around a small table loaded with drink, laughing.

It was Jed's job to settle in, it was his role to laugh with these men, but it rankled Raleigh nonetheless to see him with his head back and a glass in his hand. Three gun racks had been arrayed against the edge of the patio, each with a brace of fowling pieces. The liveried boys stood at ease by each rack, hands at their sides, like soldiers. Raleigh could see that Zeb and his son were drunk. Their eyes swam around in their heads and they spoke at maximum volume.

"Nice to have a third again," said Johnny. "Collings wasn't much of a shot, but he got lucky sometimes."

"Your brother is a fine shot, Johnny." Turning to Jed, Zeb said "My younger son, Collings, has begun his studies at Hampden-Sydney College."

"Keeping him out of the war," Johnny said, laughing.

Jed looked at Raleigh with a sly grin, but also a widening of the eye.

The man with the pigeons walked into the field.

One of the liveried boys motioned to Raleigh, and handed him a satchel with percussion caps and shot shells.

"You know what to do? Just load the one he ain't shooting, then hand it to him."

Zeb was explaining the rules: "I'd like to eat these birds, gents, so make it count. We'll shoot in order. You'll start, then me, then Johnny. Then I'll start, then Johnny will start. There's twenty-four birds in there. Hang on—Andre! You got twenty-four birds?"

"Yessir!"

"There's twenty-four birds in there. The lead shooter makes the call to pull. Understood? Wagers? Shall we?"

Jed nodded.

"Five dollars a bird? Shall we go higher? Too low for you, I can tell by the expression on your face. What would suit you? A prize? A prize for the winner then, how about $500? Two fifty from each pocket?"

Jed smiled.

"Let's shoot," said Johnny.

Jed looked his piece over, held it to his shoulder, breeched it. It was a fine gun, in excellent condition. He nodded. Raleigh loaded both guns, and set the spare on the rack.

Zeb called out to Andre to make sure he was ready with the birds.

Jed, standing at the edge of the patio: "Pull!"

Andre threw the bird, and it tumbled for a moment before it got the air under its wings, then it darted, zigzagging, with tremendous speed. Jed slapped his trigger, and the wings folded. The bird was down.

"Well shot!"

It was Zeb's turn, and he, too, got his bird.

Johnny missed, and Jed, who had the second shot at it, knocked the bird down.

Raleigh swapped the guns and reloaded. The men took their time. A cook brought out a tray of sliced ham and cheese and bread, and the white men ate and wiped their hands and took long draughts of cider and walked back to the edge—"Pull!"

Jed was winning and Johnny seemed especially frustrated. He blamed his boy.

"Why are you loading these guns this way? Keep doing it and I'll string you up."

The boy brought out a soft rag with which he wiped the stock where the sweat from Johnny's cheek had moistened it.

Jed thought back to the blood on Zeb's shirt when he'd arrived. Competitive young man, lacking in control, dangerous as hell.

They'd shot eighteen birds, Jed had scored eight of them, on two misses by Johnny. Zeb had yet to miss, and was at six. Johnny was at four.

Johnny called "pull!" The pigeon hung in the air, and then instead of taking flight, it swerved low as if it wanted to fly back into the box. Johnny shot, and Andre cried out and fell to his knees.

"Goddamnit," said Zeb.

Andre was moaning in the yard, clutching his shirt to his face.

"Go see if he's all right," said Zeb, and his gun boy, who hadn't moved, stepped off the patio.

Johnny looked disgusted.

The boy called back: "He shot in the face, suh!"

"I can see that."

Andre was clutching the shirt to his face, and then looking at the blood in the shirt.

"Take him," said Zeb with a dismissive wave of his hand. "Then come back and give those pigeons to the cook. Put the last pigeons back in the dovecote. I suppose eighteen birds will feed us."

He turned to Jed, who was nervously looking down the range at the shot man being led away. Andre moaned in a weakened, animalistic way.

"Nice shooting, Mr. Sullivan. Luck?"

"We keep birds at Villa Amador."

"Aha." He was counting money out. "Johnny, pay up. Two hundred and fifty each. I should make you pay the whole thing after that." Zeb gave his son a good-natured smack on the back, and they walked into the house.

Marie sat in the sitting room adjacent to her bedroom at the Collings's mansion on Franklin Street, at her desk—a letter writing desk suited, Marie thought, to the absentminded twisting of ladylike curls and the composition of love poems. There was no room on it and as a result, piles of papers radiated out from the desk and across the carpet. There, all the way over by the chaise, were her drawings, annotated and corrected next to a drift of letters. A stack of books on the gardens of Europe was shaded by the hanging fern. Squarely in front of her, on the shining, pale wood, a condescending reply from a prominent landscape designer in New York, expressing his lack of interest in her backwoods project to restore the church. He'd written: "While I wish you the best in your project"—he didn't—"I cannot agree that the bucolic expression of religiosity has any grounds beyond the nostalgic in this age." Nostalgic! Of course those with no respect for the past view reverence as nostalgia. Have you no sense of the honor that carrying forward the ideals of our forebears bestows upon you? Have you no idea what it is to feel obligated? Connected? This is my land, and these are my people we are talking about, and yet he goes right ahead and calls it nostalgia. Scolds me: "You cannot stop the turn of the wheel, Mrs. Newcombe, despite the wishes of your stunted secessionists." That last—the stunted secessionists—made her blood boil. A man ought to have more respect than that. I wrote him as a hopeful pupil, and this! She was copying the passage into a letter she was writing to Calvert Vaux, expressing her surprise that efforts to lift up the souls through applied beauty and restoration of architectural masterworks would elicit such rudeness. Clearly, she and Mr. Vaux were on the same side. He understands that people cannot be relied upon to lift themselves up without example. Someone must lead them. Someone must show them. Without access to beauty how can they know beauty? To leave people to wander is to abandon them to their wildest, lowest instincts. They need guidance. Should she say as much?

She never knew how to talk to Yankees.

One of the maids shuffled to the door from the hall, and with her eyes on the floor muttered: "Your man is here to see you Mrs. Newcombe."

"Tandey?"

"Your man from the Hundred."

Keeping her pen in her hand, and without turning her chair, she gestured that he should be sent in and tilted herself in that direction to receive him, making it clear that she was being interrupted, and that she would not allow him much of her time.

"What is it, Tandey?"

He stood, just past the threshold, with his hat in his hands. The filigree of his ridiculous costume caught the light from the window, and he looked like a plump grandfather convinced by a little girl to dress up as one of the footmen so she could play at being Cinderella. The pride with which he held himself in his jacket as it rose up his forearms and stretched across his back only made him more ridiculous.

"Ma'am, we need to order up some pullets, while we still can, and we need to get some molasses, and some coffee, and we moving through them kegs like you ain't never seen. Could you, please, Miss Marie, make orders? Or send me in and I'll do it."

"Why are you here to ask me about this?"

He stood, dumbfounded.

"Why not simply tell Mr. Newcombe? Why not have it taken care of?"

"Mr. Newcombe?"

Was he playing at stupidity?

She waited for him to continue.

"Mr. Newcombe . . . he . . ." Tandey was searching for the angle, the gears were spinning, "you the only one I trust with matters of the home, ma'am, it's our business, your business, and I don't reckon Mr. Newcombe want to be bothered with it, anyway, seeing as he's got company and he busy with getting Johnny ready to go off and shooting, and so forth."

"A visitor? You recognize this man? Is he military?"

She held out hope that Mr. Newcombe might, among his ill-formed network of half-wits and former employers, have found a string to pull to afford her more militaristic son some passage into a rank she felt he deserved and relieve her not only of her anxiety about Johnny ending up in a position unbefitting to a Collings, but also of her defensive duties—standing up to the denigration of her husband—implied by her mother, but barely hidden when it came from her sister—was hard work.

"No ma'am, I gather he from Brazil. Ain't seen him before. He brought his servant with him, sleeps out there in the stable loft and brushing his horses."

"Do you know him? The boy?"

"The man who sleeping in the barn?"

"Do you recognize him?"

Tandey looked down at his feet.

"I don't reckon I do," said Tandey. "But knowing people ain't my concern, I know the house, and that's what I need to know."

"And we need things."

"Ain't nobody keep a handle on things the way you do, ma'am."

"And Temple?"

"How do you mean, ma'am?"

"Is she working? Does she do what you ask her to?"

"Temple catching up, she'll be just fine."

Marie had turned back to her desk, and was writing out notes for Tandey—a note to a grocer, a pass that allowed him to travel around the city and back to the Hundred.

"She's got bad blood in her, you know. Her brother, after all, shot Oliver Bodkin."

Tandey didn't say anything.

"You've never believed that, have you, Tandey?"

"I couldn't say, Miss Marie."

"And you don't believe he died in the fire, with Mr. Bodkin?"

"I never thought on who died in that fire, never paid it no mind."

She had finished the notes and handed them over to Tandey with a nod.

Did the girl know her own self? Marie wondered if Temple saw the Bodkin features on her own face. Had she stood at the Old House before it burned down and stared into the portrait of Master Mr. Bodkin, seen her face in his face? Marie was young when Flora, the Bodkin concubine, died and her ghost or his guilt or both chased Master Mr. Bodkin to the city. Young but aware, and she remembered. Quiet in the parlors of wealthy women, needlework chastely on her lap while the news slipped out. There, with tea and little sweets, wrapped in finery and lit by the streaming afternoon light through the beveled glass panes, the women expressed and implied. Bodkin had been news, his disintegration a spectacle. That family, the standard, the origin, the Bodkin line like a sill plate on which Virginia set her cornerstone. That he remained immeasurably wealthy, even grew more so while so clearly befouled, infuriated them and sped their tongues. "I hear he sold one hundred slaves the other day!" Met with gasps. "As I understand it, his son has completed school, but is staying in Boston." Or: "Who is taking care of the horses?" Answered: "He sold most of the horses, too." And someone's husband was at the auction, and someone had ridden a Bodkin horse at a hunt once, and found it intractable. Because now they would lie and say that that which they had coveted all their lives had never been anything at all. Not just Bodkin. In those parlors among the women Marie learned of every noble planter's seed dropped into every slave girl within a hundred miles—save for by the husbands of anyone who happened to be sitting in the room. These matrons were long practiced at polite omission. Marie had heard it all. She knew these men well before she'd spoken to any of them. She feigned introspection, asking herself if her knowledge of her class had pushed her search for a husband afield as an antidote to the corruption. She'd found a wild, untamed man, a real and actual man of action, unpolluted by generations of sloth and dalliance. And Bodkin's Hundred, as well. How naive she'd been.

"Thank you, ma'am," said Tandey, waiting at the threshold to be dismissed. She nodded to him and returned to her letter.

CHAPTER FORTY-SEVEN

The Dinner

In the morning, Jed limped over to Raleigh's little campfire, leaning on his cane, and sat on the crate. Low flames licked at a pot of water. Jed was wrapped in an extravagantly patterned cloth they'd bought in Richmond—"An alternative to a dressing gown," Raleigh had said, "very dramatic."

Raleigh was at his shoulder, brushing his hair, applying beard oil, ostentatiously looking for stray hairs to trim with a pair of silver scissors. The act gave them a chance to talk.

"The house," said Jed, speaking low "is in chaos. Last night they threw roasted birds down the middle of the table and we ate with our hands. They drink constantly. Zeb's got these hangers-on, rough people, I guess they work for him. They sit there at the table. I'd be offended if I were who I'm saying I am. There's saber marks on the newel-posts, on the mantel. They fence with sabers in the hall. The maids scurry around like mice, hugging the walls."

"I noticed," said Raleigh, "a general decay. Buildings need paint. People living in a combination of fear and freedom. They act like they're working, but I get the sense that they aren't sure what they are supposed to do."

"I think that's exactly what it is. The missus has gone off to town, to Richmond, to tend to her father. He ain't well."

"You think it's true?"

"You mean do I think it's a welcome distraction? From the way Johnny talks about her to Zeb it sounds like she might be gone. I looked in her rooms—not a single piece of jewelry left on the premises."

Raleigh laid a hot towel across Jed's cheeks, reached for the razor: "You were going to rob her."

"I wasn't. But that's neither here nor there. There weren't any jewels. Not even a locket. Not even an ivory comb. Was she the mast of this ship?"

"It makes sense. She'd know more about running things than Zeb would. Zeb was a slave catcher, but her blood is blue. She's always had help. Have you seen Temple?"

"There was no one serving us. Just the cook brought out a trencher of roasted pigeons. After Johnny fell asleep with his face on the table and started snoring, Zeb laughed and took me into the library for whiskey and cigars. One of the ferns in there ain't gonna make it, after all the whiskey I dumped in there. I don't know how they live like this. I saw a girl in the pantry through the door about the age you described."

Jed looked at Raleigh.

"Actually. She does look like you. She's got that forehead, she's mulatto, like you are."

"Mulatto?"

"Sure."

"How do you mean?"

Jed put up a hand, signaling for Raleigh to stop his razor work. Half his face still covered in shaving soap. "Mulatto."

"I'm not mulatto."

"Who were your parents?"

"I don't know."

"Look here, at your arm. What color is that?"

Raleigh looked, but couldn't answer.

"There's milk in your coffee, Raleigh, that's all I'm saying." Raleigh returned to shaving him.

They watched Mack and Gilly amble through the pathway in between the slave quarters. Mack was absentmindedly rubbing his belly and turning his head back and forth, looking into doorways with a hungry menace. Gilly, all awkward angles and bones, his elbows jutting, was focused dead ahead, staring at the two of them. When he saw that Jed and Raleigh were returning his gaze, he tipped his hat and chuckled.

"Breakfast time, Mr. Sullivan," Gilly called, "come up to the house."

Jed nodded, took a towel and wiped his face, and leaned into the cane to support his weight as he rose.

On the sideboard there was bread and butter, jam, coffee, and ham. Jed poured himself a coffee and cut himself a slice of bread.

"There's a party today, Mr. Sullivan," said Zeb, already seated. "I hope you'll stay on for it. Some of the boys are joining up. The cavalry!"

"If it'll give me another chance at your stock, I'd be delighted."

"We might find something for you yet," said Zeb.

Young men from the neighboring plantations started arriving about noon, and Tandey served punch on the lawn, underneath the pecans.

One of the liveried boys appeared by Raleigh's fire and said that he was needed in the kitchen.

"The kitchen?"

"Sent to tell you they need you."

At the old kitchen, his first home, he found Mack waiting for him.

"Come carry a pig," he said. "This way, got them in the springhouse."

Raleigh tried to stay behind Mack, as if he were following, though he knew well the way between the kitchen and the springhouse.

"Cut these pigs yesterday," said Mack. "Killing is my favorite part, always has been."

Raleigh wanted to run, but what then? Mack was a filthy, tattered man. Bloodstains and mud were crushed into his shirt. His beard was a tangled mess, spotted with dried tobacco juice. He'd burst a blood vessel in his right eye, and it was as red as a cardinal.

"Hang on a second, here," said Mack. He pulled a ceramic flask from his a pocket and took a pull. He squinted at Raleigh, who was trying to look subservient. "I know you from somewheres."

Raleigh didn't respond.

"I do. Gilly said so, too. He noted it first, I always like to give him credit, seeing as how he ain't so smart."

Raleigh shook his head, mumbled a "no sir."

"You son of a bitch, I do." He brought the flask around fast, and it hit Raleigh square in the jaw so hard that Raleigh swooned, seeing light and darkness at once. Mack had him by the neck of the shirt and threw him, stumbling, through the door of a stone shed. The door slammed shut behind him and he heard Mack laughing.

"Like I need help carrying pigs. It's going to be right fun watching you swing. Glad you're back. Good for a colored to have a little lesson before he hangs, though."

Raleigh threw himself against the door, to no end. He clawed at the stone walls until his fingertips bled. The heat was oppressive, and the close air in the room stank. There in the corner he saw a small dirt-encrusted bowl, which he grabbed and used to scrape away some of the floor, only to hit a mesh of heavy iron rods. You couldn't dig your way out. This space was built for cruelty. There were no accommodation for life at all: no water, barely any light. This room was made to remind you that your life was entirely dependent upon the gestures of your captors. Raleigh's jaw ached where Mack had punched him, and he sat on the floor and rubbed it. He had to get out of here: They knew. They'd kill Jed.

This meant she was here, didn't it? They wouldn't bother with this if she weren't here, would they?

He rose and called out, knocked on the door and called again. In the yard, his cries sounded muffled and distant and went mostly unnoticed and entirely ignored.

"Gentlemen! Gentlemen!" Zeb called out to the crowd gathered in the shade in front of the New House. "Ladies. Neighbors. Friends."

His neighbors kept on talking, so he picked up a second silver punch cup, and banged it against his own until folks turned to look at him. Tandey, by the punch bowl, grimaced at the disregard for the silver he worked so hard to maintain.

"My friends," started Zeb, beaming about at the small crowd. "We are gathered to send off our sons. We will eat, and we will toast them, and we will celebrate their inevitable victory and their glorious futures defending our rights, our lives, our traditions, and our land. Before we eat, a toast!"

Jed raised his glass with the others.

"A toast!" said the crowd.

"Gather the men!" said a woman.

"Yes. Gather them."

Soon, six flush-faced young men in cavalry costumes, with Hardee hats, bright scarves, and sashes hung with sabers were smiling in a half circle. They were bolstered by one another, and where they might have been shy individually, they felt strong and daring together. One of them drained his punch cup and called out to Tandey for more.

"Yes," cried the others, "bring us more punch."

Tandey scrambled to fill their cups as they handed them to him.

"Boys!" said Zeb. "No. I misspeak. For these are men! Men! I know I speak for everybody when I say that it is with the greatest respect that I salute you. I admire your youth. I wish I was in the fight myself, but failing that, I send you." He was slurring. "The cavalry will be glad to have you and happy to see you. We need men with your . . . your courage, your strength. They are upon us. Threatening to end what we hold dear. Go and fight! But first, feast."

To Jed, they looked ridiculous. He was ashamed that he had once spent his youthful energies chasing glory. He saw naïveté and privilege, and he wanted to erase it. He wanted the polished swords rusted and pitted, the strong horses weakened by thirst and overworked. He wanted to see in the faces of these boys the despair built up after days of futility. These children who had never seen hardship. They thought so highly of war. Heroism, thought Jed, is a trick, an enticement. Jed remembered the men he'd seen driven mad with thirst, men who had buried their faces in filthy water and shat themselves to death.

This way to glory.

Now they were arrayed around the tables in the lawn, and Jed was politely fielding questions regarding his progress and his thoughts. He was doing well, he said. Finding much of promise.

"I think it's a damn shame," he said, convincingly. "People ought to be ashamed."

This was met with wide approval. Jed was looking for Raleigh, and growing more nervous as he failed to see him. The young liveried boys were to and fro among the small crowd, the cook poked his head out of the kitchen, but Raleigh was nowhere to be seen. He heard Zeb over his shoulder.

"When this is finished," Zeb was saying, "when the fighting is done, I expect you'll find yourself accepted by the academy. Proved yourself. There's a future ahead of you, son, you're just at the beginning. Once you find Jubal Early, when you get up near Manassas, you'll be fine. You're to be his aide-de-camp, I have it on his word."

There came a scattering of gravel under hooves as a horseman arrived on the driveway, and asked, without apologies, for Marie Newcombe.

Zeb rose, furious, embarrassed to have his wife's absence pointed out, embarrassed that the horseman had asked for her instead of him.

"I'll have your hide, what is this?"

"I have a letter for her."

"Well, she ain't here, goddamnit, and you have interrupted these gentlefolk."

Zeb was walking toward the rider, his right hand clenched in a fist.

"I have a letter from Collings, her son. He's hurt."

There was a gasp.

"Give it, then."

Zeb handed the letter to Johnny, who had come to his side.

"It's a letter from Collings."

"I gathered that."

"He was in the militia. Mustered by the president of the college. They ranged up to Rich Mountain and yesterday Collings was captured by General McClellan."

"Yankee dogs." Zeb spat on the ground.

"McClellan sent them home. He told them: 'Boys, secession is dead in this region, go back to your college, take your books, and become wise men' and then he let them go. Paroled them. Sent them back! Collings says he hurt his foot."

"Hurt?"

"He says that he has it still."

"Has it? You mean he almost lost it."

Zeb looked at Johnny, and Johnny at Zeb. The Newcombe with first blood spilled in this war was the last one anyone would have thought to take up arms.

"Organized by the president of the college, it says."

Zeb stormed toward the house through the nervous guests, Johnny at his heels.

"Father, I'll go," said Johnny.

"Gilly will take a horse and some money and ride to the college. He'll find Collings and get him a doctor if he needs one. I'll go tomorrow. You get to Richmond and join your muster. Don't set aside your promises."

"But he's hurt!"

"People get hurt. It's a war. People get hurt."

The rest of the party were left dangling, wondering what to do now. There were a few feeble attempts to continue the party, but they were short lived, and the people soon pressed last coins into the hands of the young men, gave them parting gifts of trinkets for luck and recollection, and left. The young cavalrymen rode off toward Richmond in a bunch, less happily than they had expected to. That left Jed, leaning against a tree, smoking, watching Tandey gather the food. There was an entire suckling pig left uneaten.

"I guess we could go ahead and eat that this evening," said Jed. "Put some salt and vinegar on that, it'll be all right."

"I's thinking the same thing. Yes indeed," said Tandey, with overblown obsequiousness.

"You got any greens?" asked Jed. "It's been a long time since I had a good bunch of greens with a streak o' lean and some onion."

"In Brazil? That's how you eat 'em there?"

Jed laughed.

"I see what I can do."

"My boy around? I'd like to go over the tack with him, make sure we're set for tomorrow."

"If'n I see him, I'll send him your way, sir."

"But you haven't seen him?"

"No sir."

"You tell him."

"Yes sir."

Tandey was nodding his head so hard by this point Jed figured it was about to fall off. Something was afoot.

Gilly clattered out of the barn, already riding hard, knobby knees sticking out, hat pressed down on his head, bound for Hamden-Sydney and the injured son. One down, thought Jed.

Raleigh, imprisoned, beat with weakening fists upon his door, but no one came. Had he already died? This would be hell, wouldn't it? A good first step toward hell? Trapped. Unable to give help. Robbed of your mission. A feeble being scratching at the walls of your impenetrable cage—it seemed so literal, so tangible. He'd figured the afterlife would be more unknowable. He reassured himself that he was not actually dead, he was simply captured. He called out in a raspy, torn voice.

Jed took a walk around the plantation, pretending to stroll and ready with the information that he'd been told to stretch out the injured foot. He was looking for Raleigh, but trying not to call attention to himself or his search. Finding no sign of him—and finding his things still arrayed around the fire and set up in the barn—made him nervous. In his room Jed pulled his revolver from his saddlebag and made sure it was loaded. He sat in thought. He wanted to talk to Raleigh. There was danger in the air, these people were threatened, and unhinged, and far too drunk. If Zeb had simply sold him the girl, they'd be gone. They needed a new plan.

He heard the dinner bell, rose, and slipped his pistol into his belt.

The roasted pig was splayed upon the table, still in the shape of a pig but boned out, and with all the meat chopped and piled inside, dashed with vinegar, salted, spiked with pepper. When Jed walked into the dining room the holes in the head of the pig where the eyes had been seemed to stare at him—voided sockets taking the measure of the man.

"Gentlemen," said Jed, mostly to the pig.

Zeb lurched sideways, very drunk now, and spun toward him. There was weight in the pocket of Zeb's waistcoat, a small pistol. He had in his hand a long match, and as he spoke he methodically lit each candle on a massive candelabra.

"Mr. Sullivan," he slurred. "D'you'know Mack?"

Mack grinned. He was rubbing the knuckles of his right hand, which looked as if they'd been recently put to use. Did Zeb not remember that they'd eaten together last night? It was a threat.

We're caught, thought Jed. *Raleigh is missing, and they have figured us out.*

Jed bowed, leaned on his cane, and limped to a chair which faced Mack across the intricate white tablecloth, perfectly stitched and sewn into repeating patterns with threads of pink so pale as to be almost white. A dowry cloth, thought Jed, the kind of fabric that comes in a rich bride's trunk.

Zeb turned to throw the match in the fireplace and knocked a glass of wine over, which caused Mack to laugh. Neither moved to clean up the wine. Zeb righted his glass, poured himself some more.

Mack tipped a bottle of whiskey from the table into his wineglass and drank so fast that the whiskey poured in rivulets into his scraggly beard.

The table was set for ten, and Jed plucked a glass from one of the place settings and poured himself some whiskey. Seeing that Mack and Zeb both had hunting knives next to their coffee spoons, he drew the long-bladed knife that had been by his side since he was a boy. He held it in his hand, admired it, drank the whiskey. He felt the pull of his revolver against his belt.

Zeb swayed over the flower of red wine sopping the brilliant white cloth and clumsily looked about. "Too many plates."

He roared: "Plates!"

Temple, head down, scurried in from the pantry.

"Three plates."

Zeb took the two plates closest to him and threw them against the wall.

"Have at it," he slurred.

Mack chuckled a vicious little gurgling laugh and stabbed a hunk of the young pig.

Jed did not like his odds.

Temple had picked up the rest of the extra plates and slipped out of the dining room and into the pantry. Jed watched the door swing shut behind her.

"Come back here," said Zeb.

Temple ducked into the room, and he indicated a place next to him for her to stand, at the corner of the table. With each of Temple's steps there was a muffled clunk as her shackle hit the floorboards. Zeb chewed some pork, took some wine, wiped his face, and looked at Jed.

"She needs chaining, because she used to like to run. But she's good. I could sell you her."

Jed knew that to reach for his gun was to invite a shot, but something was going to happen. And if something is going to happen, then it already has happened. Never wait. The way out is the way forward. But how to begin? Flip the table onto Mack? He'd get shot by Zeb before he could turn on him. They were ready; they were drunk. That was both good and bad.

"Why the change of heart?" Jed asked.

"What would you give me for her?"

"A price?"

"A price."

"What did you have in mind?" Jed looked her over. He was stalling for time, and he hated it, but he had to figure something out. Zeb did not intend to sell him anyone. Zeb was toying with him, letting Jed know that the game was over, and making him continue the masquerade out of cruelty, which was all he understood.

She was the image of Raleigh, wide forehead, light skin, big, open eyes. Her face was like a windstorm. She was trying to figure out what was going on and whether Jed was frying pan or fire.

"We suspect she's a mulatto. Don't rightly know. *Partus sequitur ventem*, only part of the provenance that matters."

Jed nodded, tried to appear interested without appearing excited.

"She'll do anything. I don't want her anymore. Not that she isn't worth it. I'll send her with the shackles. Look, I've wrapped the chain in velvet so it doesn't ruin the floor."

Zeb stood up and pushed Temple over to the other side of the table, closer to Jed. What was he doing? Mack thought it was funny, whatever it was. She stood before Jed, and Zeb showed him her ankles, which were cut and bruised where the shackles were closed around them. The velvet on the chain was opulent, a deep purple.

Zeb reached for his knife, and with a movement so fast that Jed gasped, he cut Temple's shirt down the front and ripped it open.

"She's in excellent condition, as you can see."

She stood, quivering in the candlelight, staring blankly behind Jed.

Zeb dropped into his chair with an air of nonchalance.

Mack was chewing a piece of the pork.

Jed took his knife and slowly moved it into the pile of pork in the middle of the table. He stabbed a chunk, brought it to his plate, and set the knife down so that the handle was pointing to Temple. He hoped she noticed.

"She's all you're offering me?"

"Look at her, she's beautiful. Tell me what you'll pay."

"She's not what I'm here for."

"Isn't she?"

Looking up, Jed saw Temple's face flushed with rage. She was looking right at him. Their eyes met, and she looked at the knife. All he had to do was nod. He did.

She took the handle, spun, and plunged the knife into Zeb's throat. Zeb cried out, surprised, too drunk to understand what was happening as blood plumed from the wound.

Mack was still forming the curse word he was set to yell when the heavy end of Jed's cane came down on his head. He reached to the wound, and stared dazedly at the blood on his hands for too long. The bullet from Jed's revolver hit him in the chest and blew him backward in his chair.

Temple stood back, trying to pull up her shirt, which was in tatters. Zeb was still alive, clutching at his throat, blood shooting through his fingers. He couldn't focus, he couldn't speak. Temple leaned in, her face in front of Zeb's.

"Can you hear me? Can you still see?"

She deftly cut the cord holding the key to her shackles.

"You look me in the face," she said. "This is the happiest I've ever been, watching you die."

Jed looked around and said, "We should go."

"Did Rose send you?" Temple unlocked her shackles and left them where they fell.

"Sorta. We gotta find Raleigh."

She gasped.

"My brother?"

"I hope they . . ."

"I know where."

There was no lock on the outside of the jail, just an iron bar sunk into the stone. Jed had given Temple the extravagant fabric he'd worn as a robe, and when she opened the door and stood, burning in a sheath of bright sunlight out of the west, the last light of the day, she looked, to Raleigh, in despair on the floor, like Athena.

He sat up.

"Temple?"

"Brother."

They ran to the barn, knowing that at any moment someone would sound an alarm. Raleigh grabbed the bedrolls from the hayloft, and the few things in the tack room, then saddled the horse he rode in on for Temple. He found another saddle and whistled for Snap, who bounded up. On the gravel in front of the house, Temple cried out to wait. Tandey stood in the doors of Bodkin's Hundred.

She held out her hand.

"You can come with us."

"No, girl, I can't."

"You could. You're welcome."

"It ain't that. I head out, then they know it was y'all. I figure y'all been gone a couple hours already before the boys in there got into this fight, I don't see how I coulda been here to see them kill each other and been gone with you."

He smiled.

"You'd do that for me?"

"Ain't just for you."

Temple smiled, and the evening light caught every gold thread wrapped around her. She dug the heels of her bare feet into the roan and clucked at her to move on.

Tandey stood with his hat in his hand before Marie's desk.

"He and Mac were right drunk. Upset, too, about Collings getting hurt. I was in the pantry. I hear them get to yelling, and I can't figure out what about, but it was hot, and then there's a great shuffle and a bump sort of and then I walk to the door, thinking I better go in there and see what is happening and I open the door and the gun goes off and Mack is on the floor with his chest half exploded and Mr. Newcombe, he is clutching at his neck. Blood everywhere. I run to him, gathering up the tablecloth to try and stanch it. I tried, but he got him good, got him right in that pig-killing part of the neck, you know. Few seconds and I don't think there was any blood left in him at all."

"Where were the houseguests during this?"

"Everybody left when we got the news about Master Collings."

"The Brazilian?"

"I ask the livery boy when they left and he said they left a couple hours before. I didn't see 'em go. Bought that young house girl and left." He didn't want to say Temple's name.

"Bought her?"

"I guess so. That's what they tell me."

"All right, Tandey."

Marie Collings shook her head. Her husband's death was no surprise. She looked into the future—she was a widow now, which meant she could inherit and own—and she liked what she saw.

Tandey's story wasn't true. She didn't care to know the truth.

Tandey got in the shay—he loved the pair of horses that pulled this wagon, and he smiled at them and whistled a little song that got them moving. He steered gently toward the shops where he had established credit the week before. He charged food, shot and powder, two barrels of good red wine, and overalls of tough canvas.

They wrapped up the clothes and wrote down the debit on Marie's account. Two blocks away, Tandey changed out of his uniform and put on the overalls. He took the passes that Marie had given him from the pocket, and threw the livery costume in the gutter. He pointed his horses to the Great Dismal Swamp.

CHAPTER FORTY-EIGHT

Bull Run

July 1861

Jed, Raleigh, and Temple moved slowly through a stand of loblolly pines, letting the horses lead them through the clutter of the forest.

"We might have been better off heading toward Danville," said Jed. It didn't matter. Outside of Fredericksburg they saw a freight roll by, stuffed to the walls with soldiers.

"Feels better heading North, though," said Raleigh.

On Saturday, they took to the road and found it clogged with strange tides of traffic, jovial families, women with baskets of produce and bushels of peaches, farmers leading dairy cows.

They made an out-of-the-way camp by a creek in a woods, from which they heard distant voices, laughter, thunder.

"Cannons," said Jed. "That's cannon fire. I'm going to walk over, and find a shop."

He looked at Temple.

"You're gonna need some boots. Let me measure your foot." He squatted before her and gestured to his forearm. She pressed her heel against his wrist. He put his hand against his sleeve at the tip of her toes and nodded. "Y'all sit tight."

"Temple," said Raleigh, after Jed left.

"Don't."

"I should have come back."

"You'd be dead. I'd be dead. We're all about a breath away from dead anyway. You probably shouldn't have come back at all."

"I should have tried."

"You did try. You did more than try. You came back. We made it out. If you'd done it by yourself, he'd have killed us. It was a good thing you brought Jed Stokes."

"I wish it had been better."

"Doesn't mean anything. Saying that."

Raleigh nodded. Sat with his elbows on his knees.

"It's a stupidity," said Temple, "to try to wish yourself into someone else's place. I understand it. I felt it when Oliver died. Why me? I thought you were dead, too. I was glad you weren't there. I was glad that you weren't suffering, and sad that you were dead. I'd wish that fate had taken me instead, but then I'd think of you there, and what would have happened to you, and I'd take it back. It's just magic, anyway, that thinking. It doesn't do anybody any good."

They waited in the pines by the creek, feeding the little fire and listening to the roar of the cannons in the distance.

Jed came back with a flour sack over his shoulder from which he pulled a bundle of clothes, a fresh piece of beef wrapped in paper. He had purchased a handful of salt and some riding boots and socks.

"Bought you some clothes."

They were men's clothes—pale trousers and a work shirt.

"See if them boots fit," said Jed.

Temple's ankles were sore, but the boots made them feel secure, and they were close to her size. She nodded and thanked Jed.

They pierced slices of beef with green branches and held them out over the fire to cook.

"Can't get a straight answer. Ask the butcher what's happening and he tells me that the Union is gonna ride right through the Confederates and on down to Richmond. It's going to be over tomorrow. The man in the general store told me that the Confederates are going to whip those Yankees and send them on home. They've got Jackson coming in, he says, from the Valley. It's a real war, is all anybody agreed on. Folks walking toward it with picnic baskets, and that doesn't sound like any kind of real war. We'll just wait and see, I guess. It's gonna rain before too long here. Other side of the trees," he nodded, "there's a run-in barn in a pasture. Let's wait out the rain there. We'll be up early, nobody will notice."

They left the horses hobbled by the stream, and slept in the run-in against the back wall with their saddles. The next morning they found the horses grazing along the edge of the fence, ate biscuits and drank coffee by the creek. The rain had turned the dust to mud, and the guttered and puddled road was riddled with signs of traffic; wagon wheels and feet and horseshoes had all left marks.

"Thank you for the clothes," said Temple.

Jed nodded.

"Why did you help us?"

Jed looked up the road and rocked in the saddle, slowly, holding the reins with a light touch. He patted his horse before spoke.

"I wanted to do something. I've been looking for my own life for a long time. I don't think I ever found it. I thought maybe I could set it right for y'all. Seemed like a real thing to do."

The wounded came away at a steady pace from where the battle had been. Some were in wagons, laid out, moaning and soaked. Some were walking, dangling an arm uselessly or leaning on a compatriot. Blood-soaked men with fearful eyes stood in the trees on the side of the road staring into nothing. As the travelers neared the battlefield, the effects intensified. Fences had been trampled or had their planks taken and repurposed. They saw a farmhouse with one of its walls gone. The chimney on the other side of what had been a comfortable room was intact, and there by the hearth was a rocking chair, set as if for a play. The ground everywhere was beaten and torn. There were scraps of fabric and leather, discarded powder horns, buttons in the mud. All the grass was gone. The trees looked twisted, burned, their leaves shaken off, their boughs blasted with cannonballs.

"Middle of July and not a leaf in sight," said Jed.

Great puddles stretched in every depression. There were doctors and thieves walking in the fields. To their right a bridge had been smashed by a cannon and a wagon was overturned. In the creek below men worked to pull the dead from the mud.

Dead horses were everywhere, and the horses they rode flared their nostrils and widened their eyes and moved with great fear and careful trepidation.

Soldiers pulled cannons back toward the collections of tents, where fires were burning.

A man in a clean suit pulled up his cabriolet as they passed and called out, addressing Jed: "That's that, then, eh? The war won?"

Jed didn't answer so he spoke again.

"Yankees will think twice before they march into Virginia again! We won!"

Jed shook his head.

Temple straightened in the saddle and said: "You think everything will continue as it has been."

The man in the cabriolet opened his eyes wide and looked not at her but at Jed, hoping that Jed, as a white man, would put down this impertinence. Jed grinned, looked up and down the road, and with calm determination placed his hand upon the gun on his hip. Temple continued:

"You think this story is your story, but you have been tricked, or you have tricked yourself. You believe you have a right to comfort and complacency. You believe this is your history. That it will grind on in your favor, but everything can change. Nothing is set. You believe that if you simply put one foot in front of the other that the ground will catch you, you believe that the natural way is your way, that god is with you, that the river flows only for you, but your empire is over. This is over. Yesterday is passed and tomorrow the story moves forward. You can't win."

She pressed her boot heels into the flanks of her horse and trotted northward along the muddy road.

Acknowledgments

It takes a lot of enthusiasm to make a book, and I am much obliged to the following: Madison Smartt Bell, Mark Elliott, Dwight Garner, David Hollander, Sarah Smith, Ed Trask, D. Watkins, Carrie and Will Watman, West Watman, Sharr White, Beau and Lexi Woodrum, and Laura Whitehurst.

Thank you, Bernard Schweizer and Heresy Press. You made this book better.

Thank you to the de Groot Foundation.

Thank you, Rachael, for everything.

Other Heresy Press Titles

Nothing Sacred: Outspoken Voices in Contemporary Fiction
ed. Bernard Schweizer and James Morrow
Deadpan by Richard Walter
The Hermit by Katerina Grishakova
Animal: Notes from a Labyrinth by Alan Fishbone
Unsettled States by Tom Casey
Devil Take It by Daniel Debs Nossiter
Alice, or The Wild Girl by Michael R. Liska
The War On Words: 10 Arguments Against Free Speech—And Why They Fail
by Nadine Strossen and Greg Lukianoff

Newsletter

Don't miss the Heresy Press Newsletter: https://heresy-press.com/newsletter/

Mission Statement

Heresy Press promotes freedom, honesty, openness, dissent, and real diversity in all of its manifestations. We discourage authors from descending into self-censorship, we don't blink at alleged acts of cultural appropriation, and we won't pander to the presumed sensitivities of hypothetical readers. We also don't judge works based on the author's age, gender identity, racial affiliation, political orientation, culture, religion, non-religion, or cancellation status. Heresy Press's ultimate commitment is to enduring quality standards, i.e. literary merit, originality, relevance, courage, humor, and aesthetic appeal.